The Betrayed

Echoes from the Past
Book 7

By Irina Shapiro

Copyright

Contents

Prologue

His dark eyes were huge with terror and incomprehension. Tears of fear and rage slid down his cheeks and the muscles in his neck strained as he tried to break the restraints, but they were fastened securely. An unnatural hush fell over the crowd, the silence pulsing with expectation. The men watched in mute fascination as the executioner drew a sturdy iron nail from his pocket and held it against the sun-kissed skin of his victim's wrist. A few looked away, either from squeamishness or shame, but no one left, and no one moved to stop what was about to happen. A bloodcurdling roar tore from the man's heaving chest as the first nail was driven into the elegant wrist. Shaking violently with pain and shock, his bowels let loose and a stream of vomit erupted from his mouth. Undeterred, the executioner made his way to the other wrist and raised the hammer.

By the time the deed was done, the man was no longer screaming. His head hung down, his chin resting against his shoulder. Crimson droplets of blood fell, as if in slow motion, painting the snow a violent red. No one moved. No one spoke. No one could find the strength to look away from the gruesome scene, which had been written and directed by their ignorance and hatred. The minutes must have ticked by, but time stood still for the men who watched their victim with bated breath. He wasn't dead, not yet. His eyes were partially open, his lips moving, either in prayer or in a desperate plea for help, begging for mercy from those who had betrayed him.

Chapter 1

April 2015

County Leitrim, Ireland

The weather was gorgeous, spring sunshine bathing Lough Gill and the surrounding woods in a golden haze. Parkes Castle stood proudly on the shore of the loch, its gray stone walls as massive and impregnable as they'd been in the seventeenth century when the castle was built. Several people strolled along the ramparts, gazing out over the stunning countryside and posing for photos. A few of them directed curious glances toward the tent erected just beyond the car park, but most lost interest after a few seconds and returned to their sightseeing. The owners of the castle had instructed the staff to inform those who asked that an archeological dig was in progress, but nothing of interest had been found yet. Disclosing that crucified remains had been discovered would surely send nosy tourists flocking to the excavation site and distract their attention from the main attraction.

A small group of people surrounded the trench, peering into its exposed depths, which still contained the splintered and rotted remains of the cross. The excavation had taken just over a week, which, in archeological terms, was quick as lightening. Having unearthed the remains, Quinn was eager to return to London and begin working on the new case. There was no need to excavate the entire cross. She'd taken several samples of wood to be sent to the lab, and the UCD School of Archeology in Dublin had been notified of the find, but only after the skeleton had been carefully removed from the cross, and the bones labeled and bagged. Quinn had readily agreed to share the findings with her Irish counterparts, since technically, she was on their turf.

Quinn stood and stretched her back after having crouched by the trench for nearly half an hour. She'd never seen anything like this, at least not in person. She'd unearthed many ancient skeletons over the course of her career, but none of them had been victims of crucifixion, buried in a shallow grave in what must have been the woods outside the castle walls.

Quinn turned to Gabe, who stood off to the side, Alex in his arms. Alex's face was turned upward, his mouth open in wonder as he watched a pretty bird fly overhead. He lifted a chubby hand and pointed but, at only seven months, didn't have the word for what he was seeing, so only made a sound of wonder.

"Bird," Gabe said patiently. "Bird."

"Bah," Alex repeated, his eyes round with awe. "Bah."

"We need to make sure there are no similar burials in the vicinity," Quinn said. "It's entirely possible that this execution wasn't the only one of its kind."

Gabe shook his head, the bird forgotten. "To excavate this area would take months, if not years. That kind of undertaking would require a flexible budget and unlimited manpower." He turned to Rhys Morgan of the BBC, who was standing at the edge of the trench, staring mournfully into the pit.

"I can't authorize that kind of expenditure. We'll leave the rest to UCD. Perhaps the school can apply for a government grant. Surely they'd like to know what lies beneath."

"They can file the necessary paperwork, but you won't have any answers in time for the program," Quinn replied. Once her analysis was complete, the new episode of *Echoes from the Past* would begin shooting within several months with an air date of November.

"Let's begin with this one, then, and see if you can learn anything that might give you a clue as to whether there might be others like him," Rhys replied, brusque as ever. "I'm absolutely fascinated. I've never seen anything like this," he added, his gaze sliding to the lineup of plastic bags containing the bones of the victim. "Could this have been a religious ritual of some sort?"

8

Quinn considered the question. "I really don't think so. I've heard of ritual crucifixion, but in most cases the person is tied to the cross rather than nailed, and they are taken down after a short while. Men are actually nailed to the cross every Good Friday in the Philippines, but they aren't left to die, and it's strictly on a voluntary basis."

"Maybe this bloke volunteered," Rhys suggested.

"I've never come across any research mentioning ritual crucifixion in this part of the world, and I'm not so sure it's a man," Quinn replied as she meticulously arranged the bagged bones in a rectangular cardboard box in preparation for transport.

"You think this might be a woman?" Rhys asked, his eyebrows lifting comically.

"I think I won't know for sure until Dr. Scott has had a chance to examine the remains and run the necessary tests. There's nothing more we can learn from this site. We're done here," Quinn said as she laid the final bag in the box and closed the lid.

"Right. Pack it up, Darren," Rhys said to the cameraman who'd been standing by, awaiting instructions. "Let's reconvene at the hotel. Three o'clock, say?"

"Rhys, we're tired and dirty, and I need to feed Alex and put him down for a nap. I'll ring you when I'm ready," Quinn replied as she wiped her hands on her mud-stained jeans. Rhys rolled his eyes in exasperation and walked away, heading toward the narrow lane that was almost completely blocked by their cars. He got in, slammed the door, and drove off without a backward glance.

"Sometimes, I think he's almost human, and then he reminds me he's really a cyborg," Gabe joked.

"Rhys has the unique ability to separate the personal from the professional," Quinn replied. "He's not happy about having a baby on his set."

Alex chose that very moment to start fussing. He pushed against Gabe and reached his arms toward Quinn.

"He wants his mum," Gabe said.

Quinn pulled off her latex gloves and reached for the baby. "Come here, my angel. I haven't forgotten about you."

She extracted a teething biscuit from Alex's baby bag and handed it to the baby. He grabbed it and began to gnaw on it happily, drooling all over his hand in the process.

It took nearly another hour to fill in the gaping trench and clear the site before they could start back to their hotel.

"I'm famished," Quinn announced as she strapped Alex into his car seat.

"There's a pub just down the road," Gabe replied as he took the wheel of the rental car. "Let's get some lunch. Rhys can wait."

"Sounds great," Quinn said. "What do you think, Alex? Want to go out for lunch?"

The baby continued to bite on his plastic teething ring, which he eyed with suspicion since it didn't taste as good as the biscuit he'd demolished a short while ago.

Half an hour later, they were settled in a corner booth at Murphy's Pub. Alex was sitting in a highchair provided by their server, gumming a piece of bread and eyeing Gabe's bangers and mash with undisguised interest.

"Give him some," Quinn suggested. "He doesn't want his baby food."

Gabe reached out and gave Alex a spoonful of mashed potato. Alex smacked his lips in appreciation and opened his mouth for more.

"I think we're going to have to start him on table food soon," Gabe said as he watched his son's pleasure in discovering this new flavor.

"I think we just have," Quinn replied. She took a little piece of cod and gave it to Alex, who ate it happily. Once the baby was satisfied, Quinn and Gabe were free to discuss the case uninterrupted.

"What are your thoughts?" Gabe asked.

"I honestly don't know. Until we have some indication of how old the skelly is, we have nothing concrete to go on."

"Surely you have a theory."

"My initial guess would be that this was a Christian person crucified by pagans, which would make the remains at least a thousand years old, but I'm not sure that theory will stick."

"Why do you say that?" Gabe asked, chewing thoughtfully.

"Because of what I discovered beneath the skeleton's pelvis."

"That bit of metal?"

"I cleaned it this morning while you were still asleep," Quinn replied. Gabe looked surprised but didn't complain about not being shown the artifact sooner. "There was no time this morning to discuss it with you," Quinn explained, "and this was something rather unexpected."

"Tell me."

Quinn reached into her bag and took out a small plastic bag, which she held up for Gabe's inspection.

Gabe let out a low whistle and reached for the bag to inspect the item more closely. "Is this what I think it is?"

Quinn nodded. "It's the Hand of Fatima. Looks like yellow gold with an opal at the center."

"So, you think the victim was Muslim?"

"Most likely. However, I would imagine that this particular amulet would be worn by a woman, not a man, but the length and width of the bones suggest the victim was male."

"Could have been a large-boned woman."

"Yes, that's possible, but what would a Muslim woman be doing in Ireland a millennium ago, and why would she be crucified?"

"Perhaps the locals thought she was a witch," Gabe suggested.

"Crucifixion was traditionally reserved for men. What would this poor woman had to have done to deserve such a harsh punishment? If she had been accused of witchcraft, she might have been burned or even stoned, but why crucify her in the woods?"

"You think that's where our victim died?" Gabe asked.

"I do. No one would dig a grave large enough to bury a cross. If someone wished to give this person a proper burial, they'd have taken them down first. It stands to reason that the victim was crucified in the woods and left there. In time, the cross fell backward, and the remains were buried beneath layers of soil and vegetation."

Gabe smiled happily. "This case is going to be fun," he announced. "Sometimes, I really love this job."

"Yes, researching a crucifixion certainly beats dating pottery sherds. Whoever this person was, their story must be an interesting one," Quinn replied.

"More for us than for them, I would imagine."

"Not an end I'd wish for," Quinn agreed.

"Will you consult with Jo?" Gabe asked carefully.

Quinn set down her fork. It would be a dream come true to work with her twin sister, but Quinn didn't think Jo would want to get involved. They'd been reunited only two months ago and were still feeling their way around one another. Having been separated at birth, they had yet to get to know each other on a more intimate level and become comfortable sharing their thoughts and feelings.

Quinn was eager to plunge right in, but Jo was more reserved and often noticeably withdrew when Quinn became too inquisitive or tried too hard to encourage a closer relationship. Quinn didn't judge her. Jo had trust issues, and having suddenly met not only her twin sister but her biological parents and half-brothers, she was overwhelmed. More so because she was still recovering from life-threatening injuries sustained during a photojournalism assignment in Afghanistan.

Quinn had to tread softly so as not to spook her skittish sister. Asking Jo to use her psychic gift was probably not a good idea. Jo shared Quinn's ability to see into the past when holding an object belonging to the dead, but unlike Quinn, who used her gift to learn more about her subjects and fill in the blanks in their life stories, Jo refused to touch anything that might trigger a vision and had no interest in exploring her unusual gift.

Quinn understood only too well. For a long time, she had felt just the same and wished she could be normal, for lack of a better word. It was only after discovering the remains of their ancestor Madeline Besson, who had been erased from their family history because of her mixed blood, that Quinn had finally made peace with her gift and decided to focus on giving a voice to people who could no longer speak for themselves.

"I'll tell Jo about the case, but won't ask for her help," Quinn replied. "If she offers, I'll gladly accept."

"Do you think she will?" Gabe asked.

"No."

"I'm sorry."

"Don't be," Quinn replied. "I'm thrilled to have her in my life and will proceed at whatever pace she's comfortable with. There's a lot to take in, and I don't blame her for feeling ambushed, especially by Sylvia."

"Has Jo spoken to her?"

"They've spoken briefly, but I believe the word that best describes Jo's attitude toward our birth mother is 'glacial.' She blames Sylvia for abandoning her and isn't interested in hearing Sylvia's side of the story. At least not yet. I'm glad to see her getting to know Seth though. They seem to be forging a genuine bond."

"She's taken to Emma too," Gabe said.

"Yes, she promised to help Seth with Emma this week."

Emma, who couldn't bear to be parted from her new puppy, Rufus, had asked to remain in London with her grandfather, who would be returning to New Orleans at the weekend. The two loved spending time together despite not being biologically related, so the solution worked out for everyone. Logan had promised to stop by as well, and had taken Seth, Emma, and Jo out for pizza last night. It gave him an opportunity to spend time with his newly found sister without the awkwardness of a one-on-one meeting. Jo seemed to feel more comfortable when part of a group, so everyone tried to give her the space she needed to get to know her family members at her own pace.

"I'm glad Emma is not here," Gabe said. "I would hate for her to see something as gruesome as that burial site. It would distress most adults, not to mention a five-year-old child. Good thing Alex is too young to understand what he's looking at."

"Not when it comes to food," Quinn replied, deftly moving her plate of uneaten chips out of Alex's reach. "I think he might be too young for fried foods. I wouldn't want him to get a bellyache."

Alex clearly did not agree and let out a wail of protest, but Quinn held fast and handed the plate to their server when she passed by. "There, all gone," she told the baby. "How about some milk?" She handed Alex his bottle and he latched on, sucking with great concentration.

"And how are things between Jo and Rhys?" Gabe asked.

Rhys, who had used his press credentials to get into Afghanistan, had been the one to track down Jo in Kabul and then follow her to a medical facility in Germany, where she'd been transported after the explosion in the mountains that nearly killed her and her guide. Ali Khan had been taken to a local facility for treatment, but Jo had been flown out to Germany, since the Americans initially believed her to be one of theirs and wanted to ensure she got the best possible care. Jo and Rhys had developed a tender friendship that had seemed on the verge of blossoming into a romance by the time Jo returned to London.

Quinn shrugged. "I wouldn't know. Neither one is talking, but given Rhys's testy mood, I'd say not great."

"Undoubtedly, Jo is feeling vulnerable right now, and probably feels beholden to Rhys for risking his life to find her in Kabul. That's not a promising start to any relationship, since they are not on equal footing. A lot has happened in her life in the past few months. Has she expressed a desire to return to work?"

"She's still recovering from the neurosurgery. Her doctor advised her not to fly as the difference in air pressure might cause a brain bleed. I hope she won't go off on some dangerous assignment as soon as she gets the all clear," Quinn fretted.

"Quinn, Jo is a grown woman. I know you're worried about her, but your sudden involvement might make her feel suffocated."

"I missed out on thirty-one years with her, and I'm trying to cram three decades into a couple of weeks, but I know that our friendship will take time to develop. We're virtual strangers, and I don't want to do anything to endanger this fragile new relationship. Don't you sometimes wish people came with instructions?"

"I sure do. Had you come with instructions, we might have got together a lot sooner, and you wouldn't have wasted eight years on that unspeakable wank—"

"Is there anything else I can get you?" the server asked, interrupting Gabe's little tirade.

"No, I think we're done here," Quinn replied, giving Gabe a sharp look. She had no desire to talk about Luke. He was the past and Gabe was the future. End of story.

Gabe paid the bill while Quinn extracted Alex from the highchair and gathered her belongings. "It's naptime for you, young man," she said, kissing his soft, round cheek. "Maybe Daddy will take you for a walk while Mummy puts in some quality time with the Hand of Fatima," she said meaningfully, smiling beguilingly at Gabe.

"Done. I can't wait to find out what you saw."

Chapter 2

September 1588

The Coast of Ireland

As he came to, he first became aware of the jagged stones digging into his cheek, followed by the thunder of crashing waves. The sea was behind him, the surf rushing toward him and licking his boots and thighs before retreating again. Somewhere above, a seagull cried, and a brisk wind ruffled his salt-stiffened hair. His eyes were caked with grit, and he was unbearably cold. He tried to move but couldn't find the strength to do much more than lift his head. A moan escaped his lips and he gave up and lay his head back down, too weak to care about the sharp stones. His lips were dry and cracked, and he was terribly thirsty. He shivered violently in his wet clothes.

After a time, fragments of thought that had been floating through his muddled brain began to form coherent memories, until the terror of the shipwreck returned to his consciousness, slowly and painfully. He flexed his fingers and wrapped his hand around a bunch of pebbles. He squeezed harder. It hurt, but he was grateful to feel pain. He was alive. The sea roared again, but as the noise subsided, sounds of a different nature met his ears. He heard anguished moans and the thudding of blows, the cries of seagulls and screams of terrified men.

Rafael forced his eyes open but couldn't see a thing as tears stung his eyes and ran down his cheeks, cleansing the delicate orbs that had been irritated by dried grit and saltwater. Everything appeared blurred and distorted, but once his vision cleared, he was finally able to comprehend what he was looking at and he felt a renewed surge of panic. The sight that greeted him was like a punch to the gut. The beach was littered with men. There were hundreds of them. Some lay perfectly still as the waves crashed over them, while others struggled to get to their feet and reach dry land. Dozens of people, locals by the look of them, poured onto the beach to join the ones that were already there, kicking and pummeling Rafael's countrymen, their eyes wild with hatred, their teeth bared. The men brandished thick wooden cudgels and knives, which they used on whoever was closest to them. Howls of pain and shock filled the desolate beach as the locals beat the survivors mercilessly or killed them outright. Blood and brain matter splattered the rocks as skulls were smashed like ripe melons. The locals who were unarmed fell on the dead and injured and tore off their clothes and boots, stuffing their pockets with whatever valuables they could get their hands on. Rafael's training superseded his fear. Luckily for him, he'd washed up further down the beach, so the mob was still some way off. He had to get away before they reached him. Once they did, there'd be no mercy and no chance of escape.

Rafael's limbs quivered like jelly, but he forced himself to crawl away from the shoreline. The pebbles cut into his hands and hurt his knees, but he kept going, his eyes fixed on the wide strip of rushes in the distance. He was sure the men would search the surrounding area once their blood cooled. On the beach, he was completely exposed, but hiding in the rushes would give him a little extra time to get his bearings. He gasped for breath as he crawled, ignoring the pain and the nausea that threatened to overtake him. Eventually, he reached the cover of the tall grass and tried to crawl deeper into the growth, looking for a hollow or a ditch where he could lie low.

Pausing to catch his breath, Rafael turned to glance at the beach. The carnage continued unabated. Several of his countrymen had managed to get to their feet and were trying to fight off their attackers, but they were no match for angry, armed men, who cut through them with ease. Rafael continued to crawl until he found an indentation in the ground. It wasn't much, but hopefully it would hide him. He lay face-down and pulled the tall grass down to cover him, hoping no one would be able to spot him from a distance. There were enough shipwrecked soldiers on the beach to keep the locals occupied for some time. Rafael laid his head on the ground and covered his ears to block out the desperate screams that tore at his soul.

Eventually, all became quiet and still. Having slaughtered the survivors, the locals departed, leaving the beach strewn with naked and mutilated corpses. It was possible that someone had survived the massacre, but Rafael was in no shape to help anyone. He shivered in his wet clothes, his teeth chattering with cold. He was thirsty and hungry, but most of all, he was terrified. What was he to do now? Even if he made it through the night, who'd help him? Where was he to go?

He reached into the tiny pocket sewn into the inside of his doublet and extracted the hamsa. The hand-shaped charm was the size of a grape, the gold thin and filigreed. A small, round opal was set into the palm of the hand, almost like a single eye, watching over its owner. The amulet wouldn't fetch much, if sold, but to Rafael it was priceless. He pressed the little hand to his lips and kissed it reverently.

"Dear God, if you can hear me, please help me," he prayed. "I'm at your mercy, now and always."

Rafael stared at the charm in his hand. The locals had filled their pockets with Spanish gold, robbing the corpses littering the beach. They'd taken crosses, rosaries, rings, and even buckles and buttons. They were sure to take his hamsa if he were discovered. Rafael considered his options for a moment. If he died, it wouldn't matter, but if he survived, he'd do anything to hold on to it. Mira had given it to him just before he left for La Coruña. It had been a betrothal gift from her mother, but Mira had pressed it into his hand, her eyes meeting his full on for the first time since they'd met.

"I can't take it, Mira," Rafael had told her. He had been touched by her generous gesture but felt awkward about accepting the gift.

"You can. Please, I want you to have it. You can return it to me on our wedding day, Rafael, and I will be happy in the knowledge that it kept you safe."

"Thank you," Rafael had said, wondering if maybe, in time, he would learn to love this girl. He hadn't been in favor of the match, hadn't been ready to commit himself to a girl he'd met only twice before, but his father made all the arrangements and the betrothal took place, the two young people studying each other shyly as they stood side by side. Mira was pretty, but at sixteen she was still a child, raised behind the protective walls of her family's home. There were reasons why señor Cortés kept Mira and his two younger daughters in near isolation, and they all knew what those reasons were.

Given the perils of day-to-day life in Toledo, it was easier to have sons, but boys came with their own challenges, as señor de Silva was fond of reminding his sons. It was his father who'd decided that Rafael would join the army.

"You'll be safe in the army, Rafi," his father had said. "You'll be hiding in plain sight. I only wish your brother could join up as well, but he's not strong enough for life in the military. His heart can't take the strain. I've spoken to señor Cortés. Ramón will be apprenticed to him until he can become a master craftsman. There's always a demand for goldsmiths."

"Father, I don't want to join the army," Rafael had argued. "I want to be a physician, like you."

"Rafi, please trust me in this," señor de Silva had replied. "It is not safe for you to study medicine. You know the reasons, but you still don't understand the danger. Physicians invite undue scrutiny, and scrutiny often leads to an investigation, interrogation, and torture. There are those who think healers are no better than witches or sorcerers. The Church never sleeps, *mi hijo*. It has eyes and ears everywhere. We mustn't attract undue attention. We must blend in. By joining the army, you show the authorities and the priests that you are a loyal and patriotic Spaniard, a young man beyond reproach."

"Father, why don't we leave Spain?" Rafael had asked, not for the first time. "Surely there are places where we can be free to be ourselves and worship openly. We can live our lives as we choose, without constant fear of discovery."

"Rafi, our family has been in Toledo for centuries. We are as Spanish as the people who'd condemn us. I will not give in to their bullying. I will not leave my home, and neither will you. This will pass, as all things pass. We must have faith. God is great. He will protect us."

As he has protected all the countless people who were taken from their homes, imprisoned, tortured, and sentenced to die on the flimsiest of evidence? Rafael thought angrily. *The fire of the Inquisition burns bright, fed by the Church, who uses men like you for fuel, men who refuse to see reason and condemn their families to lives lived in constant terror.*

But, in the end, Rafael couldn't refuse his father. He'd been brought up to respect and honor his parents, and given their situation, his father's plan was sound. A life in the army would probably be more rewarding than endless days hunched over a workbench, fashioning bits of gold into charms and rings by the light of a candle, his daily existence reduced to long hours at the workshop followed by an evening at his home, just down the street from the jewelry shop of señor Cortés.

"How I envy you, Rafi," Ramón had said. His eyes had filled with tears when señor de Silva   informed his youngest son that Rafael would be leaving them in a fortnight, but their father offered no words of comfort. He wasn't a man given to displays of emotion or physical affection. "What I wouldn't give to go with you. Just think of it; you'll get to see the world. You'll sail the high seas. You'll experience life."

"Or death," Rafael had reminded his brother. "I'm not going on a sightseeing expedition, Ramón. I'm going to fight, to bring war to people who only want to live in peace and worship as they see fit."

"If all goes well, you'll never see battle. The British will cower at the sight of the great and mighty Armada and lay down their arms. Some might even welcome the invasion. Surely, they'd like to overthrow their heretic queen who rules without a husband and has neglected to produce an heir, a woman's only God-sanctioned duty. You'll come back full of wonderful stories, a brave soldier who's ready to claim his bride."

Rafael had shaken his head. No one understood, not even his brother, with whom he'd been close all his life. Ramón had been a sickly child who grew into a sickly young man. The slightest of exertions caused heart palpitations, and he turned pale as flour and broke out in a cold sweat whenever he didn't have enough to eat, his hands shaking like leaves until the food finally fed his blood and the tremors subsided. Ramón envied Rafael his freedom, his exciting future, and in his bitterness quoted the rhetoric of the zealots, justifying the attack on England and its brave and independent queen. Ramón would have traded places with Rafael in a heartbeat, but señor de Silva would never allow it, with good reason.

"Yes, you're right," Rafael had agreed, eager to put an end to the conversation. "I will go for a nice cruise to England, see the sights, and then come back and marry Mira."

"You lucky dog," Ramón had said, elbowing him in the ribs. "She's beautiful."

"Father will find you a beautiful bride as well. Mira's sisters are lovely, and then there are the Ramos girls. They'll be ready to be betrothed in a year or two."

Ramón had smiled happily. There were few eligible young men in their community, so Ramón would have no shortage of suitable brides to choose from. Rafael had clapped Ramón on the shoulder. "Look after Father while I'm gone. He'll need you more than ever."

"I'll look after your bride too," Ramón had replied cheekily. "Just to make sure she doesn't get up to no good."

22

"Thanks, little brother," Rafael had replied. "With you here, I'll have one less thing to worry about."

Rafael buried his face in his arms as tears of fear and loneliness slid down his cheeks. He missed his father and brother desperately, but the one person he really longed for was his mother, who'd left them less than a year ago after a prolonged illness. He'd always been closer to his mother. Lucía de Silva had been beautiful and intelligent, but also warm and understanding, unlike her husband, who valued only his own point of view. "Watch over me, mamá," Rafael whispered into the wind that ruffled his hair like a mother's hand.

He burrowed deeper into the hollow that cradled him but provided little warmth. His shivering kept him awake, his thoughts swirling like fog. He hoped his father would be informed of his fate, should he die on this foreign shore, but he didn't think his family would ever learn the truth. His Most Catholic Majesty, Phillip II, had proclaimed the Spanish Navy to be invincible and sworn that England didn't stand a chance against its might. Would the king ever admit to his subjects that 'The Great and Most Fortunate Navy of Spain' had been waylaid by the English, scattered to the four winds, and blown to bits by gales the likes of which no Spaniard had ever seen?

Trembling violently in his wet clothes, Rafael wondered how people lived in this hostile climate. The sky was the color of a nasty bruise, the thick clouds hanging so low one could almost touch them. It was cold, damp, and dreary. The shoreline was rocky and narrow, not like the glorious, sun-drenched beaches of Spain, where the sand was soft and golden beneath one's bare feet, the palm trees swayed lazily, and strains of guitar music carried on the light breeze from nearby squares. There were times when he hated Spain and those who ruled it, but at this moment, he would have given anything to see its shores again.

Memories of home awakened hunger. Rafael wasn't sure what day it was, but he couldn't recall the last time he'd had a proper meal. Supplies had been running low, so all the soldiers and crew had been put on half-rations, which hadn't been nearly enough to satisfy the hungry men. To make matters worse, the soldiers had sat around and reminisced about their favorite dishes, describing the glories of suckling pig until their mouths watered, and large pans of paella, the rice flavored with saffron and thick with chorizo, shrimp, chicken, and vegetables. Doña Lucía had never made suckling pig, nor did she add chorizo to her paella, since pork was forbidden, but there were other dishes she'd made that were just as delicious. Rafael had tried not to listen to the food talk and had gone up on deck, where the cold drizzle that seemed to fall nearly every day had distracted him from persistent hunger, but the cold and wet weren't helping him now.

His stomach growled and his mouth was dry with thirst. He'd settle for a cup of hot broth and a piece of bread, but there wasn't so much as a mouthful of fresh water to be had in his hiding spot. He licked his lips to moisten them and tasted salt. Taking one last look at the golden charm in his hand, Rafael pushed it into his mouth, swallowing it. It scratched his throat as it went down, but he didn't care. He might not live long enough for his throat to heal, but if he did, he'd keep the amulet safe from the enemy in the depths of his body.

Chapter 3

It was only once the leaden sky began to darken that Rafael felt safe enough to raise his head and look around. Crows and wild dogs had congregated on the beach and were feasting on the remains of his countrymen. Gut-churning sounds drifted toward him as they ripped flesh and crunched on bones, their teeth and beaks covered in gore. Rafael turned away and stared out over the water, a mesmerizing shade of violet in the lingering twilight. The waves no longer crashed onto the beach, but rolled in gently, foaming as they rushed over the pebbles, and then retreated, only to repeat the process again and again. The storm that had sunk Rafael's ship and many others had passed, leaving behind a vast and empty horizon, devoid of anything but lavender clouds and twinkling stars.

Rafael peered into the shadows. He thought he saw something bobbing on the water but couldn't be sure. It might have been a trick of the light, or a piece of flotsam. Maybe even a bit of wood from one of the warships that had been tossed on the monstrous waves like children's toys and swallowed whole with hundreds of men still aboard. The object drifted closer, taking on a more definite shape in the gathering darkness. A man clung to a hunk of wood, his cheek resting on one arm, his eyes closed. He wasn't moving. Rafael's initial instinct was to leave his sanctuary and offer help, but he remained where he was. He wouldn't have the strength to outrun the dogs if they caught his scent, and he was terrified of being mauled to death. Instead, Rafael rested his head on his arms and tried to sleep. After hours of terror and heightened awareness of his surroundings, he was exhausted. He drifted into an uneasy sleep, grateful to escape reality for even a short time.

By the time Rafael awoke, it was fully dark. The sky had cleared, and a gentle breeze moved through the tall grass like lazy fingers. The dogs and crows had gone, having had their fill of human flesh. The beach appeared deceptively peaceful, the dead littering the shore like hunks of driftwood. The stars above looked distant and cold, not like the bright stars of Toledo that always made him think of glittering diamonds strewn across rich black velvet.

Rafael forced himself to stand up. He was unsteady on his feet and his clothes were still damp, but he was otherwise uninjured. What he wouldn't give for a dry shirt, he mused, as he took in his surroundings. He had to find shelter and food while it was safe to look. Once the sun came up, he'd be exposed once again.

Rafael froze, all his senses on high alert when he heard a dragging sound coming from the beach. He dropped into a crouch, his eyes searching the shoreline for signs of danger. At first, he thought it was a dog, but then realized the dark shape was too large and too long. It was a man, lying on his belly, his arm outstretched, one of his legs bent at the knee. The man moved his other arm forward and pulled himself up, repeating the process again and again. He crawled away from the surf and took a short break before crawling toward the rushes.

Rafael left the safety of his hollow and made his way toward the man, who was dripping wet and muttering to himself in Spanish. He advanced slowly and laboriously, but even from a distance, Rafael could sense his determination, driven by sheer will. Rafael approached the man slowly, so as not to startle him, and called out softly, identifying himself as a friend.

The man raised a hand in greeting, then collapsed back onto the beach, too exhausted to continue. Rafael helped him to his feet and dragged him toward the hollow, which suddenly seemed very far away, given the man's considerable weight. Rafael didn't recognize him, but given his age and attire, he took him to be one of the officers.

"Your name," the man muttered as he fixed a glazed stare on Rafael.

"Rafael de Silva, sir. And you are?"

"Captain Francisco de Cuéllar."

Rafael nearly let go of his burden but caught the captain under the arms just before he fell. He'd heard of Captain de Cuéllar; everyone in the fleet had. Captain de Cuéllar had been accused of disobedience when his ship broke formation in the North Sea and sentenced to death by hanging. He was to be made an example of, but clearly, he was still alive, if not for much longer.

De Cuéllar stumbled and fell to his knees. "I need to rest."

"Let's get you to the rushes, sir. We're too exposed here."

The captain nodded and got to his feet, then staggered toward the rushes, supported by Rafael. He collapsed to his knees as soon as they reached the deceptive safety of the hollow, his breathing labored.

"Sir?" Rafael called to him, but the captain lay on his side, closed his eyes, and sank into a fitful sleep.

Rafael lay down next to the captain and pulled some rushes over them both. They offered no warmth or safety but provided minimal cover. He studied the man's face by starlight. De Cuéllar appeared to be in his early forties, a handsome man with a trim beard and a hoop earring in his left ear. His tangled hair hung to his shoulders and his deep-set eyes were offset by heavy black brows. He was an imposing man, even in his weakened condition, and Rafael felt strangely reassured by his presence.

Rafael trembled with fatigue, but sleep wouldn't come, so he gazed up at the stars, trying to figure out if the celestial formations were the same in the north as they were in the south. The constellations didn't look familiar, and it seemed to Rafael as if this wild land slumbered under a different sky.

A strange rasping sound distracted him from his astronomical study, and he sprang to his feet, instantly dropping into a crouch and peering through the long grass toward the beach. Something white and long was moving toward the hollow. Rafael's initial terror was quickly replaced by pity. The thing was another man. He was completely naked, his pale skin scratched and covered with livid bruises. He must have been stripped, beaten, and left for dead. Rafael helped the man to their hiding place, and he curled into a ball next to the captain. His eyes were open, but his gaze was unfocused, and he didn't seem aware of Rafael's presence.

"What's your name?" Rafael whispered. "I'm Rafael de Silva, and this is Captain de Cuéllar."

The man didn't respond. He was shaking with cold and shock, his teeth chattering like a bone rattle. Rafael removed his damp doublet and covered the man. The shaking subsided after a time and the man fell into a deep sleep, his breathing shallow and uneven. Rafael wrapped his arms around himself and tried to rub some heat into his stiff limbs. It was only September. How could it be this cold? He tried to recall the searing caress of the sun as he'd walked along the narrow streets of Toledo, keeping to the shade to ward off the heat, his face beaded with perspiration beneath the wide brim of his hat, and his feet broiling in his leather boots. For just a moment, Rafael could almost feel the warmth of those summer days and wished he were in Spain, walking down a familiar street toward his father's house, his mouth watering at the prospect of a good meal.

Captain de Cuéllar mumbled something and opened his eyes, gazing at the sky for a long moment before turning to stare at Rafael. His pupils were dilated, his expression blank. After a while, he shut his eyes again and slipped into unconsciousness. Rafael pressed his ear to the captain's chest and listened to his heartbeat. It was steady, which was a good sign. He'd pull through. He needed rest and food.

Rafael almost laughed at the idea. How nice it would be if some friendly locals took them in and allowed them to sit by a roaring fire while their hosts offered them bucket-sized helpings of something delicious and hot. And wine. Lots of wine. Rafael swallowed back the saliva that flooded his mouth and willed himself not to think about food. It would be his undoing. He shut his eyes, determined to fall asleep. Eventually, he succeeded.

It was still dark when Rafael woke, but a narrow sliver of pearly gray shimmered on the horizon. He was stiff with cold and needed to empty his bladder. He took care of business, then came back to check on his companions. The captain was breathing deeply, his chest rising and falling as he slept. His face was relaxed, and the deathly pallor of last night had been replaced by a scarlet flush. The nameless man lay motionless beneath Rafael's doublet, his face still as an effigy. Rafael moved closer and touched his hand. It was cold, the fingers stiff. He pressed two fingers to the man's neck, but there was no pulse. Rafael said a silent prayer for the soul of the departed and took back his doublet, which was now dry. He pulled it on and moved closer to the captain, distancing himself from the corpse.

We have to go, Rafael thought suddenly. *We can't still be here come morning.*

He shook the captain gently. "Captain, wake up." It took a few tries before Captain de Cuéllar finally opened his eyes. "Captain, we have to find a better hiding place," Rafael said. "We're too exposed here. The locals are bound to come back in the morning."

The captain nodded and slowly got to his feet. He didn't ask about the other man, just crossed himself and turned away, surveying their surroundings. "That way," he said, and the two men stumbled off, moving away from the beach and toward a clump of trees in the distance.

Chapter 4

April 2015

London, England

Quinn pushed Alex's pram down the corridor, thankful he'd fallen asleep just as they arrived at the mortuary. The familiar smell of death and carbolic accosted her, and she tried not to breathe too deeply as she continued toward Dr. Scott's office. This time, she'd made an appointment, since finding him in the middle of an autopsy was not a sight she relished. She'd seen plenty of human remains, but in her line of work, they were mostly brittle bones and empty-eyed skulls. Fresh cadavers turned her stomach, and their organs, displayed in various containers independently of the body, made her want to run for the door and into the fresh air, where gentle sunshine shone from a cloudless sky and the city pulsed with life. She tried not to dwell on how easily life could be snuffed out, but she knew the reality—here today, gone tomorrow. It was important not to put things on hold and assume there'd be time to return to them later.

Quinn had briefly questioned her decision to go on the pill after she'd weaned Alex. Perhaps she shouldn't put off having another baby. There was never a perfect time; one simply adjusted, as they had done with Alex, who hadn't been planned. Gabe was ready for another child, but he hadn't been the one to suffer the crippling symptoms of preeclampsia or undergo an emergency cesarean section in the middle of the night. It had taken months for Quinn to start feeling like her old self again, and she wasn't ready to relinquish the freedom of being alone in her body. Besides, Alex was only seven months old. There was time yet.

"Quinn," Colin Scott called out as he saw her walking down the corridor. "Good to see you. And how's our honorary archeologist?"

"He's well. Taking a nap," Quinn replied. "I think I'll speak to Rhys about billing Alex's hours as a consultant on the program," she joked.

"His input is invaluable."

Quinn followed Colin into the lab, where the skeleton they had excavated in Ireland was laid out on the slab. "Where's Dr. Dhawan today?" Colin's assistant, Sarita Dhawan, normally performed most of the tests on the skeletal remains and logged them into the system. She was usually present when Quinn came by, and the lab seemed strangely empty without her.

"Sarita's in Mumbai. Her brother is getting married next week. She showed me her wedding sari. Absolutely gorgeous— peacock blue embroidered with gold thread," Colin said. "She didn't say so outright, but I think there's someone her parents wish her to meet."

"Really? A prospective bridegroom?"

"I think so. I hope it works out for her, as long as I don't have to lose her as my assistant," Colin added, grinning. "I don't think she wants to move back to India. She loves it here."

"And speaking of weddings, have you and Logan set a date?" Quinn asked as she parked Alex's pram by the far wall, where the fluorescent lighting wouldn't disturb his sleep, and pulled on a pair of latex gloves.

Colin's face fell and he shook his head. "We were going to get married this summer, but I don't think that's going to happen now."

"What? Why?"

"Logan has managed to secure a spot for Jude at the Winthrop Rehabilitation Centre. After Jude's overdose, he doesn't want to take any chances on an outpatient methadone program. He wants to help your brother get clean and stay that way."

"How much does this facility cost?"

"More than Logan can afford. Much more. Sylvia's offered to pay half, but Logan doesn't want her to dip into her retirement savings."

"I'm sorry, Colin. You must be disappointed."

"I am, but I support him in this decision. Jude needs help, and not the kind of help the NHS can provide."

"Do you think it's possible to fully rehabilitate a heroin addict?" Quinn asked, hoping against hope that Colin would assure her it could be done.

"I don't know," Colin replied with a sigh. "It takes a very strong person to swear off the one thing they can't resist. Jude wants to get clean, but he's weak, and he's vulnerable."

"He needs to stay away from Bridget. She's his kryptonite."

"It's not Bridget he can't resist, it's the heroin. There will always be another Bridget, and another Harry."

"Who's Harry?" Quinn hadn't heard that name before in relation to Jude.

"Harry's his dealer. Or one of them, at any rate. But we all have our weaknesses, don't we?" Colin said.

"That we do. I just hope they won't ultimately destroy us. So, what can you tell me about our victim?" Quinn asked. Colin was clearly ready to change the subject, and she hoped to be finished at the mortuary before Alex woke from his nap.

"Not much. He was completely unremarkable."

"He? Are you sure?"

"Yes. Why?"

"I thought it might have been a she."

"Why would you think that?"

Quinn rooted in her bag and held up the bag containing the Hand of Fatima. "I found this beneath the body. This is more of a feminine symbol, in my experience."

"It might not have been his," Colin said.

But it was, Quinn mentally replied, feeling a deep sadness steal over her at the thought of that frightened young man and his desperate need to keep the amulet safe.

"Anyway, what we have here is most definitely a male skeleton. The victim was in his late teens or early twenties at the time of death. According to carbon-14 dating, he lived sometime in the mid-1500s. I didn't find any traces of past injuries. He was a healthy young man."

"Were you able to obtain any DNA from the hair?" Quinn asked.

"Yes. Thankfully, one of the strands had an intact follicle that yielded some results. According to DNA sequencing, he was primarily of Iberian descent with traces of North African and Middle Eastern heritage. He had dark hair, dark eyes, and olive skin. He was of average height and build for that time period. He was right-handed, and the ridges on his wrist indicate that he practiced some sort of manual labor. Given where he was discovered, I'd say he was a soldier, and the ridges were created by wielding a sword."

"And his diet?"

"He enjoyed a plentiful diet during his formative years, mostly meat based, so it's likely that he came from a well-to-do family."

"Is it possible to tell if he ate pork?"

Colin grinned. "Now you're asking for miracles. I can tell if the diet was predominately fish, meat, or plant based, but I can't tell if he enjoyed his bacon."

"Anything else you can tell me about him?" Quinn asked, disappointed.

"Not really."

"What ultimately killed him?"

"Exposure, dehydration, and shock, which probably led to cardiac arrest. The nails appear to have been driven in sideways to penetrate the wrist. The pain would have been excruciating, and as there was no footrest on the cross, his weight would have put additional pressure on his already mutilated wrists. Had his feet not been tied firmly to the vertical bar, his ligaments would have torn, and he would have fallen off the cross."

"So, what you're saying is that this young man suffered a horrific, prolonged death."

"What I'm saying is that he must have royally cheesed someone off."

"I agree with you there," Quinn said as she accepted the folder containing a printout of the results. "This is only the second time the remains of a crucified individual have been discovered. The first time was in 1968 in Jerusalem, and the only reason the remains survived was because the family must have taken the victim down and buried him. Most victims of crucifixion were left on the cross as a warning to others, and then thrown into a pit along with other decomposing remains."

"My guess is that after this man died, someone pushed the cross down and buried it in a shallow grave. Based on your photos, the cross wasn't large, just tall enough to crucify this poor bloke. And whoever disposed of him didn't care to be bothered with taking him down and burying him in a proper grave. Over time, the remains were buried deeper under layers of soil, rotting vegetation, and branches, which is why no one found it until now. How did you come across it?" Colin asked.

"The remains were found about a quarter of a mile from Parkes Castle, which is one of the most popular attractions in County Leitrim. The owners decided to expand the car park to accommodate increased traffic during the tourist season. The remains were discovered when the workers began clearing the woodland. The curator of the castle called Rhys's *Echoes from the Past* hotline after the Garda ruled it out as a recent crime. He loves the program and thought the added publicity generated by the episode wouldn't do the castle any harm."

"Well, I can't wait to see how you spin this," Colin said. "You have an amazing talent for taking a few random facts and molding them into a riveting narrative. It's almost as if you know exactly what happened to these people."

"I only come up with a plausible theory and then see if the facts fit," Quinn replied. She was saved from further explanations by Alex, who woke from his nap and sat up in his pram, looking around with annoyance.

"Look who's up," Quinn said as she smiled at the baby. "It's almost time to feed him, so I'd better get going."

"My regards to Gabe," Colin said as he walked Quinn to the door of the lab. "I'll let you know if anything else turns up, but I think this is about all I can tell you about this fellow."

"Thanks, Colin. See you soon."

Chapter 5

Jo Turing slid into a corner booth and ordered a pot of Earl Grey and a scone. She liked this little café. She could watch life going by while enjoying her tea. She liked watching life. In fact, she felt most comfortable behind the lens of her camera. Quinn would probably say she was hiding, and to some degree she'd be right. Jo had been hiding for a long time, ever since the night her adoptive brother Michael had forced himself on her and shattered all her illusions of safety, family, and love.

That night had broken something in her, and she'd never been able to put herself back together, not entirely anyway. But perhaps there had been something wrong with her even before that. She'd never quite fit in with her adoptive family, had never felt like she was truly wanted. Her mother had assured her time and again that her fears were unfounded and that her parents loved Jo as much as their biological children, but for Jo, something had always been missing. Maybe that something was in her and not in those around her, who could never love her enough to quash her doubts. There had been people who came close, like Jesse Holt. He'd been patient and kind, and loyal, but she'd left him as soon as he began talking about a future together, about starting a family. She hadn't been ready to settle down, so she'd run off to Paris, a place where a person was practically guaranteed to find adventure and romance. She had found a measure of both, but not enough to make her feel whole.

Perhaps she'd never been whole, even as a small child. Being abandoned at birth had haunted her, making her feel unworthy and suspicious of all those who professed to love her. She supposed some would say that being adopted by the surgeon who saved her life as an infant was the ultimate validation of worth, but she'd always felt more like a charity case, a theory that proved to be fact the night of the rape. Her parents' immediate concern was for Michael, who'd get struck off the Medical Board if accused of the crime. Michael's career had to be protected at all cost. Jo's feelings came second.

Jo had never forgiven her parents for that decision and carried the pain of their betrayal still. She'd left them all behind, changed her name, and made a life for herself. She was an award-winning photojournalist, a woman who was fiercely independent and widely admired by her colleagues, but she was also a woman without roots. She hadn't gone to her father's funeral, still incapable of dealing with Michael's remorse or Karen's haughty derision. She didn't need her siblings, and they didn't need her. They were strangers to each other now, people who had shared a childhood but no longer had anything to bind them together. The problem was that after years of setting herself apart, she didn't seem able to form a lasting bond with anyone. There had been several lovers since Jesse. She'd liked them, and had enjoyed the physical aspects of the relationship, but when the romance fizzled out, she'd felt no regret, no sense of loss. She'd felt relief. She'd discovered that she liked being on her own—but suddenly, she wasn't.

Two months ago, she'd woken up from an induced coma to find herself at Landstuhl Regional Medical Center in Ramstein-Miesenbach, Germany. She'd been frightened and confused, relieved to be alive. And then Rhys Morgan had shown up, followed by Quinn. Jo had felt so many emotions, they seemed to trip over each other and knock her off balance. She'd been amazed, excited, embarrassed, confused, and apprehensive all at once. She still felt much the same. There'd been a parade of new faces, and suddenly, she had a family again. She had a twin sister, three half-brothers, and biological parents who were miraculously still alive, unlike her adoptive parents, who had passed years ago.

Jo exhaled loudly and took a sip of her tea. She'd been trying to come to terms with her feelings for weeks, but she was no closer to feeling comfortable with this new reality. She should be happy, excited about this new future, but what she felt was overwhelming anxiety. It was as if a tidal wave were rolling toward the shore, growing bigger with every passing moment, but she stood rooted to the beach, unable to run for safety. Why did she feel so threatened? Except for her birth mother, whom she had yet to meet in person, everyone had been welcoming and kind.

They were all different, but lovely in their own unique ways. Quinn was warm and open, Logan flamboyant and affectionate. Jude had been distant, but that was to be expected given his situation. He'd been recovering from his own near-death experience when they met, and a long-lost sister was not at the top of his priorities.

She liked Colin Scott's quiet charm, and Seth's American brashness. It was easy to allow him to take charge. He was a man who got things done and expected no thanks or praise for his efforts. And then there was Gabe. The mere thought of him made Jo's cheeks feel unnaturally warm. Gabe wasn't just attractive; he was kind, intelligent, and thoughtful. There was something old-world about him, a nobility and steadfastness rarely found in men these days. He wasn't just devoted to Quinn. From what Jo could see, he was a wonderful father, a caring son, and a loyal friend to the people in his life. Jo had never longed for marriage, but if she ever met a man like Gabe, she'd gladly reconsider. Someone like Gabe came along once in a lifetime.

Jo cut the scone in half and spread it liberally with cream and jam. The first bite was always the best, so she took a moment to chew it slowly, pushing her concerns aside. Once she finished her treat, her mind returned to her unsettling thoughts. She supposed it wasn't just one thing that made her anxious; it was several. First and foremost, she was nervous about her relationship with Quinn. Her sister was all in, ready to build a bond that would last a lifetime. In theory, Jo loved the idea, but in reality, she found herself taking a step back every time Quinn took a step forward. Quinn and Rhys shared the same quality that she found so disturbing. They were the type of people who wanted all of you. They were aggressive and fearless when it came to loving and giving, but they were also adept at taking. Someone as confident as Gabe might not feel threatened by an all-out frontal attack, but Jo was too emotionally fragile to allow someone to corner her like that. She needed time to find her own comfort zone and draw her own boundaries.

Jo finished her tea and pulled out her mobile. What was it with this constant need to check her phone? She'd enjoyed being out of reach while in Kabul, but as soon as she'd returned to London, she'd become a slave to technology once again. Suddenly, there were things that needed to be addressed, and inquiries that had to be answered. Jo checked her voicemail, not overly surprised to find a message from Rhys. He wanted to take her to dinner tomorrow. But did she want to go? She wasn't sure.

Rhys was attractive, charming, and solicitous, but he was also aggressive, passionate, and demanding. He reminded her of the Big Bad Wolf. If she were to get involved with him, he wouldn't settle for just a part of her. He'd want all of her, and he'd want it yesterday. Rhys had no patience. He was the type of man who took sensual pleasure in everyday life. He loved good food, fine wine, and stimulating company. Rhys wouldn't settle for a casual affair. He wanted it all, and he'd made that quite clear.

But did Jo? And did she want it with him? Would she have been less intimidated if it'd been Gabe who tried to pursue her? Probably. Which wasn't to say that Gabe was any less intense. Perhaps she simply liked him more. Anyway, it would be rude to refuse Rhys's invitation. He'd been so kind to her. Jo selected Rhys's number, pressed the button, and waited for him to answer, immensely relieved when the call went to voicemail.

"Rhys, I'd love to have dinner with you. Ring me."

She disconnected the call and selected the next number. Quinn had left her a message as well. She wanted to show Jo the Hand of Fatima she'd discovered beneath the human remains she'd excavated in Ireland. Jo wanted to see the artifact but had no desire to touch it. She had sensed Quinn's disapproval when Jo had told her she didn't use her gift to see into the past, but she wouldn't be pressured. She had enough to deal with in the present; she had no desire to live other people's lives and feel their pain, because it was very rare that people led happy lives. That much they had in common.

Chapter 6

September 1588

Connacht, Ireland

The sky began to lighten gradually, the shades of gray shifting as the darkness dissipated. It was nothing like the apricot glow of an Iberian sunrise, but then this unfamiliar land was nothing like Spain. It was thickly wooded, and the early morning was as cold and damp as the coldest of winter days in Toledo. The men stopped to rest by a narrow stream. They hadn't walked far, but they were both panting with effort, their bodies depleted after their ordeal.

Rafael cupped his hands and drank until his stomach felt like an overflowing wineskin, but it felt good, invigorating. He washed his face, hands, and neck. Amazing how a small thing like washing made him feel more human. He ran his wet hands through his hair. When clean, his hair was soft and wavy, but this morning it was matted and coarse from the hours he'd spent in sea water.

Captain de Cuéllar drank a little, but even that small amount made him retch, his stomach not ready to hold anything down. He wiped his mouth with the back of his hand and tried again, taking small sips from his cupped hand. The captain extracted a handkerchief from his pocket, wet it in the spring, and used it to clean his face and neck. His face had a greenish hue beneath his fading suntan and his eyes were glazed with fatigue, but his gaze glowed with determination. "We should press on. It'll be fully light soon," he said.

"Yes, sir."

They walked on until the sky began to turn a watery blue and the woods came awake all around them. Birdsong filled the air and the undergrowth shivered restlessly as small forest creatures left their subterranean homes and scurried in search of food. It grew warmer once the weak sunshine penetrated the darkened hollows and dense thickets. Rafael reflected on how pleasant dry clothes felt against his skin. Even his boots had finally dried out, no longer squelching as he trudged along behind the captain, who appeared lost in his own thoughts.

By midmorning, Rafael spotted a stone structure through the thinning trees. "I think that's a church, sir."

"Surely the priest will help us," the captain said, his steps quickening with renewed optimism.

"I wouldn't be so sure," Rafael mumbled, vivid images of yesterday's carnage flooding his mind.

The captain hadn't seen what Rafael had seen, hadn't heard the desperate screams of dying men or the crunch of splintering bones. To go into battle where both sides were evenly matched was honorable; to butcher helpless men in cold blood was barbaric. The Irish were supposed to be fellow Catholics. How could they justify killing their brothers in faith in such a heartless manner? Rafael didn't feel much sympathy for Catholics, knowing only too well what the Church was capable of and what it did to those it considered heretics, but the men on the beach had been foot soldiers, not firebrands of the Inquisition, whose true goal had been to kill and torture in the name of Christ.

It was Phillip II's mission of divine faith to bring the Inquisition to the shores of England and unleash the priests on the millions of Protestants he considered fit only for the pyre. Rafael was secretly glad the mission had failed, but he hadn't expected to find himself stranded in a Catholic country inhabited by people who were just as ruthless and pitiless as his own countrymen. He was no safer here than he'd been in Spain, posing as a good Catholic. His kind wouldn't be welcome here either. His people didn't seem to be welcome anywhere.

But perhaps the captain was right, and the clergy here was more moderate, Rafael mused as he followed the captain toward the building. If they didn't find assistance in a church, there'd be little hope of finding help among the locals. Rafael felt a stab of disappointment when the church finally came into view. It was a ruin, the stones blackened with soot. It must have been destroyed in a fire.

Captain de Cuéllar stopped walking and stared at the ruins, a strange gurgle erupting from his swollen lips. "*Santa María*," he whispered, and crossed himself fervently.

Rafael peered at the ruin, wondering what had shocked the captain so. And then he saw them—a dozen corpses hanging from beams laid across the roofless walls of the church. The victims had all been stripped naked but were without doubt Spanish soldiers. As their bodies rotated in the soft autumn breeze, their faces came into view, and Rafael hastily looked away, unable to bear the gruesome sight. The captain wasn't as squeamish. He stood his ground, his feet apart, his shoulders back, his gaze on the dead.

"Hail Mary, full of grace. Our Lord is with thee. Blessed art thou among women, and blessed is the fruit of thy womb, Jesus. Holy Mary, Mother of God, pray for us sinners, now and at the hour of our death. Amen," the captain recited. He crossed himself again and Rafael followed suit. His heart broke for the executed men and the families they'd left behind. Death was inevitable, sometimes unavoidable when you were a soldier, but to be left hanging, naked and desecrated in a Catholic church with no one to mourn your passing or bury the body, was unspeakable.

"Come, de Silva," the captain said as he headed toward the church.

"Surely you don't intend to go inside," Rafael protested.

"There might be something there we can use," the captain replied.

Rafael nodded and followed the captain into the ruin. The tiny church had nothing to offer. It had been gutted by flames. Only the stone walls had withstood the destruction and the charred interior was now the final resting place of the hapless victims.

Rafael wished he could cover their nakedness to spare them the indignity of their death. He nearly lost his balance when he tripped on a fallen beam, but the captain grabbed him by the arm and pulled him behind a crumbling wall.

The sound of lowing came from just beyond the church, and several cows eventually came into view, herded by an old woman. She was alone, so the captain stepped out from behind the wall and smiled at her.

"Can you help us, *señora?*" he asked in Spanish.

The woman stopped walking and looked at them with interest. She didn't appear to be afraid, only surprised by their presence. She shook her head, then pointed toward the road and shook her head again, dragging a finger across her throat. It was a clear warning.

"*Gracias,*" Captain de Cuéllar said.

The woman nodded and continued on her way.

"She might tell someone she saw us," Rafael said.

"She might," the captain agreed. He was deathly pale, and his forehead was beaded with perspiration despite the cool weather. "I don't think I can keep walking, de Silva. I need to rest." Rafael's eyes slid fearfully toward the church, and the captain took his meaning. "Let's go deeper into the woods, away from this terrible place."

They ambled along for a half-mile or so before finding a fallen tree to sit on. Rafael was weak with hunger and wished there were berries or nuts he could toss into his empty stomach, but nothing looked edible. The captain closed his eyes and leaned against a tree trunk. He looked like death. His breathing was ragged and his mouth slack.

Please don't die, Rafael pleaded with him silently. *I don't want to be left on my own. I'm scared.*

"I'm scared too," the captain said, making Rafael wonder if he'd spoken out loud. "It's all right to be frightened, son."

"What do we do, Captain?"

"We keep going."

"Where to?" Rafael asked. What would be the ideal outcome in this situation? If they returned to the beach, they had a chance of being picked up by one of their ships, but here, in the woods, they would die of hunger and exposure.

"We will find help," the captain assured him. "I've no doubt there are good Christians in this country. They will give us succor."

When he heard a rustling in the trees, Rafael sprang to his feet and grabbed for what would have been his sword had he still been wearing one. "Someone's there," he hissed.

The captain peered into the foliage from beneath hooded eyelids. "Show yourself," he demanded. He would have sounded commanding had his voice carried farther than that of a mewling kitten.

Two men emerged into the clearing. They wore the tattered remains of their breeches, and their torsos were covered with dirt and scratches. They breathed a sigh of relief when they saw Rafael and the captain.

"Juan," Rafael exclaimed and threw himself at the nearest man. "Oh, Juan, thank God you're alive."

Juan embraced him. "I've never been so glad to see anyone in my life, Rafael."

"This is Captain de Cuéllar," Rafael announced, as if they were all enjoying a cup of wine at a social gathering. "Captain, this is Juan González and…"

"Paco Laredo," the second man supplied. The two men drew themselves up and bowed to the captain, respecting his rank.

"Gentlemen," the captain replied. "At ease."

The two men sank to the ground. They looked as exhausted as Rafael felt. "Are there any other survivors from our ship?" Rafael asked. He didn't know the second man, but Juan González had been one of his mates aboard the *El Gran Grin*.

Juan shook his head. "The locals butchered nearly one hundred men, back that way." He indicated the direction they'd come from. "They robbed them first," he added. "Took everything, even their breeches."

"We're doomed," Paco Laredo moaned.

"Shut up, Paco," Juan hissed. "We're not dead yet."

"But we soon will be. I almost wish I'd drowned when the *Juliana* went down. It would have been a peaceful death."

"It's not too late. You can still drown yourself, señor Laredo. There's a creek that way," the captain replied, pointing toward the creek where they'd had a drink earlier. "It's not very deep, but if you lie on the bank and submerge your head, you'll accomplish the task."

Paco seemed unsure if the captain was serious and wisely remained silent.

"Do you have a plan, Captain?" Juan asked.

"Not as yet," the captain replied.

The men fell silent, sitting on the ground as if they were awaiting their execution. Perhaps they were.

Chapter 7

April 2015

London, England

Quinn shut the book and tenderly brushed a tendril of curly dark hair out of Emma's face. She looked way too serious for someone who'd just listened to a fairy story. Emma's eyes had a faraway look, but she seemed upset despite the happy ending.

"Would you like one more story?" Quinn asked. Emma clearly wasn't ready to go to sleep, and Quinn hated to leave her if she was worried about something.

"Why do you dig up dead people?" Emma asked, her gaze troubled.

"It's my job."

"I know that, but why do you *want* to do it? You could have had another job. You could have been a nurse or a teacher, or a fashion model."

Quinn chuckled. "I don't think I could have been a fashion model, but yes, I could have had another job. But I love history, and I want to tell people's stories."

"Will someone dig up my mum someday?" Emma asked, her voice small. She mentioned Jenna less and less, having been only four when her mother died, but occasionally something would jog her memory and she'd start asking questions and wouldn't stop until she found some sense of inner peace.

"Is that what you're worried about?"

"I don't want her disturbed. Daddy said she's at peace, and I want her to stay that way."

46

"Sweetheart, no one is going to disturb your mum's grave. Daddy and I study people who died hundreds of years ago."

"You're still disturbing their peace," Emma argued. "Who is this new person you're studying?"

"He lived a long, long time ago, in the sixteenth century. He didn't have a real grave; he was buried in the woods. Perhaps I can discover who he was and then he can be laid to rest properly, with a headstone with his name on it."

"Would he know if that happened?" Emma asked.

Quinn sighed. These were difficult questions, but she and Gabe had decided that they would always try to give Emma the most truthful answer they could.

"No, he won't know, but I will."

"But you will show him on television without his permission."

"Sweetheart, history belongs to everyone. We can't ask those who came before us for permission, but we can tell their story and hope that people will learn from it, and sometimes, even right a wrong."

"Would you want people to tell your story?" Emma asked sullenly.

"I don't know," Quinn answered truthfully. "I never thought about it."

"Well, maybe you should," Emma said, and turned to face the wall. "Goodnight."

"Goodnight," Quinn said, feeling absurdly hurt by Emma's dismissal. She returned the book to its proper place, turned out the light, and left the room, going to check on Alex before heading to bed herself. Alex was fast asleep, his arms raised as if he were surrendering. It was his favorite pose and it always brought a smile to Quinn's face.

"I hope you still like me," she whispered as she leaned forward to give the baby a tender kiss. Alex smiled in his sleep, making Quinn feel marginally better about her parenting skills.

"Did Emma ask for one more story?" Gabe asked. He was stretched out on their bed, arms behind his head.

"No, she wanted to talk about archeology."

"Really? Do you think she's interested?" Gabe asked, pleased by the prospect of Emma following in their footsteps.

"No, she thinks we are grave robbers who have no respect for the dead and exploit them to gain fame and fortune."

"Seriously?"

"Something like that. She's worried someone will disturb Jenna's grave."

"I never imagined something like that would even come up."

"Neither did I. I guess we have a lot to learn about children."

"Were you thinking about graves when you were five?" Gabe asked.

"No, but then no one I knew had ever died. It wasn't until my grandmother Ruth died that I came face to face with losing someone I loved. I was older than Emma though. Emma will carry the scars of losing her mother and grandmother for the rest of her days. Perhaps it'd be good for her to visit their graves."

"I thought it would be too painful for her to return to Edinburgh so soon after the accident," Gabe said.

"Maybe we should ask her."

"Yes, I think you're right. I'll work it into the conversation one of these days. If I ask her too soon, she'll think there's a reason to worry, based on what she said to you."

"Never thought I'd be having these conversations with a five-year-old. I wonder if Alex will be as precocious," Quinn said.

"Hopefully, he'll have no reason to think about death and loss until he's much older. It's only natural for Emma to ask these questions. She's trying to understand, that's all."

"Yes, I suppose you're right. It just surprised me is all, being accused of doing something dishonorable."

"Perhaps it is," Gabe replied, his expression thoughtful. "We think our research is benefitting humanity, but we are disturbing the final resting places of those who came before us. Would you want your remains examined on TV?"

"That's exactly what Emma asked me," Quinn said. "And my honest answer is no, I wouldn't."

"So, you're giving up archeology, then?" Gabe asked with an indulgent grin. "It's not too late to change careers, you know."

"Emma said I could have been a fashion model," Quinn replied, watching for Gabe's reaction.

"And she's absolutely right. That or a bus driver. You're the best driver I know."

Quinn swatted Gabe with a pillow, but he managed to catch her by the wrists and pulled her on top of him, planting a kiss on her lips as he tossed the pillow aside. "Tell me about the latest victim of your exploitation, Madame Bones."

"Colin pronounced him to be completely unremarkable," Quinn said, rolling off Gabe and snuggling next to him instead.

Gabe turned onto his side and propped his head on his palm, his brow creased with disapproval. "I beg to differ," he replied. "Colin is not seeing the whole picture. I think it's remarkable that not only was this man crucified in a place not known for crucifixions, but he was still on his cross when we found his remains. Have you learned anything about him from the amulet?"

"His name was Rafael de Silva."

"A Spaniard? A survivor of the Armada?" Gabe asked, his eyes shining with curiosity. The defeat of the Spanish Armada was one of his favorite events in British history after the Wars of the Roses, in which his ancestors had fought, first as Lancastrians and later as Yorkists. He'd been extremely reluctant to part with Guy de Rosel's sword, which had been found buried with his love, Kate, whose remains had been discovered beneath the kitchen tiles of his ancestral home. The sword had been reburied with Kate when her remains were interred next to those of Guy and her husband, Hugh de Rosel, only last month.

"Tell me what happened, Gabe—the abbreviated version," Quinn added, seeing the eager look on Gabe's face that meant he could lecture for an hour if unchecked.

"Well, we've all learned about the defeat of the Spanish Armada at school, but few people know or care what happened to the survivors. Thousands of Spaniards came ashore after their ships smashed on the rocks and sank just off the coast of Ireland. Many died by drowning, but many survived."

"They didn't fare too well, if what I've seen is anything to go by."

"No, they didn't. The Spanish mistakenly believed that the Irish, being staunchly Catholic and discontented after years of being trampled into the dirt by Queen Elizabeth's government, would offer assistance, but they miscalculated badly—not that they ever intended to make landfall in Ireland. The ships were driven off course and sidelined by a series of gales that decimated what was left of the Spanish fleet. About two dozen vessels went down off the West Coast of Ireland. The English Lord Deputy of Ireland, William Fitzwilliam, issued a proclamation stating that harboring or assisting any survivors of the Armada was punishable by death. He openly sanctioned the use of torture to relieve the Spaniards of their possessions and weapons. Thousands were killed, but some survived. There are some who claim they're 'Black Irish' because of the Spanish blood introduced into their bloodlines by the Spaniards who settled in Ireland. Pete McGann seems to believe that story and tells it proudly."

"Does Pete have Spanish ancestors?" Quinn asked.

"Not as far as I know. Besides, there's no evidence to suggest that enough Spaniards survived the massacre to make a marked difference in the population, but don't tell Pete."

Quinn chuckled. "I won't, but one could reasonably argue that a surviving Spaniard might have taken his wife's name in order to blend in and spare their future children from being ostracized and persecuted."

"Yes, that's one theory. At that stage, they weren't overly concerned with the preservation of their ancestral lines, only with survival. So, what happened to Rafael de Silva?"

"Rafael survived the sinking of the *El Gran Grin* and washed up on the beach in Connacht. As many as eight hundred men washed up on that same beach, according to my research. Many were already dead, but the ones who survived were attacked by the locals—stripped, robbed, and killed, their bodies left for the animals and the crows. Several hundred more washed up a short distance away. Can you imagine the scene?" Quinn asked, shuddering at the memory of what she'd seen. "It must have been mind-blowing to see all these people suddenly spit out by the sea. Anyway, de Silva crawled into the rushes and hid, and was eventually joined by a captain of one of the other vessels. They managed to get away from the beach under cover of the night and came across two other soldiers later that day."

"Do you still believe de Silva was Muslim?" Gabe asked.

"Yes, I do. He swallowed the Hand of Fatima for fear of it being taken off him. It was given to him by his fiancée just before he left for La Coruña, from where the Armada set sail."

"Interesting choice of hiding place," Gabe said with a chuckle.

"The soldiers were being stripped naked, so there was nowhere else he could have hidden it. Carrying the amulet on him was an act of incredible bravery to begin with."

"Or an act of unspeakable stupidity, given what would have happened to him had he been discovered with it."

"Probably a little of both. Had it been found, he would have been put to death immediately, and it wouldn't have been a quick and painless death. He would have been made an example of and probably tortured for information about other Muslims in the ranks."

"Do you think there were others?" Gabe asked.

"Don't you?"

"Given the sheer volume of soldiers and crew that sailed with the Armada and the number of ancient families in Spain who were of Moorish descent, I think it very likely. So, what happened to him?" Gabe prompted.

"I don't know yet, but I mean to find out. I've made plans to see Jo tomorrow. I offered to show her the charm."

"Is that wise?" Gabe asked carefully.

"She didn't say she didn't want to see it."

"I think Jo's afraid to disappoint you, but it's clear she has no desire to embrace her gift. Until a short while ago, you'd have done anything to lose your ability to see into the past. Don't push her, love."

Quinn nodded. "You're right, as usual. I'm just so excited to have someone I can share this with. I know, I need to tread carefully. Jo's been different since we returned from Germany."

"She's at home now and feeling less vulnerable. She needs time to establish relationships with all these new people in her life, and she needs to do it on her own terms."

"Gabe?"

"Hmm?"

"I really hate it when you're right," Quinn said, grinning at him.

"You should be used to it by now."

Quinn grabbed the pillow Gabe had tossed aside earlier and smacked him over the head, giggling madly. He grabbed it from her hands, tossed it aside once again, and deftly flipped Quinn onto her back, pinning her beneath him. "You know what else I'm right about?" he asked, his voice low and silky.

"No. What?"

"How much you're going to enjoy what comes next."

Chapter 8

September 1588

Connaught, Ireland

The wind picked up during the course of the evening, whispering ominously in the trees above his head as Rafael tried in vain to get to sleep. His body was pressed to Juan's. Paco was nestled between Juan and the captain. It had been decided that since Rafael and the captain still had their shirts and doublets, they'd provide whatever warmth they could to the men in the middle. Juan's bare chest was covered in gooseflesh and his bare feet were cold as ice against Rafael's shins.

Paco snored softly, but the captain's breathing was ragged, his face flushed with fever. He'd put on a brave face during the day, but the hours spent floating in the icy waters of the North Atlantic had taken their toll. Rafael's father would have prescribed bed rest, hot broth, and an infusion of willow bark to relieve the fever, but other than resting on cold, hard ground, there was nothing Rafael could suggest that would help the man. He hoped the captain was strong enough to fight off the illness on his own.

"Why aren't you sleeping?" Juan asked as he pressed himself even closer to Rafael.

"I can't."

"Neither can I. Every time I fall asleep, I see Pilar's face."

"It's only natural for you to think of your wife," Rafael replied. *Especially when you're not sure if you'll ever see her again.*

"Pilar is near her time," Juan replied. "She might have had the baby already, for all I know. It breaks my heart to think that I will never see my child."

54

"Don't lose hope, Juan. We're not dead yet."

"No, we're not, but unless we find food and shelter soon, we will be. It's only September, and it's already so cold."

Rafael nodded. It grew bitterly cold once the sun went down. September in Spain was a golden month, the tail end of summer that lasted well into October. The blistering heat of July and August gave way to pleasant, sunny days and cool, fragrant evenings. September in Ireland seemed to herald the beginning of winter.

"If I die here, Pilar will never know what became of me. She won't be able to remarry," Juan whispered.

"Do you want her to?" Rafael asked, surprised by the direction of Juan's thoughts.

"I don't want her to spend what's left of her youth waiting for a husband who won't come home. I want her to be happy, and I want my child to have a father."

"I never imagined that a man would want his wife to remarry. Surely you'd want her to remain loyal to you."

"What good would that do me if I'm dead? No, I want my Pilar to know love, both emotional and physical."

"Juan, how did you know what to do on your wedding night?" Rafael asked. It was an embarrassing question, but a dark forest seemed as good a place as any to ask.

"Pilar wasn't my first."

"But lying with a woman who's not your wife is a sin," Rafael replied, shocked by Juan's unflinching honesty.

"Dying a virgin is a sin, if you ask me," Juan replied.

"Was it different with Pilar?"

"Because she's my wife?" Juan thought about it for a moment. "Yes, it was different. It wasn't only about me. I wanted to give her pleasure."

Rafael raised himself on one elbow and looked down at Juan. "Women derive pleasure from their marital obligations?"

"You really are naïve, aren't you, Rafael? Of course, they do, if you teach them right. If you're gentle and patient, they learn to like it. They open up like a flower," Juan explained.

"I never would have thought."

"How old are you, anyway?" Juan demanded.

"I'm eighteen."

"You don't know what you're missing, my man."

"What am I missing?" Rafael asked.

"An older brother. My brother took me to a brothel when I was fourteen. I was afraid I wouldn't know what to do, so he had a woman in front of me. I watched and learned, so when it was my turn, I didn't disgrace myself too badly."

"Did your brother watch?" Rafael asked, curious about this unheard-of intimacy between brothers. Rafael had never so much as taken a piss in front of Ramón.

"Yes. I didn't mind. It made me feel like a man. Afterward, my brother got us a bottle of Madeira and we got drunk."

"What happened after that?"

"How do you mean?"

"Did you two go back to the brothel?"

"We went about once a month. That's all my brother could afford in those days. We always shared a whore. It was cheaper than getting two women."

"What if your priest found out?" Rafael asked. He still couldn't wrap his mind around such debauchery.

"Rafael, priests are men. They try to suppress their urges, but don't always succeed."

"Are you saying some priests have carnal relations with women?"

"I'm saying that men are men. My uncle is a priest," Juan added. "He kept a mistress for years. She bore him two daughters."

"Was the woman not disgraced and whipped through the streets?"

"No, you idiot. My uncle found her a husband as soon as she got with child the first time. The man received a handsome incentive, if you know what I mean, and my uncle continued to see her until he grew tired of her."

"What would happen if he was discovered?" Rafael asked.

"He'd probably just get a slap on the wrist. What do you think would happen? Did you think the bishop would have him defrocked? Or castrated?" Juan chuckled softly.

"I'll castrate *you* if you don't shut up," the captain growled. "Have some respect for your wife, González, and stop talking about whores."

"I'm sorry, sir," Juan replied, making a face at Rafael.

"Go to sleep, you two. We move out tomorrow."

"Move out to where, sir?" Juan asked.

"Anywhere. We can't stay here," the captain replied.

The captain turned his back to them and pretended to sleep, but Rafael could tell by his breathing that he was awake. As the only officer among them, he felt responsible for the men, but he was probably just as scared and confused as the rest of them, as well as being ill.

Chapter 9

There was frost on the ground when they awoke at dawn, and a thick mist swirled around them, shrouding them in a cloud of icy moisture. Pedro and Juan shivered with cold, but the captain's face was unnaturally pink, his forehead beaded with perspiration. Rafael bit back a complaint about his clothes being damp. At least he still had clothes, and for that he was grateful. His stomach growled, but he made no comment. Everyone was hungry.

"How're you feeling this morning, sir?" Rafael asked the captain.

"Fit," the captain lied smoothly. "And how about you?"

"Not too bad, sir," Rafael replied with forced cheerfulness.

"Let's go, then."

"I think this is where we part company, gentlemen," Juan said as he rubbed his arms to warm himself up.

Rafael stared at him in disbelief. "What do you mean? Where are you going?"

"Paco and I have decided to return to the coast," Juan replied.

"And what, pray tell, do you intend to do there?" Captain de Cuéllar demanded.

"We will wait to be picked up by one of our ships. We have a much better chance of being rescued that way than by trudging through hostile territory in nothing but rags, Captain."

"Oh, you think so?" the captain asked, his voice rising an octave in irritation.

"I do. And if more of our men wash ashore, we can help ourselves to their clothes before the locals get there. We might even come across some supplies. If we remain here, we'll surely die."

"Suit yourselves," Captain de Cuéllar replied. "De Silva, will you be going with your friend?"

"No, sir," Rafael replied.

"You're a fool, Rafael," Juan said. "You'll die out here."

"I wish you luck, Juan, but I'll take my chances with the captain."

Juan shrugged. "Go with God."

"And you as well," Captain de Cuéllar replied, and turned his back on Juan and Paco.

The two men walked away, disappearing into the mist within seconds.

"Do you really think we have a chance of survival, sir?" Rafael asked as he followed the captain through the dense wood.

"I think there are good Samaritans everywhere. We just have to find one."

"And then?"

"And then, we'll reevaluate the situation. Come, de Silva."

The two men walked on. Rafael thought they were heading southeast but wasn't sure. It was hard to tell in the mist. They had been walking for what seemed like hours before the mist finally burned off and brilliant sunshine streamed through the trees, the shafts shimmering like arrows of light shot from heaven. Rafael stared at the canopy above his head. He'd never seen such a phenomenon. In Toledo, the sun glared more than shone, and it was all around, a constant presence, not a fleeting brightness that felt like an omen of good things to come.

"There's something magical about this place," Rafael said. "Mystical. It's almost as if we're not alone in these woods."

"We likely aren't, but it's not goblins you have to fear, but men with swords and lengths of rope. Keep walking, boy."

Rafael trudged along. He kept an eye out for anything edible, but although he saw a tree with clusters of red berries, he had no way of knowing if the fruit was edible. Same went for the mushrooms. He'd spotted a few colorful caps peeking from the undergrowth. Mushrooms grew in moist, dark places, but some fungi were poisonous, and eating even one could result in death. He noted with some surprise that he was no longer as hungry. It was as if his stomach had given up on the idea of food. If only he didn't feel so lethargic.

They stepped out of the woods and onto what looked like a dirt road.

"Shall we risk it, de Silva?" the captain asked. "Perhaps we'll come to a village."

"Where we will be welcomed?" Rafael asked, his voice laced with doubt.

"Maybe not welcomed, but hopefully not chased off with torches and pitchforks. Come."

They continued to walk, moving along at a reasonable pace. After some considerable time, they spotted several people coming toward them. Rafael thought the captain would wish to hide in the woods, but he continued to walk and raised his hand in greeting. The party consisted of two young men, a woman, and an old man who was riding a donkey.

"Would be helpful if we knew some English," the captain said wistfully.

"I speak a little of their tongue," Rafael replied. Under normal circumstances, he wouldn't readily admit to speaking English, since it would raise questions about his reasons for learning it, but at the moment, this clandestine knowledge was only of benefit if it helped them survive. The captain looked surprised but asked no questions.

"Hail them, then," he instructed.

"Good morrow," Rafael said shyly once the locals came within hearing distance.

"Good morrow," the young woman replied civilly. "Where are you headed?"

"Is there a village nearby?" Rafael asked. "We are in search of food and shelter."

The young woman looked like she was about to answer when one of the men, possibly her brother, shoved her out of the way and stepped forward. The other followed suit. The woman said something to them, but they ignored her and advanced slowly, knives drawn, teeth bared as if they were hunting a wild animal.

"Don't kill them," the woman cried. "'Tis a sin, no matter what the Lord Deputy says. The English wish to damn our souls."

"Shut yer gob, woman," one of the men growled without turning around. His eyes were fixed on the captain and the glint of gold around his neck. The captain drew back in alarm, but it was too late. The men charged, brandishing their knives. Rafael didn't think he had any strength left, but a surge of energy flowed through his weak limbs and he dodged thrust after thrust, desperate to stay alive for another day. Captain de Cuéllar let out a cry of pain as one of the young men sank the blade of his knife into the captain's thigh.

"Stop it at once, ye daft eejits," the old man on the donkey commanded. "Murder is still a sin, last I checked. Seems yer sister is the only one with any sense 'round 'ere."

The two young men drew back, hanging their heads like whipped dogs.

"Hand over yer valuables and ye will not be harmed," the old man said. Evidently, last time he'd checked, theft no longer qualified as a sin. "Now!" he commanded, making it clear that if they refused, his sons, or whoever they were, would finish what they'd started.

Rafael had a few coins, which he handed to the woman. Captain de Cuéllar might have resisted had he not been wounded. He could barely stand, and a dark stain bloomed on his velvet breeches. The two young men relieved him of his doublet and purse and removed the thick gold chain from around his neck.

"No," de Cuéllar protested when the woman hung the chain around her neck. "That contains a holy relic."

No one paid him any mind, nor would they have even if they'd understood what the captain had said. A holy relic only made their find more valuable. The young men stared at the coins. They likely couldn't estimate the value of the money, but they recognized gold when they saw it. De Cuéllar had more than forty golden crowns on him, as well as nearly one thousand ducats.

"Take off yer clothes," one of the young men demanded. "Both of ye."

"Leave 'em be," the woman pleaded. "Let's be on our way. Their clothes ain't worth nothin'.""

"I want to see them humiliated," her brother retorted.

"I think they've been humiliated enough," the old man said, his eyes glinting with greed. "Now, 'and over the coins."

The young man reluctantly handed over the loot, and the old man bit down on a coin and nodded approvingly. "Pure gold, this. Be gone," he said, grinning at Rafael and Captain de Cuéllar. "It ain't safe on the road," he added with a phlegmy chuckle.

Rafael wrapped his arm around the captain's waist and helped him to walk. The captain moaned but clamped his teeth together and continued to hobble down the road.

"These people are savages," he groaned as soon as they were out of earshot.

Rafael nodded, but didn't reply. The Spanish had committed acts of savagery against his people for decades, but their pain didn't count. To the grand inquisitors, they weren't human or worthy of compassion. Perhaps the captain didn't realize that his brethren were just as savage, perhaps even more so. The Irish had no pity for them because they were the enemy, Catholic or not, but the Spanish had turned on people whose Spanish heritage went back generations and who only wished to live in peace, which was much worse.

Rafael walked the captain over to a stout tree on the side of the road and helped him to sit down. His breeches were soaked with blood, but they had nothing to use as a bandage save their shirts. Rafael was about to tear off a strip of linen when the captain held up his hand, forestalling him.

"No, de Silva. You need your shirt. I'll be all right."

"Then allow me to clean your wound, sir," Rafael offered. He collected some leaves and used them to cleanse the wound. Thankfully, it wasn't deep, but it looked painful.

De Cuéllar rested his head against the trunk and shut his eyes. His earlier flush had been replaced with a grayish pallor that gave the captain the appearance of a day-old corpse.

"Does it hurt very badly, sir?" Rafael asked.

"It's just a scratch," de Cuéllar replied stubbornly. "It's the loss of the necklace that pains me. It was precious to me."

"I'm sorry, sir," Rafael said, his hand subconsciously moving to his belly. He still hadn't moved his bowels and was secretly pleased that his hamsa was safe in his gut. It might remain there if he died, but at least no one would take it from him and melt it down for the gold, or throw it into the flames, fearful its heathen magic would infect them.

64

"Someone's coming," the captain said, his voice low.

Rafael whipped around, instinctively stepping in front of the captain to shield him from attack but breathed a sigh of relief when he saw a boy of about twelve walking toward them. The boy kept his gaze on Rafael as he approached, then shyly raised his hand in greeting. He carried a parcel wrapped in cloth beneath his arm. The boy slowed his steps as he came closer to the men, his freckled face tight with anxiety. Rafael stood his ground, curious what the boy might want with them. They had nothing left to take.

The boy gave Rafael a wobbly smile and placed the parcel on the ground, pointing toward it and inviting Rafael to open it. Rafael turned to the captain, who nodded his consent. Rafael carefully untied the ends and gasped in surprise. The parcel contained several slices of oat bread, thickly spread with butter. The boy untied a brown pouch from his hempen belt and handed it to Rafael. It was a skin full of milk. His smile widened. He seemed pleased by the stunned reaction of the strangers and indicated that they should eat.

"Thank you," Rafael said.

The boy nodded, still smiling.

Rafael handed half the food to the captain and fell on his own portion. Bread and butter had never tasted so good, and he took a long swallow of milk to help the thick bread go down. He thought he could eat and eat but got full after a few large bites, his stomach having shrunk after weeks on half-rations and three days of starvation. He wished he had something to wrap the rest of the bread in to save it for later, but there was nothing, so he broke the slice in half and laid it buttered side to buttered side, then stowed it in the pocket of his breeches. He took one last sip of milk and passed the skin to the captain, who was still eating. He was taking small bites and chewing the bread slowly, savoring the unexpected bounty.

"*Gracias, chico,*" he said to the boy, bowing to him deferentially. The boy seemed to understand and nodded happily.

He picked up the cloth the parcel had been wrapped in from the ground and held it out to the captain, then pointed to his leg. Captain de Cuéllar wrapped the cloth around his wound tightly, staunching the trickle of blood. He bowed to the boy again, and the boy smiled.

"Is there a village near here?" Rafael asked. It was unclear where the boy had come from or how he'd known they were there.

The boy nodded. "Just over that hill. Don't go to the village. It's not safe."

"Where should we go?" Rafael asked.

The boy pointed southward. "That way. Godspeed." He retrieved the empty skin and walked away, leaving the two men where he had found them.

"There are kind Christian people here, but they fear reprisal for helping us," the captain said, his gaze warm with gratitude as it followed the retreating boy until he disappeared from sight.

"I suppose so, sir," Rafael replied. He was deeply grateful to the boy, or more accurately to his mother, who must have sent the parcel; however, they were far from saved. "Sir, perhaps we should retreat into the woods so you can rest a while," he suggested.

"No, we will continue on. I'm fine. Don't fuss."

"As you wish."

They continued down the road in the direction the boy had indicated. It was slow going, with the captain hobbling along and stopping frequently, but Rafael supposed it was better than sitting around. Moving gave them a sense of purpose, and the food had done wonders not only for their bodies, but for their spirits as well.

Chapter 10

April 2015

London, England

Jo savored the crisp, fruity bouquet of the wine. It'd been a long while since she'd had a drink, not since before the explosion that had nearly killed her. She hadn't been allowed any alcohol while she was on medication, so this was her first grown-up meal, as she thought of it. Rhys sat across from her, enjoying his own glass of Pinot Noir.

"You look happy," he observed.

"I am. This is a lovely place."

"I'm glad you like it. What do you think of the food?"

"Delicious," Jo replied.

"How about something decadent for dessert?"

Jo shook her head. "I'm done. But you go ahead."

"I never eat dessert by myself," Rhys said. "It's not the same when you can't share the pleasure with someone."

"All right, I'll take a bite. I wouldn't want to deny you the pleasure."

"I knew you'd come around," Rhys said with a grin. "The chocolate soufflé is exquisite."

"Chocolate soufflé it is, then."

Rhys was right, of course. The soufflé was so light, it dissolved on Jo's tongue and she consumed more than she should have, but watching Rhys savor the sweet was a sensual experience in itself. This was a man who understood pleasure. A shiver of anticipation ran through Jo. Would he make his move tonight? They'd seen each other several times since she returned from Germany. Rhys had sent her flowers, taken her to lunch, and stopped by with home-baked goodies. He'd taken her for a walk in the park and they'd seen a film, but this was the first time their meeting had felt like a date and all her earlier reservations melted away. She didn't want the evening to end and was glad she'd worn one of her favorite dresses. The ruby-red satin contrasted beautifully with her dark coloring and the plunging neckline revealed just enough to hint that this wasn't just a dinner between friends.

When the bill arrived, Jo reached for her purse, but Rhys moved the leather folio out of her reach. "Absolutely not," he said. "You're my guest."

"Thank you. Next one's on me."

"That's a deal," Rhys replied as he slid his credit card into the designated slot. "I'll look forward to it."

Having paid, Rhys helped Jo on with her coat before escorting her outside. The sky was full of stars, the crescent moon suspended just above the dome of St. Paul's cathedral. The pavement was bathed in the glow of a nearby streetlamp, and they had the street entirely to themselves, as if they were actors who'd taken the stage for their intimate scene. Jo hesitated. This was the moment she'd been anticipating and dreading in equal parts. She peeked at Rhys from beneath her lashes, wondering how this night would end.

Rhys raised his hand to hail a taxi, and another shiver of anticipation ran through Jo. So, he was automatically assuming they'd go to his place. She didn't mind; she was game. It'd been a long while since she'd been with anyone, not since before taking the assignment in Kabul. There'd been plenty of European journalists staying at her hotel, but no one she'd liked enough to take to bed, and the rampant gossip had put her off. It seemed that all they did was play musical beds and then boast of their conquests at the hotel bar, drinking their weight in beer and wine just to pass the time. Brief periods of excitement were punctuated by days of inactivity when nothing worth reporting in the West happened. She supposed that was why she'd gone into the mountains with Ali. She'd been looking for her own story, her own angle. Anyone could report on political unrest and suicide bombings, but no one had dared to photograph the poppy farms or go after the drug lords who supplied ninety percent of the world's heroin. She'd nearly died for those photos, and the bitter disappointment of losing them when her camera melted in the explosion still rankled. It'd all been for nothing. A total waste.

A taxi pulled up to the curb and Rhys opened the door, holding it open as he leaned in to give Jo a chaste kiss on the cheek. "Thank you for a lovely evening, Jo," he said, smiling into her eyes. "Sleep well."

Jo had no choice but to get into the car. Rhys shut the door and gave her a friendly wave as the taxi pulled away, leaving her speechless with surprise and disappointment. He'd been as casual in their parting as if she were a business associate or an acquaintance. She had yet to figure out what she wanted from Rhys in the long term, but she was accustomed to being the one to decide while the other party waited in trepidation for her next move. Rhys had taken the choice out of her hands, and she didn't care for the way that made her feel. Jo's cheeks heated with humiliation as the pleasant fullness in her stomach suddenly turned acidic and made her feel ill. She wasn't used to rejection and now realized how badly it stung.

Nighttime London slid past the window of the taxi, but Jo barely noticed it. Desolation swept over her, making her feel weepy. She didn't want to go home. She couldn't face her silent, empty flat. She fumbled in her bag for her mobile and scrolled through the list of contacts. She found the one she was searching for and made the call.

"Tim? It's me," she said softly. "Yes, I know, it's been a long time," she said in response to his exclamation of surprise. "Are you free tonight? Okay, see you soon."

Jo ended the call and tossed the mobile back into her handbag. She fished out a compact, powdered her face, and refreshed her lipstick before running a hand through her hair. She wouldn't be alone tonight.

Chapter 11

Tim turned onto his side and propped his head on his hand, looking down at Jo with a soft smile. She reached out and brushed the blond forelock out of his eyes. She liked to see his eyes. She felt infinitely better than she had two hours before when Rhys casually dismissed her from his presence. She'd known Tim for years. He was a fellow photographer she'd met on assignment in Haiti. Tim was intelligent, witty, always up for a shag, and very much married. His wife, Stephanie, knew of Tim's dalliances, but didn't seem to mind as long as he came home to her in the end, and their arrangement seemed to work for them. Jo had briefly wondered if Stephanie played the field as much as her husband. She didn't care much about Stephanie's feelings, but thought it only fair that she played by the same rules as her husband.

"So, what really brought this on, Jo-Jo?" Tim asked as he studied her face. "It's been a long while since you've required my services."

"I didn't fancy being alone tonight."

"You've never minded being alone before."

"No, but things have changed. A lot's happened since I saw you last."

"Yes, I heard about Kabul. I'm glad you're all right, Jo-Jo."

"I'm not sure that I am."

"Tell me," Tim invited. He was a good listener, and someone who never betrayed a confidence. Jo suddenly realized that she'd invited him over not so much for sex as for conversation. She was in dire need of a confidant, and Tim was the closest thing she had to a trusted friend—besides her agent, Charles Sutcliffe, who could be useful in certain situations but not when it came to matters of the heart. Charles's black-and-white view of the world didn't sit well with her own shades-of-gray perspective, and she had no desire to see the disappointment in his eyes or the telltale pursing of his lips, which was becoming his usual expression when dealing with her.

"I've found my birth family, Tim. Or more accurately, it has found me. My twin sister, Quinn, came to the hospital in Germany. Since then, I've met my biological dad and two half-brothers. I have yet to meet my biological mother and my other half-brother, who's currently unavailable."

"Sounds promising," Tim said. "Aren't you glad?"

"It all sounds good on paper, but real life and real feelings are never as straightforward, are they?"

"So, what's troubling you? Are they a bunch of tossers?"

"Not at all. My dad is American, believe it or not, from Louisiana," Jo said, imitating Seth's southern drawl to pronounce the name of the state. "His family had a plantation and owned slaves before their Civil War."

"Plenty of Brits owned slaves," Tim replied, misunderstanding Jo's comment. "You can't hold that against him."

"I don't. I'm just giving you a bit of background information. My father has a son, Brett, who lured my pregnant sister to a family tomb and locked her in when she discovered that we're descended from one of the slave women the master had bestowed his attentions on. Seems he wasn't too pleased to learn he had Negro blood running through his veins. Brett's now serving a ten-year prison sentence for attempted murder."

"Ah, so it's that kind of birth family," Tim joked. "And there I thought they were going to be dull as dishwater."

"No, they're anything but. My half-brother Logan is engaged to his partner Colin. They're lovely, both of them. Logan is by far the most pleasant surprise of all. His younger brother, Jude, recently OD'd on heroin and nearly strangled himself with a belt while shagging his strung-out girlfriend. I met him briefly, but

I don't think he's at a point in his life where long-lost sisters are a priority."

"And what about your sister?"

Jo sighed dramatically. "Quinn is remarkable."

"As in remarkably irritating?" Tim asked, picking up on Jo's tone.

"Sort of. Quinn doesn't realize how lucky she is, Tim. She has amazing, loving adoptive parents who think the sun shines out of her bum, birth parents who want nothing more than to be a part of her life, a husband who practically walks on water, and two adorable children," Jo replied. "She also hosts a top-rated TV program and has a boss who dropped everything to travel to Kabul to look for Quinny's missing sister. I have never met anyone who's more loved or appreciated."

"You make it sound like a bad thing."

"It's not; it's just that I don't think I can ever live up to her expectations. She is so eager to get to know me, to bring me into the fold. And I want that; I really do. But some primitive, insecure part of me wants to run away and hide in a cave until the danger passes."

"Jo, please don't hate me for saying this, but love breeds love. There's a reason people flock to your sister."

"She's warm, caring, and selfless, and I feel like she sucks the air out of the room as soon as she walks in."

Tim shook his head and grinned, amused by Jo's petty jealousy. "You silly cow. Here you have someone who's desperate to love you and you're scared shitless because no one has cared enough before to try to break through that wall you've erected around yourself. Do you want to spend your life alone, Jo?"

"No. I want what my sister has, and that makes me angry."

"Why does it make you angry?"

"Because I don't know how to go about getting it."

"Maybe you should start by not trying to find reasons not to like her. Sounds to me like she's desperate to have a relationship with you, and she's willing to do all the work. Let her. I know you can't knock down your protective wall overnight, but maybe just lower the drawbridge and raise the portcullis enough to let someone in."

"Problem is, once you let someone in, they tend to want to stay."

"Would that be so terrible?"

Jo opened her mouth to reply but was surprised by the sob that tore from her chest. Silent tears slid down her cheeks and she allowed Tim to pull her close, burying her face in his shoulder.

"Jo, you're going to have to let someone in sometime, or you're going to die alone."

"I nearly did," Jo whimpered.

"You've been given a second chance. Don't waste it, love."

Jo nodded into Tim's shoulder. "You're right. I just don't know where to begin."

"You've made a start already. You admitted how you feel. I know that wasn't easy for you. What do you think the next step should be?"

"I suppose I should meet my birth mother." Jo sniffled and wiped angrily at her streaming eyes.

"Then do it." Tim opened his mouth as if to say something more when his mobile buzzed. "Gotta fly," he said after reading the new text.

"Go home to your wife, Tim," Jo said. "I'll be all right."

"You know, Jo-Jo, there are better things in life than being all right. There's such a thing as being happy."

"Are you happy?" Jo asked, peering at Tim in the dim light of the bedroom.

"Believe it or not, I am."

Tim bent down and kissed the tip of Jo's nose before getting out of bed and giving her a glorious view of his sexy bum. He pulled on his clothes and slid the mobile into his back pocket.

"See you again soon?" Tim asked, smiling.

"Don't count on it," Jo replied, smiling back.

She turned onto her side and closed her eyes, finally tired enough to go to sleep. She was already breathing softly by the time Tim let himself out of the flat.

Chapter 12

Jo towel-dried her hair and pulled on a comfortable old jersey and a pair of leggings. She'd woken late, and the only proof Tim had been there was the scent of his cologne on the pillow. Jo made coffee and popped two pieces of bread into the toaster, then carried her breakfast to the lounge and sat down on the sofa. She had some decisions to make about her new family, but her thoughts strayed to Rhys instead. A part of her was still hurt by his rejection, but in the cold light of day she was glad their evening had ended when it had. She'd enjoyed her romp with Tim. It was easy and uncomplicated, the type of sexual experience she was most comfortable with. As she took a bite of toast, Jo wondered how she would feel if Rhys had been the one she had slept with last night.

She'd have enjoyed the physical side of things; she was sure of that. She'd been with enough men to tell when someone would be a good lover. Rhys would be better than good, she decided. He was a giver by nature, not someone who took what he needed and moved on. Even a one-night stand would get Rhys's full attention in bed; it'd be a matter of pride for him to know that he'd left the woman satisfied and wanting more. But she didn't want a one-night stand with Rhys. Things could get awkward if the two of them weren't on the same page. At this point, Jo wasn't even sure they were reading the same book. What did Rhys want from her? Love? Friendship? The satisfaction of knowing he'd helped someone in need? She didn't need his pity or his patronage. If they came together, it had to be on her terms. Relationships were always on her terms, and they ended on her terms as well. But she couldn't play this game with Rhys; he was too close to Quinn.

Jo folded her legs beneath her and wrapped her hands around the warm mug. Had things with Rhys gone differently last night, would she feel happy? Awkward? Desperate for him to leave? Would she feel suffocated if he suggested spending the day together? It'd been a long time since she'd spent a day with a man—lunch, dinner, an entire night, sometimes even breakfast afterward, but she hadn't spent an entire day with anyone since Jesse. Those days had never been a hardship. Being with Jesse had felt easy and natural.

Jo felt a familiar pang of regret. Jesse had loved her, and she'd loved him. He had made her feel treasured and safe, something she hadn't felt with anyone else since. It'd been a long time since she'd asked herself if she'd made a mistake letting him go. She had been too young to get married, but he would have waited had she asked him to. He would have understood. Instead, she'd run away, left the country, and changed her name. Perhaps Tim was right and the wall around her was too high and too thick. She couldn't blame her impregnable defenses on her parents' betrayal or Michael's crime against her. Many people suffered at the hands of those they loved, but they didn't allow their pain to define them, to rule their lives. *Am I damaged beyond repair?* Jo asked herself as she stared at the milky light of the misty morning.

Perhaps, but it wasn't too late. She could still turn things around. Maybe, after years of running away, it was time to confront the people who'd caused her so much pain. The first person who'd betrayed her had been her birth mother. Sylvia had left her, ill and alone, when she was less than a day old. Jo didn't want to speak to Sylvia or see her, but if she were to confront her demons, her birth mother would be the first person on her list.

"Right," Jo said out loud to herself. "Sylvia, here I come."

Chapter 13

September 1588

Connaught, Ireland

As the pain of the captain's wound intensified, the men pushed deeper into the woods and settled by a shallow creek. There were still several hours of daylight left, but the captain needed to rest, and Rafael was tired of walking aimlessly and fearful of being set upon by the locals. He cleaned the captain's wound and washed out the bloodstained bandage, hanging it to dry on a low branch.

"Leave the wound uncovered, sir," Rafael advised the captain. "The fresh air will help the blood to clot."

"Are you a physician now?" the captain asked, but did as Rafael suggested and kept the fabric of his breeches away from the still-bleeding cut.

Rafael left the captain to rest and wandered off, scouring the area for any plants that might prove helpful. He wasn't familiar with the flora of northern Europe but hoped something might look familiar. His father used eucalyptus, garlic, and apple cider vinegar to treat a festering wound, but none of these remedies were readily available in an Irish forest. Rafael bent down and picked up a sprig of a weed-like plant. It had jagged leaves and tiny yellow flowers, and looked like celandine, which was of the poppy family. His father administered a potion made of brewed celandine leaves to his patients for the purpose of cleansing the liver. Rafael hoped that if applied locally, it might prevent a wound from festering. It certainly wouldn't do any harm. He collected several more springs and headed back toward the makeshift camp.

The captain was slumped against a tree, his eyes closed, but roused himself as soon as Rafael came near. "All right?" he asked as he watched Rafael approach.

"I found some celandine. I'd like to apply it to the wound," Rafael said, showing the captain the plant.

"Go on, then."

Rafael worked the sprigs between his hands until they formed a sticky mush, then pressed the pulp into the raw-looking wound. The captain gasped and went pale but allowed Rafael to continue with the treatment. The bandage was almost dry, so Rafael wrapped it around the leg to secure the poultice. He then washed his hands in the creek and reached for the bread he'd saved for supper.

"I'm not hungry," the captain protested when Rafael held out half the bread to him. "You have it."

"Sir, you need your strength to recover. I won't take no for an answer." Rafael's stomach growled, undermining his resolve, but he held out his hand until the captain accepted the food.

The captain broke his portion in half and handed one of the halves back to Rafael. "Eat," the captain said.

Rafael didn't argue. Since he'd eaten a few hours ago, the hunger that had been dormant had roared back to life and Rafael was secretly glad he'd get to enjoy a few more bites of the bread, although it wasn't nearly enough to fill his belly.

The captain took a tiny bite and chewed slowly, savoring the meal. Rafael was tempted to wolf the bread down but followed the captain's example and ate very slowly. The bread lasted longer that way, and he felt almost sated by the time he was finished. Rafael washed down his meal with water from the creek, then stripped off his doublet and shirt and washed his upper body. The water was icy, but it felt good. He wished he could shave. Stubble had quickly grown into a thick beard and his skin itched unbearably, but neither man had a knife. Rafael dressed and returned to the captain.

"You know something of healing?" Captain de Cuéllar asked.

"Not really, sir," Rafael replied. He had no way of knowing the captain's views on medicine and had no wish to arouse his suspicion.

"You needn't fear me, son," the captain said. "I don't believe healing to be a form of witchcraft. To help a fellow human being is divine, in my opinion."

Rafael nodded. He wouldn't be drawn into a theological discussion. The sentiments might seem harmless enough, but many a man, and woman, fell for a sympathetic ear and found themselves accused of heresy and tortured until they admitted to their crimes. Some were executed, their guilt based on nothing more than a whisper from a malicious rival, or a confession obtained by means that would make anyone confess to anything just to make the unbearable pain stop for even a second. No, he wouldn't fall for that.

"How is it that you speak English?" the captain asked, his shrewd gaze fixed on Rafael's face. He'd know a lie if he heard one, so Rafael answered as truthfully as possible.

"My father believes an educated man should speak several languages. I can also speak Latin and Greek," Rafael replied. He only knew the Latin he'd heard in church and seen in his father's medical texts and didn't speak a word of Greek, but if he admitted to the captain that his father had insisted on him learning only English, he'd be opening himself and his family up to suspicion, since the captain might think he'd been planning to jump ship and remain in England. In truth, Rafael wasn't even sure why his father wished to teach him English. It wasn't as if señor de Silva ever entertained the possibility of escaping to England.

"Your father is a wise man, de Silva. What does he do to earn his living?"

"We heard you were sentenced to hang," Rafael said instead of answering.

"Yes, I was. I was accused of disobedience."

"Did you intentionally break formation?" Rafael asked. He was curious about this man, who seemed so selfless and brave in the face of certain death.

De Cuéllar shook his head. "I wasn't on the bridge when that happened. The first mate misread the signals and broke formation."

"Why did you not tell that to the tribunal?" Rafael asked, mystified. "Surely they wouldn't have sentenced you to death."

"They would have executed the first mate," de Cuéllar replied.

"But it was his fault."

"It was my ship, my responsibility. I should have been there."

"You can't be on the bridge all the time," Rafael argued.

"No, but I should have been there at that time. I felt ill and went to lie down for a bit. I neglected my duty."

"Were you scared?" Rafael asked. He had no right to ask the captain such a prying question, but having spent several days with the man, Rafael felt that a certain intimacy had developed between them.

"Not of dying, no. My one regret was that my children would be ashamed of me. They'd have to live with my disgrace for the rest of their days. My execution would have robbed them of their honor."

"Why was the sentence not carried out?" Rafael asked. "I mean, I'm glad it wasn't, sir," he added, embarrassed by the clumsy question.

"I thought they'd hang me the day after the tribunal, but for some reason, the powers that be decided to wait. Perhaps they wished to make an example of me at a later date. I spent nearly two months in the brig, awaiting my fate. And then the ship went down in the storm and many good men died, while I was washed ashore and given another chance."

"Is that what this is?" Rafael asked. He hadn't meant to sound sarcastic, but he couldn't muster the same optimism as the captain, whose resolve seemed unflappable.

"Never lose hope, Rafael. We will survive this. We will return home, you and I."

"How can you be so sure, sir?"

"I have faith. Great faith."

"What was in your locket?" Rafael asked.

"It was a holy relic. That locket had been passed down from generation to generation, from father to son. It held a splinter from the true cross, Rafael. That bit of wood had touched the body of our Savior."

Rafael nodded. He strongly doubted the bit of wood had come anywhere near Jesus Christ, but wisely chose not to point that out. "You must be heartbroken to have it stolen from you."

"I am. I was going to pass the relic to my oldest son, but maybe it will bring salvation to the woman who took it. I must trust in the will of the Lord. Perhaps my family has held on to such holiness long enough."

"You're very generous of spirit, sir," Rafael replied.

He admired this man, perhaps because he was so different from his own father. Rafael loved his father and wished only to make him proud, but señor de Silva didn't have the courage or faith of the captain, despite his refusal to leave Spain and seek a safe harbor for his family. He was a man who lived in perpetual fear, dreading every knock on the door and praying daily for a reprieve from discovery, believing that God kept him alive as a reward for his stubbornness. Rafael understood something of his father's perverse nature, but it also angered him and incited secret rebellion in his breast. Captain de Cuéllar believed his God would save him because his God was merciful and forgiving. Señor de Silva feared his God would condemn him and turn away from him in his hour of need if he tried to save himself and those he loved.

"I'm not generous, nor have I lived an unblemished life, but I try every day to be the best man I can be. That's the only way I can be at peace with myself. Now, go to sleep, young de Silva. You need your rest, and I need mine. Tomorrow is another day, another trial of faith and courage."

"Goodnight, sir," Rafael said and curled into a ball. *I wish I had your courage*, he thought as he drifted off to sleep.

Chapter 14

The day was bright and sunny, the kind of day Rafael would normally rejoice in, but the trilling of birdsong and the sun shining through the thick green canopy overhead only made him more desperate. They'd been wandering around for days, hungry, tired, and cold. Their only hope of survival lay in the goodwill of strangers, and that was thin on the ground. The captain assured Rafael that his wound felt infinitely better, but he had difficulty getting to his feet and could barely walk. And where were they walking to, anyway? Rafael asked himself glumly. It wasn't as if they had a destination.

Rafael felt a familiar pressure in his abdomen and excused himself to attend to private business. He hadn't moved his bowels since swallowing the hamsa, so he'd need a moment. He squatted behind a thick trunk. It didn't take long, since there was barely anything in his stomach. Rafael pulled on his breeches and retreated to the creek to wash his hands. He cleaned the amulet thoroughly and admired it for a moment, secure in the knowledge that the captain couldn't see what he was doing. The bright blue opal glittered in the sunlight, winking at him like a playful eye. He wished to keep the charm close, to take it out when he felt despair to remind himself that God was watching over him, but given what had happened to the captain's possessions, there was only one thing to do. He placed the hamsa in his mouth and swallowed it with a handful of water. He hated to do it, but what choice did he have? Rafael returned to the captain.

"It's time we were on the road," Captain de Cuéllar said and turned in the direction they'd been walking the previous afternoon.

Rafael didn't bother to ask questions. The captain didn't have answers, and it was senseless to keep pointing out the perils of their situation. They had to keep moving. Perhaps Juan had been right to return to the beach, Rafael mused as he walked next to the captain. Juan and Paco could be aboard a ship, heading back to Spain at this very moment. Or they could be dead, lying on the beach, their remains picked over by hungry crows. He supposed he'd never know what became of his friend, and the thought saddened him. It would've lifted his spirits to discover that Juan had been rescued and was on his way back to his wife and child.

They walked the whole day, stopping periodically so the captain could rest. His face was a sickly shade of green, his breathing labored and shallow.

"Perhaps we should stop for the night," Rafael suggested, but the captain shook his head stubbornly.

"We keep going."

It was only when the purple shadows of twilight began to pool between the trees and the first stars appeared faintly in the sky that they saw the square tower of a church. The captain smiled and pointed toward the building. "We go there."

Rafael trudged along after him, terrified of what they'd find within. What if there were more corpses displayed for the entertainment of the locals? He was at the end of his tether, and if it weren't for the captain's endless faith, he might have given up by now and found a peaceful place to die.

The church looked gray and solid in the dusk, its windows aglow with candlelight. The heavy wooden door was closed but not locked, and the two men entered on silent feet, fearful of the reception they'd get. The inside smelled of wood, incense, and candlewax, achingly familiar smells that nearly brought tears to Rafael's eyes. He didn't believe in Christ the Savior, but he'd attended mass since he was a small child as part of his family's quest to appear Christian. He'd enjoyed the singing and the pageantry of the Church since the rituals of his own faith were always conducted in secret. As he followed the captain down the nave, Rafael wondered if his life would have been different if he believed in Christ.

A young priest knelt before the altar, his head bowed, his face illuminated by the flames of two thick candles that bracketed the altar. He appeared to be deep in prayer. He crossed himself, rose to his feet, and turned when he heard their approach. The priest's smile faltered when he realized he wasn't in the company of his parishioners, but he held his ground. Rafael thought they should leave before the priest called for help, but Captain de Cuéllar continued to advance toward the altar, his gait painful and slow.

"*Bonum vesperum*," the priest said, hailing them in Latin. "*Sani salvique*." *Good evening and you're safe*, the priest had said. Could he be trusted? The captain seemed to think so.

"Thank you, Father," he replied in Latin. "We would be most grateful for your assistance."

"Come," the priest said and beckoned for them to follow him into the vestry. "You can't be seen here. It's too dangerous."

The vestry was surprisingly spacious and nearly empty of furniture. There was a bench against the wall and a small table with what appeared to be the parish register on it. A brass candlestick with a tall white candle stood next to the register but wasn't lit. The priest used his own candle to ignite the wick and invited Rafael and the captain to sit on the bench as he stood facing them.

"My name is Father Liam," he said. "May I know your names?"

"I'm Captain Francisco de Cuéllar, and this is Rafael de Silva," the captain answered for them both in halting Latin. "We were shipwrecked north of here just over a week ago. We are in desperate need of aid, Father."

The priest nodded. "You must be tired and hungry."

"That we are," the captain agreed.

"Stay here. I will return presently."

The priest closed the door behind him, but it was only when Rafael heard the scrape of a key in the lock that he thought the

86

offer of help might be a trap. "He's locked us in, Captain. He means to turn us over to the mob," Rafael whispered.

Captain de Cuéllar leaned against the wall and stared at the candle flame, his face impassive. "He is a man of God, Rafael. Have faith."

My people have been persecuted by men of God for centuries, Rafael thought bitterly. *Pardon me if I don't have faith in the clergy.*

Rafael walked over to the door and tried the knob. The door wouldn't budge. It was made of solid wood, fitted with iron hinges. But even if they managed to force the door, they had nowhere to go. They hadn't eaten since the bread ran out and Rafael felt too weak and too hungry to keep walking. He couldn't begin to imagine how the captain managed to keep moving.

"How's your wound, sir?" Rafael asked.

"It pains me, but it's on the mend."

"Really?"

The captain shrugged. "It's what I'd like to believe."

Both men tensed when they heard stealthy footsteps approaching the vestry. They seemed to belong to only one person and Rafael exhaled in relief. The priest unlocked the door and came in, shutting the door firmly behind him. He had a basket slung over his arm, the contents covered with a piece of cloth.

"Please," he said, motioning them toward the table. He moved the register to the bench and displayed the contents of the basket. There were two small loaves of bread, several slices of ham, a hunk of cheese, and four apples. There was also a skin of beer. Father Liam gestured toward the food. "Enjoy," he said.

Rafael tore his loaf in half and filled the middle with pork and cheese. His father would have been horrified to see what he was eating, but at this moment, he didn't care. He was desperate for sustenance, and if he had to fill his belly with pork and cheese, he would do so with pleasure. Rafael took a bite and rolled his eyes in ecstasy. Captain de Cuéllar smiled at him and took a bite of his own meal. They ate in silence, passing the skin between them until all the beer was gone.

"You can sleep here tonight, but you must leave before first light. The villagers will kill you if you're discovered," the priest said with brutal honesty. "They're under orders to kill all the survivors of the Armada. Many of your countrymen are already dead."

"Is there anywhere we can go where we'll be safe?" Captain de Cuéllar asked.

"You must get to O'Rourke's territory. Sir Brian is a good Christian man who's no friend to the English. He will help you."

"And how far is it to O'Rourke lands?' Rafael asked.

"It's several days' walk from here. You must stay out of sight if you hope to reach safety," Father Liam admonished them.

"Thank you, Father," the captain said.

"It is the least I can do," the young priest replied. "I will come back and rouse you before dawn. Now, take your rest. You look like you need it," he added ruefully.

There was nothing to lie on but the narrow bench, so both men opted for the floor. They lay side by side on the hard stone. The vestry was cold, but not as cold as sleeping in the woods would have been and they were grateful for this small comfort. Their bellies were full, and for the moment, they had hope.

"Goodnight, de Silva," Captain de Cuéllar said. "Today has been a good day."

"Yes, sir," Rafael replied. Perhaps their luck was finally turning.

Chapter 15

April 2015

London, England

Quinn checked on the scones and turned off the oven. She'd never been someone who enjoyed baking, even though her mum had baked every Sunday while Quinn was growing up, but since they'd moved into the new house, she'd discovered a sudden desire to pursue new hobbies. Some she enjoyed, like entertaining, and others she detested. Puttering about in the garden was at the top of her list of dislikes. It was much like dusting—as soon as you finished, new dust settled, and new weeds sprang to life days after a patch had been weeded. Quinn took the tray of scones out of the oven and set them on the worktop to cool.

The doorbell chimed precisely at eleven, and Quinn hurried along the corridor to let Jo in. She had been pleased when Jo rang and asked if she could come round, so Quinn had promptly invited her for tea and scones. She'd always liked elevenses. It was the perfect time of day to enjoy a cup of tea or coffee and have a little something to tide one over till lunch. And it was a time when no one else would be at home and she and Jo could enjoy a nice chat. Alex had gone down for his nap a half hour before and would hopefully sleep until at least noon.

"Something smells amazing," Jo said as she stepped into the house. "Is Rhys here?"

Quinn laughed. "No, I take full credit for the wonderful smell. I baked us fresh scones."

"Did you make them from scratch?" Jo asked.

"Yes. It's not that difficult once you get the hang of it. First time I baked scones, they could have been used as missiles."

"You really are a marvel," Jo said. It was a compliment, but the words were tinged with sarcasm, which Quinn chose to ignore.

"Hardly. I just have a lot of time on my hands these days."

"What about the case you're working on?" Jo asked as she followed Quinn into the kitchen.

"Most of the work happens in my head," Quinn confessed. "Once I know what to look for, I try to find facts to support what I already know to be true." Quinn poured them both tea and transferred the scones to a pretty plate.

Jo accepted the tea and reached for a scone. "How do you do it, Quinn?" she asked.

"Do what?"

"Handle the artifacts."

"How do you mean?"

"It's not like going through some dusty old records. It's personal. It's painful."

"I admit, at times, it's more than I can handle, but I find satisfaction in being able to tell the stories of people who can no longer speak for themselves. Have you never handled an object long enough to learn its secrets?" Quinn asked.

"I've unwittingly picked up items that had belonged to the dead several times, but I couldn't hold on to them for more than a few minutes."

"Why is that?" Quinn asked. She could understand Jo's reluctance to see into the past, but the way Jo winced when she spoke of holding the objects made her think Jo's reaction was influenced by something more than mere distaste.

"I couldn't take the suffering. You must have a high tolerance for physical pain."

"I'm not sure I follow," Quinn replied, confused. Experiencing the suffering of the individuals she saw in her visions often left her gutted, but the pain was emotional, not physical.

"Don't you feel their pain?" Jo asked, staring at Quinn over her half-eaten scone.

"Not physically, no. Do you experience physical pain?"

Jo nodded. "I do. When I was eleven, Dad took me to the hospital, and we went down to the mortuary, where a postmortem was in progress. I was told to wait in the pathologist's office. The deceased's belongings were on the desk, in a plastic bag. I knew I wasn't supposed to touch anything, but there were these cufflinks, and they had an interesting design—very unusual. I took one of the cufflinks out of the bag to get a better look."

"What happened then?"

"I felt a searing pain in my side. It was like nothing I'd ever experienced before. I cried out and dropped the cufflink. It took a few minutes for the pain to finally subside, but my side felt sore for hours afterward."

"And you think you felt the pain of the deceased?" Quinn asked, still trying to wrap her mind around this interesting development.

"The man who owned the cufflinks had been attacked while he was walking home late one night. He was stabbed in the side. He bled to death," Jo replied, her voice flat.

"Did it ever happen again?"

"A few times. I tried on a ring that had belonged to my aunt, my mother's sister, June. She died of a heart attack at forty-six. I touched a pocket watch that had belonged to our neighbor's grandfather. His Spitfire went down over the Channel in 1942."

"My God," Quinn said, watching Jo with renewed interest. "Your ability is different than mine, and different than Brett's.

Brett and I never really talked about it, but I think he would have mentioned experiencing excruciating physical pain. He saw, not felt, of that I'm certain."

"The pain frightened me so much, I learned to avoid picking up anything that might have belonged to someone who died. People don't like it when you touch their things, or objects that belonged to those they loved, so I found it surprisingly easy. I haven't had an episode since my teens."

"Fascinating," Quinn said. "I suppose that makes your gift more powerful."

"Powerful or not, I have no desire to make use of it. I prefer to look at my subjects through a lens. It affords me a degree of emotional detachment."

Quinn nodded. That didn't surprise her in the least. Jo seemed to crave emotional detachment the way others craved intimacy. Quinn couldn't imagine going through life keeping everyone at arm's length, but she had no right to judge. She'd had a very different experience growing up.

"Let me see it," Jo said suddenly.

"See what?"

"I want to see the charm you found in Ireland."

"Jo, the person it belonged to was crucified."

"I know. I need to see if it will happen again, now that I'm older. I'll hold it for just a second."

"All right, if you are sure."

Quinn went to the study and returned with the plastic bag containing the hamsa. It glinted in the light from the lamps above the worktop, its opal center as fiery as it must have been when the amulet was first crafted. Jo reached for the bag and held it up, examining the little charm through the plastic.

"It's exquisite," she said. "I've seen a number of these in the Middle East."

"So have I. They sell them in every shop. Some are made of gold and precious stones, others of silver. And there are many cheaper versions that are used as keyrings, wall ornaments, and other trinkets."

"It must have belonged to a woman," Jo said. "This is too feminine to have been worn by a man."

"It had belonged to a woman, but she'd given it to a man as a keepsake," Quinn replied. She didn't want to give anything away, curious what Jo would experience when she held the hamsa in her hand. She was nervous, too. If Jo truly felt the pain as the victims had felt it, this experiment could go horribly wrong.

Jo carefully extracted the amulet from the bag and dropped it into her palm. The sisters stared at her hand, transfixed.

"Well?" Quinn finally asked after several tense minutes had elapsed.

Jo placed the charm on the granite worktop and took a shuddering breath. "I saw a dark-eyed, dark-haired young man. He looked Hispanic, and his clothes were very old-fashioned. Tudor era, perhaps. He seemed lost and frightened."

Jo suddenly reached for a scone and wolfed it down in three bites. She took several large gulps of tea before speaking again. "I'm sorry, all at once I felt a gnawing hunger, the type of hunger that permeates your every waking thought. I am not one for mindless eating, but I feel as if I could eat a dozen of these."

"Yes," Quinn said, nodding. "That makes perfect sense. He was starving. Did you feel anything else?" she asked eagerly.

Jo shook her head. "I felt bone-weary, but the predominant feelings were of overwhelming fear and crippling hunger. I felt no other physical discomfort. Perhaps I've outgrown the more extreme side effects of the visions."

Quinn retrieved the charm and returned it to the bag. "I suppose that's a good thing. I don't know what I would have done had you felt as if iron nails were being driven into your wrists."

Jo smiled sheepishly. "I wouldn't have let it get that far, but I suppose I wanted to see what you see. And now that I've seen him, I feel great sadness. He was hardly more than a child. Tell me about him. Who gave him the hamsa?"

"His name was Rafael de Silva, and the charm was given to him by his fiancée shortly before he sailed with the Spanish Armada. It was meant to bring him protection and luck."

"Clearly, it didn't work," Jo scoffed.

"No."

"Unless he gave it to someone as a gift, or as payment. I almost hope that's the case."

"I can't see that he would have done that. Given the hatred and mistrust the other Spaniards felt toward anyone who wasn't Christian, Rafael would have been risking his life by even admitting to having the charm. He swallowed it to keep it safe."

"That's one way of doing it, I suppose," Jo replied, grinning.

Quinn stared at Jo, amazed that she hadn't considered the possibility that had just occurred to her. "The charm was found below the body, in the dirt. It's quite possible that it was still inside his body when he died. Once the soft tissue decomposed, the metal object would have fallen to the ground, landing around the pelvic area, which was where I found it."

"That makes perfect sense," Jo agreed.

"But, if the charm was safely hidden, why would anyone want to crucify this poor young man?" Quinn asked, trying to find a theory that fit.

"I can't begin to imagine what he must have endured in his short life. No wonder I felt such fear in the few moments I held the charm."

"His story is not one that had a happy ending. And speaking of happy endings, how was your date with Rhys?"

Jo shrugged and looked away, focusing her gaze on the kitchen window. "It was nice," she muttered.

"I'm sorry. I shouldn't have asked. It's none of my business."

"It's okay, Quinn. You can ask, but I'm afraid there's nothing to tell. We had a nice meal at a restaurant of Rhys's choice, and then he kissed me on the cheek and sent me on my way."

"Were you hoping for more?" Quinn asked carefully.

"I *expected* more. I must have misread the signs. Think you can shed any light?"

Quinn lifted her cup to her lips and took a slow sip. It was a delaying tactic, but she wasn't sure how much she should say. More than anything, she wanted to forge a close relationship with Jo, but Rhys was not only her boss, he was a dear friend who'd confided in her and allowed her to see a side of himself he shared with few people. She had no right to betray his confidence by gossiping about his pain.

"Jo, Rhys is a very private person. He doesn't discuss his personal life with me." *Unless he has no choice*, Quinn thought, recalling the night she'd found Rhys sprawled on his bed, cold and unresponsive. He'd tried to drown his pain in sleeping tablets and alcohol after his fiancée miscarried their baby and had its remains incinerated before Rhys even got to the hospital. She'd then walked out on him after a heated argument in which she implied that the child hadn't been his. Rhys had managed to pull himself together, but he'd carry the scars of his loss for the rest of his life.

"But you do know something?"

"Rhys went through a difficult time a few months ago. I think he's still trying to come to terms with what happened. Perhaps he wants to take things slow. I'm sorry, but I can't tell you any more than that."

"I admire your loyalty, Quinn," Jo replied coolly, making Quinn feel like a worm. "I really should get going. Thanks for the tea."

"Jo, would you like to come for dinner next Saturday? I can invite Rhys," Quinn said, hoping that would be an added incentive.

"Sure, why not. I'll ring you."

Jo gave Quinn a quick peck on the cheek and walked out, leaving Quinn feeling as if she'd betrayed her sister somehow by not gossiping about Rhys.

Chapter 16

Jo slung her bag over her shoulder and headed toward the nearest station. Having reached it, she changed her mind about taking the Tube and continued walking, eager for physical exercise and a chance to marshal her thoughts. She'd enjoyed the little experiment with Quinn. Talking about the past and the unfortunate Rafael de Silva had allowed them to bond in a way that didn't make Jo uncomfortable. She admired Quinn's desire to tell the stories of the common folk who'd been forgotten, their names erased from history. Jo liked to tell stories as well, only she preferred to see the world from a distance, a tactic that allowed her a modicum of control.

Of course, that approach didn't always work, given the fiasco in Kabul, but she did care about shining a light on places and individuals who were struggling for survival in some of the darkest corners of the world. In a way, her chosen profession was more relevant than Quinn's flights into the past. After all, did any of these stories break new ground? Hadn't they learned about these historical events at school? What could Quinn add to the plethora of information on each given subject besides the sad story of one man or woman? She simply put a name and a face to a well-documented time in history, giving her narrative a more personal angle.

Some psychics might be brave enough to tell the world what they saw, but Quinn preferred to keep her ability a secret, and Jo didn't blame her. Not everyone could deal with that type of exposure, or the ridicule that would inevitably follow the revelation. Quinn would be a laughingstock in scientific circles, a pariah. If the truth came out, her program might get cancelled altogether, the BBC not wishing to align itself with a psychic unless the context was purely fictional. *Is that what I am?* Jo thought as she strolled along. *A psychic?*

The idea was intriguing. She'd always hated her unwelcome ability and worked hard not to access it, even by accident, but what if she were to try? Would she see exactly the

97

same things as Quinn if she spent time with Rafael de Silva, or would she see a different set of memories? Perhaps it was safe to try now that she knew she wouldn't get nailed to a cross, so to speak. And what of Brett Besson? What was his gift like? Quinn said they'd never openly discussed it, but it would be interesting to compare notes.

Jo filed away the question for later. Brett wasn't a topic Quinn wished to discuss, and Jo could hardly blame her after what she'd endured at his hands. Seth and Kathy Besson were in the process of filing an appeal, hoping Brett would get acquitted on a technicality, since Seth had beaten a confession out of his son in order to get to Quinn on time. She would have died had Seth not pummeled his son within an inch of his life, but that very desperation could now be used to undermine the conviction against Brett. He'd confessed under duress.

Tired after the long walk, Jo found a café and ordered a cup of tea and a turkey sandwich. The hunger she'd felt after holding the charm for only a few minutes still gnawed at her, even after eating several scones, and she felt unpleasantly weakened by the experience. She settled at a corner table and gazed out the window, watching the passersby as she enjoyed her meal.

She had been born with a gift that enabled her to look into the past, but she would gladly exchange this ability for one where she could examine the living. How different her life would be if she could hear the thoughts of those around her. Jo supposed she was curious about Rhys, especially now that Quinn had implied that he'd suffered some great personal tragedy. Rhys always seemed so cool, so in control. What would it take to make a man like him unravel? And what would make a man like him throw caution to the wind and rush off to Afghanistan to look for a woman he hardly knew? Was it unrequited love for Quinn or was it a despair so deep that he needed to feel his life threatened in order to value it once again?

She was sure Rhys had been hurt in Kabul. She'd seen his careful movements when he visited her at the hospital. There were no marks of violence on his face, but his hand had strayed to his side several times as if to contain the pain and his grimace had betrayed the depth of his suffering. Had Rhys been set upon, or might he have been in the vicinity of an explosion? And had risking his life given him the absolution he craved? Had he been able to work through whatever it was that ailed his soul? She hoped so, because she genuinely liked Rhys, and even if they never saw each other again, she wanted to know that his quest to find her had benefitted him as well.

And Quinn… She supposed Quinn was the one person she really wished to understand on a deeper level. They were twin sisters, they'd shared a womb, and an adoption experience that had left Jo scarred and broken. Quinn had found a way to turn her anger and confusion into something positive, whereas Jo used it as a shield. She was in awe of Quinn's ability to trust, especially after her boyfriend of eight years had cheated on her and broken up with her via text. She had such unwavering faith in Gabe. Such commitment to another human being could only exist when the person giving her trust was utterly secure in herself and her place in the world.

Jo supposed that despite Luke's betrayal, Quinn's experience of men had been very different from her own. Every man Jo had known, since the time she was a small child, had been a selfish, lying bastard—every man except Jesse. But Jesse had been smitten with her, maybe even a little obsessed. She'd been young, emotionally fragile, and hesitant to commit. Would he have remained true to her if she'd married him and allowed herself to settle into a life of domesticity? Would he have still loved her after she had several children and was no longer a girl, but a woman who had other priorities besides satisfying him in bed and helping him in his work? Perhaps that was why she'd run, because she hadn't really cared to discover that Jesse had cloven feet, just like every other man in her life.

Her father had had affairs. She'd heard her parents arguing many times, late into the night, her mother threatening to leave him if he didn't end his latest fling. He usually did, but not because he loved his wife. It was because he was already bored and ready to play the devoted husband for a while until a new flame sprang to life in his heart, or more accurately, his prick. By the time Jo was a teen, her parents had no longer shared a bedroom, and her father stayed out several nights a week, telling his wife he was "at the hospital," when they all knew it was a euphemism for saying he was staying at the current girlfriend's flat.

By his own admission, her biological father, Seth, had cheated on his wife and destroyed their marriage. Seth and Kathy had got back together recently, a development that had made Seth happy, but would he do better the second time around? Was it possible for someone who'd cheated once to stay faithful for any length of time? Were second chances really an opportunity to do better or just another chance to fail miserably?

Most men she'd come across in her work indulged in casual affairs, secure in the knowledge that their wives would never find out they'd shagged someone in Kabul or Tokyo. Was it possible to have a loving, committed relationship for the rest of one's life? Did Gabe, who was attractive and urbane, never stray, even in his thoughts? Was he still content, having won the woman of his dreams? The fact that Quinn didn't appear to be plagued by these doubts was what intimidated Jo and made her grudgingly admire her sister. What was the first step to such unwavering sense of self? Perhaps it was being honest, and Jo hadn't been honest with Quinn, not by a long shot. But was she ready to bare her soul?

Chapter 17

Quinn glanced at the kitchen clock as she stowed the remaining scones in a container and rinsed out the mugs. If she were lucky, Alex would nap for another half hour. Once he woke, she'd take him for a long walk. Alex needed the fresh air and she could use the exercise. In the meantime, she could ring Jill. They'd spoken several times since Quinn had returned from Germany with Jo but hadn't seen each other due to their conflicting schedules. Jill, who'd closed her vintage clothing shop in Soho at the beginning of the year, had just started a new job, working as a forensic accountant for an international conglomerate. It had been Jill's dream to have her own business, but even though things hadn't worked out, she wasn't bitter or disappointed. She'd bravely moved on and was settling into her new position. Quinn hoped Jill wouldn't be too busy to talk for a few minutes.

"Quinn!" her cousin exclaimed when she picked up the call. "I was just thinking about you."

"Must be telepathy, then. How are you? How's the new job?"

"Job's all right. When it comes to accounting, it's like riding a bike; once you get on, you immediately recall how to pedal. To be honest, I enjoy the predictability of it, because the simple beauty of a perfect balance sheet can gladden the heart."

"Do I sense a note of sarcasm?"

"Well, maybe just a little," Jill admitted. "I do miss the shop sometimes, but I'm determined to make a go of this."

"I'm glad to hear it. I'm having a little dinner party next Saturday and I'd love it if you and Brian could join us. I want you to meet Jo," Quinn added nervously. Jill was her best friend, her childhood partner in crime, adolescent confidante, and honorary sister. She'd been there for all the important moments in Quinn's life, but they'd barely seen each other since Quinn's quest for Jo had begun.

Jill sighed. "All right. We'll be there."

"Jill, what is it? Don't you want to meet my sister?"

"No," Jill replied, surprising Quinn with her bluntness. Jill wasn't one to mince words, but this was harsh even for her.

"Why? I'd like my sister and my best friend to get to know each other."

"I won't remain your best friend for long," Jill replied in a sulky tone.

"What are you talking about? You've been my best friend since we were little."

"That's because *she* wasn't around to spoil things."

"You can't be serious. Are you jealous of my relationship with her?"

"Quinn, all I've been hearing for months and months is Jo this and Jo that. It's like the sun rises and sets on Sister Jo. I understand how important she is to you, but you're piling an awful lot of expectations on this woman. You hardly know her."

"I'm getting to know her, and it'd be nice if you gave her a chance. Jill, Jo will never replace you. Never. Now, tell me you'll put this childish jealousy aside and keep an open mind."

Jill exhaled deeply. "All right. I will put this childish jealousy aside and meet Jo. But I won't like her," she added. Quinn could tell by the tone of her voice that she was smiling.

"Fair enough. See you next Saturday."

"Okay."

Chapter 18

September 1588

Connaught, Ireland

"It's time to go," Father Liam said.

Rafael rubbed his eyes and ran a hand through his tangled hair. It seemed as if he'd just fallen asleep, and already it was morning. His head ached and his neck was stiff. Rafael rolled his shoulders to get the crick out, but it didn't do much good.

Captain de Cuéllar got to his feet with some difficulty, using the bench to support his weight.

"Are you all right, Captain?" the priest asked.

"Spending the night on a stone floor didn't do my back any favors," the captain replied in Spanish, then switched to Latin for the benefit of Father Liam. "I'm just fine, Father. I thank you for your help."

"Here," the priest said as he handed the captain a cloth-wrapped parcel. "I'm afraid that's all I can spare."

"You've done more than enough," the captain replied. "We'll be on our way, then."

Father Liam extinguished the candle before leaving the church. "Best not to draw attention to ourselves," he explained.

Rafael shivered as he stepped outside. The sky was black as tar, the stars cold and distant. A biting wind moved through the trees, the leaves rustling ominously overhead. There wasn't a glimmer of light from the cottages in the distance. The world felt deceptively safe, but the cover of darkness wouldn't last long. Having eaten the night before, Rafael felt more energetic and hoped they'd cover a good distance this day. The prospect of help lit a tiny flame of hope in his chest, and for the first time in days, the fatalistic pall he'd been under lifted a bit, allowing him to breathe easier.

They parted company with Father Liam in the graveyard. "Go with God. I'll pray for your safe passage."

"God bless you, Father," the captain replied. "I'll never forget your kindness. Come, de Silva."

Rafael followed, eager to get as far from the village as possible before the inhabitants began to wake. Neither man spoke until ribbons of light began to appear in the east, casting a blood-red glow onto the puffy clouds.

"Promises to be another fine day," the captain said as he hobbled along. "We'd best get off the road now."

They veered off into the woods but continued to walk parallel to the road to keep their bearings, stopping around midday to rest.

"Let's see what the good father gave us, shall we?" the captain said as he unwrapped the parcel. There were four hard-boiled eggs and half a loaf of bread. "Here." The captain gave Rafael half the food.

Rafael looked at it with longing. He would have happily eaten everything in one go, but he helped himself to one egg and returned the rest of the food to the captain. "Let's save it for later."

The captain nodded. "We'll be glad of it in the evening," he agreed.

After a brief rest, they set off again. Hour after hour, their surroundings remained the same—dense woods, endless sky, the smell of the sea carried on the stiff breeze, and an occasional whiff of chimney smoke. A fortnight ago, Rafael had still been aboard his ship, hungry, frustrated, and homesick. The mood had been bleak, the anger of the men palpable, but at least there had still been the prospect of home, of a reunion with family. Their loved ones would forgive them the humiliating defeat, glad to find their husbands and sons alive. But now, countless men were dead, either drowned or murdered, the survivors hiding in forests, freezing and starving. How quickly one's reality changed, Rafael thought as he trudged along. His earlier burst of optimism seemed to have dissipated, leaving him feeling deflated once more.

He tried to imagine what Ramón might be doing at that very moment, or Mira. What did she do from day to day? She probably helped her mother with household tasks. Perhaps she was sewing a new gown or embroidering a tablecloth for their future home. Rafael tried to summon an image of domestic bliss, but all he felt was a hollowness in the pit of his stomach, even when he allowed his mind to stray to their wedding night. The prospect of lying with Mira did nothing to lift his spirits, or any other part of him. Why didn't he want her? There were women he found desirable. He meant them no disrespect, but his mind played cruel tricks on him, teasing him mercilessly until he thought he'd burst into flames with wanting to touch them. His fantasies were always followed by nagging guilt. It was a sin to touch oneself or spill one's seed for any other purpose than procreation. Men of his faith didn't use whores or lie with women outside of marriage. Mira would be his one and only if he ever made it back to her.

Rafael sighed. His father had said Rafael would learn to love his wife, as his father had learned to love Rafael's mother, and Rafael had to trust his judgement. It was not as if he could choose his own bride. Marriages were arranged by the families, and once an agreement was struck, there was no going back. Breaking the betrothal contract would bring shame on the family, and on the bride. Rafael's only way out was death, and he was dangerously close to being free. The grim thought made him chuckle.

"How's your wound, Captain?" he asked, desperate to focus on something other than his melancholy.

"On the mend. That poultice you fashioned seems to have helped. Where did you learn to do that?"

Rafael didn't reply. "Is that a lake, sir?" he asked as he peered into the gap between the trees.

Captain de Cuéllar followed Rafael's gaze. "I believe it is. Looks lovely, doesn't it?"

From their vantage point, the lake looked tranquil and pure, the pale-blue sky mirrored in its glassy surface. The water glowed in the autumn sunshine and the banks looked soft with thick grass.

"I think I'm going to have a bath," the captain announced. "Join me?"

"The water's probably cold," Rafael replied, but the prospect of dipping into that perfect pool beckoned. He longed to feel clean and wash his filthy clothes. Of course, if he washed his garments, he'd have to sit around naked until they dried—not an appealing prospect. He mentally thanked his mother for her forethought in refusing to allow his father to circumcise him. His father had been adamant, his had mother said, but she'd threatened to drown the newborn Rafael in the bath if her husband didn't give her his word that the child would remain untouched. After days of arguing, they'd reached a compromise. Señor de Silva would hold off until Rafael turned thirteen, then give the boy a choice. If Rafael chose to be brave, his father would perform the circumcision himself, since it'd be too late to have the ritual ceremony. If he chose the coward's way, his father would respect his decision, if grudgingly. The same agreement had also applied to Ramón.

On Rafael's thirteenth birthday, his father had called him into his study. "Well?" he said. "Have you made a decision, son?"

"I have," Rafael replied. His insides shook with trepidation, but he was going to stand his ground. He wasn't doing this only for himself, but for Ramón as well. If Rafael agreed to be circumcised, Ramón wouldn't be left with much of a choice. "I do not wish to be circumcised, Father—not if it will put my life in danger."

"Coward," señor de Silva spat out.

"There's a difference between cowardice and self-preservation, Father. My death at the hands of the zealots will accomplish nothing. I'll be just another dead heretic. If that makes me a coward, so be it, but the decision is mine, and I've made it."

"It should never have been your decision to begin with," his father growled. "I blame your mother, but what can you expect from a woman? All she cares about is the safety of her sons, but our lives are at the mercy of God. He decides whether you live or die, not you. If it's his will that you should die for your faith, then you should be willing to lay down your life."

I don't see you taking any risks, Rafael thought angrily. *Perhaps you're not as willing to please your God as you say you are.* "I've made my decision, Father," he said instead and walked out of the study, right into the warm embrace of his mother.

"Thank God, Rafi. I was so afraid you'd give in to his bullying."

"Perhaps Father is right and I'm nothing more than a coward who only wants to save his own skin," Rafael said.

"You're not a coward. You're the bravest boy I know, and the smartest. Your father's judgement is often clouded, especially when it comes to his children. Men are often more concerned with their pride than the safety of their loved ones. Come, let's have a glass of wine in the courtyard to celebrate your birthday. Your father will come around in time. You'll see."

Señor de Silva didn't come around and the subject came up again after Rafael's betrothal to Mira. "You can't go to your marriage bed uncircumcised. Mira will tell her mother, and then everyone will know that I was too much of a coward to circumcise my sons."

Rafael felt the weight of his father's expectations, and this time, he could hardly refuse. His father was right. Mira would tell her mother, and her mother would tell her husband. Within a day, everyone in their community would know, and the de Silva family would be treated with derision and suspicion. They might even be cast out if their faith came into question.

"All right, Father," Rafael said. "When I return from England, you may perform the ritual. I will not object."

"I will have your brother watch me do it. Perhaps it will inspire him to man up."

"Perhaps," Rafael had replied, hoping Ramón would hold out until his own betrothal.

Rafael shook his head in disbelief as he thought back to that last conversation. He'd survived a shipwreck, the massacre on the beach, and days without food or shelter. It'd be quite amusing if after all that the lack of a foreskin was the thing that got him killed. "Thank you, mamá," he said inwardly, and followed the captain toward the lake.

Captain de Cuéllar picked up the pace as they drew closer. It was now late afternoon and the banks of the lake looked like a good place to spend the night.

"Sir, is that a village?" Rafael asked, once the other side of the lake came into clear view.

Captain de Cuéllar stopped and peered at the opposite shore. "I believe it is. I don't see anyone though, and there's no smoke coming from the chimneys."

"Perhaps it's abandoned."

"We'll observe the settlement more closely once we're in range," the captain replied. "Perhaps we should wait for the cover of darkness before approaching."

Rafael agreed and they settled in to wait. By unspoken agreement, they finished the food. If they met with danger, they'd need their strength to fight or run. If the settlement was deserted, they'd simply take shelter and go to sleep. Rafael savored the remaining egg and bread and tried not to fret about where their next meal would come from.

"God will provide," the captain said once he finished his own food and brushed the crumbs from his breeches.

"Yes, sir," Rafael replied, without much conviction.

The lake turned a lovely shade of lavender once dusk began to gather over the lonely settlement, but the wooden huts transformed into ominous black husks in the gathering darkness, the windows like empty eye sockets in featureless faces. No sounds of human habitation disturbed the silence of the evening, and no chink of light sliced through the gloaming.

"There's no one there, sir," Rafael said, and he stood, ready to cover the distance between their vantage point and the deserted settlement. "We can take shelter for the night."

"Wait," the captain said, holding up his hand. "There's smoke coming from the farthest chimney."

Rafael squinted into the distance. He couldn't see any smoke, but now that the captain mentioned it, he smelled it. The aroma of burning wood filled him with longing. He couldn't recall the last time he'd felt truly warm and fully dry. Every morning, his clothes were damp with dew and he woke up shivering and covered in gooseflesh.

"We'll proceed cautiously and see who's there," the captain said.

They followed the shoreline of the lake until they approached the nearest hut. The houses were abandoned, the thatch roofs rotted through, and the hearth stones crumbling. There was an unpleasant smell of decay. The hut closest to the woods was surprisingly intact and a thin curl of smoke rose from the chimney. The shutters were firmly in place, but Rafael thought he could just make out the glow of a flame through a crack in the wood.

"Perhaps we should leave," Rafael suggested in a whisper.

"And pass up the chance of a warm fire?" the captain replied, smiling. "We will make our presence known and see what happens."

He approached the hut and knocked softly on the door. There was no answer at first, but eventually the door opened a crack and a frightened face stared at them from within. Then the door was yanked open and two more curious faces appeared behind the first man. The occupants of the hut were clearly Spaniards and their relief was palpable.

"Gentlemen, may we come in?" Captain de Cuéllar asked.

The three men stepped aside, allowing the captain and Rafael into the hut. The men were as bedraggled as Rafael and the captain. Their clothes were in tatters and they looked hungry and worn out. But they were alive, and they were comrades-in-arms.

"Captain Francisco de Cuéllar and Rafael de Silva, at your service," the captain said, bowing stiffly.

"Julio Fernández, Pedro Serrano, and Alfonso Pérez of the *Santa María de Visón*," Fernández announced. "You're welcome to share our shelter, *señores*."

After the initial introduction, the men exchanged basic information, eager to discover more about their new companions and to share their stories. Rafael learned that the three men were older than him by a few years. Pedro Serrano and Alfonso Pérez were common soldiers, but Julio Fernández held the rank of *cabos de escuadra* in the Tercios, an elite infantry unit. As a corporal, he outranked the other two men, but with the arrival of Captain de Cuéllar, he had to step down as leader. Pedro Serrano and Alfonso Pérez seemed genuinely welcoming, but Julio Fernández had a watchful air about him that wasn't lost on the captain, who addressed Julio when he spoke as was due his rank.

Rafael remained quiet, happy to allow the captain to do all the talking. Instead, he sat down by the fire, holding out his hands to the flames. He had never been so happy to feel the gentle caress of heat on his extremities. He edged closer and eventually the fire warmed him through, making him feel drowsy. The captain continued to converse with the men, sharing the details of their shipwreck and escape from the beach, but Rafael was hardly listening. Their story was similar to his own, and he had no desire to relive the suffering of those first few hours when he'd thought death was imminent and was frightened out of his wits.

"De Silva and I are going to Chieftain O'Rourke's territory," the captain explained. "We were told we'd find assistance there. Come with us."

Pedro Serrano and Alfonso Pérez glanced at Julio Fernández, who answered for all of them. "We can leave at first light."

"I would like to clean up before we go," the captain replied. "The lake looks inviting."

The men agreed to bathe first thing in the morning, so they could look more presentable when they arrived at their destination. Feeling warm and snug, Rafael had no desire to wade into icy water, but the captain was right, they looked like a band of convicts rather than soldiers of Spain.

Rafael's eyes burned with fatigue, but he wasn't ready to go to sleep, so he studied their companions from beneath hooded lids. With his patrician features and decisive manner, Julio Fernández fit the part of ranking officer. Pedro Serrano had the thick body and short neck of a born fighter, his ham-sized fists as intimidating a weapon as any sword. He appeared to give Julio his support, but there were several times when his eyes flashed with annoyance at something Julio said and he ventured to disagree with him, doggedly proving his point.

The only one of the men Rafael warmed to was Alfonso Pérez. He had a face like a potato, his doughy features not enhanced by large, protruding ears. His small, dark eyes glowed with good humor and he didn't seem to notice the undercurrents between Julio and Pedro, or maybe he simply chose to ignore them. Alfonso smiled at Rafael when he caught him looking and rolled his eyes in response to Julio's cocky remark. He wasn't thick, just not interested in vying for control, something Rafael understood only too well.

"Well, I'm for my bed, gentlemen," Captain de Cuéllar said. "I can barely keep my eyes open."

"Goodnight, Captain," the men replied, and took their places on the floor. Within minutes the small hut was filled with the sounds of slumber and Rafael allowed himself to drift off, comfortable in the knowledge that he was safe, at least for the night.

Chapter 19

It had taken three days of hard walking to finally reach the lands of Sir Brian O'Rourke, but as Father Liam had predicted, they had been welcomed as friends. A young lad they'd met on the road had escorted them to the chieftain's home, which was grander than anything Rafael had expected to find in the middle of such wilderness. The castle was built of gray stone, its circular tower rising above the crenelated battlements of the curtain wall. A gentle slope lead to a shimmering lake on one side, and dense woods and treacherous bogs encircled the castle on the remaining three sides. The castle wasn't as large as some Rafael had seen in Spain, but it looked formidable.

Sir Brian himself came out to welcome the men. His hair must have been a violent shade of red in his youth, but now it was streaked with gray, as was his ginger beard. He wasn't a tall man, but his wide shoulders and barrel chest gave him the aura of a man who'd stand his ground and not back down from a fight. Sir Brian's bright blue eyes shone with compassion and admiration as he beheld the survivors, who were barely standing upright after days of walking on empty stomachs, sustained by nothing more than water from the streams that crisscrossed the heavily forested land.

Sir Brian was accompanied by a younger man, whose auburn hair, blue eyes, and solid build proclaimed him to be an O'Rourke. The man wore a long tunic over woolen hose and scuffed leather boots, attire the Spaniards would normally associate with a peasant, but his sword was a thing of beauty, and he clearly held a position of respect. An elderly priest, introduced as Father Joseph, stood to Sir Brian's right, and translated his speech into Latin for the benefit of the Spaniards. The priest was a tall, cadaverously thin man with wispy white hair that fringed his egg-shaped skull. His beaky nose reminded Rafael of a vulture feasting on the remains of a dog he'd seen once when walking outside the walls of Toledo.

"Welcome, gentlemen," Sir Brian said, smiling warmly at the men. "A few of yer countrymen have already found their way to Casa O'Rourke. They're enjoying their stay." Sir Brian laughed at his own wit and pointed to the auburn-haired man. "This is Kieran O'Rourke, my nephew and the captain of my guard." He didn't say anything more about the man, but the implication was clear. They were uninvited guests, there only by the grace of Sir Brian's generosity, and they had better behave. Sir Brian smiled and continued. "Ye lot look in need of sustenance, and a wash wouldn't do ye any harm," he added, wrinkling his pointy pink nose.

"Mary," he called to a young dark-haired girl who'd emerged into the yard, "take these gentlemen to the kitchen and tell Mistress O'Toole to serve them broth and bread. And instruct Siobhan to find them beds and fresh clothes."

"'Twill be done, Sir Brian," the girl responded.

Sir Brian turned back to the men. "When ye haven't eaten for days, ye need to start slow, or ye'll make yerselves ill. Broth and bread now, meat later," he promised with a wink. "And ale. Ye'll need ale." The priest translated Sir Brian's words to the best of his ability and the men nodded their thanks.

"I wish the old coot would stop yakking and let us eat," Pedro murmured, earning himself a look of reproach from the captain, but the other men appeared to share Pedro's sentiment, nodding in agreement and gazing at Mary as if she were the answer to their prayers . Under other circumstances, they might have had more lascivious thoughts when faced with a pretty girl, but they were too hungry to focus on less immediate desires.

"*Gracias*, don Brian. You're very kind," Captain de Cuéllar said.

"My enemy's enemy is my friend," Sir Brian replied with a throaty chuckle. "Isn't that so?"

"Indeed, it is," the captain replied after the priest explained what the chieftain had said.

Pedro and Alfonso sighed with relief when Sir Brian bid the men a good day and left them to get settled. "Thank God. I thought he'd never stop talking," Pedro said as they turned to Mary.

Pedro and Alfonso barely looked at her, but Julio's eyes narrowed in appraisal as he bowed to her from the neck, smiling sardonically. She was a waif of a girl, maybe twelve or thirteen, and blushed furiously under Julio's intense gaze.

"Ye can follow me," she said. She sounded breathless, and quickly turned away, clearly uncomfortable under Julio's scrutiny.

Mistress O'Toole welcomed them with less enthusiasm than Sir Brian had, but fed them all the same, then shooed them out of her kitchen, wrinkling her nose in much the same way the chieftain had. They hadn't bathed since dipping in the lake several days ago and their clothes reeked of stale sweat and, in the case of the captain, dried blood and pus. After their meal, a different woman, this one in her forties and wearing an odd headpiece that covered all her hair and ears, led them to the uppermost floor of the castle, where they were allocated sleeping quarters and provided with pitchers of hot water and clean garments. Rafael fell into bed as soon as he washed and changed, but not before he thanked the Lord for surviving long enough to enjoy this bounty.

Supper with Sir Brian was an informal affair, which suited the men just fine. They looked awkward in their borrowed shirts and britches, which were made of homespun fabric and more suited to farmers. Only Captain de Cuéllar had been given finery befitting his rank. He wore a clean linen shirt, a leather doublet, and wool breeches, and sat next to the chieftain, his appearance much improved by a bath and a shave. They all sat around a trestle table in the great hall, a cavernous room with an enormous fireplace and mullioned windows. At least a dozen sets of antlers were displayed on the stone walls, their presence a testament to the men's hunting prowess. The hall was lit with dozens of candles and sweet-smelling rushes were strewn across the floor, the dried grass giving off a faint herbal scent that Rafael found pleasing.

Lady O'Rourke sat on the chieftain's left side. She was a stout woman of middle years and had a ruddy complexion, but her smile of welcome was warm, and she had fine blue eyes that shone with kindness. Father Joseph sat to her left and was so occupied with translating the conversation that he barely had an opportunity to touch his food.

A plump young woman sat next to the priest. She'd been introduced as Sir Brian's daughter, Shannon. She shared her father's fiery coloring and her mother's plainness. Her cheeks bloomed like roses, perhaps from shyness, and her gaze was fixed on her plate. Rafael's gaze slid to Julio's face, but the man paid no mind to Shannon. Instead, he listened intently to what the priest was saying, nodding eagerly.

"English settlers, she brought in," the priest said angrily, no longer translating, but airing his own grievances against the queen. "And where do ye think they were settled? Well, I'll tell ye—on land confiscated from the monasteries. That's right, land that belongs to the Church," Father Joseph vented. "Consecrated land given over to farming. But I wouldn't expect anything less. Spawn o' the devil, she is," he spat. "She'll burn in hell, of that ye can be certain, gentlemen. The good Lord will see to that."

"Our own noble families have been disgraced," Sir Brian chimed in. "Irish titles abolished, as if generations of history could be erased with a stoke of a quill. Well, we didn't stand for that, did we, Father?" Sir Brian cried, slamming his fist into the table. "We fought for what's ours. Rose up against the heretic queen and will do so again. 'Kill the Spaniards on sight,' she commanded. I'll not execute brave, God-fearing men, men who hold the same views as me and mine. I'll have ye know we've taken in as many as three dozen men to date, and more are coming every day."

Rafael couldn't help noticing Kieran O'Rourke's grimace of distaste at Sir Brian's proclamation, but he remained silent, devoting himself to his meat and ale. He seemed to be a man of few words, but clearly held a position of respect within the household. The few times he looked up, his gaze drifted to

Shannon, who blushed even more rosily when singled out by his attention.

"Where are the rest of the men?" Julio asked. They hadn't seen any other Spaniards when they'd arrived, and Sir Brian had mentioned that there were several dozen men on the premises.

"We can't house that many men inside the castle. I had one of the barns converted into a barracks. Ye can meet yer countrymen on the morrow."

"How many men are there?" Julio persisted.

"There were nearly forty, but several succumbed to their injuries," Sir Brian replied, and the priest translated.

"Chieftain, is there any word of our surviving ships?" Captain de Cuéllar asked. "We greatly value your hospitality, but our ultimate goal is to return home."

"There's a ship that put in for repairs about twenty miles north of here. I forget her name," Sir Brian replied.

"Then we must rendezvous with the ship," de Cuéllar said to the men, his eyes lighting with hope. "We should leave first thing tomorrow."

"Captain, with all due respect, we are too emaciated and exhausted to undertake another twenty-mile trek. I, for one, would prefer to remain here," Julio Fernández said, looking to his friends for support, which they readily gave.

"Then I will go on my own," the captain announced. "I will ask the ship's captain to wait and I will return for you."

"I'll go with you, Captain," Rafael said. The captain was older than all of them, and the only one who'd been wounded. To let him go off on his own seemed cowardly and unfair.

"You stay here, de Silva. I'll be fine," he said, smiling at Rafael. "You've earned your rest."

Rafael opened his mouth to protest but closed it before he said something he'd regret. He couldn't bear the thought of going back out into that endless forest. He was too depleted after his ordeal. Given leave to remain at the castle, Rafael turned his attention to food and drink, allowing the conversation to flow over him like an incoming tide. Once the main course, something called griskin that tasted like pork, was cleared away, Sir Brian glanced affectionately at his wife and daughter.

"All this rebellious talk has distressed the ladies," he announced. "I think they would enjoy some music. Won't ye, *acushla*?" he asked, singling out Shannon.

"Aye, Father, I would."

"'Tis decided, then. Feirgil, give us a song," Sir Brian called out to a curly haired young man seated at the other end of the table. "'Tis quite selfish of me, but I keep Feirgil here with me at the castle. I have a great fondness for music, and Feirgil is very obliging. Aren't ye, laddie? He's just composed a new planxty for us. 'Tis about a *leanan sidhe,* per Shannon's request."

"And what is that?" Captain de Cuéllar asked as the young man fetched his lute.

"The *leanan sidhe* is a beautiful fairy maiden who takes a human lover," Shannon explained, blushing to the roots of her hair. Before she could elaborate on the story, she was silenced by Father Joseph, who glared at her with disapproval, either because she'd spoken out of turn or because he didn't hold with fairy maidens taking lovers, human or otherwise.

The song was sung in Gaelic, so the Spaniards didn't glean a word of the poetry, but the haunting notes of the melody and Feirgil's gentle voice left everyone spellbound, and not a little forlorn. Having finished the song, which was unusually long, Feirgil looked to Sir Brian, who bowed his thanks.

"The good Lord bless yer unique talent, lad. That was beautiful. Well, it's off to bed with me," he said.

The women immediately sprang to their feet and followed Sir Brian from the hall. Everyone else followed suit.

Rafael retired to the tiny room he was to share with Julio. Julio wasn't his first choice of roommate, but Rafael didn't dare utter a word of complaint, even when he'd first seen the room and realized there was only one bed. Soldiers slept side by side all the time. This was no different. As long as Julio didn't snore, they'd get on just fine. Rafael undressed and slid beneath the counterpane.

"These people are savages, and they live like pigs," Julio grumbled as he turned onto his side, eager to talk. "I've never seen such primitive conditions."

"They fed and clothed us, and they've given us shelter, Julio," Rafael replied.

"Because they recognize our superiority. They have much to learn from us. Their women look like pigs too," Julio continued. "I suppose if you live in a pigsty, you can only appreciate pigs. O'Rourke's wife is shaped like a sack of grain, and his daughter better have a handsome dowry, or no self-respecting man will marry her."

"That's unkind."

"I don't have to be kind. No one understands what I'm saying anyway. Even that dotty old priest only understands Latin. Tomorrow, I think I'll visit the kitchens."

"Why, are you still hungry?"

"Yes, hungry for a woman. There were some comely wenches there. That Mary creature was all right to look at, but she's not been blessed with a bosom. Flat as a plank. The buxom one had a face like curdled milk. Come to think of it, I don't even care. I won't be looking at them long enough to remember their faces."

"Goodnight, Julio," Rafael said, and turned away from the man. He didn't like Julio and hoped he wouldn't have to share a room with him for long. If he were honest, he wished he and the captain had never met up with Julio and his friends at the settlement. The other two men were all right, especially when on their own, but Julio Fernández had a mean streak that he didn't bother to hide. Having come from a wealthy family, Julio oozed entitlement from every pore, and his good looks only made him more obnoxious.

I hope these Irish señoritas have their wits about them and won't be taken in by a pair of dark eyes, Rafael thought as he drifted off to sleep.

Chapter 20

April 2015

London, England

Rhys accepted a mug of tea from his PA and swiveled away from his desk to gaze out over the London skyline. He loved the view, but the gorgeous weather of the last few days had given way to a damp, foggy morning. Familiar buildings loomed out of the gloom, their edges blurry as if the glass and concrete were melting into the mist. Rhys took a sip of tea and wished he'd picked up an espresso instead. He felt tired and irritable. The fatigue was due to lack of sleep, but the irritation was all down to Quinn. She's sent a text last night, inviting him to dinner the following Saturday, and made sure to add that Jo would be coming as well.

Rhys sighed and propped his feet up on the credenza beneath the window. To refuse Quinn's invitation would be churlish, but to accept would imply that he was still interested in Jo romantically. Quinn hadn't asked him about his date with Jo outright, but he almost wished she had. He felt a need to explain, to state his reasons out loud and to reassure himself that all was still well between them. He hadn't meant to lead Jo down the proverbial garden path; he'd simply realized that a relationship between them would never work and decided to extricate himself before things went too far. In fact, when he'd invited Jo out to dinner, he'd planned for something completely different.

He'd chosen the restaurant carefully—an establishment that was trendy yet classy, small enough to guarantee an intimate atmosphere, and known for its superb food. He'd left several bottles of Sauvignon Blanc chilling in his fridge for when he and Jo returned to his place for a nightcap and made sure he had fresh milk and all the ingredients he'd need to cook her a sumptuous breakfast should things proceed in that direction. But over the course of their dinner, something had changed, and it wasn't Jo. It was Rhys's reaction to her.

Seeing a therapist had been his mother's idea. Well, not directly, because his working-class hairdresser mother didn't hold with such posh ideas and senseless waste of money, but she'd said something to Rhys that had stuck with him when he'd gone home to Wales for Christmas after the heartbreak of losing Hayley and the baby.

"You've always had a hero complex, Rhys," his mum had said when she joined him for breakfast on Boxing Day.

"A hero complex?" Rhys had nearly spit out his tea, but his mother had simply studied him over the rim of her own cup, waiting for the words to sink in.

"I think it's because your dad died when you were just a baby."

"I'm sorry, Mum, but I don't follow," Rhys had replied. He loved his mother fiercely, and although she came out with some questionable theories sometimes, he always listened to whatever she had to say with interest and respect.

"You are not like your brother," his mum had gone on. "Owain is practical and hardworking."

"And I'm not?"

"Don't put words in my mouth. You are both those things, but you're so much more. You've always been a dreamer, a storyteller. You were desperate to write a different ending to my story even when you were a small boy. You saw me struggling and you wanted to save me, unlike Owain, who thought only of his own needs. You longed for me to be rescued. Well, I was. Your stepfather is a wonderful man and I thank God every day that I wasn't too stubborn to give him a fair chance when he came calling. What I'm saying is, you are drawn to women who need saving, Rhys. You want to be their hero, their knight in shining armor."

His mother had exhaled sharply and shaken her head, looking at him as if he were a lost cause. "It's all those stories you read when you were a boy, stuck at home during the summer holidays with your library card and your inhaler. You're searching for a damsel in distress, Rhys. What you need is a woman who'll be your equal, who'll challenge you, drive you mad with her opinions, and even save you from time to time. What you need is a partner, not a cause."

Rhys had stared at his mother open-mouthed, his breakfast forgotten. In her own no-nonsense, brutally honest way, she'd hit the nail right on the head. He did have a hero complex, a deeply rooted desire he'd given in to once again when he'd dashed off to Afghanistan to search for a woman he'd barely known. The purpose had been threefold, he'd later come to realize. He got to run away from his own pain, impress Quinn, and rescue a beautiful damsel who'd see him as her gallant savior.

His feelings for Quinn were complicated, but he knew one thing for certain—he loved her, had loved her since the moment he found her sitting beneath a tree in a park, her eyes fixed on a point beyond his shoulder, lost in a trance. Perhaps at that moment he'd thought she needed rescuing as well. Over the past few years, he'd come to love her as a surrogate daughter, not a desirable woman. There was no physical attraction between them; perhaps he'd lost interest in her the moment she rescued herself, but he valued their friendship more than he could say. It was solid, and real, and rare.

And then came Jo. He had been attracted to her from the start. Perhaps because she was Quinn's sister, or maybe, as his mother and his therapist had rightfully pointed out, he was a sucker for a damsel in distress, and Jo was certainly that. Given Jo's sad start in life and her subsequent struggles to fit into her adopted family and then recover from the pain of her brother's assault, Jo was damaged, and Rhys has fallen for it—hard. He'd be happy to rescue her, but what Dr. Gibson had patiently explained, as if Rhys were a sensitive child, was that injured birds and lame bunnies eventually recovered and needed to be set free, not smothered with affection.

"I don't want to get hurt again," Rhys had told Dr. Gibson at their last session.

"Then perhaps you should ask yourself why you're attracted to this woman. Would you still be drawn to her if you didn't think she needed you?"

"I don't know," Rhys had replied truthfully.

Over dinner, he'd come to see Jo through the eyes of a man who was ready to question his motives and feelings. She was fragile, despite her willingness to go into war zones and risk her life for a story. And she was emotionally unavailable, a woman who closed herself off to the possibility of ever truly trusting someone. She'd go to bed with him, he was sure of that, and she'd give herself to him without reservation, but she'd never allow him into her heart, not entirely. She'd bolt at the first sign of trouble, or maybe at the first sign of real intimacy.

"I've been down this road too many times," Rhys had told the therapist.

"Then perhaps you should try walking a different path."

"What about Jo?"

"What about her?"

"I don't want to lose her," Rhys had replied.

"You can't lose something you don't have, Rhys."

He'd seen the truth of that. So when he and Jo had left the restaurant and stood outside in the cool April evening, Jo's face lit by starlight and the golden glow of the restaurant's windows, instead of inviting her back to his place, where he'd planned to make tender love to her, he'd hailed a taxi and bit his tongue when he saw the bitter disappointment in Jo's eyes. She'd wanted to be with him, had planned on it. But as the taxi pulled away, Rhys had

124

felt no regret. He'd wanted to sleep with her, very badly, but that wasn't all he wanted. He wanted more, and the next time he became seriously involved with a woman, he'd have it.

He turned back to his desk, reached for his mobile, and opened Quinn's text. He'd go to dinner, but all he could offer Jo at this stage was friendship. It was entirely up to her whether she decided to accept it. Rhys typed his response and sent it. It was time to get to work.

Chapter 21

April 2015

London, England

Quinn tucked Alex's blanket around his sleeping form and tiptoed from the room. She longed to kiss him, but Alex was a light sleeper and she was afraid to wake him. Emma was already asleep, having read a story to Gabe. She still asked to be read to before bed, but from time to time she preferred to read a story herself. The stories were simple and used words that were easily accessible to a five-year-old, but it was a start, and Emma was proud to be able to read the stories out loud.

Gabe was already downstairs, two glasses of wine on the coffee table in front of him. Quinn sat down and propped her feet up on the table, sinking gratefully into the sofa. "I'm tired," she said. Gabe handed her a glass of wine and she took a sip. "Thank you."

"How's your research going?" he asked. "Find anything useful?"

"I have, actually. Francisco de Cuéllar's name pops up quite a bit in reference to the survivors of the Spanish Armada. Of course, most accounts are brief and impersonal, but I did find a copy of a letter he wrote, so I was able to get some sense of the man. Or maybe I had a sense of him already."

"What's he like, then?" Gabe asked.

"He's precisely the type of man you'd want by your side in a crisis. He's calm, levelheaded, surprisingly optimistic, and not someone who indulges in endless complaining or self-pity."

"If I'm ever in a crisis, I hope I'm lucky enough to find someone as saintly as the captain to stand by me," Gabe joked. "What about de Silva?"

"Rafael de Silva is not mentioned anywhere, but I can't say I find that surprising. He was a foot soldier. I don't imagine he wrote any accounts of his ordeal, or if he did, they haven't survived."

"Was he literate, do you think?" Gabe asked.

"Yes, he was. His father was a physician, and Rafael spoke some English. He was well educated."

"Have you seen any actual indication that he was Muslim?"

"He reflected on not being circumcised, an omission his father resented bitterly. It seems Rafael's mother had forbidden her husband to circumcise the boys for fear of persecution. The father tried again when Rafael was thirteen, but the boy refused. He eventually agreed to be circumcised in time for his wedding, to spare the family shame. I looked up the practice—khitan, as it's called—and it's usually performed when the child is seven days old but can also be done later. In some cultures, the khitan is performed when the boy reaches puberty. Also, I sensed hesitation about eating pork, but he overcame his reservations fairly quickly. Given his situation, I'd say eating pork was the least of his problems."

"Do you think his family would have adhered to dietary laws in Toledo?" Gabe asked. "It would be noticed if the family avoided pork and reported to the local authorities. They would have been arrested and tortured."

"Yes, there is that, unless everyone in their household practiced the same faith and they bought pork for show but didn't consume it. Of course, if they threw the pork away uneaten, that would arouse suspicion as well," Quinn pointed out. "Neighbors were only too happy to denounce each other, thinking their religious zeal would keep them safe from persecution."

"It was a frightening time for people who weren't Christian. There were countless Christians who were accused of heresy as well. People were terrified to set a foot wrong. The Inquisition did a fine job of obliterating decency and charity. Life became all about survival, and if betraying your neighbor bought you a reprieve, then the choice was obvious."

"It sounds just like Nazi Germany, doesn't it?" Quinn said.

"Hitler certainly didn't invent persecution or genocide, he just improved on it," Gabe replied with a wry smile. "He made it more efficient and had it meticulously documented."

"Every time I delve into a new case, I'm reminded how lucky I am to live in this time and place. We're so blessed not to have to worry about hiding our true beliefs and customs for fear of persecution."

"Yes, we're very lucky," Gabe agreed.

"Gabe, do you ever wonder what type of person you might have been if you had lived in the past?"

"A very different one, I suppose."

"Do you think you might have been a soldier?" Quinn asked. "I can't imagine you raising a hand to anyone on someone's orders."

"We're all capable of violence, Quinn."

"Are you saying you could kill someone?"

"I'm saying that if I found myself in a situation where I had no choice, I'd most likely do it. Wouldn't you?"

"I've never thought about it, but having seen what I've seen, I think murder is justified when it's in self-defense. Sometimes, it's kill or be killed."

"Exactly, and I'm not a martyr. I would much rather live with the guilt than die with a clear conscience."

"We like to think that we're civilized and advanced, but we're not so different from the people who lived hundreds of years ago, are we?" Quinn asked.

"I'd like to believe we've learned something from history, but there are certain human traits that will live on forever, such as the mob mentality. Most villagers would not have executed a Spanish survivor on their own, but when part of a mob, they felt absolved of responsibility for the crime. It's always easier when you're going along with someone rather than making the decision yourself."

"Yes, you're right. I hope we'll never have to find out for ourselves how merciless a mob can be."

"Your thoughts are turning awfully morbid," Gabe said as he pulled her closer. "You're safe, Quinn."

"I know, but my ability to see into the past always brings me in contact with violence and death. I can't say I blame Jo for not wanting to pry into people's lives."

"I think Jo would do well to see to her own life," Gabe remarked.

"What do you mean?"

"They say the unexamined life is not worth living," Gabe replied.

"Gabe, you hardly know her."

"I know what I see, and what I see is a woman who runs away from things that make her uncomfortable. It's only a matter of time before she runs from you."

"I'm going to bed," Quinn declared, setting her glass down with finality.

"Are you angry?"

"I'm always angry when you're right," she retorted. "I think I'll spend an hour with Rafael now."

"All right. I won't disturb you," Gabe promised, and reached for the remote.

Chapter 22

September 1588

Leitrim, Ireland

"What the devil is going on?" Julio growled as he stared out the narrow window of their bedchamber.

Rafael peered over his shoulder. The yard below was full of activity. People were streaming through the open gate and there was much talk and laughter among the women. The men greeted each other with more restraint, and although Rafael couldn't hear what was being said, the conversations seemed amicable. Several people carried braces of large birds and there appeared to be a whole herd of sheep just outside the gates.

"They've come to kill us," Julio cried. "That red-headed Satan has invited the whole village to come to our execution. Look how pleased they are at the prospect."

"Sir Brian has offered us his protection. Why would he do that and then kill us?" Rafael asked. He tried to sound reasonable, but Julio's fear had spread to him and settled in his gut like a stone. Having seen the frenzied slaughter on the beach, he no longer trusted anyone.

"Don't be a fool," he said to Julio and turned away from the window. "Why would they bring livestock and birds? Whatever is happening has nothing to do with us."

"And you'd know, would you?" Julio snarled. "Maybe they mean to have a celebratory feast."

Rafael didn't reply. He left the room and went down to the kitchen. He'd ask Mary. She was a friendly girl who smiled easily and seemed eager to help.

The kitchen was a hive of activity. At least a dozen women were hard at work, plucking, chopping, stuffing, basting, and rolling out dough on the massive oak table at the center of the cavernous chamber. Mary sat next to another young girl, a large basin before them. They expertly plucked the geese and tossed the feathers into the basin. As soon as it filled up, a young boy emptied the basin into a sack and set it back in time for the girls to fill it again. Mary caught sight of Rafael and smiled.

"Good morning, señor de Silva," she exclaimed, giggling as she tripped over the unfamiliar form of address. "Have ye come to help us?"

"Is something happening today?" Rafael asked. He tried to sound casual, but his voice quivered with anxiety.

"It's Michaelmas," Mary replied.

Rafael smiled and shrugged. He had no idea what Michaelmas was, or why there was such a sense of excitement in the air, but the women appeared to be preparing a feast for an army.

Mary shook her head in disbelief. "Do they not celebrate Michaelmas in yer country?" she asked.

"What's she saying?" Julio demanded as he appeared behind Rafael. He looked pale and nervous, but not knowing what was happening must have been driving him mad.

"I think today is their *Fiesta de San Miguel*," Rafael replied. He breathed out a sigh of relief. This had nothing to do with them. Everyone was excited for the feast day.

"Out!" Mistress O'Toole called out to the men. "'Tis chaotic enough in 'ere without the two of ye underfoot."

Mary giggled. "I'll explain later. I've much work to do."

Rafael gave Mary an informal bow and left the kitchen. Julio strode off toward the great hall, but Rafael decided to go

132

outside. He was curious and thought himself safe as long as he kept to the fringes of the crowd. He stepped into the yard. The crowd that had been there earlier had dispersed for the most part, the men having gone inside. Some of the women still milled about, chatting and laughing. Several children chased each other across the yard, shrieking with laughter and earning looks of disapproval from their mothers. The younger children, some of whom still wore baby gowns, yanked on their mothers' hands, desperate to join in the fun. One little girl broke free of her mother's hand and took off after the boys, promptly falling into a puddle and getting her smock all wet.

"Stop keening like a banshee," her mother admonished her. "Ye've got no one to blame but yerself, now do ye? And I don't have a spare gown with me," she complained, shaking her head at the state of her daughter, who was crying so hard she was all red in the face. "What am I to do with ye, ye silly lass?" She scooped up the child and walked away from the group of women, who continued with their conversation as if there hadn't been any interruption.

Having lost interest, Rafael looked toward the gate to see if anyone else might be coming for the feast. A young woman dressed in a light blue gown walked through the gate and across the yard. She wasn't wearing one of the strange headpieces the other women wore and her braid, which was as bright as a copper coin, snaked over her shoulder and came nearly to her waist. A basket filled with something shiny and black was slung over her arm. She caught Rafael staring and laughed at his ignorance, her blue eyes crinkling at the corners.

"Blackberries," she said, holding out the basket so he could get a better look. "For the Michaelmas pie," she added, as if that explained everything.

"I've never seen these blackberries," Rafael replied, trying to repeat the name of the berries just as she'd said it.

"Here, try one." She picked out a plump berry and held it out to him. It didn't look appealing in the least, but it seemed rude

133

to refuse, so Rafael accepted it and popped it into his mouth. It was surprisingly juicy and delicious.

"Best enjoy it while ye can," the girl said, looking up at him impishly.

"Why?"

"Can't eat blackberries after today," she replied cryptically.

"What will happen if I do?"

"Satan will have pissed on them."

"What?" Rafael asked, feeling foolish in the extreme. He must have mistaken her meaning.

"It is said that the devil was so angry, he pissed on a blackberry bush on the Feast of St. Michael, so it's unwise to eat them after today."

"That's a strange story," Rafael replied with a smile. She was having fun at his expense, but he didn't mind.

"Oh aye, it's true. But today, we must have blackberry pie. It's special."

"Why's that?"

"On Michaelmas, a ring is baked into one of the pies. The lass who finds it will be wed within the year."

"Do you hope to find it?" he asked.

The girl's smile vanished, and it was as if a cloud had passed over the sun. "No, I don't. Well, I'd best be getting on."

"Wait, what's your name?" Rafael called out to the girl, but she'd already disappeared into the castle, her braid flying behind her.

Rafael walked toward the outer wall and sat down on the steps leading up to the battlements. To some, it would feel strange to be someplace but not feel a part of it, but he was used to the feeling. He'd felt isolated all his life. Instead, he watched with interest as the men began to emerge from the castle, minus the braces of birds, and head toward the gate. Snatches of conversation drifted toward him, and after a time he deduced that Michaelmas was a quarter day and some of the men had paid their rents to their chieftain in food. Having done their duty to their lord, they were headed to the fair, where they'd sell their livestock and purchase supplies for the coming winter. Everyone seemed to be in fine spirits, and Rafael felt an unfamiliar peace steal over him. No one paid him any mind, so he enjoyed watching the comings and goings, eager to learn something about these people he found himself amongst.

"Sir Brian has invited us to the Michaelmas feast," Alfonso said as he approached. "There's to be roast goose and something called Michaelmas pie."

"Yes, I know all about that," Rafael replied.

"Never met a pie I didn't like," Alfonso said. "Or a feast, for that matter. Any occasion that calls for food and wine is all right in my estimation."

"Whatever you say, Alfonso," Rafael mumbled. He'd just spotted the girl in the blue gown, but she wasn't looking in his direction. She was speaking to a dark-haired man who seemed to be angry with her. The man was considerably older than her and was well dressed, his velvet breeches and tunic setting him apart from the peasants who wore clothes made mostly of homespun fabric. The man gestured and Rafael caught the glint of gold on his finger. *He must be someone of importance*, he thought, still watching the altercation and wondering if he should come to the young woman's aid. She shook her head stubbornly in response to something the man said and walked away, leaving him to look after her, his lips pressed into a thin line of displeasure, his hands on his hips. He shook his head in exasperation and disappeared indoors.

Chapter 23

Sounds of merriment spilled from the open doorway of the castle, along with guests who needed a breath of fresh air or were desperate for the privy. Many never made it and relieved themselves in the first dark corner they could find, breathing out a sigh of relief and then returning to the feast to carry on with their eating and drinking. Through the open doorway, Rafael could see the servants bustling from the kitchen to the great hall and back, bringing platters of food and taking away empty platters, buckets of bones, and limp heads of geese that had been consumed almost whole. The wonderful smell of baking pies filled the air, making Rafael's mouth water. Julio, Alfonso, and Pedro were all at the feast, along with the other Spaniards who were staying at the castle, but Rafael had made his excuses and retreated to his room once the feast began.

Last night, he'd fallen on his first meal after weeks of near starvation, but his body hadn't been ready to handle such bounty. He felt unwell and had supped tonight on a slice of buttered bread and a cup of milk. He needed to take things slow and eat small, simple meals, or so his father would have said had he had a patient who'd presented with Rafael's symptoms. The bread had helped him to feel better. It absorbed the bile his stomach produced and reduced the queasiness that had plagued him since last night's supper.

Feeling stronger, Rafael had left the safety of the room and made his way to the battlements. He was surprised to see that there were no sentries posted at the gate or the watch towers. The gates were wide open, but no one was coming in or out. Rafael walked along the wall until he reached the side facing the lake. The glassy surface of the lake shimmered like silver in the moonlight, its banks bathed in the pale light that gave the scene an otherworldly appearance. Had someone told Rafael that was what heaven looked like, he would have gladly believed it, for the beauty of the landscape took his breath away.

He tried not to think of the beach at Connaught where he'd washed up a fortnight ago. Had anyone bothered to bury the bodies of the butchered men, or had they been left to rot? How could God sanction such a massacre and then lead the survivors to a place of such rare beauty, where the locals feasted as if nothing had happened only miles away from their home? How was a mere mortal like him to make sense of any of this, and what was he to do now? Captain de Cuéllar had left at dawn, determined to rendezvous with the ship that had pulled in for repairs down the coast. Would the stranded men be granted passage home, or would they be left here over the winter, a burden to Sir Brian and his clan, strangers in a strange land?

Rafael reached into the inner pocket of his newly cleaned and mended doublet and extracted the hamsa. It glittered in the moonlight, the opal staring back at him like a milky eye. Rafael closed his fingers around the amulet. Had it kept him safe and delivered him to this oasis, or had it been some other invisible force? Was he alive because of the captain, who had refused to give up and led him to safety? He said a quick prayer for Captain de Cuéllar and the success of his mission. The man could barely walk, but he wouldn't be deterred, so strong was his desire to return home and resume his duties.

"Hiding?" a soft voice asked just behind him. Startled, Rafael dropped the charm onto the stone walkway.

The girl with the braid picked it up and studied it, her face creased with concentration. "What is that?" she asked. "I've never seen the like."

"It's eh…nothing," Rafael replied. "Can I have it back, please?"

The girl reluctantly gave the amulet back to him and gazed up at the pale moon that was reflected in the still perfection of the lake. "This is my spot," she said softly.

"I'm sorry. I'll go."

"Stay."

Rafael wasn't sure what to do. This girl had seen and touched the hamsa, but she didn't seem frightened or appalled. She likely had no idea what it meant, and he wasn't going to be the one to explain it to her. She seemed melancholy as she stared out over the moonlit lake.

"Are you all right?" Rafael asked.

The girl nodded. "Just overcome with the beauty of the evening is all," she replied, her voice a whisper on the wind.

Rafael struggled to come up with something relevant to say, but nothing sprang to mind, so he remained silent.

"The stars look like a swarm of fireflies, don't they?" the girl observed. "Do ye have fireflies in Spain?"

"Yes, we do. May I ask your name?" Rafael said shyly.

"It's Aisling. Aisling O'Rourke. And you are?"

"Rafael de Silva, at your service. It's a pleasure to meet you, señorita O'Rourke. Are you kin to Sir Brian?"

"Aye," Aisling replied, her mouth turning downward in a pout. "What was that ye just called me?"

"Señorita. It means—" Rafael paused. He'd assumed the young woman was unmarried, but perhaps she wasn't. Maybe that was why she hadn't expected to find the ring in the pie, because she was already wed.

"There ye are. Come back inside, Aisling," the man he'd seen her with earlier demanded as he strode toward them. "What d'ye think ye're doing, lass?"

"I needed a breath of air," Aisling replied. She seemed to shrink into herself as the man approached, as if she wished to be invisible. "Good evening to ye, Master de Silva," she said, and turned toward the man.

He glowered at Rafael but said nothing. Instead, he grabbed Aisling by the arm and half-dragged her toward the steps leading down into the yard. Rafael waited a few moments, then followed the couple. For some reason, the beauty around him suddenly felt counterfeit. He knew nothing about Aisling, nor did he have an inkling of who the man was, but the one thing he knew for certain was that he had no right to interfere. The ways of these people were foreign to him. Perhaps the man was her father, or her husband. He clearly had a claim to her.

Rafael returned to his room, pleased to see that Julio was still at the feast. He stretched out on the bed, looked at the moon that shone through the narrow window, and thought of home.

Chapter 24

April 2015

London, England

Jo stopped in front of the house and gazed at the innocuous façade. Behind the black door lived the woman who'd haunted her dreams since she was a child, the woman who'd been the monster under the bed. Jo had never thought she'd get the chance to meet the one person who'd caused her more damage than anyone else in her life, but here she was, ready to face her demons.

She hadn't told Quinn she was coming to see Sylvia. This was something she needed to do on her own. It would either be the first step to healing or the beginning of a new phase that could be even more detrimental than the previous one. The person she'd hated since childhood had been nameless and faceless. But now she had a name and a face to go with the nightmare, as well as the painful knowledge that this woman had lived a happy life, completely unaffected by her past choices.

Having worked up the courage, Jo finally rang the doorbell and listened to it reverberate through the house, a joyful peal that was so at odds with her mood. It took mere moments for the door to open. Sylvia stood stock still, studying the daughter she'd abandoned with a hunger that made Jo uncomfortable. She'd seen photos of Sylvia but seeing her in person was a wholly different experience. She was smaller than Jo had expected, less intimidating. Her hazel eyes, so like Quinn's, were filled with apprehension, and her dark shoulder-length hair was peppered with gray. Sylvia wore a moss-green dress, accessorized with a tasteful scarf in shades of green, burgundy, and beige, and her low-heeled burgundy shoes matched her outfit to perfection.

"Please, come in," Sylvia said at last. "I don't imagine you want to do this on the doorstep."

Jo followed Sylvia into the front room. Like the woman herself, it was understated and classy. Several framed photographs were displayed on a console table. There was a photo of Sylvia with a man who must have been her husband, one of Logan and Jude as children, and a recent portrait of Emma and Alex. There was also a picture of Quinn, looking thoughtful, her face slightly averted from the camera.

"Would you like some tea or coffee?" Sylvia asked. She seemed nervous, and Jo was glad to have caused her discomfort. It'd be unfair if the woman remained unfazed by their meeting.

"No, thank you. I just want to get this over with."

"This doesn't need to be unpleasant," Sylvia replied.

"I can't see how it can be anything but." She realized she was being antagonistic but couldn't help herself. All her carefully rehearsed sentiments flew out of her head, leaving only hurt and anger behind.

Sylvia sat across from Jo and folded her hands in her lap. "Go ahead. Say what you've come to say. I'm ready." She looked like a woman who was about to be executed and was resigned to her fate, which took some of the heat out of Jo's words.

"I will never forgive you for what you did."

"I don't expect you to. But the fact that you're here means you're open to having a conversation."

"How could you do it?" Jo cried, unable to control herself any longer. "How could you leave me like that?"

"Jo, I will tell you exactly what I told your sister when she put me on trial for my crimes. I was a seventeen-year-old girl who'd just given birth to twins. I was frightened and in pain. You were clearly very ill. I panicked. Would I do things differently if I got the chance to do them over again? Yes. Will I apologize for the choices I made when I was seventeen? No. I did what I thought was best at the time. Both you and Quinn were adopted by good

141

families and were given a better life than I could have ever given you. You got the best medical care Leicester had to offer and won the heart of its star pediatric surgeon. If you subtract the emotional from the factual, you still come out way ahead."

"You abandoned me," Jo retorted.

"I was in no position to be a mother to you."

"Did you not feel the slightest bit of love toward me?" Jo asked. She sounded like a petulant toddler, but the question came out unbidden.

Sylvia shook her head. "Jo, as you know by now, it wasn't a planned or wanted pregnancy. The babies in my womb were interlopers, aliens. I saw you as a punishment for my mistakes, a judgment for my behavior. I didn't even know who fathered you, nor could I admit to anyone, least of all my father, that I'd shagged three men within the space of a half hour. I was ashamed, I was scared, and I was desperate to make it all go away. I know you believe I've walked away from this without a scratch but abandoning you two left scars on my soul. I could never be truly honest with my husband, or my sons. I spent decades keeping secrets—secrets that ate away at me even when I thought they were long buried."

Jo stared at the woman who'd given birth to her. She wasn't nearly as hateful or callous as Jo had expected her to be. True, she hadn't offered an apology, but she'd gone out of her way to let Jo know that her decision hadn't left her unscathed.

"I've hated you all my life," Jo said, grasping at the last threads of her anger.

"Is it at all possible for you to stop?" Sylvia asked.

"I don't know. How do you stop hating someone?"

"I suppose in much the same way you stop loving someone. Sometimes it's a gradual process, and sometimes it happens overnight. You look at them, and the fierce emotion you felt

142

toward them is gone. I think you hate me a little less than you did ten minutes ago," Sylvia added with a shy smile.

"I can see why Quinn decided to forgive you."

"She was angry too, for a long time. The way I see it, we have three options. We can have nothing to do with each other after this meeting. We can be casually civil to each other if we run into each other socially, as I'm sure we will, since we now have Quinn and your brothers in common. Or we can try to forge a friendship and see where it takes us."

"I'm not ready to be friends with you," Jo replied. Sylvia hadn't suggested anything Jo hadn't considered herself, but she suddenly felt cornered and desperate to get out of this house. The things Sylvia had said resonated with her, not because she forgave her, but because they were so similar to some of the things Jo had said to herself, the reasoning she'd conjured up for giving a child away without destroying one's conscience. Sylvia's sentiments opened the door a tiny crack, allowing Jo to believe that perhaps there was still a chance things could be made right.

"I understand, Jo, and I will respect whatever you decide. I am very happy to have met you, and I am glad you're home safe after your ordeal."

"Thank you," Jo mumbled as she stood to leave. She felt like she needed to add something more but wasn't at all sure what to say. "I'll see myself out."

She walked briskly toward the door and stepped out into the beautiful spring afternoon, taking a great gulp of air, as if she'd been suffocating. The curtains in the front window twitched, Sylvia's silhouette momentarily shadowing the gauzy fabric. If Jo had been hoping for closure, she hadn't got it. If anything, she felt more unsettled than ever.

"Are you all right, love?" asked a middle-aged woman walking her dog past Sylvia's house. She looked at Jo with compassion and reached into her bag for a pack of tissues. "Here." She held out the pack and Jo accepted it gratefully.

She hadn't realized she was crying, but the woman's kindness nearly undid her. Great sobs tore from her chest, tears blurring her vision and her hands shaking as she tried to blow her nose.

"Would you like to come in for a cuppa?" the woman asked. "I live just there. Nigel's already done his business, so we can go in."

"Thank you," Jo replied. She'd collected herself somewhat and was embarrassed by her uncharacteristic outburst. "You're very kind. I'm all right now."

"Well, if you're sure. It's no trouble."

"Really, I'm all right," Jo assured her. She tried to return the packet of tissues to the woman, but she waved Jo's hand away.

"You keep them, love. I've got another pack in my bag. Perhaps you should ring someone," she suggested. "You shouldn't be on your own when you're upset."

"I'm going to call my sister," Jo replied, suddenly realizing that she was desperate to talk to Quinn.

"That's a sensible idea. There's nothing like having a chinwag with your sister. Always helps me. Well, take care."

The woman walked away, dragging a reluctant Nigel behind her. Jo shoved a crumpled tissue into the pocket of her coat, pulled her mobile out of her bag, and called Quinn.

"Hi, Jo," Quinn answered cheerfully.

"Can I come round? I need to talk to you," Jo blurted without any preamble.

"Of course. Are you all right?"

"I will be," Jo replied, and ended the call. Suddenly, she knew exactly what she needed to do.

Chapter 25

"Wasn't that delicious?" Quinn asked Alex as she spooned the last of the homemade baby food into his mouth. "That's right, little man. I made it just for you." She wiped Alex's mouth and hands and lifted him out of the highchair. "Now you are going to take a nice long nap, and I will spend some time with your aunt Jo," Quinn continued as she carried the baby up the stairs and toward his room. "What do you think of that?"

Alex didn't seem to have an opinion on the matter, so Quinn settled him in his cot and turned on the monitor. Alex instantly reached for his favorite stuffed animal and pressed a finger into the bear's nose, laughing happily when it made a squeaky sound. "At least this one doesn't light up or have a siren," Quinn mumbled as she tucked the baby in and closed the curtains. "Sleep well, my darling," she crooned as she bent down to kiss the baby. "I'll see you later."

"Bah," Alex said.

"How about 'Ma'?"

"Bah."

"We'll work on that later."

Quinn closed the door and returned downstairs. She put the kettle on and rummaged in the cupboard for a packet of chocolate biscuits, but it was nowhere to be found. Chocolate biscuits were Emma's favorite, so their absence was easy to explain. Quinn gave up on the cupboard and turned to the refrigerator. Maybe she could make some sandwiches, if she could find anything to put in them. She really needed to get to the shops. The kettle boiled just as the doorbell rang.

"Hi. Are you all right, Jo?" Quinn asked as she invited her inside. "Would you like some tea?"

"I'd prefer something stronger," Jo replied.

145

"All right. There's whisky."

"That will do."

"What's happened?" Quinn tried again as she brought out the bottle of whisky and two glasses. She didn't want a drink, but it seemed rude to leave Jo to drink alone.

"I went to see Sylvia," Jo replied as she shrugged off her coat and tossed her bag onto the worktop.

"What on earth did she say to you?"

"Nothing that didn't need saying," Jo replied, and reached for her glass. She tossed back the whisky and held out the glass for a refill.

"Slow down, sis," Quinn said. She poured Jo a finger-worth of the spirit and put the bottle away. Jo wouldn't be getting drunk on her watch.

"I've spent my life hating Sylvia," Jo said, her gaze fixed on the now-empty glass. "I blamed everything on her, all my problems. But do you know what I realized today?" She didn't wait for an answer. "I realized that even though I'd never met the woman, I'm just like her. I'm selfish, cold, and incapable of loving anyone."

"You got all that from one meeting with her?" Quinn asked, wondering what Sylvia could have said or done to unnerve Jo to such a degree. "Sylvia is not the mother I would have asked for, but she does have her good points."

"Yes, she's honest; I'll give her that. And unapologetic."

"Jo, what's this all about?" Quinn asked gently.

"I didn't tell you the whole truth, Quinn. At first, I was afraid you'd judge me, but then I realized I had no desire to rake it all up again, not after I'd done such a fine job of burying it so deep. But everything is different now, and I feel exposed—turned inside out, if you will. The past just keeps coming at you until it

146

becomes the present and the future. Sylvia made me realize it's high time I faced my own mistakes."

"We all have things we'd prefer to keep hidden. You're allowed to make mistakes, and you're allowed to move past them."

"Is there such a thing as moving past your mistakes? Sylvia is almost fifty and her mistakes are still haunting her after all these years. I want to make things right, Quinn, and I can begin by being honest with you."

"Jo, I will support you in whatever way I can," Quinn replied. "And I won't judge you. I promise."

Jo nodded and reached for Quinn's untouched glass. She tossed back the contents and set the glass on the worktop. Her cheeks were flushed, and her gaze was glassy and slightly wild.

"You've been relentless and fearless in your pursuit of your birth family, and I've benefited from your efforts. I thought I was happy not to know my birth parents or siblings, but now that I've met Seth, and Logan and Jude, and even Sylvia, I see what I've been missing. No matter what happens from this point on, I know that there are people out there who have welcomed me and made me feel like I belong. I've never really experienced that before, not even when I was a child."

Quinn remained quiet, letting Jo talk. She was working up to telling her something important and Quinn didn't want to interrupt or give her a reason to change her mind. Jo needed to unburden herself, and Quinn was there to listen.

"I told you there were no consequences to what happened with Michael, but that wasn't strictly true. Michael didn't use a condom the night he came to my room, and he was too drunk and stupid to pull out in time. My father, being the pragmatist that he was, called in a prescription for the morning after pill as soon as he discovered what had happened. The pills weren't readily available in those days, but he was Dr. Ian Crawford, he could get his hands on anything. He instructed me to take the pill right away, but I flushed it down the toilet. It was a foolish thing to do; I admit that, but I was angry and hurt. I believed that my father was protecting Michael rather than looking out for me. I suppose I wanted to spite him."

"You got pregnant," Quinn said, finally grasping the magnitude of this confession.

Jo nodded. "I did. My parents tried to talk me into terminating the pregnancy, but I refused, really dug my heels in. In retrospect, I think the only reason I wanted to keep the baby was because I was desperate to hurt them. I thought I'd feel vindicated. What could be more of a punishment than having to stand by helplessly and watch their son's child growing inside my body? They'd failed to protect me and had been more worried about Michael's career than what he'd done. They tried to sweep the whole thing under the carpet and continue as if nothing had changed, so I set out to prove them wrong. I realize now how foolish I was, and how selfish, but at the time, I wasn't thinking rationally."

"What happened to the baby, Jo?"

"I was able to conceal my pregnancy until the end of the school year. I felt angry and defiant, but I didn't feel any different physically. The pregnancy didn't feel real to me at all until the baby began to move, and even then, I felt no connection to it. I ignored it. As soon as school let out for the summer holidays, my father packed me off to a 'retreat,' as he called it, for unwed mothers. You wouldn't think they'd still have such places, but he found one in Ireland. Since abortion wasn't legal there, there were still those who preferred to hide their shame and were comfortable enough to afford a place like St. Monica's Home for Mother and Baby."

"St. Monica is the patron saint of mothers," Quinn said. "Was it an awful place?"

"No. It wasn't at all like those horrid convents run by bitter old nuns whose only pleasure in life is inflicting misery on young women who've allowed themselves to sink into sin. It was a posh

148

manor in the countryside, where the women were looked after by caring staff. Money goes a long way, even in a situation like that. I made friends with some of the other girls. The three months I spent at the home were peaceful and pleasant, and I allowed myself to forget why I was really there."

Jo's eyelashes shimmered with tears, and Quinn reached for her hand but didn't ask any questions. Jo needed to tell her story in her own time.

"The baby was born in August. I had an easy labor. The whole thing lasted about three hours from beginning to end. There was a pediatrician on staff, and he took the baby away as soon as it was born. My father thought it best, and I didn't disagree. I didn't want to see the baby or hold it. I felt no love toward it. I was happy to finally be rid of it. Is that awful?"

"No, it's not. You were sixteen. Hardly more than a child yourself. And the baby hadn't been a product of love, or even desire."

"No, it wasn't. I never saw it, Quinn. I left the retreat a week later and returned home in time for the new autumn term. It was as if the whole thing had never even happened."

"What became of the baby?"

"It was given up for adoption. To be honest, I never gave it another thought, and I was comfortable with that decision until I met you. Seeing what you'd gone through to find our birth parents, and the void left in your life from not knowing where you'd come from, I suddenly began to wonder what happened to my child and if I'd caused it years of pain and insecurity. I always believed my child was better off without me, but neither of us was better off not knowing our birth parents, were we? Sylvia might not be what we wished for or needed, but she's a flesh-and-blood woman, and despite my anger toward her, I want to get to know her. Is that perverse?"

"No. I could have walked away from her, but I keep coming back. She frustrates me, annoys me, and baffles me, but she's still my mother, and I want her in my life. There's a part of me that needs her, and I think she needs me as well."

"Is it too late to find my daughter?" Jo asked, her gaze begging Quinn to say it wasn't.

"I don't know, Jo. I suppose it depends on what you hope to accomplish. Do you want to find your child in order to ease your guilt, or do you want to be a part of her life?"

"I want to know her. Do you think she'd wish to know me?"

"I think there's only one way to find out."

"Will you help me find her?"

"If that's what you want."

"I wouldn't know where to start. My father handled the adoption, but he's gone."

"Hold on." Quinn left the kitchen and returned a few moments later with her computer. "Let's see if St. Monica's still exists."

"I highly doubt they'd just hand over the information."

"No, but it's a start. Where was it located?"

"Not too far from Dublin, I think."

Quinn Googled St. Monica's Home for Mother and Baby near Dublin. Several entries popped up. "It closed six years ago," she said. "The manor house is now a care home for the elderly."

Jo exhaled loudly. "Now what?"

"Did the home handle the adoptions or did they liaison with an independent agency?"

Jo shrugged. "I have no idea. I never asked any questions. By the time the baby was born, I only wanted my life back. I

150

trusted my father to ensure the baby was placed in a good home. That was enough for me."

Quinn closed the computer and pushed it aside. "Jo, there are ways to find a person. I found you."

"What do you suggest?"

"I suggest you take some time to think about what you want. If you are ready to find your daughter, then we will leave no stone unturned; however, if you decide it's best for everyone involved to leave things as they are, no one will think any less of you. This is a big decision."

"Quinn, I've made up my mind. I must find her," Jo said forcefully. "Will you help me?"

"Of course. I'll be with you every step of the way."

"Thanks, Quinn." Jo pulled her into a warm hug. "I appreciate your support."

"You'll always have it, no matter what."

Chapter 26

"I'm going to ring Drew Camden in the morning," Quinn said as she snuggled deeper into her favorite spot on the sofa. "He was able to help me find Jo. I think he'll make real inroads into finding Jo's daughter."

"I suppose," Gabe replied noncommittally.

"Do you have a better idea?"

"Yes. Don't do anything until Jo's given this matter some serious thought."

"Meaning?"

"Meaning that she seems to have made a life-altering decision based on nothing more than momentary impulse. Let's assume for a second that she has no trouble finding her daughter. What then? Will she commit to being a mother to her, or will she barge in, disrupt the lives of this girl and her parents, and then disappear again? She admitted that she'd given this child no thought over the past fifteen years. Who's to say that once she satisfies her curiosity, she won't lose interest?"

"That's a pretty grim view of Jo's motives, Gabe."

"Perhaps it is, but you yourself said that Jo doesn't appear to have any lasting relationships in her life. So, if she's not ready to commit to taking part in her daughter's life, she shouldn't cause her this kind of emotional upheaval. I have an American student who calls this type of behavior a 'seagull mission.'"

"And what would that be?" Quinn asked, raising an eyebrow at the odd comparison.

"It's when someone swoops in, shits on everything, and takes off."

"Gabe!"

"Come on, Quinn. Can you look me in the eye and tell me that Jo is doing this for the right reasons?"

Quinn's gaze slid away from Gabe's blue stare. No, she couldn't say that, and if she were honest with herself, a part of her agreed with Gabe. Jo had nearly died in Afghanistan. She'd woken up frightened and alone in a German hospital and had done what anyone in her situation would do—took stock of her life and found it wanting. Establishing a relationship with the daughter she had given away fifteen years ago would make for instant family—or, if Jo wasn't emotionally prepared to deal with the reunion, cause unnecessary pain for the child and her adoptive family.

"I think you are right, to some degree," Quinn finally conceded. "Which is why I need to help her. I don't think she should be pursuing this on her own. Besides, once this quest becomes more than just an idea, it will seem more real to her and she'll consider the consequences of her actions."

"I hope you're right, Quinn. You seem to have an awful lot of faith in her."

"And you have none."

Quinn reached for the remote and turned on the TV, putting an end to the conversation. She was angry with Gabe, but she was also angry with herself for falling into this emotional trap. Gabe was nothing if not clear-eyed when it came to her family, and to date, he'd proven to be correct on most counts. She loved Jo fiercely, but she didn't really know her sister—not yet. Except for Logan, none of her siblings were at all what she might have expected had she known she had a twin sister and three brothers. She resolutely refused to think about Brett, but Jude was frequently in her thoughts.

"I think I'll go visit Jude tomorrow," Quinn said. "Will you mind the children?"

"Of course," Gabe replied. "I'm sure he can use a bit of company."

153

"You've changed your tune," Quinn replied. Gabe's history with Jude blinded him to Jude's despair and his inability to conquer his addiction.

"Just because I don't trust him around the children doesn't mean I don't wish him well. He's struggling, I know that, and I genuinely hope he can find the strength to overcome his dependency on heroin."

"Me too. I wish I could help him somehow."

"Just be there," Gabe replied. "The rest is up to him."

"That's the problem."

Chapter 27

Winthrop Rehabilitation Center was housed in a red-brick manor about twenty miles south of Cambridge. The beautifully landscaped property was gated, and a camera was mounted on one of the pillars, its electronic eye focusing on Quinn for a few seconds before the gate slid open. She'd called to make an appointment before arriving and was asked for her license plate number and make of vehicle. Unexpected visitors were turned away. She checked in at reception, where she had to present two forms of identification and was issued a visitor's pass. She felt a sense of violation when her bag was searched but complied without a word.

"I do apologize, but there are those who'll try to sneak in contraband for their loved ones. They don't think they're doing any harm, but they're only setting them back in their recovery," the security guard explained as he handed back her bag. "Have a pleasant visit."

Quinn found Jude in the garden. He was sitting on a wrought-iron bench, his eyes closed, earbuds in his ears. His head bobbed gently to the music he was listening to and his foot tapped to the beat. He looked no different from any other young man, but it'd been only a few months since he'd survived an accidental overdose and near strangulation. Quinn hoped he'd lost his taste for erotic asphyxiation after his near-death experience, but somehow, she doubted it.

Jude's eyes opened a fraction, as if he were waking up from deep sleep, but then flew open when he saw her walking toward him down the path. "Quinn!" he exclaimed with pleasure. "What a surprise. This place is so boring, I'm losing what's left of my mind."

"Well, thanks. And there I thought you were actually happy to see me," Quinn replied with a smile.

"I am. No one except Mum and Logan comes to see me, and this joint's full of recovering drug addicts—the most miserable people on Earth. We're not allowed so much as a fag or a drop of alcohol. It's torture."

Quinn took a seat on the bench and handed Jude a small package. "I brought you some treats. Chocolate is the next best thing to drugs, right?"

"Not really. I wish you'd snuck in a bottle of lager."

"Against the rules, I'm afraid."

"I know." Jude sighed. "But a bloke can hope."

"How have you been?" Quinn asked, taking in Jude's healthy color and fuller face.

"Fine, I s'pose. They feed us well. They should, given the fortune they charge to rehabilitate junkies like me," Jude said bitterly. "I feel awful. Logan's sinking his life savings into this place. I'm not worth it, Quinn!" Jude exclaimed. "I should have died. I'd have made everyone's life that much easier. I see the pain in Mum's eyes every time she comes to see me, and the expectation in Logan's. He wants to believe I'm cured, fit to go back out into society."

"And are you?"

"I'm not fit for society. I'm not fit for anything. I'm a fuck-up, Quinn."

"You are not. Stop talking rubbish. We all have our vices."

"Yeah? What's yours?"

Reliving the lives of those who are long gone and getting crushed beneath the wheels of the train wreck that was their lives, Quinn thought miserably. "I can give you a list as long as my arm," she said.

"Yeah, that's what I thought; can't come up with a single one. Helpful to know my two siblings practically walk on water. Makes me want to hurl. And speaking of siblings, how's Jo?"

"She's well," Quinn replied carefully.

"You paused. What's up? Come on, dish some dirt. Surely I can't be the only tosser in this family."

"I thought you'd met her."

"Very briefly. I didn't have family relations on the brain at the time, if you know what I mean. She's fit, I'll give her that."

"Fit?"

"You know, hot. Get with the lingo; you're not that old."

"Right. I'm still getting to know her. She's not an easy person to get close to."

"You don't say. Logan thinks she's distant."

"Yes, I suppose she is. There's a reserve there that's difficult to break through, but I'm trying. Despite her aloofness, she feels like family."

"Like your bro in New Orleans did?" Jude asked, smiling cruelly. "Sorry, that was a low blow. How's that going, by the way?"

"My father is in the process of filing an appeal."

"Are you angry with him?" Jude asked, going to the heart of the matter.

"Yes and no. I can't fault him for wanting to help his son. I'd do the same for one of my children."

"Really? Even if they were guilty of attempted murder?"

"Yes, even then."

"So, I s'pose nearly topping myself with heroin is not as bad as it gets, in terms of parental disillusionment."

Quinn didn't take the bait. She knew what Jude was doing. He wanted her to reassure him that he hadn't lost the love of his family despite his failings. He longed to be comforted, revealing something of the softness beneath the brittle shell, but Quinn was in no mood to coddle him. Feeling sorry for him would only enable him to continue on this path of self-destruction.

"Jude, here's an idea. Stop feeling sorry for yourself, get clean, and get out of this place. You have your whole life ahead of you; don't waste it. Making one mistake doesn't make you a hopeless failure; it makes you human. No, it's not fun being sober after years of living high, and no, it's not easy to own your mistakes and take responsibility for your own wellbeing, but guess what? Everyone does it. It's called being an adult."

"Wow, tell it like it is, sis!" Jude exclaimed, but he wasn't offended by her honesty; he was smiling into her eyes. "Thanks, Quinn. Thanks for caring. Not many people do."

"Have you spoken to Bridget?" Quinn asked. Jude's girlfriend was partially to blame for his overdose and near death. She was an enabler, a seductress whose siren call Jude couldn't resist.

"Nah. Can't talk to anyone on the phone, and only immediate family is allowed to visit. Those are the rules. Besides, Bridget's toxic."

"Are you through with her, then?"

Jude nodded. "We're finished. Besides, I'm in love."

"Are you?"

"One of the nurses. She's so strict, she can put any jail warden to shame. Suddenly, I can think of other fun things to do with a belt. She can spank me anytime," he joked, arching his brows suggestively.

158

"I think that's my cue to leave."

"Was it something I said?" Jude chuckled at Quinn's discomfiture. "Lighten up. Just messing with ya. All the nurses are draconian in here, to save us from temptation, I think. I'm glad you came," he said, his voice softening. "Bring the kiddies next time. I'd love to see them."

"There will be no next time. You're getting out of here."

"I'm getting out of here," Jude repeated. "Make sure to throw me a wild welcome home party."

"Will do. I hope you're up for juice, ice cream, and balloons." Quinn gave Jude a kiss on the cheek and stood, ready to leave.

"I'll see you soon, yeah?" Jude said, his voice hopeful.

"Sooner than you think." Quinn could feel his gaze on her as she walked away, and for some reason, she wanted to cry.

Chapter 28

October 1588

Leitrim, Ireland

After a period of rest and decent food, Rafael felt physically stronger, but the burden of worry hadn't eased. Captain de Cuéllar had returned to the castle, exhausted, ill, and bitterly disappointed to have missed the Spanish ship. He'd seen it in the distance, hovering on the horizon as it set sail for home. The ship had been their last hope, and now the men had no choice but to prepare themselves for the long northern winter.

Captain de Cuéllar tried to hide his despair, but his soul was shattered. The inevitability of spending the winter in Ireland weighed heavily on his mind, and despite his usual optimism in the face of adversity, he didn't believe anyone would return for them come spring. They were on their own, in a place where one man's sympathy was the only thing that stood between the survivors and certain death.

"We must find a way home, de Silva," the captain whispered urgently when Rafael came to visit him in his chamber. He looked gaunt and exhausted, but his hollow cheeks were flushed, and his eyes burned bright with fever. The captain's beard and hair seemed to have grown more silver since the day he'd washed ashore, and deep lines of worry were etched into his forehead. "Sir Brian is a good, God-fearing man, but thirty-odd men to house for the winter is a great burden on his resources. What has he to gain by helping us?"

"Must everything be about gain, sir?" Rafael asked.

"A leader must make choices, son. Sir Brian's first responsibility is to his people. With winter coming, there's little we can contribute. Field work is finished for the year, and the men are not accustomed to this unfamiliar terrain. All we are good for is chopping wood and telling stories by the fire," the captain said with disgust.

"Surely we can make ourselves useful come spring. There will be fields to till and crops to plant," Rafael argued.

"And what do you know of farming? Most of our men come from cities. They don't know a hoe from a scythe. And the ones who come from farming families are too few in number to make any difference to the clan. No, my boy, we must find a way to return home. This isn't our place, de Silva. This isn't our destiny."

Rafael didn't bother to argue. He wasn't about to engage in discourse about destiny with a man who could barely keep his eyes open, although he had his own opinion and it didn't quite align with that of the captain. No man wanted to believe his destiny was to die a pointless, painful death. The men who had drowned when the ships smashed on the rocks or were beaten to death on the beach couldn't have imagined such an awful end would be their destiny. Every man needed to feel that his life mattered and he'd been put on this earth for a purpose, a beloved son of a benevolent God, but perhaps there was no great plan and life was just a series of random events brought about by circumstance, luck, and one's own ability.

"We must find a ship," Captain de Cuéllar rasped.

"Yes, sir," Rafael replied, placating the man. As the captain had rightfully pointed out, everything in life was about profit and loss, and no Irish captain in his right mind would agree to take a bunch of stranded Spaniards home at the onset of winter, especially when they didn't have a handful of coins between them.

"I'll leave you to rest, sir." Rafael's words were lost on the captain, who was already asleep, his breathing labored and his face tense even in repose.

Eager for a bit of solitude, Rafael left the castle and ventured beyond the wall and into the woods. Autumn had arrived, and the forest had changed from a verdant green to dazzling shades of crimson, persimmon, and golden yellow. The ground was covered with a thick quilt of fallen leaves, and the woods smelled pleasantly of pine and resin. Rafael walked along, enjoying the calming peace of the forest. The castle was sizeable, but there were always people about, and he couldn't manage a few moments of privacy even in his own bedchamber. Julio behaved as if the room had been provided for him alone and treated Rafael like an interloper.

Rafael sat down on a fallen log and reached for the hamsa. He'd prayed many times since leaving home, but not once had he been able to speak the words out loud. He supposed it made no difference to God, but he felt an overwhelming need to raise his voice to the heavens, to feel free, even if it was only for a few minutes and in the middle of an Irish forest. Rafael stood and faced what he believed to be east. The prayer had to be recited in the direction of Jerusalem. He took three steps back, then three steps forward, as tradition demanded, then stood still with his feet together and began to speak. He kept his voice low, should anyone come upon him, but loud enough so that the words could be clearly heard by the Divine Presence.

"Blessed are You, Lord our God and God of our fathers, God of Abraham, God of Isaac and God of Jacob, the great, mighty and awesome God, exalted God, who bestows bountiful kindness, who creates all things, who remembers the piety of the Patriarchs, and who, in love, brings a redeemer to their children's children, for the sake of His Name."

A deep peace settled over him as he continued to recite the prayer, which had several verses. The words flowed from memory, and for just a moment, he felt as if he were standing next to his father and brother, his head bowed and covered with the black and white *tallit*.

"He sustains the living with loving kindness, resurrects the dead with great mercy, supports the falling, heals the sick, releases the bound, and fulfills His trust to those who sleep in the dust. Who is like You, mighty One! And who can be compared to You, King,

162

who brings death and restores life, and causes deliverance to spring forth!"

Deliverance. That was what he was truly praying for. His people had prayed for deliverance from persecution, but this time Rafael prayed for a way home. Had he had no one to return to, he wouldn't care where he ended up, but there were people waiting for him, people who would be heartbroken should they never discover what had become of him and assumed that he lay in some unmarked grave in unconsecrated ground. There were no Jewish cemeteries in Spain, not anymore, but when a member of their community died, prayers were recited and rituals were performed so that the departed had all he needed on his journey to the afterlife, and to the Lord.

"Amen," Rafael whispered as he finished the prayer and returned the amulet to its hiding place.

Having had his fill of solitude, Rafael turned his steps toward the castle. He'd almost reached the edge of the woods when he heard muffled cries and the unmistakable sounds of a struggle. The voice sounded feminine, and the screams were punctuated by ominous silences. Rafael grabbed a stout stick, in case he might need a weapon, and hurried toward the screams. He caught sight of something black and gleaming through the trees, and then a flash of blue. It took his brain a moment to comprehend what he was seeing.

Julio Fernández, clad in his black leather doublet, had a girl pinned to the ground, his hand clamped over her mouth to muffle her cries for help. He was fumbling with the skirts of her blue gown in a frantic effort to gain access. The girl's face was turned away, but Rafael saw her bright hair. It had escaped its binds and lay in a tangled mess around her head, the color blending with the orange carpet of fallen leaves. Julio shifted his weight to push the fabric up to the girl's waist. The milky white of her thighs contrasted sharply with Julio's brown hand. The girl struggled desperately, but she was no match for a trained soldier. Julio yelped and yanked his other hand away from the girl's mouth as she bit his finger and cried out again. She tried to throw him off, but Julio was too heavy.

"*¡Cállate, puta!*" Julio growled savagely as he ground her face into the leaves. "Shut up, whore!" he said again, this time in broken English.

The girl's eyes were huge with fear and she whimpered like a wounded animal when she spotted Rafael among the tress. He could only imagine what went through her mind at the sight of him. Rafael held up his free hand to show her he meant no harm.

"Fernández, get off her. Now!" Rafael exclaimed as he advanced on Julio.

"*¡Chingate!* Fuck off!" Julio growled. "This is none of your affair."

"It's very much my affair."

"I'll deal with you once I'm done with her," Julio panted. "Better yet, you can have her afterward. You'll enjoy it, I promise," Julio wheedled in the hope that Rafael would agree, and Julio could still take his pleasure.

Rafael raised the stick and brought it down hard on Julio's back, making him cry out in pain.

"*¡Hijo de la gran puta!*" Julio hissed.

"Kindly leave my mother out of this," Rafael replied hotly. "If you don't return to the castle this minute, I will tell our host how you chose to repay his kindness. I doubt you'd survive long on your own, Fernández, assuming Sir Brian even allowed you to leave. If I were him, I'd string you up from the nearest tree."

Julio gave the girl a vicious shove before getting to his feet and tucking his exposed organ into his breeches.

"*¡Qué guapona! Cuánto me apetece!*" Julio said in a conciliatory tone, his handsome mouth twisting into an evil grin as he assured Rafael he'd enjoy the girl. "We can share," he added.

Anger like molten lava flooded Rafael's gut. He grabbed Julio by the upper arms and slammed him against the trunk of a nearby tree. "You will apologize to the lady and swear that you'll never come near her again."

"Apologize?" Julio laughed. "You must be joking. Look at her, she's nothing but a worthless skivvy."

Rafael drove a fist into Julio's jaw. Julio let out a muffled gasp as his head smashed into the tree and a trickle of blood appeared at the corner of his mouth. He looked dazed.

"I said, you will apologize, you worthless piece of shit."

"Fine, I'll apologize," Julio conceded when Rafael raised his fist again.

"You will not touch her or any of the other women ever again," Rafael hissed.

"But I will touch you, *puerco marrano*," Julio snarled. "You will pay for this, when you least expect to."

Rafael's blood ran cold at Julio's well-chosen words. *Puerco marrano* was a vicious insult, usually reserved for Jews. Did Julio suspect, or had he simply used the most degrading slur he could think of?

"My apologies, lady," Julio spat out in his accented English. "I will not trouble you again."

"Now, go."

Rafael released the man, but remained strategically positioned between Julio and the girl, giving her time to compose herself. Julio shoved Rafael as he pushed past him and glared at the girl. Clearly, he blamed her for getting caught. He staggered off, his hand pressed to his bruised face.

Once Julio was gone, Rafael turned to the girl. He'd seen her before in the kitchens but had never spoken to her. She was around fourteen, with hair the color of a ripe orange. She was small and slight, but generous breasts swelled above the bodice of her threadbare gown. Her wide blue eyes swam with tears as she adjusted her skirts and tucked her hair back into a cap that had come off during the struggle.

"Are you all right?" Rafael asked, averting his gaze to give her a moment to collect herself.

The girl nodded. "Thank ye, sir. I'm indebted to ye."

"You owe me nothing. I beg forgiveness for the inexcusable behavior of my countryman. He won't trouble you again."

The girl nodded. Her heart-shaped face was pink with cold, or maybe with indignation, but her mouth stretched into a tiny smile. "May I know yer name?"

"Rafael de Silva, at your service. What is your name?"

"Eilis." The girl didn't offer a surname, but given her coloring, she had to be related to Sir Brian in some way.

"Are you an O'Rourke?" Rafael asked.

Eilis shook her head. "Oh no. I work in the kitchens. I'm naught but a servant, sir. O'Toole is the name."

"Like the cook?"

"Aye. She's my granny."

"I see," Rafael replied, but he didn't see at all. He couldn't quite understand the notion of a clan or why some people were O'Rourkes and others weren't. Perhaps families with different names were formed when outsiders married O'Rourke women and remained on O'Rourke territory. For a brief moment, when Julio had pushed Eilis's face into the leaves, he'd thought it might have been Aisling beneath him, since the girl resembled her somewhat.

"Ailish," he pronounced her name experimentally, liking the exotic sound of it. To him, it sounded like 'elfish.' There was

166

something elfin about her. She was like a wood sprite, completely at home in the forest, her coloring a reflection of the nature around her.

"How is it that ye speak English, Master de Silva? The rest of the Spaniards don't," Eilis asked as they began to walk back toward the castle.

"I learned the basics as part of my education, and I've picked up many new phrases since coming to the castle. I have no difficulty understanding some people, but there are others whose speech is beyond me," he confessed.

"That's because they're not speaking English," the girl explained. "That's the Gaelic ye hear."

"I'm afraid it sounds rather unpronounceable."

"It can be," she replied with a grin. "The English call it barbarous, which is in keeping with what they think of us. Ye must find this place very different from yer home."

"I do, but there's a unique sort of beauty here."

"Really?" Eilis asked, surprised.

"I have never seen trees this color," Rafael admitted as he looked up at the flaming canopy above his head. "The colors remind me of a roaring flame."

"Because they're red?"

"There are so many different colors within a fire: red, orange, yellow, and even blue. To me, no two trees look the same. Each one is a tiny flame, but from a distance, it's like a great forest fire, the flames leaping against the vast expanse of blue."

"When it's not pissing down with rain," Eilis said, making Rafael laugh.

"Yes, when it's not pissing down with rain. Your country seems to have an inexhaustible supply of water."

"It's the rain that makes everything so green and lush," she replied. They had reached the outer wall and Eilis turned to him. "I think it's best if I go in by myself. I thank ye again. I won't forget yer kindness, Master de Silva."

"Good day to you, *señorita*."

She grinned at him and headed toward the gate, leaving him to stare after her.

Chapter 29

By the time Rafael returned to his room, Julio had collected his few possessions and cleared off. Rafael was relieved, but Julio's fighting words rang in his mind. He didn't know the man well, but he'd spent his life on the lookout for those who could hurt him and his family. Julio was, in Rafael's opinion, the worst kind of Spaniard: vain, cruel, and entitled. He was also vengeful. He wouldn't forget the insult quickly, if ever. Julio Fernández would welcome a fight to release his aggression but being made to apologize to someone he believed to be beneath him was the greatest insult Rafael could have inflicted on him. Julio's family was noble, and he had been raised like most noble Spaniards to believe that the rules of decency or laws of man didn't apply to the likes of him. As a ranking officer in the Tercios, he believed himself to be military elite and wasn't overly popular with the other men, who resented his high-handedness and sense of entitlement.

Rafael sat down on the bed and exhaled loudly. He'd made an enemy this day, and the day wasn't done yet. He wouldn't go to Sir Brian, but he would have to tell the captain what had transpired. Julio Fernández couldn't be allowed to get away with what he'd tried to do. Justice had to be meted out. Julio had assaulted a defenseless girl, but he'd also placed all of them in danger. If Sir Brian found out what had happened, he would evict them, turning them out to face a harsh winter with no shelter or supplies.

A timid knock on the door distracted Rafael from his turbulent thoughts. "Come in," he called, but no one entered. Instead, another knock followed. Annoyed, Rafael went to the door and yanked it open. Aisling was standing outside, a thick bundle beneath her arm.

"Good day to ye, Master de Silva," she said shyly.

"Good day. Come in," Rafael invited, stepping aside from the door, but Aisling shook her head and remained where she was.

169

"It wouldn't be proper. I came to thank ye for coming to Eilis's aid, and to beg a favor of ye."

"Of course. Anything I can do."

"Have ye told anyone?"

"Not yet, but I plan to inform Captain de Cuéllar. He can speak to Sir Brian. Julio Fernández will be punished, have no fear."

Aisling's face suffused with color and she shook her head vehemently. "Please, don't. Just let the matter drop."

"What? Why?"

"Once word gets out, everyone will assume Eilis has been despoiled. Her reputation will be ruined, her future destroyed. She says the man never—well, ye know—so no lasting harm was done."

"I see," Rafael replied. "If that's what you wish."

"It's what I wish," Aisling said, her eyes blazing with resolve. "There are other ways to punish someone."

"All right, then. I won't breathe a word."

"Thank ye." Aisling held out the bundle to him. "Please, take this."

"What is it?"

"It's my way of thanking ye. It's a cloak. It belonged to my father. I thought, with the winter coming, ye'd need something to keep ye warm."

"Thank you. That's very kind. I will wear it gladly."

"Good." Aisling gave him a small curtsey and disappeared down the passage, leaving him somewhat bemused. He'd got the situation all wrong and could have done more damage than Julio had already inflicted. What a fool he was not to consider the consequences to Eilis, who was obviously important to Aisling O'Rourke.

Rafael shut the door and unrolled the bundle. The cloak was made of thick gray wool. It was a bit worn in places, and had been fashioned for a stouter man, but it was the best gift Aisling could have given him. He was always cold, and it was only October. Rafael carefully folded the cloak and hid it beneath his pillow, since he had no trunk or valise of his own. Any of his countrymen would be happy to find such a warm garment, and he had no intention of parting with it.

There was another knock. Perhaps Aisling had forgotten something or changed her mind about the cloak. Not waiting to be invited in, Alfonso entered the room.

"*Buenos dias*, Rafael," he called out genially. "Seems Julio doesn't care to share a room with you any longer. I'm your new bedmate."

"I have no problem with you, Alfonso," Rafael replied. He wasn't sure how close a friendship Julio and Alfonso had, but Alfonso had proven himself to be an easygoing, unassuming young man. He'd been enlisted in the army by his father, who had great aspirations for his son's military career, but all Alfonso really wanted was to play at dice and drink wine.

"Nor I with you," Alfonso replied as he set a sheaf of paper and an inkpot on the small table by the window.

"There's no way to get a letter home," Rafael said, watching as Alfonso carefully laid a quill atop the paper.

"I know. To be honest, I wouldn't send a letter home anyhow. My father would probably berate me for getting shipwrecked, blame me for the spectacular defeat of our illustrious navy, and demand that I return to Spain immediately."

"Not a very realistic request, given our present situation," Rafael replied.

"He's not a very realistic man. Actually, the paper is for something entirely different."

"Oh?"

"Rafael, have you ever read *Lazarillo de Tormes?*"

"Yes. Why?"

"Because it's brilliant. I can't believe the author wished to remain anonymous. Had I written anything so entertaining, I'd want to shout it from the rooftops. What about the works of Lope de Vega? He's my favorite playwright. What a wit!"

Rafael glanced at the carefully stacked sheets of paper. "Are you saying you wish to write a play?"

"I am going to write a chronicle about what happened to us, mi amigo. I'll document our adventures in this hostile land."

"Alfonso, I hate to douse your fire, but you won't find eager readers for your chronicle unless you record a somewhat imaginative interpretation of events, one bordering on fantasy. Spaniards don't want to read about the defeat of their invincible navy or hear about the suffering and humiliation of their brave soldiers at the hands of pitchfork-armed peasants. If you're looking for literary success, I suggest you write something that makes people feel good."

Alfonso stared at Rafael, his mouth open in surprise, then grinned sheepishly. "And that's why I need an agent, Rafael. I have no mind for business matters, which is why my very pragmatic padre gifted me to the army. What do you say? I will write a work of staggering genius, and you will find me a wealthy sponsor who'll finance my success. I will give you fifty percent of all profits. Between the two of us, we can be a literary triumph."

Rafael slapped Alfonso on the shoulder, smiling at his innocent enthusiasm. "Why don't you get started on your masterpiece and then we'll see if we can make you as famous as Lope de Vega. And I can certainly see why your father thinks you have no head for business. Perhaps the army was a good choice after all," Rafael replied, teasing Alfonso good-naturedly.

"Really? You think so?" Alfonso's face drooped comically. "I'm not a very good soldier, Rafael, but I like telling stories. I have so many ideas."

Alfonso settled himself at the table and dipped the quill into the inkpot, his face taking on a dreamy quality as he gazed out the window, his mind already on his narrative.

"Buena suerte, Alfonso. As your agent, I expect to be the first to read the finished play."

"Of course," Alfonso mumbled, Rafael already forgotten.

Rafael left Alfonso to his literary aspirations and decided to go check on the captain. With nothing to do all day, time weighed heavily on his hands and he almost envied Alfonso his burst of creativity. At least it would give him something to focus on besides their unfortunate circumstances.

The captain's room was on the ground floor and was vastly more luxurious than the stone cell Rafael had been relegated to. The high bed boasted thick velvet hangings in deep red to keep out the draft and there was a nightstand, a small writing desk, and two chairs placed conveniently before the hearth, where a merry fire burned bright, filling the room with a pleasant warmth. Rafael knocked on the partially open door and was bid to enter.

The captain sat in one of the chairs, fully dressed, and in the company of Lady O'Rourke, who had taken a personal interest in his recovery. Father Joseph stood behind Lady O'Rourke's chair, his face creased with disapproval. The captain held Lady O'Rourke's hand in his own, palm up, and stared at the lines etched into her hand.

"Ah, señor de Silva, do come in," Lady O'Rourke called. "Did ye know the captain is a gifted fortune-teller?"

"My lady, I'm no such thing. It's merely a silly diversion to pass the time."

Father Joseph then translated, emphasizing the word silly.

"But yer predictions are so accurate," Lady O'Rourke gushed. "Why, ye're infallible."

"Hardly," the captain replied. "Everything I told you is painfully obvious to anyone who cares to look." He released the woman's hand and she stood, clearly reluctant to leave.

"I will see ye at dinner, Captain," she said, blushing like a young maid.

"I will look forward to it," the captain replied gallantly. "Sit down, de Silva," he invited as soon as Lady O'Rourke had left the room in a swish of skirts, followed by the sour-looking priest.

Rafael took a seat. He welcomed the delicious embrace of the heat and moved his feet closer to the fire. His boots were worn so thin, he felt as if he were walking around barefoot most of the time.

"Fortune-teller?" Rafael asked once their hostess was out of earshot.

"Don't ask," the captain scoffed. "I don't know what possessed me to tell the ladies about it. Now they won't leave me in peace."

"Can you really tell fortunes?" Rafael asked, shocked. The captain was so proper in his manner that this interesting ability simply didn't fit with the image Rafael had of the man.

Captain de Cuéllar sighed and shook his head, smiling shyly. "I was a sickly child, de Silva. My parents didn't think I'd live to see ten summers. My nurse was of Moorish descent, but her family had been servants to mine for generations and my parents protected her, despite her refusal to relinquish her heathen faith. I trust this will go no further," the captain said, as though suddenly realizing what he'd unwittingly admitted to.

"Of course, Captain."

"Well, Noor was a great one for telling fortunes. Her grandmother had taught her, and my mother often asked her to read her palm, especially when she was worried or upset. I begged Noor to tell my fortune. My mother forbade her to do it, thinking she'd see nothing but death, but Noor felt differently. She read my palm in secret and told me I'd live a long and healthy life and rise rapidly in rank once I joined the army. At the time, this seemed fantastical to me, but her prophecy came true. I began to grow stronger, and by the time I'd reached the age of twelve, my father began to plan my military career."

"Your nurse taught you to read palms?"

"She did," the captain replied with a wistful smile. "She said it would make me popular with the ladies."

"I see she was right in that as well," Rafael replied, grinning. "Will you tell me my fortune?"

"I most certainly will not," the captain replied gruffly.

Rafael understood only too well why the captain refused. Just as his parents had believed the old nurse would see no future in young Francisco's palm, the captain feared he'd see nothing but death in store for the men.

"I only do it to amuse our hosts. We have nothing with which to repay their hospitality. Now, off with you, de Silva. I'd like to be alone for a little while, if you don't mind."

"Of course, Captain," Rafael replied, and let himself out of the room. It still bothered him that Julio Fernández would get away scot-free with nearly raping a young girl, but he had to respect Aisling's wishes. He swore softly as he walked down the dim corridor and out into the autumn chill. People like Fernández always got away with everything because of their wealth and

175

status, even in a place such as this, where they were nothing more than burdensome guests.

Chapter 30

April 2015

London, England

Quinn set aside the charm and shook her head in dismay, annoyed with herself for jumping to unsubstantiated conclusions. Upon seeing the Hand of Fatima, she'd immediately assumed that Rafael was of Moorish descent. The earliest examples of the hamsa in Spain were the numerous depictions in the Alhambra, the fourteenth-century Moorish fortress near Granada. The five fingers of the hand were believed to represent the five pillars of Islam: faith, fasting, prayer, pilgrimage, and tax, but the amulet wasn't exclusive to the followers of Islam.

While on a dig in Jerusalem, Quinn had seen plenty of hamsas of all shapes and sizes sold in shops specializing in Judaica. The hamsa was sacred to the Jews, as well, and had been originally called the Hand of Miriam and used to ward off evil. Many charms, both Muslim and Jewish, were set with a stone, or an eye, in the palm of the hand as protection against evil. The Jewish hamsa, however, was believed to have Kabbalistic origins and was one of the few amulets permitted to the Jews, whose faith didn't allow charms or symbols as they could be used in divinism or magic rituals. In modern-day Israel, the hamsa was as common a symbol as the Star of David.

Rafael's dark looks had been initially misleading, but most Sephardic Jews had the olive skin and dark coloring of their native Spain, unlike the Ashkenazi Jews, who were fair-skinned and often had the light hair and eyes common to their Eastern European homelands. Rafael looked like a Spaniard and was a practicing Catholic, as was his family, but their devotion to Christ was nothing more than a shield against the Inquisition and their only protection against brutal and merciless persecution.

Quinn reached for her laptop and Googled the origins of the name de Silva. She'd initially assumed that Rafael's ancestors had changed their name to something more Hispanic-sounding in order to allow them to hide in plain sight, but the information was there in black and white, and had been there all along had she chosen to research it sooner. De Silva had been a common Jewish surname in sixteenth-century Spain. Many descendants of the families bearing the name had dropped the 'de' after they were driven from Spain and went simply by Silva, a last name that was still in circulation today.

Rafael had been born and raised in Toledo, the capital of Castille and one of the most important cities in central Spain. Toledo had been a prominent cultural center since the Roman times and had been home not only to Christians but to numerous Moors and Jews, who had later been expelled and relentlessly persecuted if they chose to stay. Few Jewish families had remained in Toledo after 1492, and those that stayed had lived in constant fear of discovery. Why did the de Silvas stay? Quinn wondered as she replaced the amulet in the plastic bag. She'd learned from Rafael that his father had refused to entertain the idea of leaving, but he clearly hadn't been the only one. The de Silvas had been defying the edict for nearly one hundred years by then. Why, like the Jews of Germany during the rise of Hitler, had they failed to see the signs and stubbornly held on until they were tortured and burned for their loyalty to their culture and faith? Had it been worth it? Could a person truly live when their every day was permeated with fear of death?

Quinn looked up when Gabe walked into the bedroom and climbed into bed next to her. "Alex is asleep," he said with all the pomp of someone announcing that they'd made it to the top of Mount Everest. "He put up a fight. He's becoming a real rascal, that one."

Quinn nodded in agreement, but her mind wasn't on the baby, whose wily ways she was well acquainted with and more than equipped to handle.

"Gabe, if you had been a Jew in fifteenth-century Spain, or in Germany at the beginning of World War II, would you have stayed or fled?"

"Why do you ask?" Gabe asked, clearly surprised by the question.

"Because Rafael was a Jew, and his family remained in Toledo long after the Jews were driven out in 1492. By 1588, they had been in hiding for nearly one hundred years, living in constant fear, and raising their children to be secret Jews while pretending to be devout Catholics in public."

"I couldn't say," Gabe replied, his expression thoughtful. "Hindsight is always twenty/twenty, but what if something happened right here, right now? What if London, or the whole of England, became unsafe for us? Would we flee? Would we leave behind everything we know and love, turn our backs on centuries of family history, and go start somewhere else? My mind says no, I wouldn't be driven from my home so easily, but in my heart, I know I'd leave. No amount of history or tradition could guarantee the safety of our children, and they and you are my first priority, now and always. What about you?"

"I would do anything to keep Alex and Emma safe. The mere idea of them coming to harm because of my stubborn refusal to see the writing on the wall makes my blood run cold. Having said that, I can also say that there's no joy in being a refugee, not now and not then."

"'I'm a stranger in a strange land,'" Gabe quoted Moses. "Some problems are universal and have been around as long as mankind."

"Rafael was definitely that—a stranger, I mean. A fish out of water," Quinn replied. "And he was just as wary in Ireland as he had been in Spain. Things wouldn't go any better for him if he were discovered."

"Is that why you think he was crucified?"

"I think he either unwittingly betrayed himself or someone did it for him. Perhaps he mistakenly gave his trust to someone he shouldn't have, like a woman."

"Would he have done such a thing, given his upbringing?" Gabe asked.

"I wouldn't think so, but people do foolish things when they find themselves in unfamiliar situations. What really puzzles me is the method of execution. Why would anyone want to crucify him? That's awfully extreme, even for the henchmen of the Inquisition."

"Might he have been crucified by the Irish?" Gabe suggested.

"I honestly can't see Brian O'Rourke's men going to such lengths. The punishment usually fit the crime. What heinous crime could Rafael have committed to warrant such a fate? If he committed murder, they'd simply put him to the sword or hang him. I found no evidence to suggest that anyone was crucified in Ireland in the sixteenth century, or any century before or after that. Crucifixion was favored by the Romans, not the Christians."

"I'm curious what happened to the poor man. I do feel for him. Aside from drawing and quartering, that must be one of the worst ways to go."

"I'd say," Quinn agreed. "And although I might be wrong, Rafael just doesn't strike me as someone who would do anything to warrant such cruelty."

"Victims of brutal crimes rarely do. Quinn, put Rafael out of you mind for tonight. You're getting too involved, as usual."

"I know. I just can't help myself," Quinn replied, snuggling closer to Gabe. "I'm glad Echoes from the Past was renewed for a third season, but a hiatus would have been nice. These forays into the past take their toll."

Gabe pulled Quinn closer and kissed the top of her head. "Quinn, I'd tell you not to get so personally involved and view these people as nothing more than subjects of the program, but I know you can't do that. You care for them, even though they've been dead for hundreds of years. Rafael is at peace now, regardless of what happened to him in 1588—remember that."

Quinn nodded. "I know, and I will lay him to rest as soon as I find out what happened to him."

"Have you called Drew?" Gabe asked.

"Yes, I spoke to him earlier today. He's going to come round tomorrow morning. Jo thought it would be easier to talk here rather than in some public place. Do you still think helping her is a mistake?" Quinn had no desire to argue with Gabe, but some part of her wanted his blessing.

"Quinn, you are doing what any loving sister would do. It's not for me to judge whether what Jo is doing is right or wrong."

You were more than happy to judge her yesterday, Quinn thought, but decided it was wiser not to voice her opinion.

She raised her face to look at Gabe, who wore the bland expression of someone who wished to avoid a blazing row at all cost. "Say you had a child when you were in your teens and it had been given up for adoption. Would you look for it?"

"You're full of difficult questions today," Gabe replied with a sigh. "Had you asked me before I met Emma, I might have said no, but now that I know what it is to be a father, I probably would. But," Gabe paused for dramatic effect, "I wouldn't approach the child unless I was sure I was ready to put his or her needs before my own and not plunge their well-ordered life into unnecessary chaos."

"Are you referring to Sylvia?"

"No. You were a grown woman when Sylvia came along, but Jo's daughter is only fourteen. She might not be equipped to

181

deal with such an emotional upheaval, especially if she knows nothing about the circumstances that led to her adoption."

"Yes, I see your point. I wonder if Jo plans on telling her the truth."

"I sincerely hope not," Gabe replied. "At least not right away."

Gabe's lips found Quinn's temple as his hand moved to cup her breast, but Quinn shifted away from him, sending a clear message. Having seen a young girl almost get raped by Julio Fernández and then speaking of Jo doused whatever desire she might have felt.

"Just hold me," she told Gabe.

"All right," he replied with a disappointed sigh, and turned out the light.

Chapter 31

The stormy morning leached all the daylight from the kitchen, leaving Quinn and Jo to sit in companionable silence beneath the glow of the lamp above the table. Jo had her fingers curled around her mug of tea, her face as gray as the day outside. Quinn drank her own tea, her thoughts on the upcoming meeting. She hadn't seen Drew Camden since the end of last year when he'd completed his investigation into Jo. If not for him, Quinn and Jo might never have been reunited, so she had great faith in his ability, but as Jo had pointed out again and again, there wasn't much to go on.

Jo suddenly looked up, her eyes filled with panic. "What if he doesn't want to take the case?"

"Why wouldn't he?"

"I don't know. I'm just nervous, I suppose. Do you trust him?"

"I do. Drew is clever and persistent, and discreet. He helped me find you," Quinn reminded her gently, covering Jo's cold hand with her own.

Jo nodded, but Quinn's reassurances still hadn't put her mind to rest. "How did you find him? Was he recommended by someone you know?"

"Haven't I said? Drew is Brian's cousin. Brian is Jill's boyfriend. Drew Camden was a detective on the Met before a bullet to the leg put an end to his career. It shattered his knee," Quinn explained. "Once he recovered, Drew started his own security firm, but he also works as a private investigator. Don't worry."

Jo nodded. "I trust your judgment, Quinn."

"Would you like me to freshen your tea?" Quinn asked just as the doorbell rang. "Ah, that must be Drew."

Quinn went to let Drew in and invited him into the kitchen. "Drew Camden, this is my sister, Jo Turing," she announced.

"A pleasure to meet you, Jo. It gladdens my heart to see the two of you reunited."

"Thank you, Mr. Camden," Jo replied. Her gaze was glued to Drew's face as she took his measure.

"Can I get you a cup of tea?" Quinn asked. "Or a coffee?"

"Coffee would be grand, thanks," Drew replied as he took off his coat and hung it on the back of a chair. He took a seat at the table and stretched out his leg. "Still pains me when I bend it," he explained, "and this miserable weather's not doing it any favors either." He extracted a small notebook from the pocket of his coat and turned it to an empty page. "Let's make a start, shall we? I find it helps to plunge right in rather than waste time on small talk."

Jo nodded and tightened her hold on the mug. "I'm ready."

"Good. Tell me everything you remember, no matter how insignificant you might think it is. I already know you went by your birth name then—Quentin Crawford."

"Yes, that's right. I spent three months at St. Monica's Home for Mother and Baby near Dublin. My daughter was born there on August 17th, 1999. I never saw her after the birth. My father handled all the arrangements for the adoption, and we never spoke of my time at the home after I returned to Leicester. My parents preferred to pretend it had never happened, and frankly, I was okay with that because I was more than ready to get on with my life."

"I see. Anything you want to tell me about the father of your child?" Drew asked.

"No," Jo replied firmly.

"And what about your siblings? Have you asked them?"

184

Jo's reaction was immediate. She hunched her shoulders and her gaze slid away from Drew's face toward the rain-streaked window. "We're not in contact."

"They might be able to remember something you don't from that time," Drew insisted gently.

"They won't. Please do not approach them."

"Understood," Drew said. He closed his notebook, set the pen on top of it, and accepted a cup of coffee from Quinn.

"It doesn't look good, does it?" Jo asked, her voice small and laced with bitterness. "I should have asked my father about the child while he was still alive, but I never broached the subject. And now it's too late."

"I wouldn't say that," Drew replied, and blessed her with a reassuring smile. He was a bear of a man, with a full head of curly salt-and-pepper hair and warm blue eyes. He was the type of person who invited confidences and made one feel safe, protected, and hopeful.

"I'll start with the home and go on from there."

"The home closed six years ago," Jo replied, her eyes filling with tears. "It's a care home for the elderly now. There are no other leads."

Drew took a slow sip of coffee and smiled at Jo, holding her gaze. "Jo, an investigation is much like a wool jumper," he said.

"What?" Jo and Quinn asked in unison.

"All you need is to find a loose thread and pull, and then the whole thing begins to unravel. One clue usually leads to the next. The maternity home might have closed, but the people who worked there are still around. I'll go so far as to bet that some of them are now employed by the care home. All I need is one person who's willing to talk, or at least give me the names of their coworkers. Someone always knows something. It's just a matter of asking the right questions."

Jo smiled, her face aglow with hope. "So, you think it's possible to find her?"

"I think we have a reasonable chance of success. I can't offer you any guarantees, but I can promise you that I will do my level best to find your girl."

"That's all I can ask for," Jo said. "Thank you."

"Don't thank me yet. I have some work commitments this week. I will leave for Dublin at the beginning of next week and ring you with a progress report by the end of the week, whether I discover anything or not. I know you'll both be anxious."

"Thanks, Drew," Quinn said. "We'll look forward to hearing from you."

Drew heaved himself to his feet and tucked away the pen and notebook in his pocket before pulling on his coat.

"Say hello to Brian," Quinn said as she walked him to the door. "Does he still work for you?"

"He consults for me on a need-to basis. I don't require a full-time IT department," Drew replied. "It was good to see you, Quinn. Your sister is lovely." He turned up his collar, opened his umbrella, and stepped out into the pouring rain.

"Do you feel a little more optimistic?" Quinn asked once she rejoined Jo in the kitchen.

"Yes. I like him. There's something about him that I can't quite put my finger on."

"He's possessed of that quiet confidence that makes one feel reassured," Quinn supplied.

"Yes, that's it. For the first time since I decided to find my daughter, I feel hopeful."

186

Quinn was about to reply when a thin wail erupted from the baby monitor. "And he's awake," Quinn said with a smile. "If you wait while I feed Alex, I can make us some lunch."

"Thanks, but I think I'll get going," Jo said as she began to gather her belongings. She seemed eager to leave, so Quinn didn't insist. Jo had much to think about.

Chapter 32

October 1588

Leitrim, Ireland

Over the coming days, Rafael bumped into Aisling several times. She always smiled and called out a greeting before continuing on her way, either to the kitchen or to the outbuildings in the yard. Regardless of their standing within the clan, everyone seemed to pitch in with the chores and no one except Lady O'Rourke sat idly by, not even Shannon. Seeing Aisling left Rafael feeling awkward and foolish, and wishing he'd come up with an excuse to keep her from leaving so soon. There was something about Aisling that drew him like a moth to a flame. It wasn't just that she was beautiful; she was spirited and a little defiant, a trait he could relate to. Aisling reminded him of a caged bird, her eyes turned to the great sky outside her prison, desperate to fly away, if only someone would set her free.

Perhaps he was reading too much into two brief conversations, but his soul reached out to hers in a way it never had to Mira. To him, Mira seemed hollow and colorless, whereas Aisling was achingly alive and wonderfully mysterious. He longed to talk to her and learn more about her life in this foreign place, but despite his best efforts, they never found themselves alone, as they had on the battlements the day of the feast. Rafael hadn't seen much of Eilis either, but came face to face with Julio Fernández nearly everywhere he went, which irritated him beyond all measure. Julio was as cocky as ever and had surrounded himself with a group of men who were drawn to his macho arrogance and cruel tongue. Julio seemed to feel no remorse and fixed Rafael with an insolent stare whenever no one was looking, his gaze a silent reminder that his threat had not been an idle one. Julio would find a way to pay him back, of that Rafael was sure; he just couldn't predict what form his vengeance would take.

"Are you still mooning over that girl?" Alfonso asked as they approached the great hall, where supper was about to be served. The inhabitants of the castle ate their supper earlier, leaving the hall to the Spaniards, who liked to linger after the meal and talk well into the night, since there was no reason for them to be up early the following morning. Some of the men tried to help with everyday chores, but the others did nothing but lounge about, dicing and drinking for lack of anything better to do. They seemed oblivious to the fact that they created extra work for the servants and forced the castle steward to dip into the winter stores to feed the extra mouths. Sir Brian was gracious as ever, but his allegiance could be easily withdrawn if he began to view his guests as a liability, which they were quickly becoming.

"I'm not mooning over anyone," Rafael replied gruffly, embarrassed that his feelings were so obvious.

"It's nothing to be ashamed of. She's pretty and seems to like you as well."

"How can you tell?"

"You really are an innocent, aren't you, de Silva," Alfonso said, rolling his eyes toward the heavens in mock exasperation. "In a castle this size, the one girl you find attractive manages to run into you at least once or twice a day, and you think she doesn't like you? You have much to learn about women, my friend."

"I won't argue with you there, Alfonso," Rafael agreed. "I do like her, but I'm not in any position to act on my feelings. Besides, I'm promised to a girl back home."

"Rafael, decency is one thing no one can take away from you, but so is common sense. You must take what life gives you and make it fit into your warped sense of honor. You're not Julio, or others like him. You don't take what you want without any consideration for anyone's feelings. This girl clearly likes you, and if you can do something to brighten this bleak time in your life, then allow yourself this little bit of joy. If she looked at me like that, you better believe I'd be at her beck and call, and give her wherever she wanted," Alfonso added with a meaningful smile.

"And what is it you think she wants?" Rafael asked.

"I think she wants you to make a move."

"What kind of move?"

"Do I need to spell it out for you?" Alfonso chuckled heartily.

Rafael's cheeks flamed with embarrassment. He really was a simpleton when it came to women. "It wouldn't be right, Alfonso. I mean to go home and honor my obligations to my family. I won't toy with Aisling. I respect her too much."

"Right you are, Rafi. Right you are," Alfonso replied, still grinning. "Respect, that's what it's all about."

"Are you laughing at me?"

"You better believe I am. Now, let's go eat; I'm famished."

Rafael followed Alfonso into the great hall and took his seat on the bench. He accepted a cup of ale and tucked into the bowl of stew Mary placed before him. Conversation swelled around him, but he fixed his attention on the food, not in the mood for idle chatter. Since Alfonso dominated the conversation with ideas for his play, Rafael had little need to interject anything more than the occasional nod of approval.

The men around them were highly entertained by Alfonso's rapidly evolving story, talking over each other in their eagerness to offer plot twists and amusing situations from their own lives that they were willing to allow Alfonso to use in his budding masterpiece. Alfonso lapped up the attention and laughed heartily with the men, but Rafael saw the gleam of excitement in his gaze. This wasn't idle conversation for him, this was research. Alfonso wasn't nearly as oblivious or unambitious as he appeared to be. A keen mind hummed behind his innocent brown eyes, and as Rafael directed his attention to the food, he reconsidered Alfonso's advice. Perhaps Alfonso was right, and Rafael owed it to himself to seize this opportunity with Aisling, but he had no inkling of how to go about it without causing offense.

He'd seen some of the men eyeing the castle girls. They didn't speak a common tongue, but there was an unspoken language of attraction that needed no translation. The women averted their eyes and played coy, but not before making lingering eye contact and smiling in a way that left no room for doubt that they found the men appealing. Rafael had no way of knowing if these flirtations ever went beyond ardent gazes, but some of the men seemed distinctly happier than they'd been a fortnight ago. The next time he saw Aisling, he'd try to speak to her.

Chapter 33

The following day dawned sunny and bright, and Rafael longed to leave the castle and go for a walk in the woods or by the lake. He had nothing to fill his days and envied Alfonso his sudden desire to become a playwright. It kept him busy and made him popular with the other men, especially since he had named some of the characters after his friends. Rafael had to admit that the tidbits Alfonso had been persuaded to read to them were witty and entertaining. He had cast Rafael in the role of the pious priest who acted as the main character's nagging conscience. Rafael had instantly become the butt of good-natured teasing, except by Julio, who had suggested to Alfonso that perhaps the character should be martyred for his unwavering faith.

"Only if I can make Julio a lecherous villain," Alfonso had responded, making the men guffaw with laughter. Julio had stormed off, but not before he called Alfonso some choice names.

"Are you going out?" Alfonso asked Rafael as he glanced up from his writing.

"I need to take a walk. I feel restless."

"You should find a companion to walk with," Alfonso replied innocently.

Rafael was about to rebuke him but changed his mind. "Maybe I should," he replied instead. Alfonso smiled absentmindedly and returned to his manuscript.

"Alfonso, perhaps you should name your villain something else," Rafael suggested.

"Why? Julio is the perfect name."

"Julio Fernández doesn't take kindly to being made a fool of," Rafael replied. "Now's not the time to make enemies."

"Don't be silly, Rafi. It's all in good fun. It's not as if anyone outside this castle will ever read my play. I need a diversion, and it improves morale among the men."

"You don't believe we'll ever get home, do you?" Rafael asked, sensing Alfonso's melancholy.

Alfonso shook his head. "Let's not speak of it, Rafi. Go take your walk."

Rafael inclined his head in acknowledgment and left Alfonso to his literary efforts.

He was just wondering where the best place to bump into Aisling might be when he saw her coming toward him down the passage. She wore a plain gown, the russet color a muted reflection of her hair, which was tucked beneath a modest cap. Her cheeks were rosy, probably from the heat of the kitchen, and a basket was slung over her arm.

"Good morrow, Master de Silva," she called out. "Lovely day."

"Eh…yes, it is. I was just going to take a walk," he added shyly, too nervous to ask her to join him.

"The woods are lovely this time of year," she said, giving him a meaningful look. "I'm going for a walk myself." She smiled and continued toward the door. Aisling crossed the yard and passed through the gates, her gait brisk and purposeful. Rafael followed at a discreet distance, hoping he hadn't misread her meaning and wasn't about to make a fool of himself.

Aisling stopped just beyond the gates and turned back briefly, a beguiling smile tugging at her lips. Before Rafael could return her smile, she turned away and hurried along a wooded trail, her gown blending with the colors of the forest. She finally stopped, bent down to pick up something off the ground, and tossed it into her basket.

"What is that?" Rafael asked once he caught up to her. The objects in her basket were green and spherical, and fuzzy enough to be mistaken for small creatures.

"Chestnuts," Aisling replied. "Don't ye have chestnuts in Spain?"

Rafael thought about it for a moment. "Castaña? Yes, we have them," he said. "But they're shiny and brown, not like those strange things."

Aisling let out a peal of laughter and shook her head in amusement. "Ye have to peel off the outer shell to get to the nut, which is very tasty."

"I thought people only eat them at Christmastime," Rafael said as he bent down to pick up several chestnuts. He added them to her basket. "Why don't you let me hold that for you?"

Aisling handed over the basket and searched for more nuts as Rafael trailed after her. "We roast them at Christmas, but they're added to various dishes at this time of year. They're a good source of nourishment. Did ye never go chestnut picking before?"

"I grew up in a city," Rafael replied. "We purchased chestnuts at the market."

"I'm sorry," Aisling said.

"Sorry? Why?"

"It must be awful to live in a place where everyone's right on top of each other, with no open sky and no woods to get lost in. I wouldn't like it."

"We have a walled garden behind our house," Rafael said defensively. "It has a birdbath, and we often sit outside on summer evenings. It's cool and pleasant beneath the wisteria arbor," he added wistfully.

"What is this wisteria?" Aisling asked.

"It's a climbing plant that produces garlands of large purple blooms. It's very beautiful."

Aisling nodded. "I suppose I imagine every place is just like this one, never having been anywhere else."

"It's very different where I come from," Rafael said. "But it's beautiful here as well," he hastened to add.

The sky was a turquoise blue, as bright as the opal in his hamsa. The bold color appeared almost unnatural in contrast to the bright leaves that formed a riotous canopy above their heads. Through a gap in the trees, Rafael could just make out the lake. On this clear day, it sparkled and shimmered, the silvery-blue surface reflecting the glorious autumn foliage.

"Do you walk in the woods often?" Rafael asked as he followed Aisling to the next chestnut tree.

"Not on my own. Wandering around alone can be a dangerous business for a woman," Aisling replied.

Rafael felt heat rising in his cheeks. "I can't imagine what you must think of us, especially after…"

Aisling smiled up at him. "Do ye think Irishmen are any different? Men are men—slaves to their carnal urges. As a woman, I must see to my own safety. Eilis knew better than to go off on her own. She has no one to blame but herself."

"Don't say that. She's just a child."

"A child who can be abused as a woman," Aisling retorted.

"You must have a great deal of faith in me, to be alone with me like this," Rafael observed.

"Ye're nothing like that other man," Aisling replied. "Ye'll not harm me."

"How can you be so sure? You hardly know me."

"I know enough," Aisling replied cryptically.

She continued to collect the chestnuts, her expression as serene as if they'd been discussing the weather. The basket was half-full, and soon they'd have to return to the castle. Rafael wasn't sure what he'd expected, but he was taken aback by the turn their conversation had taken and puzzled by the young woman next to him. She was direct and unashamed to speak of things that women of his acquaintance would never dare to broach. No one ever spoke of carnal acts or the nature of men. The women were kept in ignorance, and even after marriage, the intimate relations between husbands and wives were governed by the dictates of the Torah. He tried to imagine having such a frank discussion with Mira and nearly laughed out loud at the thought.

"What's funny?" Aisling asked, his chuckle not unnoticed.

"You are like no woman I've ever met."

"And have ye met many women?" Aisling asked, looking at him with interest.

"No," Rafael admitted.

"I didn't think so."

"Is it that obvious?"

"It is to me." She stopped walking and looked up at the lone bird wheeling overhead. Her good humor seemed to evaporate like morning mist. "I'm to be married soon," she announced. "Uncle Brian has chosen a husband for me."

"Do you not like the man he's chosen for you?"

Aisling shrugged. "He'll never let our children starve."

"Is that a good enough reason to marry someone?" Rafael asked, silently berating himself for being so forward.

"It is in Ireland. Love doesn't survive long on an empty belly."

196

Had he heard a statement like that a few months ago, he might have argued against its validity, but having spent several weeks with barely enough to eat to keep him alive, Rafael understood the sentiment only too well. He hadn't seen much of Ireland, but the villages they'd passed and the peasants they'd come across looked impoverished and downtrodden. Even life in the castle of the chieftain wasn't as luxurious as he might have imagined. There were few comforts outside of a warm fire and regular meals, but the fare was simple, and the rooms hardly more than stone boxes.

"Is that the man I saw you with on Michaelmas?" he asked, his curiosity getting the better of him.

"Aye. He's the reeve, so he was here for the feast as part of his duties. He brought a bonnif for Uncle Brian, as a gift, the sleveen."

"I'm sorry, but I have no idea what you just said," Rafael replied, embarrassed by his ignorance.

Aisling laughed. "What I said was that he's a tax collector who brought a pig as a gift for my uncle. He's clever and knows how to get on Uncle Brian's good side."

"Ah, I see. You seemed angry with him," Rafael observed.

"He asked my uncle for permission to marry me. He should have asked me first."

"Would you have said yes?"

"No. I made my feelings plain enough before, but he's not a man to be thwarted. He'll have what he wants, one way or another."

"I'm sorry. I know what it's like to have no say in your own life. My father has arranged a match for me as well," Rafael confided.

"Ye don't love her? Surely a man has more options than a woman," Aisling said, looking up at him.

"Not always." Rafael glanced away, peering at the sky-blue water beyond. How could he explain to Aisling that there were few Jewish girls left in their town and that in order to marry within the faith he had to forego any dreams of love? His father had assured him that he'd grow to love Mira, and perhaps he was right. Mira was a young woman worthy of love.

"I must honor the wishes of my father," Rafael finally said.

"Do ye always do what yer father tells ye?"

He nodded, suddenly ashamed. He'd never defied his father in anything. Until this moment, he'd thought that was something to be proud of, but Aisling had made him feel like a child who didn't know his own mind and needed his father's guidance to make life's important decisions.

"Yer father isn't here," Aisling said as she approached him and took the basket from his hands, setting it on the ground. She lifted her face to his. Her blue eyes were dancing with mischief and a playful smile tugged at her lips. "I dare ye to kiss me," she whispered.

Longing quickly replaced shock, and Rafael lowered his head and kissed Aisling's pouty lips. She slipped her arms around his neck and pulled him closer, inviting him to deepen the kiss. He'd never kissed a girl, had never held one so close, and the feeling was heady. His body's response was immediate. Aisling pulled away and took a step back, her eyes wide with surprise.

"Forgive me," Rafael muttered, mortified.

"There's nothing to forgive," Aisling replied. Her face was flushed and her lips slightly parted, but what nearly undid Rafael was the look in her eyes. It was soft, yet unbearably sad. "I wished to know what it was like to kiss someone I actually like." She grabbed the basket and ran toward the castle, leaving Rafael aroused and confused.

That night, Rafael had a tough time getting to sleep. Alfonso was snoring happily next to him, his round face relaxed in repose, but Rafael wasn't at peace. It wasn't just the memory of the kiss that kept him awake. His body thrummed with unfamiliar sensations, his passion stoked by his first physical contact with a woman, but it was his mind that drove him mad, his thoughts going round and round until he was too wound up to lie still. He slid out of bed and huddled on the narrow window seat, his arms wrapped around his knees. An icy draft seeped in through the window frame, but the cold helped to cool Rafael's ardor and allowed him to think more clearly.

Had Aisling been having a bit of fun at his expense? She'd said she liked him, but perhaps her desire to kiss him had been driven by defiance, a need to thwart her uncle and humiliate her betrothed, even if they'd never learn of her transgression. Were women driven by the same passions as men, or was Aisling as unique in her nature as she was in her appearance? She was the most beautiful woman he'd ever seen, and the most baffling. Aisling had looked at him full in the face and conversed with him as a man would. She wasn't afraid to speak her mind or tease him. He liked that. It made her more real, more interesting. She wasn't a blank slate for her husband to write on, she was already perfectly formed in both body and mind. And what did she expect would happen now? Was he to forget the magical kiss they'd shared, or did she hope to do it again? It would be wrong of him to make advances to another man's betrothed, but he hadn't been the one to make the first move. Aisling had dared him to kiss her, and she'd pressed her body against his and returned his kiss with a hunger that took his breath away.

Rafael exhaled deeply and abandoned his frigid perch in favor of the warm bed. He couldn't predict what Aisling would do, but he knew what was expected of him. His father had raised him to be an honorable man and to treat the fairer sex with kindness and respect. Having made his decision, Rafael was finally able to rest.

"Rafael, I'm beginning to fear for my virtue." Alfonso's voice drifted into Rafael's sleepy brain.

"What?" he mumbled as he tried to force his eyes open.

"You keep poking my backside, and I could have sworn you called me 'mi amor,'" Alfonso said, barely suppressing his mirth.

Rafael's eyes flew wide open as the meaning of Alfonso's words finally penetrated. His prick was as stiff as a ship's mast, and he'd been lying on his side, probably pressed to Alfonso's back in his sleep. He must have been dreaming of Aisling. Rafael's face suffused with lava-like heat and he rolled onto his belly, deeply ashamed of his condition.

"It's all right, amigo," Alfonso said, smiling at him with sympathy. "I'll leave you in peace to take care of it."

"What do you mean?" Rafael demanded, turning his head to look at Alfonso.

Alfonso rolled his eyes and chuckled. "Would you like me to show you?" He made a lewd gesture with his hand and laughed uproariously when Rafael made a chocking sound and buried his face in the pillow. He didn't look up until Alfonso left the room and shut the door behind him.

Chapter 34

May 2015

London, England

Jo took a sip of wine and tried to relax, but the alcohol did little to soothe her frayed nerves. She hadn't really been in the mood for Quinn's dinner party, but it would have been rude to cancel at the last minute, and Quinn had clearly put a lot of effort into the evening. The lights were low and soft music played in the background, but the company could have done with some improvement. Brian Camden was likable enough, if a bit bland, but behind her forced smile, Jill appeared to be seething. Her dark gaze caught Jo's several times during the meal—appraising, judging, possibly even warning. She supposed she could understand the woman's insecurity. Quinn had been her closest friend since childhood and Jill felt threatened by Jo's sudden appearance.

Quinn made no secret of her feelings and gushed about their reunion to anyone who'd listen. Jo was flattered but also a little annoyed, since Quinn was dragging her into the spotlight, where she had no desire to be. She wasn't comfortable with the stares or the questions, or the inevitable exclamations of, "What on earth were you doing in Afghanistan? Didn't you know how dangerous it was? You might have died." Yes, she'd been well aware of the danger, and now knew how perilously close she had come to death. She had no desire to rehash those awful weeks in Germany, nor the painful details of her adoption. She valued her privacy and needed to retain some measure of control over what people knew of her private life.

And now, looking at Jill across the table, an uncomfortable thought took root in her already suspicious mind. Did Jill know about the baby? Had Drew shared the details of the case with his cousin? Jo didn't think Drew would break a professional confidence, but people often blurted the most inappropriate things when with family and after a few pints. Jill's relationship to Quinn made her fair game and opened her up to the type of scrutiny she'd tried her whole life to avoid.

Jo smiled and answered yet another inane question from Brian while trying valiantly to keep her temper in check. She shouldn't have come, especially since annoyance was not the only emotion to plague her this evening. Gabe sat on her left, his nearness causing her acute discomfort. The man took her breath away despite her best efforts to ignore the flame he ignited within her. A glowing orb of desire had settled in her lower belly, making her ache with need. What she wouldn't do to feel those elegant hands on her body and to give herself up to the sheer ecstasy of having him inside her. She wasn't the most giving of lovers and more often than not focused on her own pleasure, but she'd do anything to satisfy Gabe. She'd gladly go down on her knees and stay there until he was spent, her own needs fulfilled just by pleasing him.

An unwelcome heat suffused Jo's cheeks. She tried to douse the fire by focusing on Jill, who was grilling Rhys about the fifth episode of Echoes from the Past, which was currently in production. Rhys eagerly regaled them with tales from the set, mimicking the horrible accent some of the actors tried to put on to get the part of the Russian characters and making them all laugh.

"We've had to hire a consultant," Rhys said, smiling at his audience. "You can't imagine how difficult it is to get all the little details just right, and what it takes to get an English speaker to pronounce Russian words. Our British tongues just can't seem to bring forth certain sounds."

"So, who's this consultant you hired? Is he a self-styled Russia expert, or the genuine article?" Quinn asked.

"Her name is Ekaterina Velesova. She's the daughter of Russian immigrants and has a PhD in early twentieth century Eastern European history. Katya is very knowledgeable."

"Oh, so it's Katya, is it?" Gabe joked. "Has she been giving you private tutorials on the socioeconomic and political impact of the Russian Revolution?"

Rhys blushed like a teenage girl. "She's really lovely, actually," he muttered.

Quinn's gaze flew to Jo, but if she expected to see hurt, she'd be disappointed. Jo felt nothing akin to jealousy. It wasn't Rhys she wanted, she'd realized, despite Quinn's obvious hope that they'd get together. Rhys, for his part, had been charming but aloof all evening, treating Jo no differently than he treated Quinn or Jill, who was glaring at her again.

"Jill, can I pour you some wine?" Gabe asked, solicitous as ever. "Surely you're getting tired of mineral water."

"Thank you, no," Jill replied, her eyes sliding to her still-full plate.

Brian leaned toward her, as if offering silent support. Jo turned her attention to Quinn, wondering if she'd noticed that little maneuver.

"We have some news," Jill said, her voice so low everyone had to lean in to hear her. "We're having a baby."

"Oh, Jilly, that's amazing news," Quinn exclaimed, and instantly came around the table to give Jill a hug. "Brian, we are so pleased for you."

"I've asked Jill to marry me," Brian announced, beaming around the table. "The proposal is a long time overdue, I know, but I had to get my courage up."

"Seeing as you have no difficulty getting other things up, it should have been a piece of cake," Rhys replied, making Jill laugh happily.

"We are so excited," Jill said. "You are the first to know. We haven't even told our parents yet. We wanted to wait until after the first scan, but I don't think we'll be able to hold out that long."

"How far along are you?" Quinn asked.

"Six weeks."

"How are you feeling?"

"Bloody awful," Jill replied. "I've been sick every morning for weeks. I can't wait for the second trimester. They tell me it gets easier then."

"It does," Quinn agreed. "Oh, I can't wait to meet this baby. I'm so chuffed for you both. When's the wedding to be? Before or after the baby arrives?"

"That's up to Jilly," Brian replied. "We will do whatever she wants, whenever she wants."

"Wise decision, old boy," Gabe said, nodding in agreement. "From this point on, what you want is completely irrelevant. You've done your bit."

Quinn elbowed Gabe in the ribs, making him laugh. "I'm sorry to hear your life is filled with suffering and sacrifice."

"My life is filled with love," Gabe replied without missing a beat. "And nappies. Lots of nappies. I've also learned how to braid hair and make pigtails. If anyone is in the mood for a new hairstyle, I'm your man."

"Is that what I'll be doing if we have a girl?" Brian asked, putting his arm around Jill.

"That and so much more," Gabe replied. "I'm Emma's living canvas. I actually look very fetching in pink lipstick and blue eyeshadow," he shared, grinning. "I love having a daughter," he said, a blissed-out expression softening his face.

Rhys bowed his head, but not before Jo noticed the pain in his eyes. Did Rhys have children? He hadn't mentioned any.

Quinn must have noticed his discomfort as well because she sprang to her feet. "Shall I start clearing up?" she asked.

"I'll do it," Gabe replied, standing and putting a gentle hand on her shoulder to keep her seated. "Relax and spend time with your guests."

"Let me help," Jo said, rising to her feet. She gathered several dirty plates and brought them to the kitchen.

"Thanks for helping," Gabe said as he took the plates from her. "Quinn won't admit it, but she's knackered. She worked hard to prepare this dinner. She wanted to impress you; I think."

"Well, she has. It was lovely. I can't cook worth a damn."

"Me neither, but I've mastered boiling eggs, making toast, and heating up baby formula."

"Good man," Jo said, smiling in encouragement. She hadn't realized it, but she'd moved closer to Gabe. She breathed in his masculine scent, wishing she could wrap her arms around him and press her cheek to his chest. She wanted to feel his heartbeat and know that it beat only for her.

Gabe took a step back, putting distance between them. "Right, let me get the rest of the plates. Would you be a love and put the kettle on?" he asked, leaving her in the kitchen.

Jo leaned against the worktop and let out a tortured breath. What did she think she was doing? Her behavior, her very thoughts were completely beyond the pale and had to stop this very minute. She filled the kettle and put it on the hob before returning to the dining room. Perhaps next time Quinn invited her to dinner, she'd make up a prior engagement and spare herself this needless suffering.

"I'm sorry, but I think I'll get going," she told Quinn. "Thank you for a lovely evening."

"Won't you stay for dessert?"

Jo smiled apologetically. "I'm rather tired."

"Right. Of course. You're still recovering. I'll ring you tomorrow."

"Shall I order you an Uber?" Gabe asked.

"No, I'll catch a taxi. I'll be fine. Goodnight, all."

Jo grabbed her coat and stepped out into the fragrant spring evening. Her face felt unnaturally warm and there was a throbbing in her lower belly that she tried to ignore.

"Put Gabe out of your mind," she told herself viciously as she walked toward an intersection to hail a taxi. "He can never be yours."

Chapter 35

The morning after the dinner party, Quinn came down early. She'd had a restless night, plagued by strange dreams that left her feeling as if she hadn't slept at all, and wanted to enjoy a cup of coffee in peace before Alex woke up. She made the coffee and took it into the front room, where she curled up on the sofa. Gabe had assured her that all had gone well, but she felt hollow, especially when she considered Jill's announcement. She was thrilled for Jill and Brian, but a part of her wanted to weep. She'd gained a sister, but it seemed that she was well on the way to losing her closest friend.

In the past, Jill would have rung as soon as she missed her period, would have asked Quinn to come round to offer moral support when she took the pregnancy test, but she hadn't said a word. Jill was engaged and pregnant, and Quinn had found out about it along with everyone else, as if she were just someone Jill knew rather than her closest confidante since they were old enough to have secrets. How had this happened, and why? Was it down to Jo, or was Quinn to blame for the rift that seemed to widen with every passing day?

Quinn finished her coffee and reached for her mobile. It took two people to grow apart, and it took two people to bridge the gap. Jill was an early riser, always had been. She'd be awake right now, enjoying a cup of tea as she checked her email and scrolled through the posts on Facebook. Quinn took a calming breath and made the call.

"Hey," Jill said. "Thanks for last night. It was nice."

"Was it?" Quinn asked, plunging right in. "Why hadn't you told me? I can't believe I had to find out along with everyone else."

"You'd have found out sooner had you made time to speak to me," Jill replied calmly. "Look, I don't blame you. I know you're busy with the children and with your program. And in your spare time, you're hanging out with Jo. She's lovely, by the way, a real charmer."

"Jill, this jealousy is beneath you."

"I'm not jealous, I'm truthful, as I always have been. And here's another truth for you. Jo fancies Gabe."

"Are you so upset that you'll say anything to hurt me?" Quinn demanded. A dull headache was building behind her eyes and the coffee felt like toxic sludge in her stomach.

"Quinn, I love you. I will always love you, and I will always have your best interests at heart. Jo has zero interest in Rhys; it's Gabe she wants."

"Jo would never do anything to hurt me," Quinn retorted.

"Are you sure? You barely know her. You've built up this picture of the perfect sister, a soulmate, your other half, but she's just like Sylvia: calculating, self-serving, and sly."

Quinn pinched the bridge of her nose. Jill was being vicious, but beneath the hurt, she knew that Jill was telling the truth of what she'd seen, and perhaps she was right to some degree. Jo was what her mum would call 'spiky,' a word she had for people who were unapproachable and touchy.

"Jill, thank you," she said. "I know you're only looking out for me, and you're right, Jo is not quite what I expected. Heck, I don't even know what I expected, perhaps someone who's exactly like me, but Jo and I are as different as night and day, and it will take time for us to find a relationship we're comfortable with. But I'm always comfortable with you. Please, don't shut me out of your happiness. I want to be there for you, for your wedding, and for your baby. I'm so thrilled for you."

"I know you are," Jill replied, her tone softening. "Look, I'm sorry if I hurt you, Quinny, but if there's one thing I've learned, it's never to ignore your gut instinct, and my instinct is screaming bloody murder. Don't let down your guard too soon, is all I ask."

"I won't."

"Oooh," Jill suddenly moaned. "Got to go. I'm going to be sick." She disconnected the call, leaving Quinn staring at the phone.

She was just about to make another cup of coffee when Gabe came down the stairs, Alex in his arms. Emma followed him, still in her pajamas.

"You're up early," Quinn said to Emma.

"I'm excited for my sleepover with Maya," Emma replied. "Daddy said he'll take me."

"I can take Alex with me if you need a bit of time on your own," Gabe said. "You look tired."

"I'm all right. You two go on. Alex and I have much to do this morning."

"Such as?" Gabe asked as he settled Alex in his highchair and poured some milk into his bottle.

"I have to unload the dishwasher, do several loads of washing, put together a progress report for Rhys, and hopefully spend an hour or two on research."

"And what does Alex have to do?" Emma asked as she took a seat at the kitchen table.

"Alex just has to be his adorable self," Quinn replied.

"Hm," Emma said, and tucked into her bowl of cereal. "Why does no one want me to be my adorable self? It's clean your room, Emma. Put away your toys, Emma. Make your bed, Emma."

Quinn and Gabe exchanged looks over Emma's head. Were they really too demanding or was Emma just jealous of Alex?

"Surely there are some benefits to being you," Gabe said. "You are going on your first sleepover, while Alex is staying at home."

"There is that," Emma agreed. She pushed away her half-eaten breakfast and slid off the chair. "I'm going to go pack my stuff."

"You're only going for one night," Gabe said.

"You don't understand," Emma replied, giving him an imperious look. "I need several outfits, pajamas, my toothbrush and hairbrush, and hair accessories. I'm also bringing Emme, so I have to pack for her. Maya also has an American Girl doll. Her dad brought it for her from America. Her name is Julia, and she has loads of stuff. A lot more than Emme has."

"Right. What was I thinking?" Gabe replied, rolling his eyes. "Off you go, then."

"Are you all right? You look a bit peaky," he said to Quinn as soon as Emma left.

"I just spoke to Jill. I was upset that she hadn't told me her news first."

"I thought you might be," Gabe replied. "Quinn, things are bound to change. Jill will have her own family now."

"I'm her family. I always have been. Just because we have other people in our lives doesn't mean we can no longer be close."

"No, it doesn't, so don't let it happen. Don't let anyone come between you two."

"You mean Jo."

"I mean anyone. Jo is no threat to you," he said. The comment was innocent enough, but Quinn wondered if he was referring to something other than her relationship with Jill. Could there be a kernel of truth in what Jill had said about Jo's interest in Gabe?

210

Quinn resolutely put the thought from her mind as she slid several pieces of bread into the toaster. This wasn't turning out to be a very pleasant morning. Gabe came up behind her and put his arms around her, resting his chin on top of her head.

"Don't worry so," he said as he pulled her close. "It will all work out the way it's meant to."

"That's what I'm afraid of," Quinn muttered.

Chapter 36

After Gabe and Emma left, Quinn settled Alex in his playpen and retrieved her laptop from the study. Gabe had unloaded the dishwasher while she threw in a load of laundry, so she had a bit of time to focus on her research. The minute she came across something of interest, her mobile rang. It was Drew Camden. Jo had said earlier that she hadn't heard from Drew, which was surprising. He'd promised to ring by the end of the previous week, but it was now Tuesday and Jo was worried that he hadn't been able to discover anything worth reporting.

"Hi, Drew," Quinn said as she took a seat on the sofa, her gaze fixed on Alex, who seemed intent on separating his bear from its plastic nose. "How are you? Jo's not here, if you were hoping to catch us together."

"I'm well, thanks. Eh…look, Quinn, I wanted to speak to you first. I hope that's all right."

"Yes, of course."

"Do you have time to talk?" Drew asked, sounding awfully glum.

"Yes. Are you still in Ireland?"

"No, I'm back in London."

"Was the care home a dead end, then?" Quinn asked.

"Not at all. I spoke to several people who worked at St. Monica's at the time Jo was there. None of them remember her, but that's not surprising. Countless women passed through that place over the years. A few of them liked it so much, they came back again," he scoffed.

"Are you saying Jo had more than one baby?"

"No, I didn't mean that. Ignore that last comment. I'm just frustrated, I suppose."

"Drew, what exactly have you discovered over there?" Quinn asked. Drew was stalling, and that didn't bode well for Jo's case.

"Since the early nineties, St. Monica's worked with two adoption agencies—one in Ireland, one in England. The Irish agency specialized in international adoptions, while the British agency focused on domestic arrangements. I began with the agency in Dublin. Of course, they would never open their records to me, but the director of the agency was able to confirm that Jo's daughter's adoption wasn't handled by them. She checked for both Quentin Crawford, as Jo would have been known then, and Ian Crawford, who was her father and handled the legalities of the adoption. Neither name came up in the database. She also pulled up the files of all the babies from St. Monica's. There were only two children born in August of 1999 whose adoptions they oversaw. Both were boys, and both went to the States."

"And do you believe this woman?" Quinn asked.

"I have no reason not to. It's easier for her to tell me the truth and fob me off than deal with a court order, should Jo decide to go that route."

"So, this leaves the other agency," Quinn deduced. "Is that why you're back in England?"

"Yes. I just left the offices of the Family Circle Adoption Agency. Like the agency in Dublin, they were able to confirm that Jo's baby never passed through their hands. They handled only one case from St. Monica's that August, and the baby, although a girl, had been born on August 2, 1999. Unless Jo has the birthday wrong, this child couldn't have been hers."

"What does this mean, Drew?" Quinn asked, sensing his discomfort.

"This could mean one of two things. Ian Crawford might have registered Jo under a false name; therefore, the file would be under her alias, and since we don't know what it might have been, we can't inquire about the child. Or the baby was never adopted."

"How can we find out?"

"The only way we can discover the truth is by gaining access to St. Monica's records."

"You mean get a court order?"

"That's not really what I had in mind," Drew replied.

"Drew?"

"One of my private security clients might be able to help, but it wouldn't be strictly legal."

"Are you telling me this person has the ability to hack into the database?" Quinn asked.

"Yes, he's quite talented. Should I put this to Jo, or simply tell her that I encountered a dead end in my investigation?"

"Why would you want to keep this from her?" Quinn asked, confused. Jo had a right to know what Drew had found out.

"Quinn, if that baby was never legally adopted, then we have to assume that it either died or fell into the hands baby traffickers, in which case we'll never find any trace of her. She might have wound up anywhere in the world, and not have had a very pleasant life."

"I see." Quinn sighed. An oppressive heaviness settled in her chest and she drew a shuddering breath.

"So, I ask again, should I tell Jo the truth? I spent only a few minutes with her, but she seemed fragile. Perhaps it would be kinder to let her believe her baby is out there somewhere, part of a loving family that went through legal channels to adopt her. She'll be disappointed, but she won't be shattered."

Quinn stared at Alex, who'd lost interest in the bear and was now banging a plastic toy on the floor of the playpen, squealing with delight when blue and red lights began to blink, and an annoying tune erupted from the tiny speaker. She wanted to grab him and hold him close, to keep him safe in her arms until he was at least forty. What had happened to Jo's poor, defenseless child? And what had Dr. Crawford done to keep his son's shameful secret?

Quinn took a calming breath. "Drew, here's what I think we should do. Ring Jo and tell her that you have spoken to several past employees and were able to obtain the names of the adoption agencies, which you intend to visit this week. In the meantime, have your man see if he can find anything concrete. If he does, we can pursue the lead and see where it takes us, but if he doesn't find any trace of the child, then we tell Jo the trail has gone cold. What do you say?"

"I say that's precisely what I planned to do, but I didn't want to make the decision without consulting you first. I'll ring you when I know more."

"Thanks, Drew. And thank you for being sensitive to Jo's feelings."

"I'd rather not hurt people if I can avoid it," Drew answered gruffly. "Talk soon."

"Yeah, talk soon," Quinn replied and ended the call.

Chapter 37

November 1588

Leitrim, Ireland

"What on earth are you doing?" Rafael asked.

Alfonso was rooting around on the floor in the morning half-light, his round face flushed and anxious. "I lost my cross," he moaned.

"Was it very valuable?"

"It is to me. The lock on the chain broke, so I kept it in my pocket, but now I can't find it. I need it, Rafi. It's the only connection to home I have left."

I know just how you feel, Rafael thought. "I'll help you look."

Rafael got out of bed and let out a whoosh of air as his feet hit the icy floor. He ignored the cold and got on his knees, peering beneath the bed and examining every crevice between the stones. The cross was nowhere to be found, and they abandoned the search.

"Could you have dropped it somewhere else?"

"I don't think so. I was very careful about keeping it safe."

"Does it have any distinctive features? Maybe we can tell the others to be on the lookout for it."

"It had a small ruby set at the crossbar. It was my mother's," Alfonso whined. "She died when I was six."

"I'm sorry. It must have been very special to you."

Alfonso sat on the bed and hung his head in despair. "I'm so homesick it hurts, Rafi. Seville seems like heaven on earth compared to this damp, freezing hell. I'd give anything to see it one more time."

"Alfonso, we must not give up hope."

"There's nothing worse than false hope, Rafi, for it prevents you from accepting your current circumstances. If we are to remain here, we must think of our future. Perhaps you can marry your *preciosa*," Alfonso suggested.

"Aisling is betrothed, Alfonso. She's not mine for the taking, and even if she were free to marry, I have nothing to offer her."

"Who is this man she is to marry?"

"He is a man of position and wealth. He's the reeve."

"Then he's most definitely a better bet than you are," Alfonso replied, smiling sheepishly. "She does like you though. I see her watching you from beneath those fox-red eyelashes when she thinks you're not looking. She's smitten."

"Much good it does me," Rafael replied, and grabbed his cloak. "I'm going for a walk."

"See you later," Alfonso mumbled.

Rafael hadn't gone far when he saw the captain, who clearly had the same idea. "May I join you, de Silva?"

"Of course, sir."

The captain's health had improved greatly over the past few weeks. His wound no longer pained him, and his cheeks had lost some of their cadaverous gauntness. His gait was brisk as he headed for the gate.

"You seem much improved, sir," Rafael said.

The captain nodded. He seemed preoccupied, so Rafael stopped talking and walked along in respectful silence. "I've been conferring with Sir Brian," Captain de Cuéllar said.

"About?"

"About finding a ship to take us home."

"And is that a possibility?"

"Not at present, but I remain hopeful."

"Some of the men believe the navy will send a ship for us come spring," Rafael ventured.

"Then let them believe it," the captain replied. "Anything to keep their spirits up in the face of a long, dark winter."

"You do not believe it, sir?"

"I do not. The men who made it back to Spain will have reported that there were no survivors. Even if they thought some men had survived the shipwrecks and the murderous natives, they wouldn't know where to search for us or how many of us might have made it through the winter. We're on our own, de Silva. It's up to us to find our own way home."

"Will we?" Rafael asked, his heart in his mouth.

"We will get home or die trying," Captain de Cuéllar replied hotly. "Let's turn back, shall we?"

They walked back to the castle in silence, each lost in his own thoughts. As soon as they entered through the gate, they noticed something odd. A dozen people were pacing the length and breadth of the bailey, their eyes glued to the ground, their shoulders hunched as they shuffled along.

"Ask them what they're doing," Captain de Cuéllar said to Rafael as they approached the castle steward.

"We're searching for Sir Brian's cloak pin," the steward replied, lifting his eyes off the ground momentarily.

Rafael had seen Sir Brian wear the pin. It was crafted of braided silver and set with a sizeable amethyst.

"The pin was a gift from Sir Brian's mother to his father on the occasion of their marriage. It has great sentimental value, so we'd best find it right quick."

"Does he think the pin might have been stolen?" the captain asked after Rafael translated the steward's words for him. Rafael relayed the question to the steward.

"No one would dare," the steward replied. "Perhaps the lock wasn't securely fastened, and the pin fell off."

"I hope you find it soon," Rafael said, and followed Captain de Cuéllar inside.

People were everywhere, scouring the castle for Sir Brian's pin. Rafael came across Aisling and Eilis in the passage outside his room. Aisling smiled shyly when she saw him. They hadn't been alone since the day in the woods and had, by what seemed like mutual consent, avoided each other.

"We are looking for Sir Brian's pin," Eilis explained. "He lost it."

"Yes, I know."

"I hope I'm the one to find it," Eilis said. "Sir Brian offered a reward."

"Eilis, go check by the storerooms. Sir Brian was there just yesterday, conferring with the steward," Aisling suggested. "I'll join ye shortly."

"That's a good idea." Eilis flashed a happy grin and disappeared around the corner.

"Aisling, I…" Rafael began.

"Ye must keep yer amulet safe," Aisling said, surprising him into silence. "Several things have gone missing over the past few weeks."

"Do you think someone's stealing them?"

"Don't ye?"

"Alfonso lost his cross."

Aisling nodded, her suspicions confirmed. "What was it, that amulet?"

"It's nothing, just a pretty trinket my intended gave me."

Aisling shook her head. "It's more than that. I saw the look of fear in yer eyes when ye dropped it." She looked up at him, her eyes narrowed. "Ye're not quite what ye appear to be, are ye, Rafael? I know a pagan symbol when I see one."

"It's not pagan," he blurted without thinking.

"Mayhap not, but it isn't Christian either, that I know for certain."

Rafael felt the blood drain from his face. This was the closest he'd ever come to discovery, and he didn't know how to best handle the situation. Aisling was too observant and clever to lie to, but he could hardly tell her the truth and put his life in her hands.

"Don't worry, yer secret is safe with me. Whatever it is," she added. She looked like she was about to say something more when footfalls alerted them to someone's presence. "Meet me on the battlements after supper," she whispered, and hurried off.

Rafael entered his room and shut the door, leaning against it. He pulled the hamsa from his pocket, closed his fingers around it, and held it close to his heart. "Lord God, King of the Universe," he whispered. "Please protect me."

Chapter 38

The bailey was deserted. The inhabitants of the castle had finished their supper and retired to their quarters, and the Spaniards were in the great hall, where they'd be drinking and dicing until they either fell asleep where they sat or ran out of ale. Rafael had slipped away as soon as he finished his meal, stopping by his room to grab the cloak. The cloak served a dual purpose, to keep the bite of the November night off his skin and to hide him from prying eyes. Whatever Aisling wanted to talk to him about was best left between them.

Rafael crossed the bailey and ascended the wall walk. His steps barely made a sound, but he thought the drumming of his heart was surely audible above the mysterious sounds of the night. A pale moon hung suspended over the lake, the glowing orb silvering the smooth surface and the woods beyond and painting the normally ordinary scene with an otherworldly beauty.

Rafael spotted movement at the far end of the walk and slowed his step. He was sick with apprehension, his stomach in knots. He didn't really believe Aisling meant him any harm, but a lifetime of lying and hiding had left him wary of trusting anyone with his secret. Sometimes the deepest traps were hidden beneath the most innocent of disguises.

Aisling turned when she heard his steps. Beneath the hood of her cloak, her face was as pale as the moon, her eyes shadowed by despair. Rafael approached her but didn't say anything. Instead, he gazed up at the moon, willing his heart to stop hammering so. Aisling didn't speak either. She just stood there, a silent pillar of temptation.

The lake was still as a looking glass, a moonlit bridge stretching toward them, beckoning them to follow the path into the murky blackness of the deep. A night like this bolstered Rafael's belief in the existence of heaven, a place where all was forgiven and forgotten, where there was no fear, no pain, and no disappointment, only contentment and peace, and eternal salvation.

"I was resigned," Aisling suddenly said, her voice like a whisper on the wind.

"To what?"

"To marrying Patrick Dennehy. Uncle Brian cares for me, and he chose a man of position and means. He did his best for an orphaned niece, and I was grateful, if not happy. And now I feel like a bird in a windowless room. I am beating my wings against the stone walls, but there's no way out; I'm trapped. I think ye know how that feels."

"Yes," Rafael replied softly. "I do. Is there no way out of this marriage?"

Aisling shook her head. "Kieran will skin me alive if I back out now."

"Kieran O'Rourke, the captain of the guard? What's he got to do with it?"

Aisling sighed. "Kieran is my brother, Rafael, and he has his sights set on Shannon."

"Sir Brian's daughter?"

"Aye. Sir Brian doesn't have a son, so the clan will be left without a chieftain once he's gone," Aisling said, giving Rafael a meaningful look.

"And by marrying Shannon, your brother will be assuring his place in the line of succession."

"Exactly. He's already Uncle Brian's closest male relative, but as his son-in-law, no one will have reason to challenge his claim. If I refuse to marry Patrick, Uncle Brian might refuse to consider Kieran's suit."

"Does Kieran love Shannon?" Rafael asked. He'd noticed Shannon's reaction to the man but didn't think he'd seen an answering warmth in the captain's gaze.

"Lord no," Aisling replied. "She's a good-hearted lass, but not to Kieran's taste. He will be sacrificing something as well to obtain a position of power. I've no right to stand in his way, Rafael. He's the only close family I have, and I know one thing for certain—Kieran will always look after me, no matter what."

"So, you're a helpless pawn in the game of your brother's ambition?"

"Ye can help me."

"How can I help you?" I can't even help myself, Rafael thought bitterly.

"Help me take charge of my life, if only for a moment—a beautiful moment that will remain with me always, no matter what life has in store for me."

Rafael turned to face Aisling. Her eyes were shining with hope, and at that moment, he would have gladly promised her anything she asked for—except for the one thing she seemed to have in mind.

"We can be together, Rafael. I know this castle like the back of my hand. There are plenty of places where we can hide from prying eyes. I have only one thing of value, and I don't care to give it to Patrick Dennehy."

Rafael's heart nearly burst from his chest. Aisling wanted him to make love to her. She was offering herself to him, openly and without reservation. Any man of his acquaintance would take her up on her request. He didn't believe he would ever make it back to Toledo, and this could be his only chance to experience physical love. Aisling was so beautiful, she set his soul alight. She didn't care if he wasn't a Christian, or an Irishman. She wanted him for himself, for the person that he was.

"No!"

"What?"

"No. Aisling, you are much more valuable than you realize, and I'd gladly spend a lifetime showing you how precious you are, but I can't agree to what you're asking of me," Rafael said.

"Don't ye want me?" Aisling's eyes shimmered with tears and her lower lip quivered as she tried not to cry.

"I want you more than I've ever wanted anything, but I was raised to be a man of honor. I will not disrespect you or the man who's given me his protection in the face of certain death. I must do what I believe to be right."

Aisling balled her hands into fists and flew at him, hitting his chest, her eyes wild with rage and hurt. "Ye coward! Ye pathetic, sniveling coward. I've offered ye the one thing I have that's worth a damn, and ye humiliated me," she cried. Tears were streaming down her face, leaving tracks on her pale cheeks.

"Aisling, please—" Rafael pleaded, but she ignored him.

He watched in helpless misery as Aisling ran the length of the walk and pounded down the stairs. Her cloak billowed around her as she crossed the bailey and disappeared into the castle, the heavy door slamming behind her.

Rafael groaned with frustration and ran his hands through his hair. Why did every interaction with Aisling leave him feeling naïve and inadequate? She was the only person who seemed to have the power to unsettle him and make him question his sanity. He knew he'd done the right thing, but why did it feel so wrong, so soul-wrenching? Was he a fool to turn down her offer? Why was it that suffering was always valued more than joy? In his eighteen years, no one had ever advised him to do what made him happy or asked him what it was he really wanted. His whole life had been planned for him, but even if he managed to make it home, what awaited him when he got there brought him no comfort.

A bird in a windowless room, Rafael thought, repeating Aisling's apt description of her situation. Standing alone on the deserted wall walk, he suddenly felt a lack of air, as if a door had been firmly shut and he was left within to fight for his freedom.

Perhaps Aisling felt drawn to him because they were kindred spirits, two people whose whole lives were ahead of them but who felt no excitement at the prospect of the future, two people whose wings had been clipped to serve the goals of others.

The wind picked up and thick clouds rolled in, obscuring the moon and obliterating the shimmering moonlit path on the water. Leaves rustled in the wind, and an animal howled in the distance, its cry followed by several others. Rafael shivered and wrapped his cloak tighter about him. As he headed for the stairs, he heard hoofbeats. The sound was faint at first but grew louder and more urgent as the lone rider approached the castle. He jumped off his horse and pounded on the gates, rousing the sentry who'd been dozing at his post.

"What ye want?" the sentry growled.

"Open up, man. I bring urgent news," the messenger cried.

"Who sent ye?"

"Chieftain McClancy."

The name obviously meant something to the sentry. He unbarred the gate to admit the messenger. The torch illuminated the man's face, which was tense with purpose.

"I must see Sir Brian," he said as he threw the reins to the guard. "Now!"

Suddenly, the yard was filled with activity as men poured out of the castle to see what the commotion was about. The messenger was escorted inside and offered a tankard of ale while someone went to rouse Sir Brian from his bed. Several Spaniards stood at the entrance of the great hall, their anxiety palpable. They needed no translation to understand that whatever news the messenger brought wasn't of the joyful variety.

Chapter 39

May 2015

London, England

"See you later, Daddy. I love you, Rufus," Emma exclaimed before she ran into the house and embraced Maya as if she hadn't seen her in weeks, when in fact they'd seen each other at school only a day ago. Emma had been begging for a sleepover with Maya for several months, so Quinn and Gabe had finally agreed after conferring with Maya's mother and working out all the details. Quinn thought it a good idea, but Gabe still harbored some reservations. Emma was only five, a bit young to start spending the night away from home.

"Don't worry, Mr. Russell," Nina Carter said, noting his forlorn expression. "Everything will be fine. They're going to have a lovely time."

"It's Emma's first sleepover," Gabe replied.

"I know. Maya's as well. I will ring you if I have any questions or if Emma decides she'd rather go home, but I doubt she will. We have a full evening planned."

"Thank you for having her."

"It's our pleasure."

Gabe gently pulled on Rufus's lead. "Come on, boy. Time to go home."

Rufus didn't seem pleased with the idea of returning home, so Gabe reassured him. "We'll take the long way, boy."

Rufus trotted along, his warm brown eyes taking in every detail of his surroundings. He loved being outside. Gabe wished

Emma were with them. He acknowledged to himself that he was being irrational, but every new parenting experience came with its share of angst. Emma was old enough to ask for help should she need it or to ask Maya's parents to use the phone to ring home. *She'll be just fine*, Gabe told himself with more conviction than he felt.

Having suddenly recalled that Quinn had asked him to stop in at the chemist to buy nappies, Gabe headed toward Boots, his thoughts turning to last night's dinner. Quinn had meant well when she invited Jo and Rhys, and Jill and Brian, but Gabe couldn't help noticing the tension around the table, caused by the unfortunate pairing of their guests. Quinn's less-than-subtle attempts to bring Jo and Rhys together were painfully obvious, and he wished she'd scale back on her matchmaking. Jo and Rhys each had their own emotional baggage to deal with, and they needed to handle their budding relationship, if that was what it was, in their own way. Despite Quinn's best efforts, he couldn't help feeling that those two were not on the same page. In fact, they weren't even reading the same book.

Gabe smiled ruefully to himself. He loved that Quinn was so excited about Jo and so desperate to forge a strong bond with her, but he worried where her exuberance might lead. He'd spent time with Jo only twice before yesterday. The first time, she'd been pale and nervous, still recovering from her injuries and clearly intimidated by all the new people suddenly thrust at her. The second time, when she'd come for lunch at their place, he'd offered to take the children to the park and give the sisters a chance to talk uninterrupted, but Jo had insisted he stay. She'd looked at him with interest—feminine interest—and he'd found that a bit disconcerting. He still hadn't formed an opinion about her at that stage, but he never ignored his gut instinct, and it told him to tread carefully.

And now there was the question of her long-lost daughter. He couldn't explain why he felt so strongly about Jo's attempts to find the child, but for some reason, his intuition told him things wouldn't end well. He feared her dealings with Quinn wouldn't end well either. Jo and Quinn were like chalk and cheese, or maybe more accurately, like Sylvia and Seth.

Jo resembled Seth physically, but that was where the similarity ended. What he knew of her so far led Gabe to believe that Jo was Sylvia's daughter through and through. Perhaps it was her polite aloofness or the guarded look in her eyes whenever anyone got too personal. This was not a woman who lowered her defenses easily, or who was overly concerned with the emotional needs of others. Jo's first priority was Jo, and if someone got in her way, she'd simply walk around them, or worse yet, push them aside to make way for herself.

He'd tried to broach the subject with Quinn, but she got upset and immediately sprang to Jo's defense. She'd been through a lot, she'd been abused and betrayed by her family, she'd just had neurosurgery and was still recovering. Gabe certainly took all those things into account, but what he saw when he looked at Jo was a woman who lacked natural warmth and seemed wary of letting anyone into her heart. Perhaps that was why her relationship with Rhys had stalled. Rhys was an observer of human nature, a teller of tales. He saw things most people missed, and Gabe was certain after seeing his interaction with Jo last night that Rhys had already figured out all the things Gabe was just coming to realize.

And then there was Jill's thinly veiled animosity. Gabe couldn't help noticing the looks she'd directed at Quinn's twin. She was curious about the woman, that was to be expected, but Jill, who was usually so pleasant and easygoing, had appeared threatened by Jo and seemed to resent her presence in Quinn's life. Was this normal female rivalry, or had Jill seen something that made her wary?

After last night, Gabe was certainly wary of Jo. As an administrator and an educator, he was acutely aware of the bounds of propriety he had to observe to keep well away from any unpleasant accusations. Female students often developed crushes on their professors and sought to make the relationship personal. Gabe had managed to avoid all such entanglements in the past; he knew the signs when it came to ardent females. He'd seen those signs in Jo last night. She'd stood closer to him than necessary, had raised her face to his in a way that invited him to kiss her, and what he'd seen in her eyes was undeniable. It was desire—desire for him. He knew with absolute certainty that if he'd wrapped his arm around her and pulled her close, she would have pressed her body to his in a way that'd leave him in no doubt of what was on offer. God, what was she playing at?

Gabe tugged on the dog's leash to hurry him along. Jo was his wife's sister. She was someone Quinn trusted, perhaps mistakenly. Was what happened last night just an unguarded moment, or had she meant to get him on his own to issue her silent invitation? Might she have been testing him to see if he'd bite? Was this some sort of game for her?

He had no intention of finding out, he decided as he walked into Boots. He paid for the nappies and stepped back out into the street. He had no right to interfere in Quinn's relationship with her sister, but in his case, forewarned was forearmed, and he was taking this warning very seriously.

Chapter 40

Quinn made herself a cup of tea and took it outside into the garden. She loved having a garden, and she adored her new house, which had needed very little work aside from a coat of paint and several new light fixtures. Alex was fast asleep in his pram, his cheeks rosy from the fresh air. She settled herself at the wrought-iron table and turned her face up to the gentle sunshine. It was a beautiful day, peaceful and quiet—too quiet. It felt odd not to have Emma there. She was at an age when she talked nonstop, asking questions, making observations, and generally prattling on until one's head was ready to explode, but that was the way of little girls, Quinn mused. It was adorable really, especially when she came out with statements that were astute enough to astound her and Gabe. Emma had been asking a lot of questions about Jude, and about Logan and Colin, and their engagement. These were not easy topics to address, but neither was the sudden appearance of a twin sister. Quinn tried to answer as truthfully as she could without burdening Emma with unnecessary and inappropriate details.

"Is Jude still sick? I miss him. Is Bridget sick too? Is she with Jude? Will Logan and Colin have babies? Why can't men have babies? They have a belly, just like women. Why hasn't Grandma Sylvia come round? When will we see Grandpa Seth again? I want to go to New Orleans. You said we'd visit Disney World next time we went to see Grandpa. And I want to meet Brett. Why hasn't he come? He's your brother, just like Logan and Jude, right? And where has Aunt Jo been all this time? Why has she never come to see us before? Why doesn't she have children if she's the same age as you are? She likes Daddy. She smiles at him a lot."

"She smiles at us too, Em," Quinn had replied, taken aback by Emma's unexpected comment.

"Not in the same way," Emma had replied matter-of-factly.

Quinn chuckled to herself. What a little madam Emma was turning out to be. This morning, before going off to Maya's, she'd asked to speak to Jill.

"I have something important to ask her," Emma had said, hands on hips.

"Really? Like what?"

"That's between me and Jill," Emma had replied. "Can I have the phone, please?"

Quinn had selected Jill's number and handed her mobile to Emma.

"Hello, Aunt Jill," Emma began. "I'm very well, thank you. Mum tells me you and Brian are finally getting married," Emma said, nearly making Gabe choke on his coffee. "Am I to be one of your bridesmaids?"

Quinn couldn't hear what Jill said, but she could tell by Emma's face that it was the correct answer. "Yes, I want to very much. I have experience, from Mum and Dad's wedding," she added, in case Jill had forgotten. "And I'm older now, so I'd like a more grown-up frock, please. And flowers in my hair."

"Emma," Gabe whispered. "That's not polite."

Emma gave him a disdainful stare as she continued her conversation. "Are you going to invite Aunt Jo? I think you should. She seems lonely. She could use a good party. Are you going to have a party or is this to be a small affair like Mum and Dad's? I hope you have a party. I'd like a live band."

"All right, that's enough now, miss," Quinn said as she took the phone from Emma's small hand. "I'm sorry, Jilly. Emma's a bit overexcited."

"Oh, it's no problem at all. As a matter of fact, I'd like her to have a word with Brian. He wants to get married at the registry office," Jill said, her voice dripping with disgust.

"I gather you have some objections," Quinn said, chuckling.

"You gather correctly. I've waited too long for him to finally get his nerve up, and I intend to have a proper wedding, band and all."

"Have you a date in mind?"

"I mean to have this wedding by the end of June, before I begin to show."

"You'll have a devil of a time finding a venue on such short notice."

"Not to worry. We already have a venue. We'll have the wedding in my parents' garden. We'll get one of those party tents and set up a dance floor on the lawn. It'll be grand."

"Your parents must be very excited."

"They will be, as soon as I tell them." Jill giggled. "Got to dash. I have a wedding to plan."

Quinn disconnected the call and glared at Emma. "That was rude, Emma."

Emma shrugged. "I want to be a bridesmaid."

"Yes, I've gathered that, but you should have waited to be asked."

"Why?" she asked, puzzled. "How would Jill know I wanted to be a bridesmaid unless I told her? Now she knows, and I'm in," Emma said, making a sliding gesture with her hand.

"Gabe?" Quinn had turned to Gabe for support.

"Let's not make this more than it needs to be," Gabe had said. "Are you ready to go, Emma?"

"I'm ready, Daddy."

Quinn leaned back in her chair. Perhaps a few hours without Emma weren't that bad after all. She should use the time to discover what had happened to Rafael, but she had to admit, she was reluctant to find out. Some of her previous subjects had unwittingly brought about their own downfall, but Rafael had done nothing, so far, to cause anyone to wish him harm—well, anyone except Julio Fernández, who didn't seem like the forgiving type and might have found a way to revenge himself on Rafael after their altercation in the forest.

Rafael was kind, considerate, and honorable. His only crime was his faith, but in the eyes of some, that was the most unforgivable crime of all. Would he be betrayed by Aisling? She appeared to be the only person to know his secret. Quinn's stomach lurched at the thought of what was to befall the hapless young man, but she needed to get to the end of his story. She'd spend some time with the hamsa once Gabe returned.

Her mobile buzzed and she reached for it, wondering if Emma might have changed her mind about spending the night, but the call was from Drew.

"Hello, Drew."

"Hello, yourself."

"I wasn't expecting a call so soon."

"It didn't take long," Drew said with a heavy sigh. "My man had a gander at the records last night."

"And?"

"And nothing. Jo was registered at St. Monica's under her own name. There's a record of her admission, antenatal examinations, and the child's birth. There's even a record of payment, made by Ian Crawford, in cash. What there is no record of is what happened to the child."

"What are you saying, Drew?"

"I'm saying that I need a new lead, and I can't get that without Jo."

"How do you mean?"

"Quinn, Jo's brother and sister were in their thirties at the time of her child's birth, and both in the medical profession. It stands to reason that her parents discussed the situation with their children, possibly even asked for their advice. They may know something, but they certainly won't open up to me. And then there's the solicitor. He must respect the attorney/client privilege, but Jo is his client, as was her father. Mr. Richards may have even drawn up the adoption papers. I'm happy to continue with the investigation, but Jo needs to give me something to work with, since I've exhausted the leads she gave me thus far. Will you speak to her? I think this might sound better coming from you."

"Why do you say that?"

"Because any questions about her siblings get her hackles up, in case you haven't noticed. Something happened in that family, something she doesn't want me to know about."

"Right. I'll speak to her, Drew."

"Give me a bell once you learn anything, *if* you learn anything. Something tells me Jo won't jump at the chance to speak to those two."

No, I don't think she will, Quinn thought. "I'll be in touch."

"Ta."

"You're welcome. Bye."

Quinn set the phone aside and gazed at the clear blue sky. Jo hadn't told Drew about the circumstances that had led to her stay at St. Monica's, but Drew was a detective, he was adept at reading between the lines. He might not have deduced Michael's part in Jo's pregnancy, but he could clearly see the tension in Jo whenever her siblings were mentioned. Quinn would have to speak to Jo, but she'd have to tread carefully. She had to agree with Drew. As the child's father, Michael was bound to know what had become of it, and Karen was sure to have been told of the arrangements at the time. Jo would never agree to speak to Michael, which was completely understandable, but Karen could prove to be a good resource, if a reluctant one.

Chapter 41

November 1588

Leitrim, Ireland

By the time the messenger exited Sir Brian's study, everyone at the castle was wide awake and in a state of quiet agitation. It seemed to Rafael that the inhabitants, as well as the Spaniards, were holding their collective breath as they waited to discover what would induce Sean McClancy to send a lone man into the wilderness at that time of night. Rafael had never seen a wolf, but he'd heard them out there in the night, their howls sending a chill down his spine as he imagined their bared fangs, crimson with blood after a fresh kill. No wonder the messenger had taken a flaming torch with him, since nothing but fire would scare off the hungry beasts.

The man gave an apologetic nod as he pushed through the crowd and made his way toward the kitchens, probably desperate for a drink and a place to lay his head till morning. Sir Brian stepped out of the study and scanned the sea of worried faces.

"Father Joseph, Kieran, with me," he called out. "Señor de Silva, you too, and please ask the captain to bring along a few trusted men."

Rafael quickly translated the request and the captain called out a few names before following Sir Brian, the captain of the guard, and the priest into the hall.

"Shut the door," Sir Brian instructed Kieran O'Rourke before taking a seat by the great hearth. The fire had burned down, but it was still the warmest place in the great room, and the farthest from the door, where at least a dozen people were gathered, impatient for news.

"What's happened, Sir Brian?" the captain asked, looking to Rafael to translate. He looked grim in the light of the dying fire, his face unshaven and creased from sleep.

"A large number of English troops have been dispatched to deal with the survivors of the Armada," Sir Brian explained with the aid of the priest. "They'll be here in less than two days, possibly even sooner, if the weather holds."

Rafael's heart sank. Yesterday, the survivors had been a drain on the chieftain's resources, but today they were a threat to his life and the lives of those under his protection. Brian O'Rourke had a good number of fighting men, but even if he decided to protect the Spaniards under his care, the chances of warding off the English were virtually nonexistent, and the penalty for treason was death, for Sir Brian and all those who assisted him in harboring the fugitives.

"What does the chieftain propose to do?" whispered Alfonso, who was standing next to Rafael. He looked panicked, his head swiveling on his short neck as he looked from one man to the next, searching for a clue to his fate.

"Sir Brian, we will leave at first light," Captain de Cuéllar said, causing a ripple of shock to pass through the Spaniards who were present. "We thank you for your hospitality and boundless generosity."

Father Joseph translated. He was visibly relieved by the captain's suggestion, but Sir Brian shook his shaggy head. "No," he said, holding his hand up to silence the captain's protests. "The English know ye're here. If ye leave, ye die."

"And if we stay, you die," the captain interjected.

Sir Brian suddenly smiled, his grin self-satisfied and cocky. "This castle is impregnable. It's surrounded by a lake on one side, woods and bog land on the other three. The English can come, but they'll never breach our defenses. As long as we have enough provisions to last till spring, we can hold them off."

"Do you have enough provisions?" the captain asked, his voice trembling with hope.

"We will if we drastically reduce our number. McClancy has offered his assistance, which I will gladly accept. Come morning, women, children, and anyone who's not needed to defend the castle will leave for McClancy territory, where they will bide until summoned back."

"You must go with them," Captain de Cuéllar protested. "If captured by the English, you will be tried for treason, Sir Brian."

Sir Brian inclined his head, mulling over the captain's suggestion. "That I will, and I must admit, I'm rather fond of my head," he said, making a few men chuckle nervously. "'Tis settled, then. We leave at first light." He turned toward Kieran O'Rourke. "Kieran, inform the men and make an inventory of our weapons. And arm the Spaniards."

"Aye, Sir Brian."

"We'll need a dozen men to escort us to McClancy's. We can't leave our people unprotected."

"As ye say, Sir Brian. I'll see to everything," Kieran replied.

With that, everyone filed out of the hall, ready to either prepare for departure or find their bed. Rafael and Alfonso made their way up the stairs. There was nothing for them to do, and Rafael suddenly felt bone-weary. A few hours ago, Aisling's anger had been his biggest concern, but now the situation had changed once again, and his life was in danger. Sir Brian was foolhardy to allow the Spaniards to remain, in Rafael's opinion, but he was grateful to the man, nevertheless. The walls of Sir Brian's castle were the only thing standing between the Spaniards and certain death.

Rafael hardly slept that night, and crept downstairs long before the pearly light of dawn began to silver the sky in the east. He had no reason to keep quiet though, since the castle was a hive of activity. Preparations for departure were almost complete, and several loaded wagons stood in the yard, ready to roll out. Excited children ran around, chasing each other and pretending to fight off the English with sticks. Women simultaneously chastised their children, hurried along their husbands, and kept a keen eye on their possessions. The men-at-arms walked from wagon to wagon, issuing orders to the drivers, encouraging the women to get a move on, and trying desperately to avoid the children who were constantly underfoot.

As the first shimmering rays of the rising sun lit up the sky in the east, the gates were unbarred and the wagons rolled out, followed by a column of people who'd travel to Sean McClancy's castle on foot.

"Cowardly dogs! Imagine leaving your home behind at the first sign of danger," Julio Fernández exclaimed as he watched the exodus from the window of the great hall. "I'd put all those lily-livered *cobardes* to the sword if I were the chief. The man has no backbone, but I shouldn't be surprised. He's running scared himself. His people are only following suit."

"Be silent, Fernández," Captain de Cuéllar commanded. "You will not speak ill of our host. He saved our lives and continues to protect us still. We will stay behind and defend the castle, but I won't think ill of any man who wishes to leave. We are not their responsibility and I don't expect any Irishman to spill his blood to protect me from the English. We've come here to fight and fight we will. Señor O'Rourke will provide us with arms. The rest is up to us."

"There are nearly two thousand English soldiers marching this way, if McClancy's information is correct," Julio argued. "We don't stand a chance."

"The odds are not in our favor, I'll grant you that," Captain de Cuéllar said, "but we will do everything in our power to stay alive. We will use every resource available to us, and our greatest resource is this castle." The captain looked at the assembled men. "Now, go. Arm yourselves with whatever weapon you can obtain and see if there's anything we can do to fortify the castle. De Silva, use your knowledge of the language to spy on Kieran O'Rourke's men. We need to know if we can depend on them in a fight, or if they're open to turning us over to the English in return for their lives. Whatever happens, we will not shame Spain!"

"I suppose soiling our breeches is out of the question, then," Alfonso whispered as soon as they left the hall. "A few dozen men against two thousand. The question is not whether we're going to die, but how long we can last before they skewer us on their swords. I almost wish I'd drowned when my ship went down. It would have been a more peaceful death."

"Alfonso, how did you wind up in the army?" Rafael asked, annoyed by Alfonso's pessimism.

"Not by choice, mi amigo. It was either the army or the priesthood. I'm beginning to think I made the wrong choice."

"I think you might be right."

"I didn't fancy being celibate, but as it turned out, I'm celibate anyway, only now I have the opportunity to be used as a pincushion by English soldiers."

"You're like a cat, Alfonso. You've got nine lives," Rafael replied and left his friend to sulk. He was in no mood to bolster anyone's spirits, not when his own were so dangerously low. He supposed that under the circumstances, it was foolish to worry about his less-than-amicable parting with Aisling, but he desperately wished he hadn't hurt her feelings. Had he agreed to consider her proposal, she might have kissed him. The memory of the kiss they'd shared in the woods stood out like a beacon of light on a dark night, a beautiful memory that would stay with him for the rest of his days. He'd give anything to see her one last time, to say goodbye, but he was glad Aisling was gone. She'd be safe from the British, and that was all that mattered.

Rafael left the castle and walked across the now-empty bailey. He had his orders, but the only way he could learn anything from the Irish men-at-arms was through overhearing their conversations, and hardly anyone was about. The gates had been barred and several men were already manning the wall, but they were sullen and silent as they gazed into the distance.

Chapter 42

An unnatural hush settled over the castle once the sun sank below the horizon and lengthening shadows drove out daylight. Corridors that had been ringing with voices only hours ago were silent and dark, the rooms abandoned and eerie. Two dozen Irishmen remained, but their mood was sour, and they kept to themselves, openly blaming the Spaniards for their predicament. Several women had stayed behind as well, mostly wives of the men-at-arms, who felt it their duty to look after the men once the siege got underway.

All the remaining men congregated in the great hall, Irish at one end, Spanish at the other, each group ignoring the other and spewing centuries-old rhetoric of war. Now that the Spaniards were armed, their pride was restored, and they no longer felt like a helpless band of refugees. O'Rourke's men were able to spare eight muskets and arquebuses, which were given to men who were trained marksmen, and a dozen swords, which went to the more experienced fighters. Men who'd never seen battle, Rafael and Alfonso among them, were given shillelaghs and daggers.

Rafael regarded his dagger with interest before shoving it into his belt. A dagger wouldn't do him much good against a sword or a musket. He'd have to get within a hair's breadth of a man to sink the weapon into his flesh, and he desperately hoped it wouldn't come to that. He had no wish to look a man he was about to kill in the face, nor did he think he'd come out of such an encounter without sustaining a fatal wound himself. In truth, he might have preferred a shillelagh, which was a thick club. At least it could be used to block the thrust of a sword, unlike a short dagger, but the men who got the clubs complained viciously, making Rafael question his logic.

No one seemed to be afraid, at least not outwardly. Everyone talked over everyone else, laughing loudly, and vowing to show the coarse and uncultured Irishmen how to fight. Their foolish bluster grated on Rafael's nerves, so he left the knot of men he was standing with and headed for the door. He wanted to be alone with his thoughts, and his fears, but the prospect of his small, low-ceilinged room convinced him to go a different way. The wall walk was no longer safe, since an arrow or a musket ball could easily find its mark, so he continued up the stairs toward the tower, hoping the door was unlocked. As he passed an arrow slit in the stonework, he saw a single bird wheeling above the castle, its silhouette caught in the moonlight. He thought it was an osprey but couldn't be sure. He'd never seen one up close. He envied the bird its freedom and wished he could fly away from this oppressive and foreign place.

Rafael pushed open the door and stepped onto the narrow stone platform. A brisk wind ruffled his hair and he shivered in his thin linen shirt and doublet, wishing he'd had the forethought to bring his cloak. During the day, the view had to be breathtaking, but now, all was dark and sinister, and silent.

Sensing a presence behind him, Rafael reached for the dagger. He spun around, dagger in hand, ready to face whoever was hiding in the shadows. Aisling's eyes opened wide as she flattened herself against the stone wall, terrified by his reaction.

"I'm sorry," Rafael said. "I didn't mean to scare you."

"Who did ye think was up here?"

"I don't know. I wasn't expecting anyone, least of all you. What are you doing here? Why didn't you leave with the others?"

"I wished to defy Uncle Brian. I was furious," Aisling replied, her cheeks bright spots of angry color.

"What happened?"

"He accused Mary of stealing the cloak pin and the other items that had gone astray, and he ordered her to be punished. Mary didn't take anything. I told Uncle Brian he's a fool if he thinks she's the thief. Mary is one of the most honest people I know."

"Has anyone searched Mary's belongings?" Rafael asked.

"Aye, but my uncle said that no thief worth their salt would ever hide their loot in a place where it could be so easily found."

"But why did he accuse Mary? Surely there must be a reason."

"Mary and Shannon O'Rourke were great friends when they were younger. Uncle Brian never opposed the friendship; he's a fair man and didn't want his daughter to have airs. One day Lady O'Rourke noticed that Shannon's ring was gone and had the castle searched from top to bottom. The ring was found beneath Mary's pillow. Both Shannon and Mary swore that Shannon had given the ring to Mary as a gift, but Mary had been accused of stealing and punished. The friendship soured after that."

"How was Mary punished?"

"Her father took a belt to her in front of Uncle Brian and Aunt Iona. Shannon was made to watch. Mary tried to be brave, but after a few lashes, she was howling like a banshee, saying she'd taken the ring and to please stop hitting her. Shannon felt wretched, since she really did give the ring to Mary. She was too young to understand that it wasn't hers to give. It was too valuable a gift to bestow on the daughter of a servant. Uncle Brian could have easily said it was a misunderstanding and simply taken back the ring, but he allowed Mary to be punished, mostly to teach Shannon a lesson."

"Is there anyone else who might have helped themselves to the valuables?"

Aisling shook her head. "No one I can think of. The thefts began after ye arrived at the castle."

"You think it's one of the Spaniards who's stealing?"

"Either that, or someone is using the Spaniards as a cover. Everyone is suspicious of the foreigners and thinks Uncle Brian is raving mad for taking ye in. Perhaps someone stole Uncle Brian's pin to get his attention and make him question the wisdom of ignoring the royal decree. He's putting the entire clan at risk, not only himself." Aisling sat down on the floor and leaned against the wall. She looked tired and frightened, peering into the darkness beyond the parapet.

"So, you remained at the castle to punish him?" Rafael asked as he lowered himself to sit next to Aisling. "Seems to me you're only punishing yourself."

"I'd no wish to go to McClancy's."

"Why?"

"Because Patrick Dennehy will be there. He's Sean McClancy's kin."

"It was my understanding that the clansmen marry only within the clan," Rafael said. He thought of the clans as separate tribes, but supposed they had to mix with other clans from time to time.

"Uncle Brian and Sean McClancy are great friends. They encourage marriage between clan members. Ye've got to mix the blood to produce strong children."

Rafael nodded. His own father had said much the same thing. With their community growing smaller with every generation, it was imperative to bring in new blood to keep the children from being born sickly or mentally deficient. Marriage between first cousins had been forbidden by their rabbi, which was a blessing since Rafael had no desire to marry his cousin Ana, a venomous little besom of thirteen.

"Patrick is eager for us to be wed. Going to McClancy's would only give him a reason to bring up the wedding. He wants us to marry before the year's out," Aisling said balefully. "Besides, I'm not afraid of the English. They won't hurt me. The English don't make war on women."

Now, there you are wrong, Rafael thought, but didn't speak the words out loud. He'd never been in battle, but he'd spent enough time among soldiers to know what men did to the women of the enemy, especially when their blood was up. Men could be animals, and a pretty young woman like Aisling would not be left unmolested if taken by the English.

"Aisling, if the English take the castle, you need to hide and get away at the first opportunity. You must take to the woods. You know this land; it can be your ally."

"Ye're sweet to worry about me, Rafael, but there's no need." Aisling rose to her feet. "Are ye coming down or will ye stay up here for a bit?"

"It's too cold."

Rafael stood and found himself dangerously close to Aisling. She looked up into his face, her eyes luminous with affection. He knew it was wrong and went against every reason he'd given her for not wishing to take their relationship further, but he couldn't help himself. He pulled her close and pressed his lips against hers, his heart soaring when she leaned into him and wrapped her arms around his neck. She kissed him with all the desperate passion of an innocent young girl.

"Don't go," she whispered once they finally broke apart. "Please, don't go."

"Aren't you cold?" he asked.

She shook her head. "I meant, don't go back to Spain. Stay here, with me. Uncle Brian will be angry, but he'll come round in time."

"And what of your brother?" Rafael asked, stalling for time.

"Uncle Brian has already agreed to the match. Shannon and Kieran will be married at Candlemas. Once they're wed, there's nothing he can do."

"Aisling, this is not my place. I have nothing to offer you."

"Ye can offer me kindness, and love. That's all I need."

"You can't eat kindness and love, *mi amor.* You said so yourself."

"I don't want to marry Patrick, Rafael. I hadn't realized how much until I met ye. There's no kindness in his heart, no affection. He wants to possess me, but he has no love for me or any woman. He thinks us feebleminded and only good for keeping house and warming a man's bed."

"Aisling, if things were different—"

"But they aren't, are they?"

Aisling pushed him away, yanked open the door, and ran down the steps, leaving Rafael feeling guilty for letting her down once again.

Chapter 43

May 2015

London, England

Gabe pinched the bridge of his nose and closed his eyes for a moment. His head was beginning to ache, and he still had at least ten end-of-term papers to grade, one rubbish essay after another, the students endlessly repeating overused phrases copied from the internet and offering strikingly similar conclusions based on little more than supposition. Before Wikipedia, students had plagiarized a plethora of different sources, but now it was just one, and most didn't even bother to restate the information in their own words. Gabe pushed aside the pile of reports. Thankfully, it was a bank holiday and he'd been granted an extra day to wade through this pile of steaming horseshit.

Alex directed an accusing stare at Gabe from the playpen and promptly tossed a toy over the side. Gabe smiled. "I know, sweat pea, you'd rather be at the park on this beautiful day. So would I. Give me another hour and then we'll go for a long walk. Deal?"

The baby didn't understand a word, but Gabe's soothing tone seemed to do the trick, and he busied himself with a firetruck that made lots of noise and flashed an inordinate number of lights.

Gabe was saved from starting on the next essay by the pealing of the doorbell. "Let's see who that is," he said to Alex. "Maybe Mum forgot her keys."

Gabe tried to hide his surprise when he found Jo waiting patiently on the doorstep. She smiled brightly when he opened the door.

"Oh, hello, Gabe. Nice to see you. Is Quinn in?"

"Actually, she isn't. She went to collect Emma from her sleepover. Would you like to come in?" he asked against his better judgement. He wished Jo would just offer to come back another time but couldn't find it in himself to be rude.

"Thank you." Jo followed him into the front room.

"Quinn should be back soon if you'd like to wait. I'm in the midst of grading end-of-term reports, so I can't keep you company."

"I can only stay for a minute," Jo said. "I was in a bookshop yesterday and came across this book. I thought Quinn might find it helpful. It's about the mystic origins of the hamsa and its connection to the Kabbalah."

Jo extracted a slim volume from her bag and held it out to Gabe. Her gaze was playful, and her lips stretched into a seductive smile as she looked up at him. "I like mystical things. There's something wonderfully romantic about things that have been shrouded in mystery for centuries. There are all kinds of weird legends about the bond between twins, you know. No wonder twins always tend to be attracted to the same people. It's in their genetic make-up to want the same things."

"I've never heard that particular theory," Gabe replied, keeping his tone as even as he could. "I've heard of sibling rivalry and think it's a made-up term used to excuse petty jealousy."

Jo laughed and studied him from beneath her lashes. "That's because you're an only child. You'd be surprised how competitive siblings can get."

"Is that something you know from experience?" Gabe asked.

"I was too young to compete with my brother and sister, but they went at it hammer and tongs, those two. They were always trying to outdo each other to impress our father, for whom nothing was ever good enough. It came as no surprise to me that they both became cardiologists, just like Daddy."

"Well, I hope you and Quinn won't find anything to compete for," Gabe remarked as he began to move closer to the door. "I'm sorry, Jo, but I really must get back to those reports."

"Sorry to have interrupted you. Tell Quinn I stopped by."

"I most certainly will," Gabe replied.

He breathed a sigh of relief once he shut the door behind his sister-in-law. What in the holy hell was that about? Was she openly telling him she wanted what Quinn had or was he reading meaning into perfectly innocent comments? The twisting in his gut told him it was the former.

Gabe returned to the stack of reports, but his mind was no longer on the wonders of carbon-14 dating and its impact on the accuracy of dating ancient remains. He leaned back in his chair and gazed out the window. He needed some air, and so did Alex, who was clearly getting tired of being confined to the playpen. He pinned Gabe with his blue gaze and hurled the firetruck over the side of the playpen in obvious protest.

"Come on, buddy. Let's go for a walk," Gabe said as he walked over to the pen and lifted Alex out.

Alex smiled, displaying several newly erupted teeth. He reached out and put his hands on Gabe's cheeks, holding his face tenderly.

"I love you too, little man," Gabe said and kissed the tip of his nose. He grabbed the diaper bag Quinn had prepared for him earlier and let himself out of the house.

Once in his buggy, Alex looked around, his eyes round with wonder as a double-decker bus rolled by. He pointed and Gabe automatically said the word twice, to make sure Alex caught it. "Bus. Bus."

"Bah," Alex cried.

They repeated this with cars, birds, and a bicycle until Alex's eyelids began to droop and he dropped off. Gabe decided to keep walking until Alex woke up from his nap, since he'd promised him time on the swings. Gabe took out his mobile and selected his mother's number. He hadn't spoken to her since Friday morning and felt a bit guilty. Normally, he rang every morning, but had been sidetracked by preparations for the dinner party and plans for Emma's sleepover.

Phoebe answered on the first ring. "Gabe, I hoped you'd call this morning."

"You could have called me, Mum. I could have used the distraction."

"I didn't want to bother you. You said you had a lot of papers to grade. How's that going?"

"Slowly and painfully. Some of my students copy swathes of information directly from the internet and think I won't notice. You'd think they'd paraphrase a few paragraphs for decency's sake instead of copying them word for word."

"It's so much easier to cheat these days, isn't it, with all that technology. They don't even have to bother writing it all out. Just copy and paste, and it's done and dusted. And then they blame everyone but themselves when they get a low grade. I just don't understand these millennials. Things were so different in my day," Phoebe said with a loud sigh. "We understood the value of hard work and took pride in a job well done."

Gabe chuckled. Hearing his mother use a term like 'millennials' surprised him, but her sentiments didn't. "Mum, how are you?"

"Oh, you know. At my age, making it to lunch feels like an accomplishment."

"Come on. You're not that old."

"No, but I feel it some days. When your father was still alive, I had a sense of purpose and a well-established routine. Your father liked his meals at certain times, and he always expected a home-cooked supper. I don't need to cook anything for myself. I'm happy with a salad or a bowl of soup, which I can pick up at any café. No point making a pot of soup if I won't eat it all."

"You can invite someone over for a meal," Gabe suggested.

"I'll tell you a secret, son," Phoebe said, her tone conspiratorial. "Old people are not good company. I'd rather watch telly than hear a litany of someone's ailments. I have enough of my own."

"Mum, we'll come and see you as soon as the term is over. We'll have a picnic by the river, and I'll take you to the garden center. I know how you love that place."

"I'd like that. I miss my grandchildren," Phoebe said sadly. "Send me a new photo, will you?"

"Of course. I'll take one today. Alex has two new teeth."

"Make sure he smiles, then, so I can see."

"Mum, I need a bit of advice," Gabe said, hoping he wasn't going to regret sharing his suspicions with his mother, but he needed someone to talk to and this subject was too delicate to share with anyone, even Pete, his best mate since college. Pete would probably think it amusing and make light of Gabe's concerns.

"Tell me," Phoebe invited.

"I feel ridiculous even saying this out loud, but I think Jo fancies me."

"Can't say I'm surprised."

"Aren't you? Am I so hard to resist?" Gabe joked.

"It's not you, son. Not that you're not handsome and charming," Phoebe backtracked.

"What is it, then?"

"It's a sister thing. When we were young, before I married your father, my sisters and I always found ourselves fancying the same blokes. I suppose when the person closest to you finds someone attractive, you assume they must be worth the attention and suddenly want them for yourself."

"Mum, that's mad."

"It's human nature. Statistically, most people have affairs with family members, particularly with brothers and sisters-in-law, or close friends, rather than total strangers. Attraction tends to grow when people come in constant contact with one another and there's the 'forbidden fruit' element to make them seem so much more appealing."

"So, what do you suggest I do?" Gabe asked.

"The worst thing you could possibly do is get between those two. Their bond is fragile, and given how excited Quinn is to finally have her sister, I'd say, don't say a single negative thing about Jo, even if it's true."

"So, I do what, exactly?"

"Play dumb."

"Pardon?"

"Play dumb, son."

"I'm sorry, Mum, but I don't follow."

"You're doing a fine job of it right now," Phoebe replied, chuckling to herself.

"Mum!"

"Gabe, just as you instinctively know Jo wants you, she instinctively knows you know, and as long as there's that secret knowledge between you, the problem will persist. Pretend you don't notice. Don't take the bait. Treat her as you would one of your more forward female students."

"You mean, look through her?"

"Exactly. She will do one of two things. Either she will get the hint and transfer her affections elsewhere, or she will feel compelled to step up her game."

"I can't believe you just said, 'step up her game.'"

"I'm not a dinosaur, you know. I watch television."

"So, what do I do if that happens?"

"You tell her off, is what you do, and let her know, in no uncertain terms, that you're not interested." There was pause on the other end before Phoebe spoke again. "Gabe, *are* you interested? It can be flattering, I know, but you love Quinn. Don't you?"

"Yes, I love Quinn, and no, I'm not flattered. I feel angry and frustrated, and afraid that Jo will come between us. Quinn is so enamored of her twin that she can't see the wood for the trees. She thinks Jo is perfect."

Phoebe sighed. "You mustn't say anything to Quinn. This is one lesson she must learn for herself. She's got the right of it when it comes to Sylvia and Seth, and her brothers. She'll see Jo's true colors as well, but it will take time. They have a special bond, those two, so it will be more difficult for Quinn to separate fact from fiction when it comes to Jo, but she will, Gabe. She will. Quinn is a smart woman, and an intuitive one. She'll know soon enough if someone's after her man, and she won't take it lying down. Quinn will fight for you."

"And suddenly, I have a vision of Quinn and Jo mud wrestling," Gabe joked.

"All jokes aside—she loves you. Remember that, and don't do anything to jeopardize your marriage."

"I won't. Thanks, Mum."

"Anytime, son. Don't forget to send me that photo," Phoebe said. "I think I'll go over to Cecily's for a bit. I'm in the mood for company."

"Tell her I said hello."

"I'll be sure to do that."

Gabe disconnected the call and turned toward the park. Alex would be waking up soon. His afternoon naps lasted about a half hour. Gabe took a deep breath. The air smelled of freshly cut grass, flowers, and that lovely spring smell that always lifted the spirits. He felt better after talking to his mother. Perhaps playing dumb wasn't such a bad idea.

Chapter 44

"How was your sleepover, Em?" Quinn asked.

Emma walked alongside her, head bowed, her gait sluggish. "It was okay," she mumbled.

"Just okay?" She'd expected Emma to be full of glee and begging to schedule the next sleepover immediately, but Emma seemed oddly subdued.

"I'm tired. I couldn't sleep."

"Were you too nervous to fall asleep?"

"No. I fell asleep, but then I woke up when I heard shouting."

"Who was shouting?"

"Maya's parents. They were having a row."

"I see. I'm sure they didn't mean to wake you," Quinn said, annoyed that the Carters hadn't bothered to keep their voices down. Emma was a light sleeper, and it was only natural that she'd feel a little uncomfortable in an unfamiliar place. Hearing grownups shouting at each other would be unsettling for any child, let alone one as sensitive as Emma.

"Mum, do you love Daddy?" Emma asked. She'd stopped walking and looked up at Quinn, her little face creased with anxiety.

"Of course. Why do you ask?"

"Will you love him always?" Emma persisted.

"I'd like to think so."

"Promise me you'll never get divorced," Emma said. Her thick lashes shimmered with unshed tears and her mouth was turned down at the corners, her expression heartbreakingly tragic.

"Darling, what did Maya's parents argue about?" Quinn asked as she squatted in front of Emma so the little girl wouldn't have to look up at her.

Emma sighed deeply. "Mrs. Carter called Mr. Carter a wanker. I don't know what that means, but it's a funny kind of word, so I think it must mean something bad. She said he's useless in bed. I guess he couldn't sleep either. She said that she's in love with someone else, and wishes she'd never married him. She said she wants a divorce."

"I see. Darling, sometimes marriages don't work out, but that doesn't mean Maya's parents don't love her and her brother. They will always be their parents, no matter what."

"But they won't be together, living in the same house. Maya might have a new father, and a new mother. I don't want you and Daddy to be with other people. I want you to be together, always."

Quinn stood and pulled Emma into an embrace. Emma's arms went around her waist as Emma buried her face in Quinn's midriff. "Emma, Daddy and I love each other, and we love you. We are a family, and we will always be a family, no matter what happens."

"But you and Jo weren't always a family," Emma mumbled. "You were given to different parents. Family doesn't always stay together."

"The situation with Jo is very different. Our parents weren't married when Jo and I were born. We were given up for adoption."

"Why weren't they married? Don't you have to be married to have babies?" Emma asked. She seemed to have forgotten that Jenna and Gabe hadn't been married and that she hadn't met her father until after her mother's untimely death.

"It's preferable," Quinn replied, realizing she'd just entered a minefield. She had to be very careful about how she explained things and what she promised. Emma was right; families didn't always stay together, and although she hoped she'd never have to consider divorce, unexpected things happened all the time and children got caught in the crossfire of their parents' animosity.

"What's a wanker?" Emma demanded as they continued home.

"Oh, dear," Quinn muttered to herself. "It's an insult. Like if I say someone is a dummy. It's not a nice thing to say."

"Is Daddy a wanker?"

"He most certainly isn't."

"That's good," Emma replied, somewhat mollified. "If he's not a wanker then you won't be angry with him and fall in love with someone else. Is he useful in bed?" Emma asked, looking up at Quinn, her eyes wide with childish curiosity.

"Very. He makes me feel safe, so I don't have bad dreams. Now, how about we go home, and you have a little lie-down before lunch? I think a nap will greatly improve your mood."

"Can we have pizza for lunch?" Emma whined.

"Sure. We can have pizza. We'll order one once you wake up."

"Mum, I'd like to have another sleepover with Maya, but I want it to be at our house. Okay?"

"Okay. But how about we wait a few weeks? I think one sleepover per month is more than enough."

"I think so too," Emma replied and slid her hand into Quinn's. "Let's go home, Mum."

"Yes, let's."

Chapter 45

November 1588

Leitrim, Ireland

No one was surprised when a call from the sentries announced the arrival of the English. The troops came fast and thick, their numbers swelling from a few dozen to hundreds within a few hours. Within a day, the castle was besieged. The English set up their camp a safe distance from the wall to keep their men from being picked off by musket fire from the battlements, but it was close enough for the Spaniards to see their tents and smell their cooking fires. Hundreds of smoke columns curled into the overcast sky, and the pale peaks of canvas tents dotted the forest like giant mushrooms that had sprung up overnight. Kieran O'Rourke had predicted there'd be no cannon, and he was right. The terrain was too boggy in some spots and too densely wooded in others, but that didn't prevent the English from being armed to the teeth. Every soldier appeared to possess a musket as well as a sword.

Once the English dug in, fed their men, and grew tired of cleaning their muskets and polishing their swords, boredom set in, and the taunts began. They jeered at the Spaniards watching them from the battlements, calling them ugly names and describing in detail what they'd do to them once they were captured. Since most of the Spaniards didn't understand a word, they were spared the gruesome details, but the bluster of the past few days quickly abated, leaving the men silent and guarded in the face of impossible odds.

"It was very considerate of Sir Brian to leave us something to play with," Julio Fernández said loudly when he saw Aisling crossing the bailey on her way from the barn. She was carrying a bucket of milk, her attention fixed on not upsetting the contents. "I mean to have a go, lads."

"She's not your plaything," Rafael growled, furious that Julio would speak of Aisling, or any woman, in that way.

"Nor is she yours, from what I hear. You failed where a real man would have succeeded."

"If by success you mean overpowering a young girl and forcing her to submit to your advances, then you must be the definition of masculine prowess," Rafael retorted. "Besides, I'm not trying to seduce her," he added, deeply embarrassed that his longing for Aisling was so obvious to the others.

"Maybe you should be. Having a woman might finally make a man out of you, you sniveling milksop," Julio snapped.

"Doesn't seem to have done you any favors, Fernández. You're still the same vicious bastard you must have been when you were a boy. I wager you tore the wings off butterflies and threw stones at dogs just to show how brave you are. Or did you throw stones at people?"

"Yeah, I threw stones at Jews, but they're not people." Julio smirked, admirably rising to the bait. "And neither are women. God only created them for the pleasure of men."

"And yet, you still have to force yourself on them to get what you think is your divine right. Why don't you tell the others how you tried to rape a thirteen-year-old in the woods? You were very brave; you showed her what it means to be a real man."

The blow knocked Rafael to the ground. Blood gushed from his nose and the ringing in his ears prevented him from hearing the insults Julio hurled at him in his fury, but his murderous expression told Rafael everything he needed to know. He managed to get to his feet, but his assailant kicked him in the stomach, making him double over with pain. Stars exploded behind Rafael's eyes, breathing was agony, and his head pounded like a drum, but he kept his balance and braced himself for the next blow.

Julio looked like a bull who was about to charge the *torero* when Captain de Cuéllar came running from the direction of the privy and ordered the men who stood around watching the fight to restrain Julio. Groans of disappointment were silenced by the captain's thunderous expression.

"You're a disgrace to Spain and to your king," the captain roared. "I should have you flogged, Fernández."

"It'd be worth it just for the sheer pleasure of beating this piece of dog shit to a pulp," Julio snapped. His blood still up, he was trying to shake off the men who were holding him by the arms.

"Go to your bedchamber," Captain de Cuéllar ordered. "I'll deal with you later."

I'm not a child, Julio's furious gaze seemed to say, but he knew when he was beaten and strode off in a huff.

"Are you all right, *mi amigo*?" Alfonso asked as he put an arm around Rafael to steady him. "Why do you bother getting into it with him? You know what he's like. He likes to goad people, and earnest fools like you make for easy targets."

"I am supposed to just ignore his insults?" Rafael asked. "If I do, everyone will think me a coward."

"No one thinks you're a coward, Rafael. They know Julio is a bully and humor him rather than stand up to him. We have enough to deal with without fighting amongst ourselves."

Alfonso escorted Rafael inside and brought him to the kitchen, where Aisling was elbow deep in dough. Three other women were in the kitchen, but they paid little attention to the Spaniards, going about their business as if the men weren't even there.

"Jesus, Mary, and Joseph," Aisling exclaimed. "What happened to ye?"

"He defend your honor," Alfonso said in his broken English. "He hero. Almost," he amended, making Rafael chuckle. "Julio got in a few good ones," Alfonso added in Spanish.

Aisling wiped her hands on her apron and came toward Rafael, a small smile tugging at her lips. "Ye fought that man because of me, ye daft eejit?"

"I fought him because he has no honor."

Aisling shook her head. "'Tis about time someone stood up to that vicious turd."

"I'll stand up to him as many times as it takes to make sure you're treated with the respect you deserve."

Aisling smiled warmly and patted Rafael on the shoulder before going to fetch water and a cloth to clean his face. He wiped his nose angrily, smearing blood on his hand. His nose was throbbing, and a blinding headache was building up behind his eyes. He'd never been in a fight before and hoped he'd acquitted himself well. Now that the rage was subsiding, he felt a bit shaky and tearful.

The warm water Aisling used to clean his face felt good. Her movements were gentle and sure, cleaning away the blood and dabbing at his split lip until the blood began to clot. But the pain in his head grew worse, forcing Rafael to shut his eyes against the light streaming through the window set high in the wall.

"Ye need to lie down," Aisling said. "Help him to his room, please," she said to Alfonso, who nodded.

"Thank you," Rafael muttered in Aisling's direction as Alfonso placed an arm protectively around his shoulders and led him from the kitchen.

"No, thank ye," Aisling replied under her breath. "Ye're a foolish lad, but no one can accuse ye of cowardice. I just hope yer foolishness doesn't get ye killed."

"Go to sleep," Alfonso said once he deposited Rafael on the bed. "You look like hell."

"I feel like hell."

Rafael closed his eyes and pinched the bridge of his nose to ease the pain in his head. It didn't help. His nose was most likely broken. He could barely breathe through the swollen nostrils, his open mouth the only source of air. Alfonso and Aisling were right, he was a fool to rise to Julio's taunts. Now that he had a moment to think about it, he realized Julio had baited him on purpose. He knew how Rafael felt about Aisling and had hoped for exactly the reaction he got. Rafael had played right into Julio's hands and allowed him to show the other men that he'd knock down anyone who stood up to him. Had Captain de Cuéllar not come on the scene when he had, Julio would have beaten Rafael senseless. They weren't evenly matched, and Julio clearly had more experience with fighting than Rafael, who'd spent his youth hunched over his father's books rather than brawling in taverns.

He hated bullies, but there were always a few in every group. They tended to band together, instinctively realizing there was strength in numbers. Unfortunately, their victims never seemed to do the same, and got pummeled time and again because their friends were too cowardly to stand up for them. Alfonso had been quick to offer his aid, but only after the captain had broken up the fight. For all his talk, he was too afraid to challenge Julio.

Rafael turned away from the light and discovered that it was easier to breathe when he lay on his side. *I'll have to be more careful of Julio Fernández*, he thought drowsily. He hadn't made any enemies in the past, but he'd made an enemy of Julio the moment he came upon him in the woods with Eilis. Julio Fernández did not strike Rafael as someone who'd ever turn the other cheek.

Chapter 46

The first few days of the siege passed in strained anticipation as the defenders of the castle watched and wondered if the English had a strategy or simply planned to starve them out. Since the inhabitants of the castle had been preparing for winter, supplies were plentiful, but the English seemed to be just as well provisioned and in surprisingly good spirits. Snatches of songs could be heard in the evening as the soldiers sat around their fires, warming themselves and passing the time.

"Her Heretic Majesty must have troops to spare if she can send this many men to wait out a few dozen Spaniards," Pedro said as they sat down to their midday meal on the third day. "She must really fear us."

"Or she simply wants to finish what she started," José Méndez replied.

José, who'd already been at the castle when they'd arrived, seemed to have struck up a friendship with Pedro and they spent much of their time together. Julio, who'd been released from his room after a stern talking-to from the captain, sat next to Pedro but said nothing. A few others nodded in agreement. The mood was grim, an overwhelming sense of foreboding hanging over the assembled men. No one believed the English would do nothing and simply sit outside the castle walls, eating through their supplies and singing endless songs. They had to have something up their sleeves, as they always did.

They were just finishing their meals when Mary erupted into the hall. She scanned the men until her eyes settled on Captain de Cuéllar. "Come. Quick," she cried, and gestured with her hand in case the captain didn't take her meaning.

Benches scraped against the stone floor as the men rose in unison and hurried outside. Two Spaniards had been assigned to patrol the battlements, but there was no sign of them, leaving the battlements unmanned. The Irishmen, who'd been practicing their sword skills on the other side of the yard, came running as well, their swords still drawn.

"Mary, what happened?" Rafael asked. "What did you see?"

"I heard shots. Yer men are dead," Mary replied woodenly. Her earlier panic seemed to have been replaced by shock.

"Quick, go to them," Captain de Cuéllar ordered the men standing closest to him. "They might still be alive."

Four men made their way to the battlements, two for each fallen man. They crouched down once they reached the top to avoid being shot, but there was an eerie silence, made all the more frightening by the nearly two thousand English soldiers just beyond the walls of the castle. The rest of the Spaniards remained in the bailey, watching their friends and waiting for news of the wounded. It wasn't long until the men returned, carrying the two corpses.

"They've been shot in the head," José said once they laid the men on the ground before the captain. "English shooters must have hidden in the trees and taken them out."

The men bowed their heads and crossed themselves. "God rest their souls," Captain de Cuéllar said quietly before turning to face the remaining men. "This is a warning that they'll kill anyone patrolling the battlements. There are several other vantage points we can use that should be out of range of their muskets, even if they come close to the walls. We must keep a lookout."

"Ho, Spaniards! We have a message for you. Come and see," an English solider hailed them in heavily accented Spanish.

The men turned toward the captain, who looked angry and defiant. The Irish fighters stood off to the side, watching, their swords now sheathed, since they were in no immediate danger.

"Rafael, Alfonso, Julio, and José. Come with me. Keep your heads down."

"*Sí, Capitán*," the men replied in unison.

They ascended the battlements and crouched down, peering between the crenellations. The English were gathered at the edge of the wood, well out of musket range, watching the castle with gleeful anticipation. Captain de Cuéllar let out an oath as two Spaniards, so dirty and ragged they barely looked like soldiers of Spain, were led into a clearing that was visible from the castle walls. The men could barely walk. They were emaciated from months of near starvation and had been cruelly beaten. Their faces were bruised beyond recognition and rusty stains marred what was left of their shirts and breeches. Their feet were bare, and their hands were tied behind their backs.

An officer stepped forward and looked toward the castle. Even from a distance, his smug expression was hard to miss.

"My name is Colonel Rigby," he announced in ringing tones, in English this time. "I am in command of Her Majesty's troops, which will remain encamped here until each and every one of you has been captured. Should you choose to surrender, you will be offered reasonable terms. Should you choose to persist with this ridiculous standoff, you will all be executed as soon as you're taken. And just to show you how serious I am, I'll start with these two."

Rigby turned toward the two men, who were restrained by English soldiers, and gave the order. The men were dragged toward a full-bellied oak and forced to watch as two lengths of rope were slung over a sturdy branch. Neither man bothered to struggle as they were positioned directly beneath the branch. They were either too weak or had no hope of a reprieve at this late stage. Instead, they turned their faces in the direction of the castle, their gazes fixed on their countrymen as the nooses were draped around their necks, their lips moving in silent prayer.

"*Estamos con vosotros, hermanos,*" Captain de Cuéllar shouted. *We're all with you, brothers.*

Rafael hoped the captain's words brought the condemned men some comfort, but he doubted it. A moment later, the prisoners were hoisted up. Their legs kicked at the empty air, their bare feet desperately trying to find purchase as they gasped for breath. The men in the castle watched in helpless horror as the two prisoners continued to struggle, slowly suffocating. The English made sure their necks weren't broken when they were strung up, to prolong their suffering. It was cruel but effective. The Spanish soldiers crossed themselves and bowed their heads as a sign of respect once the two prisoners finally went limp, their struggle over.

"Surrender now, and you will not meet the same fate," Colonel Rigby shouted. "You will be taken prisoner and treated with respect."

"Why don't I believe him?" José asked sarcastically. "There are enough trees here for each and every one of us."

"We will not surrender," the captain vowed once they returned to the other men. "Our only hope of survival lies in holding our defenses. For all their bluster, they can't get to us without breaching the castle walls."

The men nodded, but no one spoke. It wasn't hard to guess what they were thinking. If the English chose to scale the walls, little could be done to stop them. Several dozen men could hardly hold off two thousand, and if the Irish decided to bargain for their freedom, the surest way to a pardon lay in handing over the Spaniards, for whom they harbored no fond feelings.

"What's the plan, Captain?" Julio Fernández asked, his earlier anger forgotten.

"The plan is to wait and see what they'll do. We must keep watch around the clock. Eight men, four vantage points, two-hour shifts."

"Yes, sir," the men replied.

"You two, take the north corner," the captain said to Rafael and Alfonso.

"Let's go," Rafael said.

"We'll be staring at the corpses of those men the entire time," Alfonso replied as he followed Rafael toward the watch tower. He looked like a turtle with his shoulders hunched to protect his head.

"Not much we can do about that. Think of it as a reminder of what will happen if we fail."

Alfonso didn't reply. They both knew their chances of ever leaving the castle were almost nonexistent. The English meant to either take them prisoner or execute them. Rafael wasn't sure which option he preferred. At least the poor men who were now swinging in the breeze had been spared years of imprisonment and suffering. They would have never been released or had any earthly chance of getting home. At least they were now at peace.

Alfonso and Rafael took up their watch. They couldn't stand upright for fear of being shot, so they crouched behind the truncated parapet, watching the English. All they could do was alert the others if the English were on the move, since they had no muskets. The minutes ticked by slowly, the men stiff and uncomfortable in their unnatural position. The English soldiers returned to their camp and went about the business of preparing supper. There was no sense of urgency one would associate with an imminent attack, but Rafael couldn't relax. His gaze kept straying to the two hanged men, whose faces seemed to be turned toward the castle despite the stiff breeze, as if in a final reproach.

"I would give anything to be at home right now," Alfonso said wistfully. "I hate this place, and I hate the army. If I ever make it out of here alive, I'll gladly join the priesthood, as my father wished. At least I'll be safe and have plenty to eat."

"And the women?" Rafael asked, grateful for the distraction. "I thought you couldn't give up the women."

Alfonso shrugged miserably. "Face it, Rafi, I'm not exactly a catch. The only women I could get would be the ones I paid for, and I don't want those. I want someone to love me," he said miserably. "I want to know what it's like to be loved."

"I love you," Rafael said, blowing Alfonso a theatrical kiss. Alfonso grinned and elbowed Rafael in the ribs playfully, nearly causing him to fall over.

"Thanks, Rafi. The only thing that makes this more bearable is knowing that I won't die friendless."

"Amen to that, *mi amigo*."

They smiled sadly at each other and turned their attention back to the English soldiers and the heart-wrenching sight of their comrades.

Chapter 47

May 2015

London, England

Rhys felt a twinge of nervousness as he waited for Katya to open the door. She'd invited him to dinner, but he wasn't sure if this was meant to be a date or just a meal between friends. He'd brought an expensive bottle of red wine but refrained from baking anything to take along as he normally did when visiting friends. He had no wish to make Katya uncomfortable. He'd let her take the lead.

Katya smiled warmly when she opened the door. She kissed his cheek and invited him into her flat, which was spacious and ultra-modern in its decor. Above the white leather sofa hung an oversized painting, the splashes of color and unique shapes instantly recognizable to anyone who considered himself a connoisseur of art. Rhys stepped closer and examined the painting, unable to believe his eyes.

"Is that a Kandinsky?" he asked.

"Yes."

"Is it an original?"

"Yes," Katya replied with a smile. "My grandfather knew Wassily well. He gave this painting to my grandfather as a gift when he married my grandmother."

"It's stunning," Rhys said.

"Thank you."

"Oh, this is for you." Rhys handed her the gift-wrapped wine bottle. "I hope you like red."

"I do. And I hope you like vodka."

"Why?"

"Because I have a surprise for you," Katya said, grinning like an excited little girl. "You've asked me so many questions about the cuisine of Imperial Russia and what the Kalinins would have eaten before the revolution left them homeless and penniless that I decided it would be a lot more fun to just show you. Come." She took him by the hand and led him into the dining room. The table was set for two and an asymmetrical candelabra made of cut crystal stood in pride of place on the table, the glow of the candles the only light in the room. Katya pointed toward the dishes on the table dramatically.

"You will begin your culinary journey into Russia with *blini* with sour cream and beluga caviar, smoked sturgeon, and duck liver mousse on toast points. For the main course, we have fillet of beef in mushroom gravy with garlic roasted potatoes garnished with dill."

"And what is *blin*—whatever you said?" Rhys asked, ready to eat whatever Katya chose to serve him.

"It's a type of crepe."

"Sounds delicious. And what do we have for dessert?"

"You will just have to wait and see, but I promise you're going to love it."

"I love it already. Thank you, Katya. This is one of the nicest things anyone has ever done for me. I hope you will allow me an opportunity to repay in kind."

Katya's blue eyes grew serious as she looked up at Rhys, her lips set in a pout. "I didn't do this so you could repay me. I did it because I wanted to."

Rhys took Katya's hand and lifted it to his lips, much as Count Alexei Petrov would have done in prerevolutionary days. He bowed over Katya's hand and kissed it lightly, making her smile.

"Then I accept your generous gesture and apologize if I gave offense."

"You didn't. Shall we begin?"

Rhys took a seat and Katya poured them both shots of ice-cold vodka.

"Russian nobility consumed plenty of wine, but there's nothing more Russian than a shot of vodka. *Na zdorovye*," she said and raised her glass in a toast.

"Salute."

Rhys tossed back the shot and felt the pleasant heat settle in his stomach. He took a bite of the *blini*, savoring the barely perceptible sweetness of the crepe, offset by the creaminess of the sour cream and the delicate saltiness of the caviar.

"What do you think?" Katya asked, her gaze eager.

"It's wonderful."

"I'm glad you like it because I serve it only to very special people," Katya said with a merry laugh. "I only buy it for very special occasions."

"I'm honored," Rhys replied, the warmth in his belly no longer just from the vodka.

"Many people think that Russian cuisine is heavy and crudely prepared, and that's true of the peasant dishes, but that could be said about the cuisine of the common people of any region. I love all types of food, but some Russian delicacies are still at the top of my list."

"They're quickly moving up my list as well," Rhys replied as he took a bite of the smoked sturgeon.

Katya poured him another shot. "Drink up, Mr. Morgan. I want you well lubricated." Rhys nearly choked on his fish, but quickly realized Katya was just joking. "Sorry. Crude Russian humor," she said, grinning.

Rhys bit back a very inappropriate reply and drank the shot instead. He felt pleasantly relaxed and utterly at ease. He gazed at Katya, who was dressed in a silk top the color of bluebells, her wavy blond hair framing her face, and candlelight reflected in her wide blue eyes. He hadn't realized how stunningly beautiful she was, or how refreshingly different from the women he normally came across.

"May I ask you a personal question, Rhys?" Katya asked after she served the main course.

"How personal?"

"Not personal enough to make you blush."

"Go on, then."

"Why have you never married?" Katya asked.

Rhys sat back and studied her across the table. It was a fairly personal question, one he'd asked himself only recently. He wanted to give her an honest answer, but not one that bared his soul. He wasn't ready for that.

"My brother, Owain, got married when I was twenty-two," Rhys said, recalling that day with remarkable clarity. "He was so happy. He said it was the best day of his life. I asked him how he knew Maren was the one and he said, 'Because I can't imagine my life without her in it.'"

"And you've never met a woman who made you feel that way," Katya said, watching him.

"No, I haven't. I've met plenty of lovely women, had relationships with several of them, but I never felt that type of certainty, or that deep of a love."

"Have you never had your heart broken?"

"There was a girl I fancied myself in love with back in Wales. I was seventeen. I thought she was my soulmate, but sadly, she didn't feel the same. I got over her quickly enough once I started uni."

"And since then?"

Rhys shook his head. He didn't want to talk about Hayley or the baby he'd lost. He mourned the child every day, but he rarely thought about Hayley. In retrospect, he realized that he'd never truly loved her.

"And what about you?" Rhys asked, turning the tables on Katya. "Why are you not married?"

"I was," Katya admitted. "I was very young when I married him, and like many inexperienced women, I mistook sexual attraction for love."

"Sexual attraction is not a bad starting point," Rhys pointed out. "It often leads to something deeper."

"It didn't with me. After several years of marriage, I realized that the only way I could remain married to Vadim was if I learned to accept a lesser version of myself. He didn't want a partner; he wanted a good Russian wifey who'd make his needs her only priority."

"So, you left him?" Rhys asked.

"Actually, he left me. He found a woman who made him the center of her universe. He's married to her now," Katya said without any rancor. "I wish them well. They have gorgeous twin girls."

"I love children," Rhys said, feeling the familiar pang of longing when the topic of kids came up. He dreamed of being a dad and hoped he hadn't missed his chance.

"Me too. That's the only thing I regret, not having a baby, but then I'd be tied to Vadim for the rest of my days, and that would make life indescribably difficult, given his obstinate nature. I would still like to have a child, but sadly, time is not on my side."

"Nor on mine," Rhys agreed.

"All right, enough bellyaching," Katya said with a grin. "I have heard of your legendary baking skills, so choosing a dessert for tonight was a matter of great importance."

"What did you settle on?" Rhys asked. At this point, he'd eat stale buns from Tesco just to make Katya happy.

"The pastry I selected is not strictly Russian, but it's one most Russians love. I think you'll enjoy it, especially with Russian-style tea."

"Bring it on," Rhys said, grinning with anticipation. "Do you have a samovar?"

"No. I have a tea kettle, but it's electric, if that makes it any more impressive," Katya replied.

"Let me help you clear the table," Rhys said, but Katya waved away his offer of help.

"You are my guest, and you will do nothing of the sort. Sit back, relax, have another shot of vodka, and I will be right back with our pudding, as you Brits like to say."

Rhys poured himself another shot. He didn't normally drink vodka, but the ice-cold spirit slid easily down his throat, settling in his stomach like a glowing orb of contentment. Katya returned to the dining room, carrying a platter of pastries.

"Oh my God!" Rhys exclaimed when he tasted the first forkful of Napoleon. The flaky pastry saturated with the lightest custard cream was heavenly. "This is extraordinary. Did you make it yourself?"

"No, I purchased it from the Russian bakery this afternoon. They'd just brought out a freshly made tray from the back."

"Where is this bakery?"

"If I tell you, I'll have to kill you."

"Some part of me thinks you mean that," Rhys replied.

"Some part of me does."

"You're a dangerous woman, Katya."

"You have no idea."

Katya stood and walked around the table, straddling Rhys in his chair. She wrapped her arms around his neck and ran her tongue along his lower lip, her seductive gaze never leaving his face.

"Does this mean we're done with dessert?" Rhys asked huskily.

"This means our night is just beginning."

The glowing orb in Rhys's belly turned to shooting flames as a hot tongue of desire leapt straight to his groin. He wrapped his arms around Katya and pulled her closer as she swiveled her hips against his, driving him wild with hunger for her. Rhys lowered his hands and cupped her round bottom. Katya wasn't stick-skinny like most of the women he came across in his line of work. She had full, luscious breasts and an ass that begged to be... Rhys forced the naughty thought from his mind and turned his attention to her breasts instead.

Katya disentangled herself long enough to pull off her top and unhook her bra, arching her back to offer Rhys one creamy breast. He lowered his head to flick his tongue against her nipple as she slid her hand downward to stroke him—not that he needed much assistance at that point.

"Come to bed, *dorogoy*," she whispered. "I have more surprises for you."

Rhys had heard that Russian women were bossy, but he wouldn't have it any other way. He lifted Katya as he stood and walked toward the bedroom, the half-naked woman still wrapped around him. As he laid her down on the bed, Katya pulled up her skirt, revealing that she wasn't wearing any knickers.

"I hope you'll like this even better," Katya whispered as she spread her legs in invitation and gave Rhys a gentle push downward.

"My favorite kind," Rhys replied as he went to work, making Katya moan with pleasure.

Chapter 48

Rhys came awake slowly, sensually, his body languid and sated from the night before. Katya was still asleep, her pale face almost luminescent in the gentle light of the spring morning. Her dark-blond lashes were fanned against her cheeks and her hair formed a golden halo on the dove-gray pillowcase. She had been passionate and generous last night, and surprisingly open, urging him to try anything he felt like. The memory sent an arrow of desire to his loins, making him think of all the delicious things he could do to wake her up.

A few minutes later, Katya stirred and opened her eyes. A small smile tugged at her lips as if she were recalling last night as well. "Good morning," she said huskily.

"Good morning."

Rhys pulled down the duvet and traced a sensual line down her body, following his fingers with featherlight kisses that began with her earlobes and ended between her thighs. Katya purred and arched her back, but Rhys wouldn't be rushed. He had every intention of driving her mad with desire before finally giving her what she craved. It took tremendous restraint on his part, but he devoted himself to her pleasure, partaking of her body only after Katya had enjoyed her first orgasm.

"Tease," Katya said once they were both gloriously sated. Her generous lips stretched into a grin worthy of the Cheshire Cat and she ran her long nails down Rhys's chest, making his skin tingle.

"Katya, what does this mean?" he asked.

"It means whatever you want it to mean, Rhys. It could be a one-night stand, or it could be the beginning of something that will be good for both of us. I think we've passed the sexual compatibility test," she added, smiling seductively.

"Is it really that simple?"

"Rhys, I'm too old to play games. When I see something I want, I reach for it. Sometimes I get it, and sometimes I don't, but I will never miss out on something wonderful because I was too afraid of rejection. If you choose to leave and never come back, I will never hold it against you, and it will have no effect on our working relationship."

"Katya, I want to come back. In fact, I don't want to leave," Rhys replied, kissing her tenderly. "I haven't felt this good in a long time. Can I make you breakfast?"

"You most certainly can. The kitchen is yours. I'll have a shower."

Katya rose from bed, her naked body smooth as marble in the sunlight. She didn't reach for a dressing gown or make any comments about not looking her best without applying fresh make-up. She appeared to be completely comfortable in her skin, a woman who saw no reason to apologize for her appearance or desires. Rhys folded his arms behind his head and watched her walk into the en-suite bathroom. He was fascinated, and unexpectedly happy.

Chapter 49

May 2015

London, England

"Go right in, Dr. Allenby," Rhiannan Makely, Rhys's PA, said once Quinn got off the lift. "He's expecting you."

Rhys looked up from a document he was reading and smiled happily. "Lovely to see you, Quinn. Have a seat. Coffee? Tea?"

"I won't say no to a cup of tea," Quinn replied. Rhys buzzed Rhiannan and asked her to bring in two cups of tea and some biscuits.

"What have you got for me?" Rhys asked, cutting straight to the chase.

"Quite a lot, actually," Quinn replied. "First and foremost, Rafael de Silva was Jewish, not Muslim, as I initially assumed. He was the descendent of one of the few Jewish families that remained in Toledo after the expulsion of the Jews in 1492."

"Have you been able to find anything about him in your research?"

"I haven't found any specific references to Rafael de Silva and hadn't expected to. He was a foot soldier, and history is not interested in the likes of him unless they do something extraordinary. Captain de Cuéllar, however, figures prominently in several articles about the post-Armada period. He left a considerable paper trail, our captain."

"Do tell," Rhys invited, his eyes gleaming with curiosity.

"Captain Francisco de Cuéllar, who was sentenced to hang for disobedience after his ship broke the Armada formation, not only managed to survive long enough to get shipwrecked off the coast of what is now known as County Sligo, but actually returned home to Spain. He wrote an account of his time in Ireland, which will go a long way to legitimizing our version of events. He spoke at length about what happened to him after he was shipwrecked, how he finally made it to O'Rourke territory, and what took place during the siege of the castle. He mentions in his account that there was another soldier with him throughout most of his ordeal but doesn't specify it was Rafael de Silva. He might not have wished to share his fifteen minutes of fame, or the more logical explanation, given that the captain was an honest and honorable man, is that he had no wish to explain what happened to his companion or be forced into a lie."

"Wait, there was a siege?" Rhys asked, leaning forward in his eagerness.

"Oh yes. Nearly two thousand English troops were dispatched to deal with the Armada survivors and marched on the castle of Sir Brian O'Rourke. Of course, they were there as much for O'Rourke himself as for the Spaniards. Brian O'Rourke had been a thorn in Queen Elizabeth's side for years, along with his good friend Sean McClancy, and his blatant refusal to follow the order to execute Armada survivors on sight was yet another provocation for the embattled queen."

"How long did the siege last?"

"I wasn't able to come up with specific dates, but I would imagine it didn't last very long."

"How can you be so sure?"

"The troops arrived at the castle at the beginning of November. What does that tell you?"

"It tells me they spent a lot of time being cold and wet while the inhabitants of the castle enjoyed warm fires and dry boots," Rhys replied without missing a beat.

"Precisely. Historically, there have been wintertime sieges, but there was much more at stake, politically speaking. Subjecting nearly two thousand men to an Irish winter for the sake of capturing a few dozen Spanish foot soldiers was madness. It was done more out of spite than any well-thought-out military tactic."

"So, you think the siege was called off?" Rhys asked.

"Most likely, which explains, in part, how Captain de Cuéllar was able to return home a few months later."

"Do you know why de Silva was crucified?" Rhys steepled his fingers in front of him, a sure sign he was in the mood to speculate. "I cannot conceive of sixteenth-century Irishmen crucifying a man as a form of punishment. Could he have been crucified by the English as a warning to the rest of the Spaniards? Perhaps he was unlucky enough to get caught outside the walls."

Quinn considered this for a moment. "The English executed two Spanish soldiers on the third day of the siege. They were hanged from a tree that was clearly visible from the castle walls. Crucifying one of their countrymen in full view of the castle would certainly be taking their threat a step further, but I simply don't see that happening. It doesn't fit with the military practices of that period. Prisoners were hanged, shot, and beheaded, but they were not crucified. Ever!"

"Would the English soldiers feel sympathy for Rafael if he admitted to being a Jew? Were Jews not relatively safe in England at that time?" Rhys asked, putting forth a contradicting theory.

"No, they weren't. I don't believe the English would have executed Rafael for his faith, but they wouldn't have welcomed him with open arms either. Jews were expelled from England by Edward I in 1290 after centuries of persecution. It wasn't until 1655 that Oliver Cromwell unofficially lifted the ban on the Jews after receiving a petition submitted by Menasseh ben Israel, a rabbi from Amsterdam, asking for permission for Jews to reenter England. By 1657, a community represented by Antonio Fernández Carvajal and Simon de Cáceres sprang up and purchased land near Mile End to use as a synagogue. And, in 1657, Solomon Dormido, the nephew of Menasseh ben Israel, was admitted to the Royal Exchange as a duly licensed broker. Normally, all the brokers had to swear an oath that made mention of Christianity, but when Dormido was sworn in in 1668, the oath was amended to exclude that part. But this all happened much later, so Rafael would not have benefitted from this new tolerance."

"Do you think he would have been aware of the ban on Jews in England?" Rhys asked.

"Probably not," Quinn conceded. "Not unless the Jews of Toledo had some contact with the community in Amsterdam, but I got the feeling they were quite isolated."

"Which brings us back to the crucifixion. Is there nothing in Captain de Cuéllar's account about this event? Perhaps a thinly veiled reference?" Rhys tried again.

"Not that I can see. The captain provided a detailed account of the time leading up to the siege. He even mentioned his annoyance with the ladies of the castle for pestering him to tell their fortunes. Apparently, O'Rourke's wife and some of her companions found the fortune-telling quite accurate and thought Captain de Cuéllar was a true seer. He then also described, in great detail I might add, his decision to leave the castle and the subsequent journey home, which took months."

"But there's a glaring omission in his narrative," Rhys supplied, "just around the time of the crucifixion."

"Yes."

"Could he have been the one who ordered it?" Rhys speculated.

Quinn nodded, pleased that Rhys had reached the same conclusion. "That's what I was thinking. Captain de Cuéllar was the highest-ranking officer among the Spanish soldiers. If anyone could order an execution, it would have been him."

"Was he a zealot?" Rhys asked.

"He was a devout Catholic, but from what I've seen, he was a kind and decent man. Honor was very important to him."

"If de Silva insulted his honor, he might have wanted him dead."

"I still don't see why he'd choose crucifixion as the mode of execution. If Rafael de Silva did something the captain deemed unforgivable or treasonous, he'd order him to be shot or hanged. So, why something so Biblical, and so brutal? If de Silva hadn't died of cardiac arrest, as Dr. Scott suspects, he might have suffered for days, dying slowly and painfully. I simply can't believe Captain de Cuéllar was capable of such cruelty."

"Men do strange things when they're drunk on power. As you say, he was the highest-ranking officer among the men. Perhaps he wanted to teach them a lesson by making an example of de Silva."

"Perhaps."

"You pity him, don't you?" Rhys asked softly.

"I do. He was hardly more than a boy. There was an innocence in him I find endearing. Rhys, do you think British audiences will be interested in an episode featuring the survivors of the Armada? The defeat of the Spanish Armada is still seen as one of the greatest victories in our national history. I don't expect people to feel much sympathy for these men, who should never have been on our shores to begin with."

"I don't agree with you there. There are numerous films and books about the trials of German civilians during and after World War II. People might hate the Nazis and the Third Reich, but they can still find pity for the unwitting victims of the regime. And Rafael was a victim, in more ways than one. He was someone who suffered at the hands of the Church, and then at the hands of his countrymen. I think his story is one that needs to be told."

"I hope you're right," Quinn replied. "Some part of me thinks he should be left in peace."

"Let me tell his story, Quinn. You know I will be sensitive and respectful of his memory. I always am," Rhys said with a self-satisfied grin.

Quinn sat back and studied him. The sun shone through the window behind him, setting his auburn hair aflame. His gray eyes looked soft and dreamy as he met her gaze. "There's something different about you," Quinn said, smiling at him.

"I got a haircut," Rhys replied.

"No, it's not your hair. It's in the eyes. I know—you look happy."

Rhys's cheeks colored delicately, and he gave Quinn a shy smile, a feat in itself for Rhys, who was anything but shy. "I suppose I am."

"Who's the lucky lady?" She didn't for a moment imagine it was Jo, so it had to be someone new.

"It's Katya Velesova," Rhys replied. "We've only just got together, but I've known her for several months now, and I really like her, Quinn. She's different."

"In what way?"

"She's smart, funny, and warm, without being needy. She's not a woman who thinks having a man in her life will solve all her problems. She doesn't have an agenda."

"Everyone has an agenda."

"They do, but Katya is someone who wants to be an equal partner, a companion, not a dependent. She's not looking to own me, and she doesn't want to be owned herself. Does that make sense?"

"Yes. It makes perfect sense. The best types of relationships are between people who give and receive without using the other person to fulfill only their own needs. It's a true partnership."

"Exactly," Rhys said, nodding. "Most women I've been with in the past saw me as a means to an end. I had something they wanted, be it financial security or the ability to further their careers. Katya just seems to want me."

"I'm happy for you, Rhys. I hope it works out."

"I'm sorry about Jo, Quinn."

"Don't be. These things can't be forced, and for what it's worth, I think you made the right decision."

"I'm glad you think so. I wouldn't want to lose your friendship," Rhys said, flashing that shy smile again.

"Rhys, you'll never lose my friendship, especially not over that. Your private life is your own. I only want to see you happy."

"Thanks, Quinn. That means a lot to me."

"And speaking of Jo, I have to get going. I'm meeting her at her flat," Quinn said, gathering her belongings.

"Is she all right?" Rhys asked with genuine concern as he walked Quinn to the lift.

"Yes." *But not for long*, Quinn thought as she stepped into the lift.

Chapter 50

The weather had turned by the time Quinn arrived. Jo's flat was gloomy, nearly leached of natural light. Jo didn't bother to turn on the lights, just sat staring out the window, a colorful pillow held against her middle like a shield against Quinn's unwelcome news. Quinn didn't rush her. Jo needed a moment to think, and Quinn needed to use the loo.

She turned on the light and her gaze fell on the rubbish bin next to the toilet. A used prophylactic was clearly visible among make-up-soiled tissues and cotton swabs. Quinn had noticed two wine glasses when she'd gone into the kitchen to put the kettle on. Jo clearly hadn't been alone last night, but Quinn didn't feel it was her place to quiz Jo about her love life. If she wished to share with her, she would. Now, Jo didn't seem to want to talk at all.

Quinn washed her hands and returned to the kitchen, where she made some tea. When she brought Jo a mug, she found her in the same position she'd left her in.

"Thanks," Jo said, her voice flat and lifeless.

"Jo, you don't have to do anything you don't want to do," Quinn began.

"I have no chance of finding my daughter if I don't provide Drew with new leads," Jo replied in a strange monotone.

"No, probably not. Without the name of the child, the surname of her adoptive parents, or the name of the agency that handled the adoption, Drew can do very little, even with his considerable experience."

"I haven't spoken to them since Mum died," Jo said, her gaze still fixed on the falling rain. "I shouldn't be scared to talk to my own sister, but the thought of coming face to face with Karen terrifies me. She was always so cold, so judgmental. And Michael…"

"You don't have to speak to Michael ever again, Jo."

"It's his child. Surely, if Dad shared any information about the adoption, he would have told him."

"Perhaps he didn't want to know," Quinn said, wondering what kind of man Michael Crawford was. She'd met Karen while searching for Jo, but never spoken to her brother, since Karen had sent Quinn and Logan directly to Jo's solicitor, Louis Richards. Quinn's devotion to Jo made her want to hate Michael Crawford, but some more rational part of her told her to reserve judgment. She'd judged Rhys, Robert Chatham, and Seth based on the story Sylvia had carefully fed her, but as Seth was fond of saying, there were three sides to every story: his, hers, and the truth. Jo's parents and sister had worked hard to protect Michael from an accusation of rape. Was it because they were blindly devoted to him, or because what happened hadn't been as black and white as Jo would have Quinn believe?

Quinn buried her nose in her mug of tea, feeling guilty for her disloyal thoughts. Rape was rape, there were no shades of gray about it. Jo had been underage, innocent, and vulnerable. Michael had been a man in his thirties. The fact that he got off scot-free only went to prove that people always blamed the victim, assuming they'd done something to provoke the attack. No matter what Jo had done, she hadn't deserved to be assaulted by her adoptive brother. She'd been just a kid when she gave birth to Michael's child. There was no excuse. Quinn would gladly go speak to Michael Crawford herself if there was any chance he'd tell her the truth.

"I'll do it," Jo said suddenly, tossing away the pillow as if she no longer needed its protection. "I will go to Leicester and speak to those two. Will you come with me?"

"Of course. You don't even have to ask."

Jo raised her head slowly and gave Quinn a look that could have turned a lesser woman to stone. Her eyes were flint-hard, her mouth stretched into a thin line. "Does Gabe know?"

"Know what?"

"Any of it. Have you told him?" Jo demanded.

"Yes, I have," Quinn replied, drawing herself up to her full height.

"You had no right." Jo's voice was low, but it sent a chill down Quinn's spine.

"I'm not in the habit of keeping secrets from him. I'm sorry; I didn't think you'd mind."

"Well, I do. It's not your secret to tell. This is my personal business, not some titillating historical tragedy to share with your husband in bed."

Quinn set her mug down and met Jo's gaze. "I said I was sorry, Jo, but Gabe is my husband, and I discuss things with him. That's what people do in a marriage. Besides, having you in my life affects him as well, in more ways than you imagine."

Jo scoffed. "You don't think I understand intimacy, not being married myself?"

"I didn't say that. Look, Jo, you're understandably upset, so I think I'll go now. If you still want me to come with you, I'll be happy to, but if you'd rather do this on your own, that's your call."

"It's not though, is it? Drew rang you first. You always know everything before I do."

"Drew thought this would sound better coming from me. I will instruct him to deal with you directly from now on."

"You do that," Jo spat out.

Quinn grabbed her bag and let herself out of Jo's flat. Jo was frustrated and upset, Quinn told herself as she stepped into the street, but her hand trembled as she opened her umbrella. This was a side of Jo she hadn't seen yet, and although she could admit her own wrongdoing, she was hurt by Jo's disproportionate reaction.

Yes, she'd told Gabe about Jo's child, but if Jo found her daughter, everyone would know anyway. Why was she so concerned with Gabe knowing the truth? Why did his opinion suddenly matter so much to Jo?

Quinn's mobile vibrated just as she was about to enter the Tube station. It was a text from Jo. It read:

I'm sorry. I shouldn't have reproached you. Please come with me to Leicester. I can't do this without you.

Quinn exhaled deeply. A part of her longed to ignore Jo's message and give herself time to think, but Jo was her sister, and she needed her help.

Quinn wrote: *Of course. Just let me know when.*

She nearly added a cute emoji to diffuse the tense exchange between them, but changed her mind and sent the text off, blinking away tears of hurt before she entered the station. This was the first time Jo had lashed out at her, but not the first time Quinn had felt a chill coming from her twin. Their relationship was still new and fragile, but there were moments when Quinn wondered if Jo even liked her.

Don't be ridiculous, Quinn chided herself as she put away her Oyster card and headed toward the platform. *Jo needs time and space to deal with things in her own way. I can be too much sometimes*, she berated herself. *I'm too eager, too persistent.*

Or maybe it's not you, a voice that sounded suspiciously like Gabe answered inside her head. *Maybe Jo is not quite what you imagined.*

Maybe not, Quinn replied silently as she took a seat.

Chapter 51

December 1588
Leitrim, Ireland

With the arrival of December, the weather grew colder and the days shorter. A sense of hopelessness and suspicion settled over the castle. Every loud sound and every sign of movement on the other side of the wall sent the men into a panic. The English couldn't be expected to do nothing forever. Winter was settling in, the cold and snow pushing the besiegers and the besieged into a suffocating embrace. The English seemed to feel just as despondent as the Spaniards and the Irish, forced to spend week after week out in the open, sitting around their fires with nothing better to do than whittle sticks. They were angry and frustrated, and baying for blood. The Spaniards often heard their taunts over the wall, insults hurled at men they hated and wished to exterminate.

The two hanged men continued to act as tree ornaments, their grotesque remains no longer resembling human beings. When the wind blew in an easterly direction, the besieged Spaniards could smell the sickening stench of decomposition and wondered how the English could bear the constant reminder of death in their midst.

Everyone was on edge, their reason undermined by the constant threat of attack. Captain de Cuéllar issued an edict stating that if any of the women were interfered with, the offender would be executed. Despite this threat, the men gazed at Aisling and Mary—the only unmarried women at the castle—with such hunger, the girls spent most of their day in the kitchen with the wives of the men-at-arms or in a locked bedchamber, fearful of being cornered in some dark passage. The Irishmen guarded their women fiercely, their mistrust of the Spaniards growing by the day. The two groups barely conversed and occupied different parts of the castle in order to avoid contact. It was only a matter of time before the Irishmen and the Spaniards turned on each other, in Rafael's opinion, and he feared the day the tensions would finally boil over.

"De Silva, would you be so kind as to ask señorita O'Rourke to join us in the great hall?" Captain de Cuéllar said, taking Rafael utterly by surprise. "I give you my word she will not come to any harm."

"W-what do you want with her, sir?"

"I only wish to speak to her, I assure you."

"I'll ask her, sir," Rafael replied meekly. He had no wish to invite Aisling into the hall. The men would be on their best behavior in front of the captain, but for a woman to walk alone into a room full of tense, angry soldiers was asking too much, and Rafael wondered why the captain wished to speak to Aisling in front of the men rather than in the privacy of a smaller chamber.

Aisling looked frightened when Rafael passed on the captain's request. "I don't wish to come," she said, shaking her head. "What does he want with me?"

"He says he only wants to speak with you."

"Why? Of what use can I be to the likes of yer captain?"

"Captain de Cuéllar is an honorable man, Aisling. He'll not let any harm befall you."

"I'll only come if ye come with me and remain by my side."

"I wouldn't have it any other way," Rafael replied. "Shall we?"

All the Spaniards were gathered in the hall, except for the ones who were standing guard on the wind-buffeted battlements, keeping their heads down to dodge a well-aimed bullet. A fire burned in the grate and the soldiers huddled close to the great hearth, shivering in their inadequate attire. Aisling was visibly frightened, but kept her head high and her shoulders back, her chin turned at a defiant angle. The captain greeted her with a courteous bow and smiled benignly, inviting her to sit. Aisling shook her head and remained standing.

"Translate for me, if you please," he said to Rafael, his gaze still fixed on Aisling, who was studying him openly.

"How long have you lived at the castle, señorita O'Rourke?" the captain asked.

"All my life," Aisling replied.

"Is there any other way into the castle besides the gate?" the captain asked. "Surely there must be ways to leave the castle unobserved."

The men stilled, clearly surprised by the captain's inquiry. This should have been a question to put to Kieran O'Rourke, not his sister, and the significance of that wasn't lost on them, especially since he was asking it openly, in front of everyone.

Aisling nodded. She looked less frightened now that she understood what he was after. "There is a tunnel that runs from one of the storerooms to a cave in the woods."

"Where is this cave?" the captain asked. "Would we bypass the English if we used this tunnel?"

"The English are camped all around that area. Anyone leaving the cave would be seen."

"Is there any other way out?" the captain asked, smiling in encouragement.

"There's a door built into the easterly side of the wall, but the terrain is boggy and unless ye know yer way round, ye'll not get very far."

"Thank you, señorita O'Rourke. I appreciate your assistance."

293

Aisling nodded to the captain and turned to leave, her shoulders hunched with tension as thirty pairs of eyes followed her progress, some gazes clouded with speculation, others with lust.

Rafael followed a few moments later and caught up with her in one of the passages leading to the kitchens. "Aisling, wait," he called.

Her face was streaked with tears when she turned to face him. She walked into his arms and buried her face in his chest, her shoulders quaking with sobs.

"What is it? What's upset you so?"

"Did ye see the way those men fixed on me? They're like starving beasts eyeing a hunk of meat. Why did yer captain bring me in there? He could have spoken to me privately."

Rafael wrapped his arms around Aisling in an effort to comfort her. He had no immediate answer to her question.

"I'm sure he had his reasons. He's a clever man," he said, trying to convince himself as much as Aisling.

"Rafael, come to my chamber," Aisling said, looking up at him from beneath tear-dampened lashes, her limpid eyes huge in her pale face. "I'm afraid to be alone. Stay with me a while."

"Aisling, I really shouldn't. It isn't proper."

"Please, Rafael."

His heart melted with tenderness. Of course, she was scared. Who wouldn't be? If it weren't for the threat of execution, half of those men would force themselves on her or Mary. They weren't bad men, but they were seasoned soldiers and they understood the odds of survival. They were scared, angry, frustrated, and losing hope by the day. They had nothing left to lose save their lives. Honor was no longer their first priority— keeping their fear at bay was. A few minutes with a woman was the quickest way to oblivion, or so he'd been told, and these men craved oblivion the way an opium addict craved his pipe, and he'd seen his share of addicts when assisting his father.

"All right." Rafael followed Aisling into the room.

The fire had died down, but the chamber still retained some warmth and was surprisingly cozy. With the shutter closed against the cold, the only light came from the glowing ambers, which cast a rosy tint on the walls. The chamber itself wasn't much bigger than the cell he shared with Alfonso, and was sparsely furnished, a fact he found surprising given Aisling's close relationship to Sir Brian, but from what he'd gathered, most people at the castle were related to Sir Brian in some way and received no special treatment. The ladies of the castle had chores to attend to, only their work didn't appear as strenuous as that of the servants, whose hands were red and raw from being constantly submerged in cold water or blistered from the fire or heavy lifting. Aisling's hands weren't red or chapped, but they were the hands of a woman who kept busy from dawn till dusk, the hands of a real woman, not a sheltered little *señorita* who did nothing but sit in the parlor with her mamá, waiting for a suitor.

Aisling locked the door behind them and turned to face Rafael. The atmosphere in the small room grew close and intimate, and Rafael's breath caught in his throat when Aisling pulled off her cap and released her heavy hair, the coppery tresses cascading over her shoulders and down to her narrow waist. He took a step back, frightened by the dangerous feelings she stirred in him. She was more forward than any woman he'd ever known, but so much more exiting and irresistible.

Aisling gazed up at him, her eyes blue pools of desire. *Will ye really reject me?* they seemed to ask as she pressed her small palms to his chest. His heart was galloping like a spooked horse, his body pulsating with all-consuming heat.

"Aisling," he whispered as he took a step toward her, knowing this time he wouldn't have the strength to refuse her.

**

295

The room was cold and dark, swathed in the murky shadows of early evening. Rafael sat on the window ledge, his forehead pressed to his knees. He shut his eyes tight, steeling himself against the inevitable onslaught of shame and reproach, but all he felt was joy, a feeling so unfamiliar to him it took him a moment to identify it. Firelit images danced in his fevered mind: the ivory curve of a breast, the hollow of a navel, long, graceful legs parted to receive him, and the unbearable ecstasy of sliding into the hot, moist sheath that was Aisling's body. It had felt so natural, so instinctive. Aisling had made small sounds—gasps of pain, moans of pleasure, sighs of contentment, and he'd matched her cry for cry, moan for moan, gasp for gasp. Dear God, how was it possible for something so base to feel so divine, and how could he bear to walk away from her now? Only death could extinguish the flame she'd lit in his heart. He'd thought he'd die happier having known love, but now that he knew what he'd be missing, death seemed like the cruelest insult, the ultimate cheat.

"Oh, Aisling, why did you have to make this so much harder for both of us?" Rafael whispered into the empty air, his breath wisps of mist in the frigid room. "What am I to do?"

He remained perfectly still, but there was no answer, no sympathy from an indifferent God. There was only a sense of foreboding tainting his brief happiness with its bitter aftertaste, and the certain knowledge that they could never be together, in this life or the next.

Rafael's eyes flew open with a start. It had to be time for his watch. If he didn't appear on time, questions would be asked, and unsavory conclusions would be reached since he'd last been seen going after Aisling. Rafael jumped to his feet and adjusted his clothing to make sure he didn't appear disheveled. His fingers instinctively brushed against the hidden pocket in his worn doublet, checking that his hamsa was still there.

He froze, his blood running cold in his veins, his breath stilling for a long, tense moment. He couldn't feel the outline of the charm, couldn't grasp anything between his fingers but pliant leather. Rafael tore at the buttons, reaching into the little pocket, probing as deep as his trembling fingers would allow. He let out a strangled cry of desperation when he realized the amulet wasn't there.

I'm a dead man, Rafael thought as he sank back onto the ledge, his earlier wonder replaced by breathless panic. Whoever had found the charm wouldn't keep quiet. They'd want to know whom it belonged to, unless they already did. Rafael took a shaky breath. His days were numbered. "Dear God," he whispered, "please keep Aisling safe. Please, oh please, don't let her get hurt because of me."

Chapter 52

May 2015

London, England

Gentle sunshine streamed through the windows of the car, and a pleasant breeze caressed Quinn's face. She was finally able to pick up speed once they left the outskirts of the city and got on the M25. Thankfully, the traffic was moving at a good clip, so they would reach Leicester in about two hours.

A week ago, Quinn would have enjoyed spending the time with Jo, but since their heated conversation a few days ago, there was a new tension between them, and resentment underscored every word of their stilted conversation. Jo was angry with Quinn for sharing her private pain with Gabe, with Drew for failing to miraculously produce her offspring, and probably with herself for letting so much time go by before asking the questions she should have asked fifteen years ago.

"Thanks for coming with me," Jo said in a conciliatory manner.

"You're welcome. Have you called ahead, or are you planning to ambush your siblings?" Quinn asked.

"With those two, an ambush works best. We'll start with Karen. She's a creature of habit, and she always liked a lie-in on Saturday mornings. Mum used to bring her breakfast on a tray while she lolled about in bed, reading or listening to music."

"And Michael?"

"I have no intention of seeing Michael. He won't know any more than Karen will, so the plan is to squeeze her for information. I did ring Mr. Richards. He said we can pop into his office any time before noon. He'll be catching up on some work and then he has a lunch engagement. We'll be back in London by midafternoon," Jo added, assuming Quinn was eager to get home.

"Sounds like a reasonable plan," Quinn said as she fixed her eyes on the SATNAV, which was indicating a delay in arrival time due to an accident on the motorway. "Bollocks. This will set us back by nearly an hour if they don't clear it up quickly."

Jo sighed and stared out the window, her face set in harsh lines, her fingers drumming on her thigh.

"Jo, I know you're nervous," Quinn began.

"Wouldn't you be?" Jo snapped. "Oh, how Karen will gloat. She's probably waited for this moment for fifteen years."

"Why does she hate you so?"

"She thinks it's my fault Mum got ill."

"How can it be your fault?"

"Stress is always a factor, and the incident with Michael, then my stubborn refusal to abort the baby, nearly sent Mum over the edge. What happened nearly tore the family apart, and my father's carefully planned coping strategy didn't quite work since I refused to comply. Mum spent months watching my belly grow, swelling with a grandchild she'd never get to hold or love. She was torn between her anger with Michael and her desire to protect me, but it was too late, for all of us."

"I'm sorry, Jo," Quinn replied for lack of anything better to say.

"Nothing to be sorry for. I've only myself to blame, or so Karen will tell you."

"Jo, what if neither Karen nor Mr. Richards knows anything? Will you abandon the search?"

"I'll have to, won't I? Can't find the child without a trail of crumbs."

299

Quinn braked as they neared the line of cars that were standing as still as if they were in a car park. She stole a peek at Jo, who was still staring angrily out the window. Did Jo really want to be a mum? She'd given up her baby nearly fifteen years ago, but she was a woman in her thirties now. Surely there had to have been other relationships, other opportunities to start a family. Quinn couldn't quite picture Jo with a baby on her hip. Even when she held Alex or chatted with Emma, she seemed awkward, unnatural. Not every woman was cut out to be a mother, and there was no shame in that. Did Jo long for a child or for closure?

Jo stared ahead and swore under her breath, cursing the traffic that was slowing them down. Watching spots of angry color bloom on Jo's milky skin, Quinn wondered what she'd be like with her daughter if she got to meet her. What was her daughter like, this unwanted child who had only been carried to term to spite Jo's parents?

"Jo, are you seeing someone?" Quinn asked as traffic finally began to move again, albeit slowly.

"Why do you ask?" Jo's head snapped in Quinn's direction, her gaze no longer on the disabled lorry on the side of the road.

Quinn faltered. "I saw two wine glasses in the sink," she replied, not wishing to bring up the used condom she'd seen in the bathroom.

"Oh, that. Tim had come round," she said with forced nonchalance. "I've known him for ages. He's married, so don't get your hopes up."

"That's a shame," Quinn replied, surprised by the wave of disappointment that washed over her. So, Jo was shagging a married man, another unpleasant thing she'd just learned about her sister. She certainly wasn't the first or the last woman to get involved with someone else's husband, but Quinn had hoped Jo would be better than that, better than the sad old cliché of the other woman who was never good enough to be 'the one.'

300

"I don't want a husband, Quinn," Jo announced, as though sensing Quinn's disapproval. "I'm not sure I even want a boyfriend, or a partner, as people are fond of calling their blokes these days. I like my freedom, but that doesn't mean I don't enjoy a good shag now and again. Tim is dynamite in bed, and he doesn't make embarrassing declarations or get jealous when I see other men. It's perfect."

"You don't have to explain," Quinn replied. Normally, she enjoyed girl talk, even if it was of the locker room variety, but for some reason, she had no wish to know more about Jo's love life, if it could be referred to as such, because Jo didn't share this information with relish, as Quinn's friends had done at uni and on various digs. Jo came off defensive and catty.

"Right. We're moving again," Jo exclaimed as the traffic surged forward. "I hope we'll get there by eleven. I want to get this over with."

Me too, Jo. Me too, Quinn thought as she focused on the road ahead. She didn't feel much like talking.

Chapter 53

They arrived in Leicester close to eleven and drove directly to Karen's residence, which was located on a leafy side street and flanked by other lovely homes that reeked of affluence and privilege. The houses were set well back from the street, their manicured lawns lush behind wrought-iron gates and flowering shrubs. Karen had either become a keen gardener or kept a landscaping pro on the payroll. The red-brick walls were smothered with ivy, and the windows were open to the May breeze, with white gauzy curtains billowing like sails.

Jo rang the bell. Her heart rattled in her chest, her breath like a sharp stone lodged in her throat. She had no wish to see Karen, and even less desire to speak to her. Karen had always been a bitch. She'd never had time to spare for her little sister, and unlike Michael, who'd got on the floor and built block towers and colored pictures, Karen had never come down to Jo's level. Michael used to call Jo 'Q,' short for Quentin, but Karen had always used her full name to imply that there was no familiarity between them, no connection. She'd resented Jo and blamed their father for foisting a squalling infant onto their fragile, long-suffering mother. Ian Crawford had been no saint, and his children knew it, but Michael and Jo had been able to forgive him his failings, while Karen had clung to her resentment.

The bell pealed inside the house, and after several minutes, clipped footsteps finally approached the door. Jo almost expected an elderly butler to answer the door and politely ask them to get off Karen's property or he'd set the dogs on them, but the door was opened by Karen herself. She'd aged, but then again, it'd been fourteen years since they last saw each other, and Karen had recently turned fifty. She still looked immaculate, even in her silk dressing gown and slippers. Karen's hair was a bit tousled but bore the lines of an expensive haircut, and her face, although devoid of make-up, was still smooth and supple. Her lips had grown thinner with age, and her eyes were a little puffy, as if she'd enjoyed too many brandies before bedtime, but Karen wasn't a drinker, or at least she hadn't been when Jo was still a part of her life.

"Hello, Karen," Jo said, hoping Karen wouldn't slam the door in her face.

"Quentin," Karen replied, her tone as warm as the iceberg that sank the *Titanic*. "I see you two have finally found each other."

"Yes, we have," Quinn said cheerfully, no doubt trying to lighten the atmosphere, as Quinn was wont to do.

"I hope your blood pressure has stabilized, Mrs. Russell," Karen said, surprising Jo with her concern. Karen always had been kinder to her patients than she'd been to family, although Quinn had never actually been her patient.

"Yes, thank you," Quinn replied. "I'm quite well."

"You may as well come in," Karen said, and moved aside to let them in. "I don't much care for airing dirty linen on the doorstep, although I'm sure you wouldn't mind."

Jo ignored the barb and followed Karen into a beautifully decorated lounge. The sun streamed through the windows and the room smelled of flowers and lemon-scented polish. The settees were upholstered in pale yellow silk, and the carpet looked as if no one dared step on it. A crystal vase bursting with lilies sat on a walnut table between the two windows, and several family photographs in silver frames were arranged on either side. There was one of their parents, taken at a function they'd attended about twenty years ago, one of Karen and an attractive man in his fifties who might be her partner, and one of Michael and his family.

Jo focused on that photo, hungry for details of Michael's life. He'd clearly remarried after the breakup of his first marriage. She couldn't recall the name of his first wife, the one who'd left him for another man and caused him to spiral out of control. His new wife looked pleasant and friendly. Her plump wholesomeness balanced out Michael's lean frame. His sandy hair was thinner and threaded with silver, and his gray eyes heavy-lidded. Middle age had softened his jowls, but he was still a good-looking man, and the creases around his mouth were a testament to the fact that he still smiled often. They had three children: two girls and a boy. The girls appeared to be in their early teens, and the boy looked around seven. All the children had dark hair and eyes, like Michael's wife.

"What is it you want, Quentin?" Karen asked, tired of waiting for Jo to state the purpose of her visit. She didn't offer them any refreshment, which meant she hoped they'd leave before the kettle had time to boil.

"You look well, Karen," Jo began. She had no desire to antagonize her sister and hoped flattery would pave the way to Karen's frozen little heart. "Not a day over thirty-five."

"Cut the bullshit. You didn't come here to have a cozy chat. Please, take a seat, Mrs. Russell," Karen said, as if drawing a clear line between her attitude toward Jo and Quinn.

Jo would have sat down just to annoy her, but she was too jittery to sit, so she remained standing, her gaze still drawn to Michael's perfect family. "Karen, there's something I'd like to ask, and I hope you will tell me what I want to know."

"Depends what it is," Karen replied, and sat down, crossing her shapely legs at the ankles.

"Did Dad ever tell you anything about my daughter? Who adopted her? I'd like to find her."

Karen blanched, but only for a moment. Her shock was quickly replaced by derision. "It's been almost fifteen years, Quentin. Why ask me this now?"

Jo almost didn't reply. She owed Karen no explanations. She only needed information, and then she'd be gone from her life, as if they'd never seen each other at all, but Karen was her only hope. "Karen, please. I'm sure Dad must have mentioned something after he returned from Ireland. Who handled the adoption? Do you know?"

"Have you seen Michael?" Karen asked, her eyes narrowing and her head tilting to the side, bird-like.

"No, but I'll speak to him next if you don't tell me what I need to know."

"You leave him alone," Karen flared. "You've done enough to ruin his life."

"Don't you think it's the other way around?" Jo cried, losing control of her temper. Karen had always had that effect on her. She could infuriate her in a matter of moments.

"No, I don't," Karen retorted. "I know what you did, and no matter what you tell yourself about that night, you'll be lying. Was the baby even his, Quentin, or did you get up the duff with someone else and blame that on Michael too? I wouldn't put it past you."

"Karen, I'm not here to accuse Michael of anything. I simply want to know what happened to the child I gave birth to. I'd like to find her."

"Why?" Karen asked, still watching Jo with that narrowed gaze.

"Because maybe it's not too late for me to be her mother. Maybe I can still forge a bond with her, if she'll have me."

Karen shook her head in disbelief but didn't spew any more bile. "I don't know what happened to her. Dad was very secretive about the whole thing. You went off to Ireland, had the baby, and returned as if nothing had happened. The baby was never mentioned again."

"And no one asked?" Jo pressed on.

"What was there to ask? It was given up for adoption. End of story. Everyone wanted to move on, no one more than you."

"And Michael? Did he never ask about her?"

"Michael wasn't in a good place. He took a sabbatical from the hospital and went traveling for a few months. He needed to move past what happened, with you, with his slag of a wife, and with our parents. He was devastated, and he needed time to heal." For a moment, Karen almost sounded kind and caring, but then, she'd always loved Mike. He'd been her little brother, her partner in crime, her study buddy once they both chose medicine, and the only person who didn't see her for the calculating shrew she really was.

"Well, thanks for your candor, Karen. Always appreciated. I won't trouble you again," Jo said.

"Quentin, I really do wish you well. I've seen your photos in the papers. You're very talented. You always were. I wish things could have been different."

"Yeah, me too," Jo replied, and meant it. Karen could have been a role model, a friend, but at this point, she was nothing more than a stranger.

"Don't talk to Michael," Karen implored. "He doesn't know anything, I promise you."

"Still afraid I'll accuse him? What's the statute of limitations on rape?" Jo asked acidly. She had no desire to press charges, but it gave her pleasure to rattle Karen.

"Please, Quentin, let him be," Karen said. She looked almost humble, but it was just an act. Karen didn't know anything about humility, or compassion. Funny that she'd chosen a profession in which she needed a measure of both.

"I'm not going to trouble Michael," Jo replied, and watched Karen's shoulders sag with relief. "Give him my best if you speak to him. He's got a beautiful family."

"Yes, he does. His wife is lovely."

"Glad you like her. I wonder if she likes you as much," Jo added, her innate bitchiness fighting its way to the surface.

"We get on," Karen replied. She looked more relaxed now that the danger had passed and was probably eager to get Jo and Quinn out of her house.

"Goodbye, Karen," Jo said, and beckoned for Quinn to join her as she walked out of the room.

Karen flung open the front door and watched them walk through. "Goodbye," she called after them just before she slammed the door shut with a bang that reverberated through the house.

"Well, that went well," Jo said as they walked down the path toward the gate.

"I hope you're not too disappointed," Quinn replied.

"I hadn't expected her to tell me anything, so no, not too disappointed. Had to try though, didn't I? Come on, let's see if Mr. Richards is still at his office. It's just gone noon."

Quinn eased the car away from the curb and headed toward the center of town, while Jo leaned back in her seat and closed her eyes against the irritatingly cheerful sun that played peek-a-boo with the leafy trees lining the street. Seeing Karen had rattled her more than she'd thought it would. It was easy to cast someone in the role of the villain when you hadn't seen them in years, but coming face to face with the past had its price. Karen seemed more vulnerable, as Jo probably did herself. Time had taken its toll on their family, and on them. Jo was no longer the angry, unloved child who wanted only to lash out and blame everyone for her problems. Or was she? Being suddenly exposed to Quinn's orderly, comfortable life begged the difficult question. Did the fault lie with her? Was she the one who caused people to turn away from her? Was she the one unable to love?

Chapter 54

Jo stood still for a moment and gazed up at the elegant façade of Mr. Richards' office. She'd spoken to him many times in the past but had never visited his practice. For some reason, the act of consulting Mr. Richards at his office made her errand seem weightier, and more hopeless. Mr. Richards had been the Crawford family attorney since his father retired in the late 1980s. He had been a family friend as well as a solicitor, but despite his friendly demeanor and unassuming appearance, he was a legal shark, and a man who would never betray a client's confidence. He wouldn't tell her anything that might compromise him, even if he were privy to the information Jo was seeking.

"Are you all right?" Quinn asked, and Jo nodded and rang the bell.

"I just want to get this over with."

Mr. Richards opened the door himself and smiled broadly, nodding in approval. "Jo, you look well. And Mrs. Russell, something of a surprise to see you here again."

"Good afternoon," Quinn replied politely, but her expression was murderous. Mr. Richards had done nothing to help when she came to him looking for Jo, and both women resented his lack of compassion.

"Please, come in. Can I offer you a cup of coffee?" Mr. Richards asked once Quinn and Jo were settled in front of his massive desk. "Sheila—that's my wife—got me one of those Keurig machines last Christmas. I seem to be going through the K-Cups at an alarming rate. Excellent cup of coffee," he said as he looked eagerly from Jo to Quinn.

"Yes, coffee would be lovely," Jo said, wishing they could just get down to business.

"Mrs. Russell?"

"Yes, please."

Mr. Richards left the office and reappeared a few minutes later, bearing a tray with three coffee cups, milk, and sugar. "There we are, then. Certainly beats having to wait for the kettle to boil." He stirred a spoonful of sugar into his coffee and added a splash of milk. "So, what brings you here? Since you've come in person, I can only assume it's important."

"It is, actually," Jo replied, inwardly annoyed by the man's cool exterior. He would make an excellent poker player if he ever allowed himself to indulge in something as base as gambling. "Mr. Richards, as I'm sure you know, I gave birth to a child in August of 1999. The baby was given up for adoption, which was handled by my father. I believe that as his solicitor, you might have some knowledge of the details. Do you?" Jo asked, pinning Mr. Richards with an unblinking stare.

Mr. Richards took a slow sip of his coffee and met Jo's gaze across the desk, his expression as inscrutable as ever. "Sadly, I do not."

"Were you aware I had a child?" Jo persisted.

"Yes, I was."

"Mr. Richards, you are my last port of call. I don't know who else to ask. My parents are gone. The maternity home where I had the baby closed down, and my sister claims to have no knowledge of anything pertaining to the adoption. Surely you must know something."

"Jo, your parents were my clients for years, and as you know, I am not at liberty to violate the attorney/client privilege. Anything I learned from them, I cannot divulge. However, I think I might be able to help," he said, smiling that tight little smile of his that she found so irritating. "Your father left a letter, to be given to you if you ever asked me about the child. I'm not privy to the contents, but I kept it safe in his file. I'll just be a moment," he said. "It's in the file room."

Quinn turned to look at Jo. "If he left you a letter, he must have wanted you to be able to find her," she said.

"Or not. You didn't know my father. He was a man who liked to play games. He might have written something along the lines of, 'You didn't ask me while you still could, and now it's too late. Good luck finding your kid.' Or maybe the letter has nothing to do with the child at all," Jo said.

Quinn was about to reply when Mr. Richards reentered the room, a crisp white envelope in his hand. "Here you are, then. I hope this helps."

"Thank you, Mr. Richards."

Jo slid the envelope into her handbag, blatantly ignoring the pointed stares of Quinn and the lawyer. She would not read this letter in front of them. In fact, she wouldn't even read it today. She needed time to work up the courage to read her father's final words to her, and quite possibly a stiff drink or two.

Quinn set down her coffee cup and followed Jo out of the office. She unlocked the car and they got in, silently buckling their safety belts. Quinn pulled away from the curb, her eyes scanning the oncoming traffic. "Home?" she asked.

"Home."

Jo leaned back against the seat and closed her eyes, sending Quinn a silent plea not to ask any questions. Quinn seemed to understand and drove back to London without ever bringing up the letter that was burning a hole in Jo's bag. She deposited Jo in front of her building and left after a brief, "Ring me later."

Jo sighed and walked toward the entrance. For some reason, she felt as if she were walking to her own execution, but then again, that was the way Ian Crawford had always made her feel, so really, this was normal.

Chapter 55

December 1588

Leitrim, Ireland

Rafael spent the next few days walking the razor-sharp edge of acute fear. Every time someone called his name or even looked at him for a second too long, he imagined that they knew his secret. He'd casually strolled through every part of the castle, peering into every corner, every stone crevice, and every crack in the wood to see if the charm might have fallen in there somehow, but he found nothing. All he saw was stone worn smooth by endless feet, wood darkened by time, and the dirt that blanketed the yard. If he'd dropped the hamsa in the yard, it'd have been trampled into the mud, which would be the most desirable outcome, but if he'd lost it in the castle, or on the battlements, someone must have found it, and that someone now knew that there was a heretic among them.

Facing east as he stood on the battlements, Rafael tried to pray, but the words wouldn't come. He had no right to ask God for help or forgiveness. He'd broken one of God's laws and had lain with a woman who wasn't his wife. Worse, he'd given himself to a woman who wasn't of his faith. Had God forsaken him? Had He abandoned him to his terrifying fate? How long would this torture go on before he was discovered and ousted in front of everyone? Tears of terror stung Rafael's eyes, but he blinked them away. He was a soldier, even if he'd never seen battle. He had to be brave, but he felt like a frightened child who longed only to be told that everything would be all right and the punishment for his transgression wouldn't be too severe.

"Dear God, I beg for your forgiveness," Rafael finally managed to whisper into the wind. "I was weak. I was frightened. I was lonely," he added under this breath. "I will accept whatever punishment you have in store for me. I should have been stronger. I should have known better. I should have had more faith."

Rafael turned back to Alfonso before the other man could notice anything was amiss, but Alfonso wasn't looking at him. He was sitting with his back to the parapet, his gaze fixed on the blood-red slash of a winter sunrise. The sky shimmered with glorious color, the frost on the treetops reflecting the crimson rays and setting the forest alight. It was an awe-inspiring sight, and a frightening one. The clouds glowed like molten lava, the fiery sky apocalyptic in its strange beauty. It filled Rafael with foreboding.

"Come, let's go break our fast," Alfonso said once their watch was over. "I can't feel my toes. I hope there's some hot broth left."

Rafael followed Alfonso along the wall and down the slippery steps. They hurried across the bailey and made for the kitchen, the only place in the castle where they could get warm. Despite fires that burned day and night, the castle was bone-chillingly icy, and the men slept ten to a chamber to conserve wood and to share the body heat that kept them from waking stiff with cold. A wood-burning brazier was used in the great hall instead of the great hearth that devoured firewood like a hungry beast but did little to warm the huge chamber. The food was rationed, and although not ravenously hungry, the men were never truly satisfied.

Rafael sighed with pleasure when the welcoming warmth of the cavernous kitchen enveloped him in its embrace. He was half-frozen after spending two hours on the wind-blown battlements. His feet were numb, and his hands were red and chapped, since he didn't have any gloves. He held them out to the fire and the blessed warmth began to spread through him, starting with his hands and moving to his tense shoulders and stiff knees.

Mary set cups of steaming broth on the trestle table and gave each man a thick slice of buttered bread. Alfonso immediately tucked into his portion, but Rafael wrapped his hands around the warm cup and bowed his head, inwardly thanking the

Lord for the food. After breakfast, he'd go to sleep for a few hours. He was tired, and there wasn't much for him to do anyway.

He finished his meal and followed Alfonso out of the kitchen and toward the stairway to their bedchamber. Alfonso was unusually reticent, and was asleep within moments, his gentle snores rumbling through Rafael's head and lulling him to sleep.

He was woken from a deep sleep by shouting from the yard below. The temperature in the room was arctic and his sleepy brain told him to ignore the noise and remain in the relative warmth of the bed, but the cries grew louder and more urgent. Rafael swung his legs over the side of the bed, swore eloquently when his stockinged feet touched the icy floor, and shuffled toward the window, pressing his nose to the thick frosted panes of mullioned glass. Had the English finally decided to attack? The thick glass made everything look wavy and distorted, so Rafael yanked open the narrow window, shivering with cold as he craned his neck to see what was amiss.

Alfonso was next to him in moments, his breath warm on Rafael's neck as he peered over his shoulder. "What's going on?"

"I don't know," Rafael replied. "I can't make out what they're saying."

The men turned away from the window and pushed it shut. Rafael grabbed his cloak while Alfonso threw a blanket over his shoulders. With no cloak of his own, he wore the blanket in its place to keep warm when outside.

"Let's go," Rafael cried. The two men hurried down the stairs and erupted into the snow-covered yard, which was heaving with angry men. Captain de Cuéllar was shouting for the men to stand down, but his commands were ignored as the men elbowed him out of the way. Someone was at the center of the melee, but Rafael couldn't see anything over the heads of the others.

"What's happening?" Alfonso cried as he grabbed José by the arm to get his attention.

Wild-eyed, José ignored Alfonso and raised himself on his toes, desperate to see what was going on.

"Stand down!" Captain de Cuéllar roared as he tried in vain to push through the crowd.

"Disperse immediately!" Kieran O'Rourke shouted as he led his men into the yard. They were armed with muskets and swords, the sight of which quickly sobered the heaving mob of Spaniards, who didn't understand the command but had no trouble interpreting its tone. "Step aside," O'Rourke ordered.

The men quieted and allowed Captain de Cuéllar to pass, moving aside to reveal Julio Fernández, who was lying on the ground, curled into a ball. His face was battered and his breathing shallow. Blood trickled from the side of his mouth and his stare was fixed on the tips of the captain's boots. His lips moved almost soundlessly, but Rafael could just make out the words of a desperate prayer.

"What's he done?" Alfonso demanded of the nearest man.

"He tried to make contact with the English."

"Why would he do that?" Rafael asked, stunned.

"Why do you think, you fool?" José growled. "He was going to betray us all in return for his freedom."

"Why?" Alfonso cried, staring at Julio as if seeing him for the first time.

"Because he's a filthy Jew!" José spat out the words as if they burned his mouth. "Paco and Juan cornered him in the tunnel. He had a white handkerchief on him and a heathen Jewish amulet. He was going to use the handkerchief to signal his surrender and the charm to protect him from harm. He's a heretic and a traitor."

All the blood drained from Rafael's face as the man's words sank in. Julio had his hamsa, and he'd been accused of being a Jew.

314

José clapped Rafael on the back when he noticed his stunned reaction. "Don't worry, de Silva, he never made it. The passage was blocked, so we are safe for now."

"Has he admitted to trying to contact the English?" Alfonso asked.

"Of course not. Said he only wanted to see how long the tunnel was, but you can't believe a word a Jew says. They're all lying pigs and will say anything to preserve their worthless skins. He's going to pay for this, that's for sure."

"How do you know the amulet belongs to him?" Alfonso demanded.

"The girl confirmed it," José replied.

Rafael followed his gaze to see Aisling standing in the doorway, huddling into her thick shawl. Her face was set in hard lines, but her eyes glowed with fierce love when her gaze met Rafael's shocked stare.

"She said she saw him praying over it on the battlements. He tried to deny it, of course; accused her of being a whore and a liar."

"I can't believe Julio Fernández turned out to be a Jew," Alfonso mumbled as he pulled Rafael away from the crowd. "Just goes to show you—can't trust anyone. He looks like one of us, but all along he was a heretic, a Christ-killer. We were defeated because of the likes of him. Maybe he summoned the storms with his amulet and brought disaster on the great Armada. It's all his fault," Alfonso cried, suddenly incensed by the magnitude of Julio's betrayal.

"You're right, Alfonso, what befell us is all his fault," Pedro cried. "He cursed our mission. Thousands died because of him. Kill the Judas!" he shouted, and the cry was picked up by the other men, who surged toward Julio, ready to tear him limb from limb.

"No!" Rafael mouthed. "No!" He was trembling, unable to comprehend what was happening. The men shoved him out of the way as they bore down on Julio, who was crying and pleading with the men who had been his friends only an hour ago.

"It's not mine," he babbled, his voice tearful and terrified. "I found it; I swear. I thought it might be worth something."

"Shut up, you lying piece of shit. The girl saw you. She has no reason to lie," one of the men shouted. "She's Sir Brian's niece, the man who gave you food and shelter, you godless fiend."

Rafael tried to block out Julio's screams as the blows rained on his head and body.

Alfonso grabbed him by the shoulders. "Get hold of yourself, man. We're all in shock, but we'll deal with him. He'll get what he deserves."

That's what I'm afraid of, Rafael thought. He stumbled off to a less crowded corner of the yard and was sick, his insides turning themselves inside out with horror. He leaned against the stone wall and stared up at the winter-white sky. His stomach was still heaving, and his legs threatened to buckle beneath him, so he sank to the cold ground and buried his head in his arms. What was he to do? The honorable thing would be to admit the hamsa was his and face the consequences, but Julio had been caught with the amulet, and Aisling, who had every reason to hate Julio, had pointed the finger at him because she wanted to protect Rafael. He owed her his gratitude, and possibly his life, but how could he stand by and watch an innocent man be tried for being a Jew? And how had Julio come by the hamsa?

Despite searching the castle high and low, Rafael was convinced he hadn't lost it. He wasn't that careless, not when his life was at stake. Had Julio stolen it? But when would he have had the opportunity? Like most men, Rafael slept in his clothes. Julio would have had to reach into his doublet, find the inner pocket, and extract the hamsa without waking Rafael, and that was assuming he'd known it was there in the first place. He'd taken off his

316

clothes only once in the past week, when he'd made love to Aisling. She'd known he had it, had seen him with it.

No, Rafael thought. *Aisling is loving and kind. She would never steal from me or frame an innocent man.* Julio wasn't innocent, not where Aisling was concerned, but would she sacrifice him to save Rafael? She would. She had, Rafael realized, and his heart swelled with love and gratitude, which were quickly overpowered by gut-wrenching guilt.

Rafael glanced toward the doorway where Aisling had stood only a few minutes ago, but she was gone, the doorway a gaping mouth in the face of the castle. He watched, with a surprising air of detachment, as Julio was led away by Kieran O'Rourke, having been rescued from the mob. Julio could barely walk, and his face looked like a slab of raw meat, but he was still alive, which was a relief.

Rafael scrambled to his feet and made his way across the bailey, heading for the great hall, where the men would be assembled by now. He had to learn more before coming to a decision about Julio, and the only way to do that was to watch and listen. What had Julio been doing in the tunnel? Was the white handkerchief really a flag of surrender, or was it just an innocent square of linen? Had Julio anything else on him besides the hamsa? Rafael stumbled along, his innards twisting and his head aching with indecision. His fate was now irrevocably and inexplicably intertwined with Julio's, and their combined sentence would be passed within the next few hours.

Chapter 56

The great hall was a roiling mass of bloodthirsty humanity. The Spaniards were up in arms, demanding that Kieran O'Rourke hand over the prisoner. The Irishman stood his ground, his arms crossed in front of his chest, watching the proceedings with great interest. He couldn't have understood much of what was said, but he got the gist of it from the expressions of rage and calls for justice.

"Ah, de Silva," Captain de Cuéllar called out to Rafael. "Come here, please. We need a translator."

"At your service, sir," Rafael replied as he approached the two groups.

"Please explain to señor O'Rourke what has happened. He seems to have misunderstood what he saw in the yard."

"What exactly should I tell him, sir?" Rafael asked.

"Tell him that two of our men thought Julio Fernández was acting suspiciously and followed him into the tunnel, which would have led him outside and straight to the English had it not been blocked. When apprehended, Fernández was in possession of the Jewish amulet. It was in the pocket of his doublet. They also discovered a stash of valuables he'd hidden behind a loose stone. It contained the items that had gone missing over the past few weeks, including Sir Brian's cloak pin. It is our belief that Fernández stole the items in order to either negotiate for his release or fund his passage back to Spain. Had he exited the tunnel in full view of the British, the castle would have fallen and all within it would have been either taken prisoner or put to death."

The captain's face was mottled with anger, but his eyes betrayed his pain. No commanding officer ever wanted to come face to face with treason or be forced to make a decision that would haunt him for the rest of his days. Rafael took a deep breath and relayed the captain's speech to the best of his ability. Kieran

O'Rourke listened patiently, nodding in understanding as Rafael stumbled over certain parts of the narrative.

"Where is this devil charm?" he asked the captain.

Rafael translated the question, and the captain extracted the hamsa from his pocket and handed it over to O'Rourke. The younger man held it up to the light from the window, studying the amulet intently. Rafael forced himself to glance away, afraid he'd reveal too much simply by looking at the charm. His hands trembled and he balled them into fists, silently praying for courage.

"I've never seen the like," O'Rourke said. "It's a pretty thing, but playthings of the devil usually are. They entice and seduce. So, it's sorcery and heresy this man is guilty of?"

"Yes," Rafael croaked. The word felt razor-sharp in his throat.

"I see. He's yers to deal with as ye see fit, Captain," O'Rourke said, bowing slightly to the captain as a sign of respect. "I'll tell my men to turn him over to ye. What will ye do with him?"

"He wishes to know how Julio will be dealt with," Rafael told the captain, all the while praying that Julio would simply be put under lock and key.

"He'll be executed," José hissed.

"Now, wait a minute, nothing's been decided," Captain de Cuéllar interjected, but the men were no longer listening to him.

"We're going to show him what Spaniards do to traitors and Jews. We're going to teach him and anyone else who thinks of betraying us a lesson they'll never forget," one of the men cried.

"Please, have mercy," Rafael pleaded, the words erupting against his better judgment. The evidence against Julio was damning, but not conclusive. There was no proof that he'd meant to parlay with the English or betray his friends, but the captain was right; had he walked out of the castle in full view of the enemy, they'd have had the means to breach the castle defenses and take everyone prisoner. Julio might not be a Jew, but he could have been the instrument of death, a traitor whose only aim was to save his own skin. He'd stolen from his friends and hosts, which could only mean he'd meant to run.

"What? You feel sorry for the Jew? Are you a Jew lover, de Silva? Would you like to take his place?" The men laughed and gave Rafael a rough shove. "Get out of here. You're still a boy. You don't understand what it means to be a man."

"Get out, you sniveling coward!" one of the men bellowed and gave Rafael a push toward the door.

Rafael walked away. He was horrified, but there was nothing he could do for Julio Fernández. These men would kill him even if Rafael admitted to owning the hamsa. Their blood was up and what they saw as a need for justice was really a desperate desire to turn their anger on someone who couldn't fight back. It wouldn't matter much if they killed one or two people. Given their collective fury, Julio Fernández would die regardless.

Chapter 57

Rafael stared in horror at the hastily constructed cross. It was made of rough beams and looked stark and sinister there at the center of the bailey. The men had worked feverishly, their fury urging them on. Captain de Cuéllar tried to reason with the men, but no one took any notice of his entreaties and some even went so far as to threaten to lock him up if he didn't stop harassing them. Suddenly, his rank no longer mattered, and it was José Méndez who took charge. He stood off to the side, watching with a master mason's eye as the men fitted the beam into the hole they'd dug in the ground and mounted the crossbar, urging them to raise it a little higher to make sure it was secure and would take the weight of a man.

"José, please," Rafael pleaded with the man. He no longer cared if he was accused of being a Jew lover or if his own loyalty was questioned. He had to do everything in his power to try to stop this madness. "Surely there are other ways."

José tore his gaze away from the cross and turned to stare at Rafael. His face softened for just a moment and he reached out and patted Rafael's arm in a fatherly manner. "I commend your compassion and courage, de Silva. It takes guts to go against the majority, but you're very young and you simply don't understand the magnitude of Fernández's betrayal."

"And do you understand the magnitude of crucifying a man?" Rafael replied hotly.

"Only too well, but God wills it, Rafael. God wills it."

"And how do you know God's will?" Rafael demanded, outraged. From the corner of his eye he could see the captain watching him with undisguised admiration.

"He let His will be known to us," José replied. He seemed to be brimming with conviction.

"How?"

"Do you know how many items Julio stole?" José asked, his eyes glinting with zeal. "Thirty. That's right—thirty. Judas betrayed our Lord for thirty pieces of silver. Fernández was going to betray us for thirty pieces of gold. He's the lowest kind of criminal—a traitor, a sellout, and a heretic. He will die this day, Rafael, so I suggest you shut your mouth and walk away before you join him on your very own cross." José chuckled and smiled broadly at Rafael's terrified expression. "I'm just joking with you, Rafi. Off with you," he said, giving Rafael a playful shove.

Rafael walked off without another word, but his insides burned as if he'd swallowed a ball of flame. Was this his fault? Was God testing him and daring him to declare himself?

"Let it go, son," Captain de Cuéllar said as he approached Rafael and laid a warning hand on his arm. "Julio Fernández deserves to die for his crimes. This is not an honorable way to execute a fellow soldier, but what he did isn't honorable either. Besides, we can't spare the wood to burn him at the stake, not with a siege in progress. The men have decided, and although I don't agree with their judgment, I must respect it."

Rafael nodded. He was going to return to his chamber, but the captain gripped his arm, preventing him from walking away. "You must be here to bear witness. We all must. You don't want to be accused of cowardice, son," the captain said, lowering his voice to a whisper. "Not at this stage. *Alea iacta est.*" *The die has been cast.* Rafael shuddered at the choice of phrase. This wasn't a game of dice; this was a man's life.

"Bring him out, lads," José called out.

Julio Fernández was dragged out from one of the outbuildings, where he'd been kept under guard by Pedro and Miguel. He blinked as his eyes adjusted to the light and allowed himself to be frog-marched toward the center of the bailey, but froze, his eyes widening in terror when he saw the newly erected cross.

"No," he pleaded. "Please, no. I'm not a traitor. I stole the jewelry, but I never meant to betray anyone. I only wanted a place to hide it."

"And the Jew amulet?" José cried.

"It's not mine," Julio sobbed. "I'm a devout Christian."

"They all are," someone called out. "Lying comes easy to them. They'll do and say anything to save themselves, those filthy cowards. And now we know that you're one of them, and you will pay for your sins."

Julio looked around in panic as the men dragged him struggling toward the cross. And then they stopped, realizing that they hadn't considered the practicalities. They couldn't lift a grown man and hold him up while someone drove the nails into his wrists, all the while standing on a rickety ladder, which would need to lean against something solid enough to hold a man's weight. They looked to José for a solution, and he offered one immediately, proving to the men that he was a born leader.

"Take the cross down and lay it on the ground, lads. Tie the bastard to the cross and nail him down, then lift the cross and slide it back into the hole."

Reenergized, the men went about their task. They lifted the cross out of the hole they'd dug in the yard and laid it flat. Julio screamed and thrashed as they forced him down. He continued to beg for mercy while they men tied his ankles and wrists to the cross, but the ability to speak left him when he saw the hammer in Pedro's meaty hands.

"Wait," José called out.

Pedro stepped aside, his expression quizzical. "Have you changed your mind?"

"Of course not."

Rafael watched in mute disbelief as José took the hamsa from his pocket. "Choke on it, you dirty Jew." He pushed the hamsa into Julio's mouth and pinched his nose with two fingers, forcing Julio to swallow the amulet. "Now, we are ready," José said, and nodded to Pedro to continue.

Julio shook his head, his dark eyes huge with fear. Tears poured down his cheeks and he tried in vain to fight against his restraints, but they were tied securely. A hush fell over the crowd as the men watched in horrified fascination as Pedro drew a sturdy iron nail from his pocket and held it against the tender skin of Julio's wrist. A few looked away, but no one left, and no one uttered a word of protest.

A bloodcurdling roar rose up when the first nail was driven into Julio's elegant wrist. He began to shake violently, and a stream of vomit spilled from his mouth, the foul smell amplified as Julio let go of his bowels. By the time the men raised the cross and fitted it into the hole, Julio was no longer screaming. His head hung down, his chin resting against his shoulder. Crimson droplets of blood fell, as if in slow motion, painting the snow a violent red. No one moved. No one spoke. No one could find the strength to look away from the gruesome scene, which had been written and directed by them and their hatred. The minutes ticked by, but time stood still as the men watched their victim with bated breath. Julio was unconscious, but he wasn't dead. Not yet.

"You look like you're going to be sick, Rafael," Alfonso said at last.

"This is not right, Alfonso."

"I agree with you," Alfonso said. "He deserves a traitor's death, not the honor of being crucified like our Lord. He should have been hanged. Even beheading is too good for the likes of him."

"It'll take him hours to die, maybe even days," José said, having overheard Alfonso's comment. "It was important to prolong his suffering."

324

"Was it?" Alfonso asked sarcastically. "Being hanged is bad enough, I would have thought."

"Seeing him up there on the cross will serve as a warning to anyone who wants to surrender to the English. Besides, hanging is too good for filth like him. He doesn't deserve our mercy," Pedro said, still holding the hammer in his hand. He seemed to have enjoyed his role in Julio's execution.

"Whatever you say," Alfonso replied, having lost interest in the discussion.

"I never suspected Julio of being a Jew," Miguel said, his gaze still pinned to Julio's gray face. "Those bastards sure know how to hide in plain sight. It's a talent they have."

"It's sorcery," José growled without turning around. "They commune with the devil."

"Which is why the Church burns them," someone replied. "To make sure they get a taste of hell before they get there."

"We can't afford to waste so much firewood. Every bit is precious," José replied, suddenly practical.

"I must find Aisling," Rafael said as he began to back away from the men, but Alfonso stopped him.

"You must stay here."

"I have no stomach for this," Rafael whispered.

"Rafael, you are a soldier of Spain, not a child. Anyhow, we're almost done here. He's not looking too good."

Please die, Julio, Rafael pleaded with the man silently. *Die quickly, for your own sake.*

After a few more minutes, the men began to lose interest and the crowd started to disperse. Rafael staggered away from the spectacle, unable to bear the sight any longer. He couldn't be around these men, men he'd talked with, dined with, and served

325

with. They were animals, barbarians, who were rejoicing in the suffering of one of their own.

The castle was deathly quiet as Rafael made his way to Aisling's chamber. The door was locked, but she let him in after he called out to her. She took him into her arms and held him tight as he cried, stroking his hair and kissing his brow until he spent himself.

"Ye must not let it break ye," she said once Rafael began to calm down. "Men do horrible things when they're scared, Rafael. Don't give them reason to turn on ye."

"Aisling, I—"

"Shh," she said. "Lie down for a spell. Ye'll feel better after ye sleep."

Rafael nodded into her shoulder and allowed her to lead him toward the bed. He lay down and she curled up next to him, her arm protectively around his midsection. He was asleep within moments, his mind desperate for respite from the horror he'd witnessed.

Chapter 58

May 2015

London, England

Quinn's hand shook badly as she dropped the hamsa onto the duvet. It lay there, innocently glinting in the moonlight, a tiny piece of gold that had sealed Julio Fernández's fate. Quinn had witnessed countless deaths, thanks to her unusual ability, but it never ceased to surprise her how brutal and bloodthirsty human beings could be. The Spaniards had been frustrated and scared, cornered like mice by a cat just waiting to pounce, but that was no excuse for what they had done to one of their own. Julio might have been an ass and worse, but he didn't deserve the horrific death his countrymen had inflicted on him.

At least it wasn't Rafael, Quinn thought, as her heartrate slowed from a gallop to a trot and the shaking subsided. Poor Rafael. She could only imagine the guilt he'd felt, and the fear. And suspicion? Quinn wondered as she took a sip of water from the glass by the bed. It was entirely too convenient that the man who'd assaulted Eilis, called her terrible names, and threatened to get revenge on Rafael had been the man caught with the hamsa and the stolen loot. Julio might have stolen the valuables. He had admitted as much, but how had he come by the amulet? What were the odds that Rafael had lost the thing he held most dear and Julio Fernández had been the one to find it and keep quiet about it? Quinn shook her head in disbelief. No, that was no coincidence, as far as she was concerned. That was a set-up. Whether Aisling had wished to get back at Julio for what he'd tried to do to Eilis, or whether she'd thought she was protecting Rafael, that hamsa had not found its way into Julio's pocket by mistake. It was planted.

"Surely you can see that, Rafael," Quinn whispered into the darkness.

"I thought you'd be asleep," Gabe said as he walked into the bedroom and shut the door behind him.

"I couldn't sleep, so I visited with Rafael," Quinn replied. She tried to sound nonchalant, but Gabe must have heard the tremor in her voice.

"What is it? What did you see?"

"I saw the crucifixion, Gabe. Dear God, it was horrific. There are no words."

"Was it him?"

Quinn shook her head. "No. He's safe, for now. I can't speak of it, Gabe. I just can't," Quinn said as she used the plastic bag to scoop the amulet off the bed without touching it. She dropped the bag onto the bedside table and stared at it, realizing that now that Rafael no longer had the hamsa, the story was at an end. She'd never find out what happened to him, never learn if he survived the siege or returned to Spain. And what of Aisling?

"Come here," Gabe said, pulling her into a warm embrace. "Forget about Rafael, at least for tonight. And forget about Jo."

"So, what should I remember?" Quinn asked playfully.

"Remember how much you love me," he whispered, his breath tickling her earlobe and shooting shivers of desire into her belly. "Remember how it feels when I touch you," he continued, his fingers light as feathers as he touched her flushed face. "Remember how it feels when I'm inside you."

"I think you might need to remind me," she said softly, her words hardly more than a sigh.

"With pleasure," Gabe replied as his lips brushed against her neck.

"No, the pleasure will be all mine."

And it was. Quinn forgot all about Rafael and her perplexing sister as Gabe made love to her, slowly and tenderly. He took his time, kissing, stroking, teasing, and pleasing her until she was quivering like a bowl of jelly, her entire being centered around her core, which was still joined to him.

Gabe rested his forehead against hers and smiled without opening his eyes. "All right?" he asked.

"Mm," she moaned.

"Again?"

"Got an early start. I have a meeting with Rhys."

Gabe opened his eyes, which were still clouded with desire, and kissed her softly. "Is that the call of the wild?"

"What?" Quinn's eyes flew open as a thin wail erupted from the baby monitor. "Right on cue," she said, reluctantly slipping out of bed and pulling on her dressing gown.

"Want me to get him?" Gabe asked, smiling at her lazily.

"You got him last time. I don't mind."

Quinn padded down the corridor to Alex's room. He was wide awake, his round blue eyes staring accusingly from between the bars of his cot.

"Come here, then," Quinn said as she lifted the baby into her arms. "What's the matter? Can't sleep? Want some water?"

Alex buried his nose in Quinn's neck and wrapped his chubby arms around her. Quinn kissed the top of his head, inhaling his sweet baby smell. "Just wanted a cuddle, eh?" she crooned as she began to walk slowly from one side of the room to the other. "That's right," she whispered. "Go back to sleep."

Alex's little body grew heavier as he began to drop off. Quinn carefully lowered herself into a rocking chair and held the baby close. "I'm so lucky to have you," she whispered into his downy head. "I'm so blessed."

Quinn closed her eyes as she continued to rock. Was there anything in the world more wonderful than holding your sleeping baby after making love to your husband? she thought dreamily. To feel safe and loved, and to know you belong. Rafael's dark, anxious eyes swam before her, jolting her out of her bubble of contentment. Would Rafael ever know that feeling? Would he live long enough to hold a child in his arms or lie with a woman who was his wife?

"I'll never know what became of him," Quinn whispered into the silvery moonlight that bathed Alex's room in an otherworldly glow.

Chapter 59

The moon was full and bright, hanging so low it skimmed the truncated tower of All Saints' Church. Net curtains billowed at the open window. The pleasant breeze of the afternoon had turned into a brisk wind, and Jo pushed the window shut before sliding into her favorite corner of the sofa and folding her legs beneath her. She instantly unfolded them and sat up, all prim and proper, the way her father had made her sit when she was a child.

You silly cow, she thought, and deliberately resumed her previous position, burrowing deeper into the cushions. The letter lay on the coffee table, a white rectangle that might as well have been an unexploded grenade. She had no illusions. This would not be a missive of love and forgiveness. This was her father's last-ditch effort to chastise her, his final judgment.

She reached for the envelope and held it suspended between two fingers, staring at the paper as if it might reveal a secret clue, but all the envelope informed her of was that the letter was for Quentin Crawford, aka Jo Turing, aka disappointment and failure, as a daughter, a sister, and a friend.

Jo took a deep breath and tore the envelope open, pulling out a single sheet of paper. She laughed out loud when she unfolded the missive. It was type-written, signed at the bottom by her father. So typical of him. He couldn't even bother to write the letter himself, make it more personal. With a hysterical giggle, she wondered if he'd had his secretary type it and then just put his signature to it, as if it were a letter to one of his patients or the medical board. In a way, it was a blessing. Had her father handled the letter himself, Jo would feel a jolt when she picked it up, and experience all the emotions her father must have been feeling when he penned his final message. As it was, she felt no physical response, for which she was truly grateful.

Get on with it, her inner voice said. *You're stalling.*

Yes, I am, Jo replied inwardly. *Some things never change.*

She held the letter angled toward the window to capture the moonlight. She had no desire to turn on the light, preferring to read her father's final words in the near darkness. Perhaps she was hiding—from him, from herself, possibly even from Quinn, damn her eyes. She was so perfect, so together. She was probably in bed with Gabe right now, sated after being thoroughly fucked. That man knew his way around a woman's body, Jo was sure of it. What she wouldn't give...

Enough, the voice said. *Just read the damn thing.*

Jo exhaled loudly and held the letter closer to her nose, her hand trembling as she began to read.

August 17, 2009

Dear Quentin,

If you are reading this letter, then I'm dead and your conscience has finally woken from a lengthy slumber. I was beginning to think it was in a coma, but I never gave up hope and instructed Louis to give you this letter if you ever came asking about your child, the child you so blithely brought into this world to punish us all for our misdeeds. If you look at the date on the letter, you will understand the significance. Today is your daughter's tenth birthday. She is well and happy, a bright spark in an otherwise dull world. How do I know that? I know because I've spent every Sunday with her for the past ten years.

Did you really think I would give away my grandchild, a baby born of my two children? The thought never even crossed my mind. I had my own plans for the baby, but as soon as Michael found out you were keeping it, he made his wishes known. This was his child, and he wanted to be its father. He was there when Daisy was born. Yes, that's her name, in case you were wondering. He was the first person to hold her after the doctor and the nurse brought Daisy to his room. He fed her, changed her, bathed her, and loved her, and he will love her until the day he dies.

He's not fit to be a father—I can almost hear you saying that, but you're wrong. It is you who are unfit. Parents know their children, and I know, as your mother knew, that what happened between you and Michael wasn't entirely his fault. Yes, he should have been stronger. Yes, he should have known better. But it was you who preyed on his vulnerability, his weakness at a time when he needed a friend. It was you who poured shot after shot of whisky that night, and it was you who made the first move. How do I know that? I guess you forgot about the nanny cam I had installed when you were an infant. I kept it running, to make sure the nannies took proper care of you and the housekeeper never helped herself to anything she shouldn't have.

You cried rape when things went too far, eager to destroy your brother, and us, for being nothing more than a foolish, gullible man who lost his head when you offered him the solace he so sorely needed. Michael has paid the price for his stupidity, but he's learned his lesson. He's a husband, a father, a damn fine doctor, and a kind human being. What about you, Quentin? What are you? Not a wife, not a mother, not a sister, or even a daughter. You are good at your job, but that's because you love the attention it gets you. The celebrated photographer. The woman who doesn't need anyone.

I don't know how old you are now, but I hope you've found love, and inner peace. And I genuinely hope you're happy. And if you do anything to hurt Michael or Daisy, I will haunt you from the grave. That, I promise you.

Your loving father,

Ian Crawford

Jo wiped away angry tears with the back of her hand, her gaze fixed on the indifferent moon. Even from the grave, he had the power to hurt her, to make her feel like a steaming pile of shit. But the worst part was that he was right—in everything he'd said. She'd wanted to hurt Michael, wanted to hurt her parents for years of making her feel like an outsider. She'd forgotten, but she had been the one who got him drunk that night, and she had been the one to sink to her knees and pull down his trousers, taking him into her mouth. They weren't biologically related, after all, and it had been fun—an experiment of sorts.

She'd never gone beyond kissing until that night, and with Michael, she'd felt safe. He'd never do anything to hurt her. He loved her. But she'd miscalculated. She'd opened a door she couldn't close in time. When Michael came to her room, she hadn't said no. She'd wanted more. She'd wanted to know what it felt like to have a man's tongue between her legs, to savor the pleasure of his fingers sliding inside her. She hadn't been ready for things to go further than that, but Michael had been too far gone. He'd been drunk and aroused, and by the time he'd pushed his way inside her it was too late to say no, too late to do anything but enjoy the sensation of him moving inside her. He should have stopped, should have left her room, but he hadn't, and she'd done nothing to stop him.

Jo tossed the letter aside. There was only one thing she could do now. She would respect her father's wishes and not go anywhere near Michael or Daisy. Her heart squeezed as she realized that she'd seen Daisy's photo that very morning. She was one of the two girls standing with Michael and his wife in the family portrait. Which one was she? The two girls appeared to be almost the same age, so she couldn't guess. She'd find out, but discreetly. She'd follow Daisy's life from a distance; it was easy enough to do through social media. She'd cheer her on, be happy for her, and celebrate her triumphs, but only from afar. Jo owed her that much. She'd never destroy her family or make any attempt to humiliate her father. Michael deserved to be happy.

Jo slowly got off the sofa, walked into the kitchen and turned on one of the burners on the stove. She set the letter alight and watched it burn until the flame nearly reached her fingers, then dropped it in the sink. The blackened piece of paper lay curled at the bottom, the typeface charred beyond recognition. Jo ran some water over the burnt paper until it was nothing more than a black stain on her steel sink. She then walked into her bedroom and pulled a hold-all out of the wardrobe. Good thing she'd had her passport reissued after her old one was destroyed in the explosion.

She finished packing and picked up her mobile. She made three calls. One to Charles Sutcliffe, telling him she'd take the assignment he'd mentioned earlier that week. One to Drew Camden, informing him that his services were no longer required, and his payment would be submitted through PayPal. And one to Tim, just because she needed to hear a friendly voice, even if it was only a voicemail recording. She then fell into bed without getting undressed and fell asleep. She had an early start tomorrow.

Chapter 60

December 1588

Leitrim, Ireland

Bluish shadows settled over the forest, swallowing the English soldiers and leaving only the glow of their cooking fires. Nothing had really changed in the past few days, but Rafael could feel a thrum of discontent coming from the English camp below. The weather had turned even colder, and as Christmas approached and the siege dragged on, the soldiers were giving vent to their frustration. Surrounded and frightened as they might be, at least the Spaniards had a roof over their heads, and the comfort of real beds and hot meals. The English were sleeping on cold, hard ground and eating salt pork and tack, the standard fare of soldiers everywhere. A few of the more enterprising soldiers set traps and managed to catch a few rabbits and other small prey, but the rest were hungry and angry.

As Rafael descended from the battlements after his watch, he tried to avoid looking at the shadowed cross in the yard. He couldn't see Julio's face, but he didn't need to. The crows had been at him already and the sight was grotesque. He wished the men would take Julio down and bury him, but no one seemed in any rush. Some still made comments about Julio, but others carried on as if he'd never existed, had never been their friend.

The kitchen was wonderfully warm after the frigid temperature outside. Aisling handed Rafael a cup of hot broth and a trencher filled with roast pork and buttered peas. The rest of the men had already eaten, and Rafael was grateful not to have to talk to any of them. He wondered where Alfonso had gone but wasn't overly worried. Perhaps he'd needed to go to the privy after their long watch. Rafael savored his meal while Aisling went about tidying the kitchen for the night.

"I'm going to turn in," she said. "I'm very tired."

"I'll escort you to your chamber," Rafael said, wiping his mouth with the back of his hand. He could have happily eaten more, but none was offered.

They walked down the dark corridors in silence, the flame of Aisling's candle casting strange shadows onto the stone walls. He didn't say anything until they entered her room and Aisling closed the door behind them.

"Aisling, how did Julio come to have my charm?"

"He stole it, just like he stole the other things," Aisling said. She removed her cap and her hair came tumbling down. It was an invitation, but Rafael wasn't ready to accept it.

"I don't believe that."

"What are ye saying?" Aisling demanded, hands on hips.

"I'm saying that you were the only person who knew I had it. Please, tell me the truth. Julio's face haunts me day and night. I can't sleep. I feel responsible for what happened to him."

Aisling's gaze slid away from him. She turned toward the bed and began to plump the pillow before pulling back the down quilt and beginning to unlace her bodice.

"Aisling, I need to know," Rafael said.

"I took yer amulet," she admitted, turning to face him. Her cheeks were pink with shame at being caught out. "I was worried someone would find it and discover the truth. I didn't know what that thing was, but I knew it was heathen and ye'd suffer for it. He was a bad man. He deserved what happened to him."

"How did you know he'd get caught with it?" Rafael asked, still trying to work out what had happened.

"I'd seen him sneaking into the tunnel. I knew he was hiding something in there. I bumped into him in the passage and pushed the charm into his pocket. He didn't even notice. When I saw him going toward the storeroom where the entrance to the tunnel is, I told the two men who caught him."

"How did you tell them?"

"I just beckoned for them to follow me. They assumed something else, but once we reached the tunnel, they saw Julio inside. He hid something behind a loose stone and then turned to leave. They drew their own conclusions. When they searched him, they found the amulet."

"You planned it?"

Aisling nodded. "Rafael, ye don't need that thing anymore. It could only bring ye trouble. I did it for ye, for us," she added shyly. "I'm not going to marry Patrick. I'll tell Uncle Brian when he returns. I'll ask him to grant ye a bit of land. We won't be rich, but we'll survive. We'll be happy."

Rafael turned and opened the door.

"Where are ye going?" Aisling demanded.

"I need time to think," Rafael replied, and headed for his own bedchamber, which was mercifully empty. He removed his boots and climbed under the blanket fully dressed. He felt wretched. He'd suspected that Aisling had a hand in what had happened to Julio beyond claiming that she'd seen him praying over the hamsa, but now he knew for certain, and the knowledge weighed heavily on him. He hadn't liked or trusted Julio, but he was no traitor. He'd used the tunnel to stash his loot, which he would probably have used to trade for goods or a passage home. Rafael didn't believe for a moment that Julio had been looking to make contact with the English.

Rafael curled into a ball and covered his head with his arms. Aisling had sent a man to his death, had stood and watched Julio's agony as he was nailed to the cross. He couldn't reconcile this merciless creature to the beautiful, loving young woman he knew, but there was no escaping the truth. In the middle of the night, when he couldn't sleep, he'd fantasized about a life with her, about children, but it couldn't be, not now, and not ever, because even if he managed to rationalize away what Aisling had done and convince himself she'd done it for love, he could never be honest with her about who he truly was. He would have to pretend for the rest of his days, go from attending a Spanish church to attending an Irish church, baptize his children, and pray to her God. He couldn't do it. He wouldn't do it. He'd rather die.

Chapter 61

The snow began to fall again three days later. At first, in the early afternoon, it came down in a flurry of light, fluffy snowflakes, but as the day wore on, it became heavier and thicker. Strong winds whipped the snow into a maelstrom, making it impossible to walk across the yard without being blinded and nearly overpowered. For the first time since the siege had begun, the watch was suspended, since there was little chance of an attack. No man could remain in the open for long, given the weather. The English were in disarray. Their canvas tents took flight, the wooden stakes torn out of the ground by the wind. Their fires were extinguished, and their supplies buried in mounds of heavy, wet snow. The Spaniards and the Irishmen retreated to the hall and huddled around the fire, which they'd built in the great hearth to ward off the chill.

The men sat in groups, some speaking in low tones, others playing at dice, and others just staring into space, wondering if their ordeal in this country would ever come to an end. Every hour, a two-man patrol climbed up on the battlements to check on the English, but the reports remained the same throughout the night. The troops were engaged in braving the elements and salvaging their supplies.

The snow continued through the night, the wind howling like a grief-stricken woman. No one left the hall, but bedded down where they sat, wrapping themselves in blankets and cloaks. Men slept on benches, trestle tables, and the floor. Rafael wrapped a blanket around himself, but it did little to keep him warm, and he slept fitfully, wishing all the while that morning would finally come.

When it did, the world looked very different than it had the day before. The snow continued to fall, but the wind had died down, leaving behind a scene of pristine beauty. Everything was silver and white, the sky a linen white as the heavy flakes continued to pile up on the ground. There was no sign of the

English camp, the tracks of the retreating soldiers erased by the heavy snow.

"They must have pushed off at dawn," Captain de Cuéllar said as he looked out over the battlements. "Too many men would have been lost to cold and hunger if they remained. The siege is lifted."

The men cheered, but Rafael felt a familiar heaviness in his heart. His gaze strayed to the cross where Julio hung, his dark hair covered with a snowy halo. The English might have left, but for him, little had changed. For the first time, he admitted to himself that he had no wish to return to Spain. He'd never openly questioned the decisions of his elders, but suddenly he felt angry, not only with his father, but with the entire Jewish community of Toledo. Why did they remain in a place where they were surrounded by people who wanted them dead? Why did they cling to something that was long gone? And why should he live his life in fear, always looking over his shoulder, fearful that the Inquisition would come for him? What sort of fool would he be to marry and bring more Jews into a world in which they were feared and reviled? No, he wouldn't go back, even if the opportunity presented itself. He would live free or die.

"All I want is to go home, Rafi. I hate this place. Even with the English gone, it's still a prison," Alfonso said as he sidled up to Rafael. "And it's as cold as a Jew's heart," he added, chuckling.

Rafael nodded absentmindedly. "I'll talk to you later, Alfonso."

He left the yard and made his way to Sir Brian's study. The door was unlocked, so Rafael let himself in. It didn't take him long to find what he was looking for. Rafael unrolled the map and pinned down the sides with his hands as he studied the image. It would take some planning, and he'd need funds to finance his journey, but now that he'd permitted himself to envision a different sort of future, he suddenly felt lighter and happier. The feeling of oppression that had haunted him his entire life had lifted, replaced with a determination he'd never known. He'd spent his life hiding, lying, and pretending to be something he wasn't, but he wouldn't have to pretend for much longer.

Chapter 62

May 2015

London, England

Soft morning light poured through the window, casting a golden glow on the most uninspired of objects and making them appear beautiful. Rhys's hair shimmered with copper highlights, and the face of his watch appeared luminous, drawing Quinn's tired gaze. Alex had woken up several more times during the night. There had been nothing outwardly wrong and he'd fallen asleep quickly once Quinn or Gabe held him, but everyone had spent a restless night, even Emma, who had got out of bed several times to ask if Alex was all right.

"You look tired," Rhys observed. "Want an espresso?"

"No, I'm all right."

"You know what makes having two kids seem like a walk in the park?" Rhys asked.

"No. What?"

"Having three kids." He laughed at his own joke and smiled at Quinn. "Sure you won't have that coffee?"

"Sure. I've already had two."

"All right, then. Let's see what we have here," Rhys said, reaching for his fashionable reading glasses. He skimmed Quinn's report and looked up, his gray eyes wide behind the lenses. "So, the person who was crucified wasn't Rafael de Silva, but Julio Fernández, who was in possession of the amulet at the time of his death."

"Correct," Quinn replied. "I'm relieved it wasn't Rafael."

"You get too attached to your subjects, Quinn," Rhys said as he stowed his spectacles in their case.

"So would you if you saw them and knew what they feel. They're as real to me as you are."

"I know. I'm sorry," Rhys said, looking contrite. "So, what happened to Rafael?"

"I'm afraid we'll never know now. The hamsa was pushed into Julio's mouth just before he was crucified, which would explain why we found it just beneath his pelvic bone. It had been in his intestines at the time of death and dropped into the dirt once the soft tissue fully decomposed. I can't learn anything more from the charm since it was no longer in Rafael's possession."

Rhys shook his head in dismay. "That simply won't do, Quinn. We need an ending to our story, preferably a happy one. Give our viewers something to feel good about for a change. What is your theory of what became of Rafael after the crucifixion?"

"I don't know what happened to Rafael, but I know what happened to Captain de Cuéllar. If we are to assume that Rafael left Ireland with the captain, then it stands to reason that he returned home and was reunited with his family. I won't go as far as to say that he lived happily ever after, but it's entirely possible that he lived an uneventful life after surviving those few harrowing months."

"Have you been able to locate any records? It would be helpful if we could show that he married his Mira."

Quinn shook her head. "Sorry, but I found no record of their marriage, or anything that might tell us when he died."

"Which could mean that he died in Ireland."

"Or it could mean that the information simply isn't available online. Unless I go to Toledo and search through church archives, I have no physical proof that Rafael even existed, except for one tiny piece of corroborative information I was able to unearth."

"Do tell," Rhys said, leaning forward in his eagerness.

"Not only did Alfonso Pérez make it back to Spain, but he managed to publish several plays. None of them have been translated into English, but I was able to find several instances where Padre Rafael was mentioned."

"Why is that significant?"

"Because Alfonso joked about naming one of his characters, a priest, after Rafael. There are also several instances of someone named Julio. Do you want to get the play translated?"

"Absolutely. It might make references to Pérez's time in Ireland and the subsequent escape. Forward the document to María Sánchez. She's a freelance translator we regularly use."

"Will do," Quinn replied. "Would it make sense to go to Spain?"

"I can't authorize a trip to Spain, since I would have to explain how you came by your information about Rafael de Silva in the first place. Our program is a docudrama, not a documentary, so as long as our assumption about what happened to our main character is within reason, no one will question it. After all, we are telling our viewers what might have happened, not what actually took place. What do we know for a fact?"

"According to Captain de Cuéllar's account, a fierce snowstorm drove the English off, putting an end to the siege, which lasted nearly three weeks. Sir Brian and his people returned to the castle just in time for Christmas, by which time I assume the cross had been removed from the yard and dumped in the woods. Julio Fernández never received a proper burial. I found references to a number of Spaniards being buried at the parish church. The two men who were hanged by the British were probably among those interred."

"And how did the captain and his men find their way home?" Rhys asked.

"It seems that their escape from Ireland was as eventful as their arrival, assuming the captain's account wasn't embellished for dramatic purposes. Perhaps Alfonso Pérez is not the only one who tried his hand at creative writing."

"Let us assume he was telling it like it was," Rhys suggested. "Captain de Cuéllar proved himself to be a sensible and resourceful man. How did he escape from Ireland?"

"Against the advice of Sir Brian, Captain de Cuéllar took all willing men and headed north to Derry, where he met with Bishop Redmond O'Gallagher, who already had several Spaniards in his care. The bishop arranged for the men to be transported to Scotland. They sailed to Hebrides, and then eventually arrived on the mainland. They remained in Scotland for several months, awaiting assistance from the Duke of Parma, who eventually arranged passage to Flanders for the men. Unfortunately, the Dutch were waiting for them when they arrived and fired on the ship, sinking it with everyone aboard. Most of the Spaniards drowned, but a small number of men survived and came ashore at Dunkirk. They eventually made it back to Spain. Captain de Cuéllar returned to active duty and served under Phillip II of Spain until 1602, after which time he settled in Madrid. Nothing is known of his whereabouts after 1606."

"For the purposes of our program, Rafael de Silva will be one of the men who returned to Spain. I think it's safe to assume he left the navy," Rhys suggested.

Quinn nodded in agreement. Rhys was right, the viewers would appreciate a happy ending, but deep inside, she didn't believe Rafael de Silva ever made it home. She could no longer see him or share his memories, but for some reason, she simply didn't believe he ever saw the shores of Spain again. Most likely, he was one of the unfortunates who died off the coast of Flanders, or perhaps he never even made it that far. She'd never know the truth, but a small part of her mourned the young man he had been, and the old man he likely never became.

"Do we know what became of the men who remained in Ireland?"

"The ones who avoided capture eventually melted into the population. Sir Brian O'Rourke and his compatriot, Sean McClancy, were both arrested on charges of treason in 1590. O'Rourke was hanged, and McClancy was beheaded. One of the charges against them was providing succor to the survivors of the Armada."

"Can't say I'm surprised. Queen Elizabeth wasn't one to allow such blatant treachery to go unpunished. She wasn't a big fan of the Irish either."

"No, she ordered her soldiers to 'Hang the harpers wherever found,' referring to Irish Catholics. She wasn't nearly as tolerant as the history books make her out to be."

"And Aisling? What became of her?" Rhys asked. "Please tell me you found something we can use."

"I did. Aisling married Patrick Dennehy in February of 1589 and had six children over the course of the next decade, two of whom died in infancy. She died in 1632. Her eldest, Ralph, was born in August 1589," Quinn added meaningfully.

Rhys's eyebrows lifted dramatically. "Ralph? August 1589? You think?"

"It's possible, but it's also possible that the child was her husband's. It would be irresponsible to suggest that she had a child by Rafael de Silva, in case she has living descendants."

"We know for certain she didn't marry de Silva, which supports my theory that he returned to Spain."

"She didn't marry de Silva," Quinn concurred.

"Excellent. I will pass this on to the writers and we will start working on a screenplay for the episode. I will need you on set June fifteenth. We'll be ready to begin filming episode six."

"I can't wait to meet the cast," Quinn replied as she gathered her notes.

"I have no doubt you'll be pleased."

"And episode five?"

"Done and dusted. Katya pronounced it to be *zamechatelno*," Rhys said, struggling with the unfamiliar word.

"And what does that mean?"

"It means 'excellent' in Russian."

"And how are things with Katya?" Quinn asked, smiling at Rhys, who was turning a lovely shade of rose.

"*Zamechatelno*," he repeated. "I'm happy, Quinn. I can't guarantee anything at this stage, but I think we're a good fit. It just feels right, you know?"

Quinn nodded. She did know. When you met the one, you always knew it, even if you didn't admit it to yourself right away. Thankfully, Rhys was mature and open enough to see a good thing and grab it with both hands.

"I'm happy for you, Rhys," Quinn said. "Truly."

Rhys just smiled.

Having left Rhys to work out the details of the program, Quinn went to meet Logan at the London Hospital canteen. They hadn't seen each other in a fortnight, and she missed his smiling face and reassuring presence. Logan was an oasis of sanity in a family that could greatly benefit from group therapy.

Logan met Quinn at the entrance and caught her in a bear hug. "Hey there, sis. I missed you. Shall we get some grub? I'm starving."

"Me too. I skipped breakfast."

"I can't promise you much in terms of taste, but you won't leave hungry," Logan joked as he led Quinn toward the canteen. They picked up a couple of sandwiches and cups of steaming tea and found a table by the window. Logan opened a packet of crisps and popped one in his mouth, rolling his eyes in ecstasy. "I could live on these. Want some?"

"No, they're addictive," Quinn said, instantly regretting her choice of words. "Sorry..."

"You've got nothing to be sorry for," Logan replied.

"How is Jude? I haven't visited him in a few weeks."

"Bored. Miserable. Frustrated. Desperate for a hit," Logan replied. "I think he's trying to sweet talk the nurses into getting him some weed, but they're standing firm."

"Is he clean?"

"For now."

"Do you think he wants to remain clean?"

"I want to eat better and exercise at least three times a week," Logan said, popping another crisp into his mouth. "Will I do it? Probably not. There's a big difference between wanting and doing."

"Are you saying you've given up on him?" Quinn demanded, outraged by Logan's flippant attitude.

"No, Quinny, I haven't given up on him, but I can't force him to get better. Only he can do that, and only if he has a will of steel. It's not easy to beat an addiction."

"No, I don't suppose it is," Quinn agreed. "I'll visit him this weekend, give him the benefit of my wisdom. At least I know where to find him."

"Have you heard from Jo?" Logan asked gently.

Quinn shook her head. "No. Her phone is turned off and there's no one at the flat. She just took off, Logan. She didn't even say goodbye. I rang Charles Sutcliffe, and he said Jo's on an assignment. He wouldn't tell me where she'd gone."

"Has Drew heard from her?"

"She left him a message and sent him payment for services rendered. I just don't understand it," Quinn complained. "One minute she was all fired up about finding her daughter, and then she just vanished."

"I think she's found her," Logan replied.

"How do you mean?"

"Whatever was in that letter made all the difference. Either her father told her where her baby had gone, or perhaps he told Jo her baby *is* gone. That would certainly account for her sudden exit."

"I don't understand it," Quinn said sadly.

"Quinn, you've got to let her go."

"She's my sister, Logan. *Our* sister."

"Yes, but you can't force people to play Happy Families any more than you can force them to give up heroin. She has to want to have a relationship with us, and from what I've seen, the jury's still out on that one. Jo will come back, and when she does, what happens next will be up to her. Until then, it's 'sayonara, baby.'"

Quinn reached out and took Logan's hand. "Whatever happens, I'm grateful I have you in my life."

"Me too," Logan said and squeezed her hand affectionately.

Quinn's phone vibrated in her pocket and she pulled it out, frowning at the caller ID. "It's Rhys. I just saw him. Excuse me a moment," she said and took the call. "Rhys, did you have a question?"

"No, I have the answer," Rhys replied cryptically.

"To what?"

"To what the next episode will be about. Meet me tomorrow at nine. I'll text you the address."

"Can you give me a clue?"

Rhys exhaled loudly. "I think you need to see this for yourself, Quinn. It's… I have no words. Don't eat before you come."

"Oh Lord, as bad as that?"

"Worse. See you tomorrow."

"Looks like we have a new case," she told Logan. "Rhys won't even tell me what it is, it's so shocking."

"You don't have to do this, you know," Logan said, looking at her with concern. "It takes a toll on you, even I can see that."

"That's what Gabe says, but it's like witnessing a car crash. You are horrified but can't seem to look away."

"Look away, Quinn, before you're the one whose life is bleeding out on the asphalt," Logan said. "You don't have to shoot up or walk across a minefield to self-destruct."

Quinn pushed away her plate, no longer hungry. She wanted to be angry with Logan for putting it to her so bluntly, but she couldn't find the energy to be mad. Logan cared about her, and he was telling her the truth as he saw it. Gabe had said much the

351

same thing, only in kinder terms. Perhaps they were right, and it was time to walk away from *Echoes*, and from her gift.

Epilogue

September 1595

Damascus, Syria

Rafael strolled down the dark street, a leather satchel slung over his shoulder. The air was warm and fragrant, and a full moon hung so low it brushed the minarets of the Umayyad Mosque. Thousands of stars twinkled against the black velvet of the sky and a gentle breeze caressed Rafael's face like a loving hand. He stopped for a moment to admire the beauty of the night. Since the day seven years ago when he'd washed up on the shores of Ireland, he'd never taken a single day for granted. He considered that day in September 1588 the moment of his rebirth, although the birth had been long and painful

Having reached his house, Rafael unlocked the door, kissed his fingers, and pressed them against the mezuzah mounted on the doorpost, as tradition demanded. He closed the door behind him and tiptoed to the kitchen. It was late; Sariah and the children were already in bed and he had no wish to wake them. Rafael poured himself a cup of pomegranate juice and carried it to a small room on the top floor that he used as his study, where he sat in his favorite chair, next to the arched window that overlooked the city skyline.

He needed to write up his notes on tonight's patient, but he could do that tomorrow. He kept copious notes on all his cases, not only for himself, but for young Rafi, who he hoped would follow in his footsteps and become a physician once he was old enough. Sariah had wanted to name the boy Abraham, but Rafael had insisted on naming the child Rafael, not after himself, but because of what the name meant. He hadn't known it while growing up, but Rafael meant 'God heals' in Hebrew. Could any name be more appropriate for a physician?

Rafael reached into his pocket and pulled out a delicate gold hamsa. He had it with him always, not because it brought back memories of Mira and his life in Spain, but because it reminded him of the journey that had led him to freedom.

After the siege ended, Sir Brian and the rest of the clan had returned to the castle. Everyone had been full of good cheer at driving the English off without firing a single shot and proving to be a thorn in the side of Queen Elizabeth yet again, a prospect that pleased Sir Brian to no end. Preparation for the Christmas feast had begun, but not everyone at the castle was in high spirits. The cross bearing Julio had been removed from the yard and carried a good distance beyond the castle walls, where it was dumped unceremoniously on the ground. No one bothered to remove the corpse or bury it, partially because the ground was frozen solid, and partially because no one cared enough to bother. The animals would make short work of Julio's remains, and they were welcome to him as far as the Spaniards were concerned.

After the crucifixion, the balance of power among the survivors had shifted, with José and Pedro taking on the role of leaders. Captain de Cuéllar still joined his countrymen for meals, but he couldn't find it in his heart to forgive the men who'd ordered Julio's death. His inability to prevent the act of barbarism that would likely haunt him for the rest of his days weighed heavily on his mind, and he concluded that he could no longer remain at the castle. After conferring with Sir Brian and Kieran O'Rourke, the captain decided to travel to Derry to see Bishop O'Gallagher, who was sympathetic to the survivors and had the means and the connections to help the men secure passage to Spain. The captain shared his plan with a select few, including Rafael. Twelve men left the castle just after Christmas, setting off on foot. Sir Brian had been kind enough to provide the men with daggers, several blankets, and bundles of food.

When it came to it, leaving Aisling wasn't hard. Their fledging relationship had crumbled, torn asunder by Rafael's guilt over Julio's death and Aisling's lack of remorse at what she had done. She thought he was upset about losing his amulet, but it was so much more than that. Rafael had meant to explain, to break the news to her gently, but instead, he simply walked away on that fateful morning, relieved to be finished with Castle O'Rourke and everyone in it.

It took nearly two weeks to reach Derry and then another several months to get to Glasgow by way of the Hebrides, after which they waited several weeks for a boat to take them to the mainland. Every step of the way, the men grew more confident. It would take time to get back to Spain, but at least their lives were not in any immediate danger in Scotland. The people weren't unwelcoming, and there was always a meal and a place to sleep to be found in any church or the home of a Catholic nobleman. Rafael never spoke of his plans to anyone. He simply watched and waited.

They arrived in Glasgow in the middle of March, and that was when he knew it was time. He didn't tell anyone he was leaving. He would have liked to say farewell to the captain and thank him for his guidance and support, but that would require an explanation, something he couldn't provide. Rafael simply stole away one night, losing himself in the narrow, twisted streets of Glasgow and then eventually moving on to Aberdeen, where he worked at the docks until he saved enough money to set off on his journey to the Middle East. It had taken him nearly a year to reach Damascus.

Rafael took a sip of juice and let out a sigh of contentment. He had a good life in Syria. There was a large Jewish community that lived side by side with the Muslims in peace. For the first time in his life, Rafael was free of persecution and fear. He'd embarked on a course of study that had allowed him to become a physician, married his beautiful Sariah, and started a family. The only thing that marred his happiness was the fate of his family in Toledo. He hadn't been able to return to Spain but had questioned every Spanish Jew who passed through Damascus, begging for news of his family. It had taken years to come across someone he'd known in Toledo, but his joy was short-lived.

"Rafael de Silva," Don Miguel had exclaimed. "As I live and breathe. Everyone thought you perished when your ship went down. How your father grieved. He performed a kriah and refused to mend his doublet for a full year. Ramón did it as well."

That bit of news nearly broke Rafael's heart. His father had not torn his clothes, as was the Jewish custom when someone beloved passed, when his wife died. It was too risky for a well-to-do man to walk around the streets of Toledo in a torn doublet. It raised questions. But he'd done it when he thought he'd lost his son. He must have blamed himself for urging Rafael to join the army. Perhaps he'd even wished that he'd allowed Rafael to study medicine.

"Tell me, is my father well? What about my brother?"

The news wouldn't be recent. Don Miguel had been travelling for seven months, but it was better than nothing. The man sighed and averted his gaze. "I wish I could bring you happy tidings, don Rafael, but I don't think your father is still with us. He was arrested on a charge of sorcery and heresy, and no one ever saw him again. Your brother tried to discover what became of him. He went to the prison week after week, but eventually gave up."

"What became of my brother?" Rafael asked, fighting back tears.

"When you didn't come back after a year, Ramón married your intended, Mira. They had a child—a son. They were still living in Toledo when I left last year."

"What made you leave at last?" Rafael asked.

"I'd rather not speak of it," the man replied, but the expression on his face told Rafael everything he needed to know. When he'd known don Miguel, he'd had a family—a wife and two daughters.

"I am sorry for your troubles, don Miguel."

The old man nodded and rose to leave. "Well, I'll be on my way."

"Won't you stay and join us for supper?" Rafael asked. It was the least he could do to thank the man for the news. "My wife is an excellent cook."

"Perhaps another time," he replied. "When we can speak of happier things."

That had been nearly five years ago, and not a day went by that Rafael didn't say a prayer for Ramón and Mira. He hoped that someday they would find their way to Syria, as so many others had.

Having finished his drink, Rafael shut the window and made his way to the bedrooms. First, he checked on the children. Rafi and Suri were sound asleep, Suri smiling in her sleep as if she were having a pleasant dream. Rafi had his arms around his pillow. Rafael kissed each child on the cheek and went to his own bedchamber. He undressed and climbed into bed next to Sariah, who was sleeping peacefully, her dark hair framing her lovely face. The mound of her belly rose beneath the embroidered coverlet, the child inside her restless and almost ready to be born. Rafael put his hand on her stomach and the baby calmed beneath his touch.

As he did every night before going to sleep, Rafael thanked God for his family and their wellbeing. He said a prayer for Ramón and Mira, and one for Captain de Cuéllar. And he praised God for guiding him to this wonderful place, where Jews and Arabs lived like brothers, and would do so for centuries to come.

The End

The Broken (Echoes from the Past Book 8)

coming January 2020

Notes

I hope you've enjoyed this installment of the *Echoes from the Past* series. I've actually never given much thought to the survivors of the Spanish Armada until a reader mentioned that he's descended from just such a person. I would like to thank Gavin Adrian Boaz for bringing my attention to the plight of those who were shipwrecked on British shores and left behind with virtually no chance of survival. Of course, Rafael and his background are entirely fictional, and not based on a real person, but Captain de Cuéllar was a real person, and I drew heavily on his letters to inform this narrative. I would also like to give a shout-out to Linda Robertson, who helped me with the many Spanish expressions used in the story. I would have been lost without her.

As always, thank you for your continued support, and if you would like to receive updates about new releases and promotions, please join my mailing list by using the link bellow. You can also reach me through my website or email. I'm always thrilled to hear from you.

http://irinashapiroauthor.com/mailing-list-signup-form/
www.irinashapiroauthor.com
irina.shapiro@yahoo.com.

And lastly, if you've enjoyed the book, a review on Amazon or Goodreads would be much appreciated.

Made in the USA
Coppell, TX
11 February 2022

73399681R00208